BETHANY GRENIER

ISBN 979-8-218-19978-4
Text ©2023 Bethany Grenier
Cover Photo, Cover and Book Design ©2023 Bethany Grenier
Cover model Hannah Fletter
-Ancestor Photos, Public Domain from a private collection.
Header page background uses a portion of the
Three of Swords tarot card Authorship: w:Arthur Edward Waite,
w:Pamela Coleman Smith was the artist and worked as an artist 'for hire.' Waite was the copyright holder and he died in 1942., Public domain, via Wikimedia Commons

Paradox
Publishing Collective

contents

acknowledgments

Thank You to my Editor, Gretchen Rumohr.
I could not have done this without you.

———

Jody, my beloved, you are a gift to me.

———

Thank you to my friends, early readers, and amazing women for always having my back and the answer I was looking for: Diana Lamphiere, Jill Gurdak, Màiri Handy, and Anisa Williams. And to my clients, who have been so supportive.

1
how soon is now?

Ember

late may, 1989

I pulled the Three of Swords tarot card today while doing my lunchtime three card spread. Because of course I did. Three swords piercing a heart, surrounded by dark clouds and unrelenting rain, just about sum up my high school experience in one word: brutal. It's one of the many reasons I sit alone at lunch. Always. I'm fine with it. The fewer people I have to talk to, the easier it is to hide what needs to be hidden. And looking around the chaotic lunchroom, I know I'm better off keeping to myself.

I'm in my usual uniform, Dress: black. Boots: black. Hair: black. Skin: pale. Lips: bloody red. I've cobbled together a wardrobe of cast-off clothing to suit my "Island of Misfit Toys" vibe, topped off with the long scarf I knit way back, in one of those *bonding moments* with one of my many foster mothers.

I notice white bread crumbs in my lap, stark against my black dress, and quickly brush them to the floor. My hands halt as two of the popular girls slow their walk as they encounter my table, "Nice Devil cards—freak!" followed by the voice of the other one: "Mirror mirror on the wall, who's the weirdest of them all?"

It's Traci, or Tammi, or maybe Tori? It's one of those "T" names that ends with an 'i' that they dot with a heart. Anyway, I don't know them, but they sure know me. They *all* know me. I am, after all, *the* goth scene at my school. That's right, it's just me, and I've put the target on my back. I don't care if it keeps them from getting near me. Whatever.

Instead of trying *and failing* to fit in, I spend my time making stuff —art, clothes, hand-knit accessories, imaginary worlds, and, you know, drama. But the drama is accidental. It's just my way, I guess.

Looking down again, I notice the laces of my Doc Martens boots are untied. I've totally modded them, a flaming heart painted on one and three swords stabbing a heart on the other, like the Tarot card. All-Seeing Eyes, pyramids, and other iconic symbols round out the imagery. The symbols haunt me though, like they hold all the secrets of the universe. I don't need *more* cryptic messages coming from the universe than I've already got—but I'll get to that in a minute. So I draw and paint my hearts and icons, shutting out the world with each new creation. If it's not visual art, I'm behind my sewing machine, instead of pretending I care about high school football or Nintendo Legend of Zelda.

No matter what I'm working on though, I spend too much of my time imagining my secret world, dreaming it to life, then drawing it in Art class. My private world is different, yet somehow familiar, existing in the same space as this world, only slightly off. Looking out the high windows along the cafeteria wall, I squint my eyes, hoping I can find just the right angle to see my secret world. I swear, sometimes that works.

Rummaging around in my bag for my walkman, my hand closes around a bulky shape. *What the...* Did some jerk slip something gross into my bag? Looking into my bag, I see that it's a large padded envelope, the corners a bit ragged and beat up. Colorful stamps of the Queen cover the upper right corner. My heartbeat picks up a little more, but this time in excitement. Mrs. B must've shoved this into my bag last night or something.

It's addressed to (dec)Em-burr wRight. He spells my name differently every single time. What a cheeky bloke! Tearing open the envelope, I stifle a squeal of delight. My British penpal, Rory, sent me a mixtape, and I just know it's going to be *brilliant*, as he would say. I quickly switch it for the Bauhaus tape I had been listening to.

I arrange my hair to cover the foam covered discs, it seems futile, but

I still try to hide the shock of bright orange. Standing up from the lunch table, I pick up my half-eaten pb&j and walk to the trash, dread growing in the pit of my stomach, wishing that Nico shared my lunch hour. Nico is rad. She's my best friend, except for Mr. Whitley. That doesn't exactly count though because he's kind of my godfather. Plus, I work for him, so there's that. But really, how many lame friends do I need when I've got Nico? Unfortunately, our only shared class is Creative Writing. I swear it's like the only thing that I'm better at than her. She's super talented and unshakable and nobody even *tries* to bully her, even though she's far from normal. It all just rolls off her back. I try to act like that, but people know when you're faking it.

"Outta my way, foozler!" I command the wannabe jock who decided to step out in front of me, harassing on his mind.

Looking only at the floor and then to my Egyptian hieroglyphics-covered book bag, I click the play button, and the music begins. The Smiths drowns out the rest of the world, including the random things I occasionally hear *about* people in my head. That's right, I hear things about people, and I really don't want to. And what's worse is that the things I hear are true. Occasionally, I'll be walking by someone, and I'll suddenly know something about them that I shouldn't. Like there's a quiet voice in the back of my mind whispering to me. And before you get too far into telling me that it's not normal to hear that stuff, I'll tell you that I'm not normal. Whether it's a secret they're keeping or a deep-seated fear, I randomly hear it. I know it as sure as I know my name, December Roisin Wright, and yes, at the beginning of every new school year, I have to tell all my teachers to please, *please*, call me Ember.

And before you ask, it's pronounced Ro-sheen.

I'm fine with not fitting in. It's the easiest way to guard my secrets—like the eight oval scars that start at my temples and work their way up to my forehead just below the hairline. They're more like blotches, really, unmistakably lighter than my skin, shimmering when the light hits them just right, fluctuating and shifting reality ever so slightly when I look at them too long in the mirror. I avoid looking at them. They leave me feeling unsettled and shaky, if you can believe that weirdness. I wear a thick fringe of bangs just above my eyebrows, covering my forehead and temples, because no matter how much makeup I wear, I can never be sure that others won't see them.

A voice rings in my ears. This time it's an unbidden memory, bringing with it the visual accompaniment, like a movie clip. I'm a little kid, playing on the monkey bars during recess, maybe in third grade. My hair hangs down, away from my face as I practice feats of daredevilry, suspended from the bar by just my legs. "Look at Ember! She has spots on her forehead. Weirdo!" A young boy's voice echoes in my mind, shouting as loudly in my memory as he did that day. I've never let the spots show since then.

I make it out of the lunchroom and pull the headphones off my ears to rest around my neck. Walking the nearly silent halls to the Art room, frustration wells up in me at the unwelcome memory replaying itself. *When will my mind ever stop showing me things I don't wanna see, not to mention seeing things at all? C'mon brain, can't we just be friends?*

Turning the handle I find Ms. Ragana eating lunch at her desk, half-heartedly sketching a figure onto a canvas in front of her. She casts her striking golden brown eyes in my direction and looks up, unsurprised to see me.

"Hi Ember. Back to work on your landscape?" She turns back to face her own drawing: her grandfather, as she'd shared with me. Taken from a photo later in his life, his hair worn in a close-cropped afro, his brown skin echoed perfectly in Ms. Ragana's skin tone. She's wearing her hair as she often does, in large braids that twist themselves into a sculptural updo.

"Yes, Ms. Ragana." As I glance in her direction, I see the oversized woven shawl she always wears, draped over her chair with one end drawn out and laying on the floor. I turn to pick it up, but as my fingers near the multicolored fabric, my mind's eye floods with images: Ms. Ragana as a young woman, likely even my age, seated in a large open room with walls covered in tapestries and what looks like hanging looms. The young woman holds a long narrow shaft of wood wrapped with yarn in her idle hands, a spindle for spinning yarn from wool, by hand. But the sight is such a strange and incongruous vision, compared to my teacher, who sits sketching.

I quickly jerk my hand back with a startled gasp. "Weird!" I exclaim without meaning to. Because what was *that*? I could only hope that she hasn't witnessed my bizarro-world moment. But of course, she has, saying, "What's that, dear?" piercing me with knowing eyes. The look she wears is inscrutable as she studies me. Then, her face opens to a smile.

"Oh—oh, n-nothing. I just wanted to pick up the end of your shawl from the floor, and I saw...well, never mind. Here's your shawl." I extend my hand, my heart beating faster at my near admission of seeing things. It's bad enough that I hear things, but lately, I see things as well, like I'm some kind of psychic or something...except the Visions that pop into my head are entirely useless, if they're Visions at all. Maybe I'm just losing my mind.

But Ms. Ragana interrupts my thoughts, saying, "Thank you, Ember. That was thoughtful of you to notice." Her eyes continue to bore into me, and I feel my pulse quicken and my cheeks flush.

"You're welcome," I reply and quickly walk away, avoiding her stare. Before I can get too far, I turn on my heel. "Ms. Ragana, do you knit? Or spin yarn?" It feels dangerous to ask the question, though I know she can't know what I've seen.

"As a matter of fact, I do, Ember. Why do you ask?" There's that inscrutable and appraising look again.

"No reason, I was just curious. I knit, too." My answer is awkward, and she smiles as though she knows the true meaning behind my question yet chooses to say nothing.

Turning away, I walk quickly to the back of the room, pulling my art from the slatted storage shelves and an easel from the corner. I set it up in front of my assigned table, sitting on, rather than behind it. Pulling my graphite pencil set out of my book bag, I begin to shade the surreal image of an ultra modern building erupting through the city's abandoned mental institution. This is what happens in both my dreams and daydreams. If I stare too long at the sanitarium, I sometimes see a haze dancing around the field of my vision. But something always distracts me, interrupting the effect. It's another of my secrets and one I hold closely, fearing that if I told anyone, I might well end up in an actual mental hospital

> ... guarded words heard in a dream
> a secret no one speaks
> is there light in the dark
> or is it a fire to burn away the secret
> leaving only ashes in my hands...

"Ugh, not today!" I mutter to myself in disgust as I drop my pencil, causing Ms. Ragana to look over at me quizzically.

"Oh, sorry, just having a disagreement with my drawing." I hide the larger unexplainable truth within a smaller truth, hoping that I just sound distracted as I pick up my pencil.

Why is this my day? Like I need this stupid song loop stuck in my head. No secret messages today, please. This is so *not what I need.*

Another secret is that I, like most people who love music, get songs stuck in my head. I read something once, while researching the phenomenon that referred to it as Stuck Song Syndrome. But when I get an earworm stuck, playing over and over, it's more like a premonition than an annoyance. Actually, it's both. But whatever the song is about comes true in some way, a warning of what is to come. I figure it's an extension of the whole "hearing secrets about people" thing.

Once, I got part of Wham's *Careless Whisper* stuck in my head for weeks just before my foster parents, or the flavor of the month as I call them, announced their impending divorce due to cheating. The divorce landed me in yet another home, with new foster parents and a new school. The song played over and over in my mind, and then it happened. And I don't even like that song. So it's an added insult to injury.

I try to ignore the ear worm and continue to shade the dramatic building eruption scene. This is different from my normal drawings of different parts of the city. There's so much diversity in the buildings, some towering, some ornate, but always at the center of my drawings is a vast squat building with a domed turret that looks like a planetarium. Tall statues guard the four corners of the buildings: two men and two women dressed in old-fashioned garb. It feels like a Temple or a public auditorium, but I can never decide what purpose this imaginary building serves. I wish I could just visit it and know what it is.

•••

"Breathe, Addi," I mumble as I walk the hall leading to a seldom-used corner of the Temple, fearing what I might find in the small room.

"Deep calming breaths." I mutter the cliche, hoping it will help. But the trite saying does nothing to cool the heat at my cheeks or the rush of blood pumping through my racing heart, pounding in my ears. I can't think.

"Foreboding? But why?" I ask myself. "It's been at least half a year since it happened. And no one's the wiser. Nobody knows, and your life is intact. Surely, she was bluffing when she claimed she was with child." But the reassuring words have no effect.

"Why can't I shake this feeling?" I whisper, trying to purge the anxiety that's plagued me all day. Now I'm drawn to this remote room, a feeling compelling me, refusing to be denied. It's foolish for me to even pay heed to such a thing. My prophetic gift hasn't ever produced this panic blooming in my chest.

I am Draíodóir, a Listener, and I certainly don't get guidance about things happening here, and now, I chide myself. Still I walk, trying to distract myself from the tightening sensation in my chest, half singing, half humming. The music is from the other world, les Dormeur, the non-magical city that lies beyond the boundaries of la Magie: worlds separated by complex spells and wards, mathematical equations, and mechanisms put in place centuries ago by the Guild of Secrets. I love the music of les Dormeur so much that I built a small crystal radio and earpiece. My secret little Maker's Corner came in handy once again. After all, what is one more misdeed, one more secret among so many others?

The door squeaks open with little resistance, casting a beam of light across the dirty floor. "Let it b—" The song dies on my lips as I draw in a sharp breath. A newborn baby, my baby, lies lifeless on the concrete floor, her birth now a certainty. Even as I tried to ignore the feeling of foreboding in my heart all day. Her blood called to mine, and now she is here: naked, pale, and near death. Motes of dust swirl in the air as energy crackles around her tiny body.

I never intended to be a father. Even before my gift awakened and I'd joined the Priory of the Draíodóir, I wouldn't have even considered children. Besides, the Vow of Chastity I pledged to the Priory ended those possibilities twofold.

This isn't just any newborn, though. This baby has power; I feel it radiating from her. But this child might as well be called "The Forbidden Child" as she was conceived in secrecy by two oath breakers. Shame heats my face at the thought: How could I have broken my word for Phaedra? No point questioning now. Done is done!

This baby will likely inherit both of our gifts if she lives. The ability to See and Hear prophetic guidance is rare. Dually gifted Oracles are born only every few generations.

The energy left in the air buzzes along my senses, jangling along my nervous system with the unease of maleficium.

This is magical energy—Phaedra tried to steal her gifts! What kind of person could take from their own child? Without another thought, I run to her. Her arms and legs are splayed at unnatural angles, her body still and lifeless. I see the small white markings around her forehead, evidence of magic: four on each side of her temples, pulsating angrily, shimmering with their iridescent haze, confirming my suspicions.

Holding my breath, I put my ear over her chest, listening for a heartbeat...only a faint whisper of a pulse. But it's not safe to perform any healings here.

I remove my linen cassock to swaddle and scoop her up. "Please don't die! Please don't die! Please don't die!" As I run, the mantra I murmur grows in urgency.

Safe in my room, I perform the healing ritual to save her. But there are also things I need if I am to succeed, both in the short term and for the long road that I now see ahead of us. "Oh my sweet girl. Please don't die!"

Catching myself, I close my eyes, take a deep breath, and pull back from the edge of panic I feel. Here she is: my daughter. So fragile, so new, so beautiful, a gift I don't deserve. I know what I must do next: I must name her. I know that Phaedra has not named her. Without a name, she is vulnerable.

I take another deep breath, trying to settle my racing heart. "I never intended to create you, but looking at you now is surreal. You are a part of me, and I'm in awe seeing your little body. But I sense your Spirit is not settled within you. How could it be after what happened? Naming you is the only way to ground you. Even in this I will fail you, with no time to do it properly, but I will give you everything I have." I exhale in defeated lament.

"But there is no time for pessimistic thoughts. I have a child to protect; she is my only focus now." Truer words I have never spoken. The words have unexpected weight laced within them, the power of VoceInvocare infusing them.

Taking a breath, I search for the quiet, blood whooshing in my ears as they attune to the silence. Magic sparks against my skin with little electric shocks, every sensation magnified. I breathe out slowly; the stillness of holding my lungs empty heightens my awareness. Energy eddies restlessly around me, the magic impatient. Taking another deep breath, pulling the power into my lungs, my vision expands in a way I've never experienced before. I sit, looking across the distance at an older, gray-haired man who resembles my father. But he is not; he is me—our visceral connection resonating in my bones. He is the future of me, sitting silently, urging me on to the task that lies before me. The expanse of our future that I see is a heady sensation as I summon my intention. I open my mouth to begin and the vision disappears, gone as suddenly as it came.

The force of my will manifests into reality through magic. "I name you December Roisin," I say, imbuing each syllable with intention and power as I press my lips to her head. "You are the ending and beginning of a new chapter, my little rose. You are my virtue lost and now regained."

•••

Through sheer force of will, he awakens himself from Onirique, the liminal space, knowing it's not really happening. It's always at this point that he can force the dream to end. He knows what comes next.

"Adair Whitley Wright, get yourself together, man," he whispers. But the days of Adair are gone, as is that life, and as he tells himself to "breathe, just breathe through it," the sentiment is no more effective in calming him now than it was that night. "Well, it seems I'll be reliving my worst memory in Onirique for the foreseeable future. The dream's coming nearly every night now. Thank the Stars and Nine Worlds for lucid dreaming," he mutters. But it's never been this vivid or panic-inducing. It escalates as their daughter's birthday nears.

He sits up, looking around his tidy room. As he takes in the tones of twilight by the rays of the morning sun filtering in through the curtains, he knows there will be no more sleep tonight. Shifting his stiff aging body and stretching his feet on the floor, he wraps a flannel robe around his body and paces the small room above his shop.

"Phaedra's trying to find her." He knows it's true as soon as the words are spoken. His gift seems to have changed over the years; he no longer hears possible futures or has an uncanny knowledge of past events. Now he simply hears the truth as he says it. He supposes it's a consequence of having left the magical world behind, but what puzzles him is the addition of the Sight to his abilities, or at least some aspects of it, anyway. It came unexpectedly, and the ability to See is not a Gift he should possess. Only the women of his world are born with clairvoyance. For what seemed like the millionth time, he surmises that it must belong to his daughter.

He'd been so reluctant to bind her gifts, her magic when she was a baby, but it was the only way they could hide in les Dormeur, the world of the sleepers. Parting the curtain and peeking out the window, he reasons that he'll lose the Sight once she regains it.

2

life on mars?

Ember

A long sigh escapes my lips as the words of the jock I'd passed in the hall echo in my ears. "Whose funeral?"

"I haven't decided yet. Volunteering?" Now that would've been a good reply if I were quick-witted. I could kick myself for not thinking of it fast enough to burn him back.

"Addlepate…" I grumble under my breath at the missed opportunity. The taunts cut me even deeper when they echo what my foster parents tell me. My stomach twists as I think about the latest set. The feeling of being tolerated always leaves me cold. People throw around the word tolerance like it's something to be celebrated, but it feels like a half step above rejection. I'm so tired of it. When will someone appreciate me for who I am? It's not my fault that weird things happen around me. I didn't ask to know when people are lying to me.

A locker slams near me and I jump like a startled cat. Lurching at loud noises is a near-daily occurrence. The decibel level of an ordinary day at school is almost too much to handle.

My thoughts trail off as I arrive at my own locker. Another stupid school day done. My fingers rotate the dial of the padlock, but my mind is someplace else. Things aren't great at the Bradshaw home. It's starting to feel like just another future memory. So many families have come into and gone right back out of my life; my shoulders slump with the realization that I'm approaching double digits in families and schools attended. I pull the padlock out of the hook, and the metal lever lifts stiffly to open the door. Looking into my locker, I groan at the number of books I need to bring home and stack them, one by one, in my bag. Their weight reminds me that I must work twice as hard to achieve the same grades as everybody else–another consequence of so many schools.

Looking at my watch, I realize that I need to motor if I'm gonna get to work on time. Mr. Whitley frowns upon tardiness, and facing side-long looks and judgments is not on my agenda today. I scowl, slam the locker shut, and head to the parking lot.

Approaching my black '74 Vespa Primavera scooter, I marvel that a piece of machinery built when I was so young still runs so well. Peeling duct tape on the seat reminds me of my long-ago foster father David and all the time we worked together on the scoot. We were nearly done when he was killed in a car accident and I was sent to yet another foster family. I sigh. "We worked hard to bring this beastie back to life after you helped me find it."

Turning the key, I put my foot onto the kick starter, pushing down with a practiced motion that causes the engine to hum to life after a few kicks. Its buzzy mosquito voice sputters until I squeeze the clutch lever and move into first gear, letting out the clutch while opening the throt-tle. Then I step onto the floorboard and hop on, gas igniting the engine into motion.

I didn't bother with my helmet in my hurry. Yeah, there will be plenty of lecturing if Whit sees me without it. Still, it's totally worth it: the wind on my face, blowing my hair back, makes me feel more alive, forcing me out of my head and into my body, silencing my anxieties about my life, my foster parents, and their inevitable rejection. I could even sing to my heart's content with no one to tease me when my notes go flat or wonky.

Breathing all the way into my diaphragm, the way David taught me to do, I get lost in the feeling of my breath traveling from deep in my belly to my mouth, enjoying the vibrations in my throat as the breath passes in, expanding my lungs, clearing my head. I exhale, letting my worries go with my breath. A rumble in the distance makes me wonder if it will be a wet ride home from work and echoes my pensive mood. Will the forecasted evening showers come early?

The familiar hand-lettered sign outside Mr. Whitley's Emporium of Curiosities and Oddities greets me as I round the corner. I release the throttle, arch my hand toward the brake, and brace myself, hoping that Whit isn't near the window to catch me without my helmet.

Of course, he's in the window, tinkering with a new display. Wait, what? Usually, he leaves displays for me so he must have something really special. I can't suppress a widening grin. Turning into the parking lot, I pull into a spot, jump off the seat, engage the kickstand lifting the scooter off the ground. Removing the key from the ignition, I throw it into my book bag and rush to the door.

Walking in, the riotous sound of bells clatter to life, setting my senses on edge. My eyes look across to the far corner of the shop, at the ceiling, the Trompe l'oeil painting of a sky with puffy white clouds. A herd of plastic rocking horses freed of their bases and now painted as fantastical beasts gallop through a field of metal Moravian star lanterns.

I groan. "Does it always have to be Fleetwood Mac? And *Rumours*? Again? It's going to be one of those kinds of days..."

More loudly, I announce, "Whit, come on! It's not the 70's anymore. It's ok to listen to records of this decade, you know."

"No helmet today, December?" Whit asks as a reply, his pointed question and use of my full first name spoken with concern. My cheeks burn under the scrutiny of his pale blue eyes, and I know I'm busted. But before I can respond, he continues, "You really should be wearing one. I'm sure I don't need to remind you of the consequences if you should have an accident without. Plus, there is also the small matter of it being illegal." The seconds seem to slow to a crawl whenever Whit chastises me. As he voices these last words, the gravity of his tone makes me hesitate before I make excuses for myself.

"Yes, I'll wear it from now on, ok? I was in a hurry, and I didn't want to be late for work." But my excuses are offered only half-heartedly. "I know, I know, you'd rather I am late than dead." I emphasize the final word, imitating his voice and its grave tone. A stern sidelong look from him is all I get for my efforts. "Sorry," I say quickly, realizing my joke didn't land quite how I intended. For someone who's a half-assed Godfather, you have a lot of opinions about how I live my life... But I can't say that out loud. It would only lead to more lecturing about his confirmed bachelor lifestyle.

I'm only trying to keep you safe, Little Rose." The return to his favorite nickname for me has me breathing a sigh of relief. I know he's let it go and isn't legit mad at me. He's been the only consistent person in my life, so I don't want to piss him off too much. My middle name means little rose in Gaelic, and he can't seem to resist using it any chance he gets. The nickname is sweet but a little too cute.

"Go ahead and change the record if you like, just no Siouxsie and the Banshees or Sisters of Mercy today. You've listened to those quite a lot lately. They're not my favorite," he says, stating the obvious. "How about that new Cure record? It's so melancholy. It's my favorite of all your records." While I want to ask him what has him in the window, I try to play it cool.

"Sure thing, Whit. And it's called *Disintegration*." I turn to walk to the record player, but my attention is quickly diverted as I notice new items on the counter—including a school folder I'd needed today. Aside from the miscellaneous new items on the counter near the front door, everything else in the shop looks pretty much as it always does. There's nothing out of place.

"Whit, I swear I'm going to nominate this place for the 'Wonders of the World.' The amount of stuff you pack in this store is astounding, especially considering how bare your apartment upstairs is. Are you somehow diverting unused space from up there down here or employing some sort of secret compression technology?" But as I finish my jibe, I see Whit's face blanch, like I've stumbled onto a real secret.

Remembering my appointment with the record player and the need for new music, I turn and head back through the twisting paths. Walking through switchbacks, I pass Whit's private office, the one forbidden room, yet another frustrating mystery of Whit.

Placing the needle on the record, I'm greeted by wind chimes sounding quietly, transitioning to the sweeping intro of "Plainsong". I close my eyes for a second, the melodic keyboards transporting me to a world much larger than the one I currently occupy. And I don't move a muscle, afraid to break the spell.

But as "Pictures of You" begins, the moment passes. I remember I have unfinished business with Whit and the new items upfront. Turning on my heel, I weave through the hidden treasures sequestered in little corners Whit carved out of the main space, a mix of antique jewelry intermixed with imported pieces. My eyes move as I do, taking in the retro clothes interspersed with my own clothing creations. The rack seems a little light, and I realize more of my designs are selling. It gives me a small thrill, especially when my BFF, Nico, buys one.

The extra income from the sales, along with generous wages from Whit, goes toward my cd collection, band posters, yarn, and candles. I'm pretty much desperate to cover the white room walls of my bedroom at the Bradshaw house. They call it my room, but it feels more like the guest room it used to be than my room. The generic floral bedspread and 1950s vanity with its medium walnut brown varnish aren't really my thing.

Another switchback takes me past a wall of 1960s glass coffee pots and cast iron pans. A display of Hopi Kachina dolls and Zuni turquoise jewelry stands near a large bookshelf. Two mid-century modern chairs with a small table between them stand at the ready for the would-be reader, and I flash back to the many hours Whit and I spent in those chairs, learning our secret language when I was little. Of course, I've long since forgotten it, but these are among my favorite memories from childhood.

Without warning, an unbidden scene flashes in my mind's eye. A little boy, so familiar, chases a tiny little girl version of myself around the shop, nearly skidding into the bookshelf. But it's not a memory; this is the first time I've seen this boy, with his long, dark hair askew. Both of us giggle as he catches me, kissing my cheek before he turns to run away, only to be chased in return. I couldn't be more than three or four, though the little boy seems a bit older. "Woah! Where did that come from?!" But I know I can't ask Whit. He'll be evasive, as usual. I'll ask a question about my childhood, and he'll shift his gaze away from me and change the subject. Well, I guess this is a puzzle for another day.

My eyes refocus on the shelf and all its books—everything from Alchemy, Natural Crystals, and the Language of Allthings. At Whits urging, I've been steadily working my way through the books of folklore stories of magical cultures. I'm currently reading about Norse mythology and Viking raiders.

A laugh escapes my throat as I remember sitting there, book propped up on top of other books so I can knit while I read— a habit that bugs Whit to no end. Our constant disagreement about multitasking never ends, but I always win– every time he tries to surreptitiously question what I'm reading, I ace his poorly disguised pop quizzes.

Having completed my daily visual accounting of the shop, looking for anything left out of place by a customer so I can tidy it, I focus again on Whit. He's redressed the mannequin with one of my customized skirts and a vintage velvet coat. Atop the mannequin's molded hair sits a pair of goggles—a new arrival from ↑↑↑.

"Excelsior!" I whisper under my breath. I'm pretty sure that's not what the symbols mean to the person who etched it, but that's what it means to me. Ever upward! The upward-pointing arrows are a powerful reminder of Stan Lee's motto, a sentiment I can get behind.

I knew it! The new window means new things delivered by Whit's mysterious inventor friend, Three Arrows. That's not his name, it's the maker's mark he uses to denote his creations. But since Whit won't tell me much about him, I've taken to calling him that, despite Whit's exasperation.

It's like Whit's trying to protect me by refusing to answer my questions about his friend. But then I have to wonder why Whit teases me with bits of information about this guy and then refuses to tell me more when he's gotten my attention. Why can't I meet him, or even know his name, for that matter? Over time, I've learned a few things. Whit had been friends with our respective parents when they were all young, so he's about my age—a detail he'd inadvertently confirmed one day as he spoke about how clever he is for such a young man. And his parents were gone, too, a sad circumstance we share. But if I press Whit for more details, his eyes get a faraway look, and he refuses to talk further. And gone is any chance to learn any more about him. Or even my own parents, for that matter. I can't fathom why Whit guards this particular friend so fiercely, his only friend outside of me.

My senses come to life, trying vainly to stretch out and feel the energy from the three arrows. I feel something, a strange connection. I don't know, but it's there whenever I touch his creations. Maybe it's just his lingering creative energy. Perhaps I'm just so desperate for another friend that I'm reading more into it than it means. There is definitely something there. I can't doubt myself now.

My mind flashes to a day when I sat at the counter, doing some assigned reading. I'd been absentmindedly running my fingers over a smooth silver ring I'd found. He'd made it, and I wanted to own it, to wear it and feel that connection. Letting the ring drop, I pushed it to the base of my finger and spun it around and around with my thumb.

As I spun it, I looked up from my reading and saw Whit enter the room. In that instant, my vision changed like a veil had been lifted. An aura of iridescent bluish light surrounded Whit, and though I blinked hard, it was still there. Still fidgeting with the ring, I pulled it off my finger, and the aura disappeared. I slid the ring down my finger again and stared hard at Whit, but it was no use. The image wouldn't return.

I begin strategizing, hoping to convince Whit to take the goggles off the mannequin. He's really into this display. He's even taken off one of his signature plaid blazers, throwing it onto the counter as he fusses with a vintage necklace on the mannequin. But I can't think of any sneaky ways to convince him to let me check them out.

That's when I spy another pair on the counter hiding amidst an array of trinkets and discarded merchandise. The ancient cash register, with its "Cash and Checks only, No Credit Cards" sign, sits in the middle of it all.

This pair is different from the others—kind of old-fashioned, like vintage motorcycle goggles, featuring oversized round glass lenses held in place on top of a rubber frame, the glass rose-tinted. The proverbial Rose-Tinted glasses. Oh, I definitely need these.

Slipping the elastic band around my head, I move the goggles into place over my eyes. Two adjustable arms hold alternate lenses. One of the dials is a compass made of clear glass, except for the directional markers and the indicator hand. There are additional markings at the center, but I have no clue what they mean.

The other dial, slightly smaller, is even more of a mystery. It seems like a second compass but has no markings on its face. Its arm that swivels around wildly stops, and a shimmering haze appears as I look at one of the treasures Three Arrows brought in. As I continue to look around the shop, the arm continues to spin. My eyes stop on Whit, the shimmering light encircling him as the arm stills again.

I say nothing and move my head further around the shop to Whit's private office when the arm once again stops. This time, though, the shimmering light is faint and barely visible. And of course, Whit won't explain what I just saw. He'll just say that I'll learn to use them in time or some other vaguery.

Whit regards me with an appraising look as I reluctantly take the goggles off. "Like those, do you?"

"Obviously! They're amazing, if not a bit mysterious in their purpose," I say, emphasizing the word mysterious, knowing Whit won't budge.

"Good thing they're for you, then. There's a hint of indulgence in Whit's voice as he sidesteps the unspoken question.

A slight squeal of delight escapes my lips and I bounce on the balls of my feet. "Really, I can have these? Oh, thank you, Whit! They're amazing."

"Now you can see the world through rose-colored glasses, Little Rose." But Whit's comment catches me off guard. There's a hint of sadness in his sentiment. I can't ever figure him out. I shrug it off, putting on the goggles again, noticing the rose-colored glass makes everything seem softer and prettier. Of course, nothing in my world has ever been idyllic, so I very much like the idea that I can choose to see the world differently—as though by filtering the world through tinted glasses, I can change my perspective.

"I know you want to meet him, Little Rose." Whit's words startle me from my reverie. He knows I'll ask, so he halts my questions before I can ask them. I look at him expectantly; maybe today is the day. But my hopes are just as quickly dashed as he continues. "It just never seems to be the right time, does it?"

"Why is that, Whit?" I ask. Whit blanches slightly at the sarcasm in my voice.

"What's the harm in letting me meet him?" And before I can stop my traitorous thoughts from betraying me, the words slip out of my mouth. "You know, I am seventeen, almost eighteen, and most girls my age have boyfriends. They are on dates, going to prom—" But I abruptly stop, realizing I've just shared my true feelings about this boy I've never even met who occupies my imagination. My imaginary life in my imaginary city with my imaginary boyfriend.

"Is that what you want? Do you want him to take you to the prom?" Whit asks teasingly.

I roll my eyes. "Um, NO! You know I don't want anything to do with that stupid prom!" I told you. I just want to meet him. I've only been asking for, like, forever.

"So, are you skipping the prom, then?" Whit asks, redirecting the conversation. I can feel my cheeks flush bright pink with embarrassment. Clearing my throat too loudly, I say, "Um, Yeah, you know I'm not a joiner." But, not to be deterred, I ask, "So, why is it then? Why can't I meet him?" I'm determined not to be swayed to another topic.

"You have enough to focus on, with school and minding your 'P's and Q's,' without adding boys to your troubles." His eyebrows knit together, and his eyes narrow. "It would be nice if you could finish high school with the Bradshaw family. I don't think the time is right yet. He's kind of in a—" But he stops like he's trying to figure out how to phrase what he wants to say.

"Self-destructive, searching, I dunno..." The words are spoken distractedly, with a hint of darkness in his words. Like he's suspicious about what's going on with his friend.

"What is it, Whit? Are you worried about your friend?" I try to sound both unaffected and caring simultaneously, but it is no use, my push snapping him back to full awareness. "It's simply not the proper time. Have I ever steered you wrong, Ember?" he asks.

"No," I answer feebly.

"Trust me, then. I promise that if you concentrate on your studies in school and here at the shop, I'll arrange an introduction—when the time is right." His voice lowers to nearly a whisper in its seriousness.

I'm so stunned by Whit's acquiescence that I nearly don't catch the part about studying here.

"Wait a sec, Whit. What are you talking about—my studies here at the shop? Do you mean those crusty old books you're always urging me to read instead of doing my homework?" My eyes narrow this time, and I look at Whit, silently appraising him. "And how soon is soon?" I ask.

"Well, my little rose, let's just say there are things they can't teach you in public school that are more important than your Government class or worse, that...nonsense book I saw you reading the other day. What was it? The Classical Dictionary of the Vulgar Tongue?" His tone is uncharacteristically disdainful, and I sense his hesitation. There's something he's not telling me.

"I found that book in a used bookstore across the street. It's from like the 1800s or something. I'm tired of being scolded for swearing, so I decided to change the way I do it."

"Hmm," he harrumphs. "I'll have to have a look at this Vulgar Tongue book."

"What's really going on here, Whit? Why all the scorn for a book I'm reading? I mean, I read all the books you tell me to; I've just added one myself. And what's so wrong with Lincoln High? What do you want me to study, anyway?"

"It's nothing for you to worry about right now. I want to add a few more books and texts to what I've asked you to read. Then you can tell me what you think of them."

But before I can catch myself, I mutter nearly inaudibly, "What in the fu—"

But Whit cuts me off quickly, scolding, "December!! Language!"

"What? I didn't actually say the word! And that's exactly why I was reading that book the other day. I just haven't found a good replacement for the f-word yet...." But I had done it intentionally, hoping to throw Whit off and maybe get more info out of him. But no dice. "And can't you just call me Ember like everybody else?"

"Even referencing the word in such a way is near enough to using the word, and it's not appropriate. I'm not so sure about these alternate words either."

"Ok, Ok, what do you want me to do? A book report about the Celts or something from your stash of esoteric books?" I quip, trying hard not to roll my eyes. Whit's request had been vague at best, per usual, and the word "texts" caught my attention. But the time for questions about arcane subjects had clearly passed. I'll press him later for further information on the matter.

"So, you like the goggles?" His abrupt change of topic further indicates that the matter is definitely closed for now.

"Very much, Whit. Thank you! I needed some for scooting around town. A bug flew in my eye the other day, and I was afraid for a minute that I might crash. And bonus, it seems like I'll be able to wear these with my helmet!"

His generosity and kindness belie the stern facade he often wears in his interactions with me. Though he doesn't say the words, I am positive he cares as much for me as I do for him. He is the closest thing I have to a real parent. There has been almost no one else to show me genuine affection. While Whit's under no obligation to stick around, he's like a godfather to me, and I'm grateful that he arranges my fosters, keeping me out of the state-run system. That would be even worse.

He never talks about his past, but it seems like his life had been on a different path before my parents died, and he stepped in to make sure I'd be ok. Running his hand over his face, he lets out a long sigh. His eyes fixate somewhere off in the distance.

Noticing his faraway look, I break the silence. "How I wish I could see what you see when you get that look in your eyes. It's like you're a million miles away."

"Not quite a million, Little Rose. Much closer, indeed," Whit's voice is as far away as his eyes have been.

"Ugh. Whit, do you have to get so cryptic? What is it that you're not telling me? Why the big secre—"

The clatter of the bells pulls my attention to Nico walking in. Her pupils are tiny, emphasizing her dramatic two-tone eyes, one amber and one sky blue shining brightly against her brown skin. She has her hair twisted into a bunch of tiny buns that she calls bantu knots. A shirt dress over another shirt, with a puffy skirt over both shirts, completes the look. It sounds like it would be a mess by my description, but it's awesome.

"Behold my new boots!" she says as she turns to show me that she's wearing the boots I recently painted for her. They're black, 14-eye Docs featuring little red hearts, each with an eye in the middle.

Whit walks by. "Hello, Nicoletta. Your special order is in."

"Hello, Mr. Whitley. Great, thanks. How are you today?"

"I'm well, and you?"

"Well as well, thank you," she says as he walks by.

"Ember, the special order Nicoletta requested is under the counter in a brown paper bag, if you could ring it up. Thanks."

I give Nico the side-eye. "What is it? Are you ready to reveal the mystery?"

"Nope."

"You're as bad as Whit with your refusal to tell me anything. I'll just enter this item into the log as Nico's mystery item," I say with emphasis, punching the numbers into the cash register. She hands me the cash, and I quickly make change.

"You never know. It might be a birthday gift for someone," Nico teases. She grabs the small bag, tucking it into her cross-body bag.

Looking at me like she's staring into my soul, she asks, "What's up, Chuckaboo? You're lookin' a little booty-hoo."

Putting the back of my hand to my forehead in jest while emphasizing the seriousness of everything, I say, "Dolorem Ipsum—"

"Ouch, it must be bad if you had to get all Latin about it. Talking about Pain Itself, and everything."

My voice is barely a whisper. "Well, yeah, It's this tarot spread I did at lunch, my normal three-card spread. Only The Hermit came up in the first position, The Tower in the second, and of course the Three of Swords in the third position. So if I'm right, whatever situation the cards point to will happen in just a few days."

"Woah, two Major Arcana cards in a three-card spread. That's pretty extra."

"Oh, I know—" But my words are cut off by a loud crash deep in the shop.

"Whiiit?"

"Everything's fine. I'm fine. Just a display toppled over..."

Returning to my whisper, I say, "Well, maybe that was it. I mean my tower card and a tumbling display. Hopefully..."

"Seems unlikely."

"Oh, I know."

But her eyes are distracted by my fidgeting with my new goggles. She reaches her hand toward them. "Well, look-a-lookie here. What are these?"

"Aren't they amazing?! Whit got them for me for scooting."

"May I?" But she grabs them before I can reply. Turning them over in her hands, she manipulates the articulated arms, extending the compass. I see the look on her face as she sees the maker's mark. Her eyes flash in recognition, and I stifle my impulse to ask her if she knows him. If I do, Whit will just interfere. But the look on her face tells me that she knows something. Handing the goggles back, she tries to appear nonchalant.

"They're cool. It'll be nice to not have the bugs fly into your eyes," she says, grimacing. "C'mon, let's go hang out. You're done here, right?"

"Nah, can't tonight. Mrs. Bradshaw will blow a gasket if I'm late for dinner. This weekend?"

"Yeah, sure. See ya mañana."

The clatter of the bells rings again as Nico departs, leaving me to ponder how best to ask her what she knows when I see her tomorrow.

Walking by again, Whit mutters to himself, "There is just something about that girl; I can't put my finger on it. But there is something oddly familiar about her...

•••

In front of him sit thirteen unique creations he's spent weeks crafting and perfecting. Each little wonder feels connected to him, especially once he sang them to life. But it's no good. There's no way he can focus his thoughts, his heart, his voice enough to access the magic. The act is second nature to him by now.

"Focus your thoughts, son." His father's voice rang out through the years in his memories.

"Focus your mind, find the silence. Your Spirit is in all that you are. It's alive in your body and bones, your blood and breath. Pull air into your lungs and it becomes a part of you. Infuse your intention, the force of your will, into your breath as it leaves your body. Then the words you speak and sing, the melodies you intone or hum now contain the full force of your will. It is the heart of Ariamancy." He looked at me with such intensity, placing his hand over my lungs, instructing me to breathe deeply and find the quiet space.

"Good, silence all the little tendrils of thought in your mind. Feel the stillness and silence within you. Ariamancy is an art form. It takes many younglings years to hone their skill. But I have faith in you."

"But Father, if I'm going to use my voice to find my connection to the magic, why would I find the silence?"

"Kenyon, my son, look at me. This is important." Though the words might've sounded chiding, they were spoken affectionately, meant to deepen his connection with his son, something he'd neglected since Magðalena's death. He cleared his mind and began again. "If you enter a room filled with noise, do you think your voice will be heard clearly?"

"No, Father, of course not."

"Of course not. But if we clear our minds and find silence to call the magic forth, we do so with intention and clarity of purpose." His father's gaze held him rapt.

"If you cannot clear your mind, the magic you manifest will not be as precise. You can certainly find your voice and sing to the magic, call it into the world without that clarity. But it is in silence that we hear and speak

and sing with the magic. Energy is a living thing. It is not in servitude to us. We must work with it, make it our ally."

"So what happens if I use the magic without that clarity? Will something bad happen?"

"That depends upon your intention, son. But in general, it simply means that whatever spell of creation you're singing to life will not be as strong and focused as it could be."

"Ok," he'd replied, overwhelmed by this new lesson. He was thirteen, excited to learn how to access the magic he'd felt in his body and bones. But he hadn't expected it to be so serious, so much responsibility.

Kenyon shakes his head, returning to the present, trying to clear his thoughts and find his quiet. These creations deserve my full attention. His fingers massage his forehead before dragging through his thick black hair. "I give up," he says to himself, defeated. "Maybe I can do this tomorrow."

3
all in my mind

Kenyon

My workbench sits in chaos, just like my thoughts, just like my life for that matter. Partially finished devices and tools clutter every surface of my workshop, but a certain amount of disorder is good for my creative process. I can't seem to get my mind together, though. My whole life feels at odds right now. I want to change everything. This house, my life, my mood, my baggage. But starting with the house seems easiest. And though I grew up here, it has never felt like a home to me. It's haunted by the fleeting dreams of the generations before me. But those have never been my dreams. I'd sell Three Arrows, the grandest home of the family's estate, if I could. But my father was adamant that it remain in the family; it's our "Seat of Power," he always said. I almost hear his voice: "Our ancestors bled for this land. Died on this land. Their bones are the foundation of this home. Our DNA is a part of this land! There is no other way to create a connection as strong as the one here."

That's likely to end with me, anyway. I'll never let love conquer me the way it did my father. He became a ghost of a man after my mother and my unborn sister died. I was there, but I don't remember– thank the Nine Worlds for that. While I will never let love in so far that it owns my soul and brings me to my knees, I'm still willing to admit that I'm lonely. I can't escape the coldness, the emptiness.

It never feels like anyone can see me. They see the money, or at least that's how it feels. I don't know; maybe I don't see them either. No matter how many women I'm with, I'm always left wanting. And yes, I know I sound like a womanizer. It's the way it turns out: Kenyon McQuiston, the cad, the one who's only out for one thing.

Still, though, this breakup with Lottie was beyond the pale. It's been months, but she's still pursuing me. I never meant to hurt her, but she just isn't "The One." She definitely wants to be and thinks she is.

Good on paper doesn't always translate to good in real life, and she just didn't do it for me. I guess I should've known better. Believe me, I tried, but between the lack of chemistry and my "commitment issues," we didn't stand a chance. I mean, why would I work so hard to force something when other women are out there?

I wish I could talk to someone about all of this. Even if my dad was here, it's not like I could talk to him. I thought about talking to Whit. He's been there for me as long as I can remember, but he's been acting strange lately, a bit distant. Maybe I'll bring it up anyway.

My hands fidget with the tiny gears of the watch I was inspired to make. All around me, books interspersed with canisters of mechanisms, gears, and an odd assortment of magical equipage help me bring this creation to life. Enchanted mechanical lightning bugs hover above me, augmenting the light streaming in the windows. And while I may have made and infused each small bug with its phosphorescence, it's still a sight to behold. I love singing the draíochta into form, first, the focus, the substance, and finally, the form, conjuring magic into the world with my hands, my voice, my mind. It's what I live for.

Staring into the distance at nothing in particular again, surrounded by so many projects in various states, I consider how many hours I've wasted just sitting here, thinking of her, wondering how much different my life could've been if she'd lived, wondering if it was my fault that she was dead. Father was always quick to assure me that it wasn't, but I could never fully remember the circumstances that had taken her. And I was the only one home when it happened, standing over her body, crying, a sick feeling in my stomach and foggy mind that refused to clear. There was no way to know what happened that day. At the very least, I feel partly responsible. I had been old enough to react, to help her, and instead of alerting someone, I stood there in shock, crying over her body.

Still holding the watch, I marvel at it: equal parts watch, moon phase observation, and planetary alignments all in one. It's nearly complete, but I find no pleasure in examining its intricacies. Instead, my mind wanders, pondering the curious old man. Though I left him hours ago, I can't stop thinking about Mr. Whitley.

Man, he was strange today. What was the rush? It's not like it was closing time. He lives above the shop anyway. Why would he be in such a hurry to get rid of me? All I wanted was to talk and hang out. I'll never forget hanging out with him and my father at the shop. Is it so terrible to spend time with me?

Clearly, he's from Elysia. Why has he exiled himself to such an odd existence in the ordinary world among les Dormeur? The sleepers. Why would anyone leave the world of la Magie? Sure, Elysia is not for everyone, with all its intrigue, gossip, and political machination. Still, there are plenty of other cities in the magical realm, the Commonwealth of Atlaria. Why would he choose a life without magic?

Memories of Mr. Whitley reach far into my childhood. The "field trips," as Father called them, were the best. Whenever they spent time together, Father seemed more animated, more engaged. Even better, she was there. They would reminisce about the old times while I would play with her. Hide and seek in the overcrowded shop was our favorite. I would run around the shop, pushing clothes aside to find her crouched in the middle of the rack. Jumping into the space next to her, my small arms wrapping around her neck, I could never resist getting as close to her as possible. I would rub our cheeks together, touching the soft skin of her face. Instinctively, my hand rubs my cheek, grazing my now-stubbly skin, tingling even now as I remember.

As the scene expands in my memory, I see my father and Mr. Whitley sitting, laughing, and joking. I can almost hear Father's laugh. But instead of pushing the memory away as a painful reminder of the man he could've been, I allow the echo of my father's belly laughs to linger. My father could've been happy. Why could he open up and share those memories, that happiness, with his friend but not me, his only son?

Rather than indulge the old hurt, my mind refocuses on the girl. How is it that I haven't thought about her until now? She was so special to me. How could I have forgotten about her? As I remember the girl who felt like home, my first love, feelings flood over me like a tidal wave, images floating into my memory like a dam bursting, like they've always been there, but they hadn't been. Had they? All I can see is her: haunted eyes and dark hair cut into a pageboy, thick bangs covering her forehead and perpetually pushed off to the side of her face, soft round cheeks and silky hair beckoning to be touched. Both girly and tomboy, dressed in embroidered jeans, sweatshirts with cut-off sleeves and chipped nail polish, she's a dichotomy.

But what was her name? It started with M?

"M.M.M," I repeat to myself over and over, but it's no use. I can't recall it. I give up. Why is it all so foggy? Is someone trying to erase her? Who would even do that? Did Father somehow take my memories from me? Could it have been Mr. Whitley? As soon as the thought occurs to me, I know with certainty that it's true. But how? And why?

And why does he live in that little emporium of treasures from an abandoned life, inconsequential minor magical items mixed with an astonishing assortment of random junk? Why does he live in les Dormeur but always wants to know everything going on here? Why does he stock his shop with items from Elysia? If Whit left this world, why does he want to keep so much of it with him? He's almost—almost greedy for it. Reminders of the life he left behind must fill the old man with sadness. Man, I just don't get him. And what about her? Where is the girl I remember? Is she the one I've been making these items for all along? Could it be her? Is she still there, hiding in plain sight? Perhaps it's time to play hide and seek again.

I brush back stray black hair, determined to figure out this mystery.

And why all the secrecy of our dealings? I mean, beyond the fact that it isn't exactly allowed to export items from here to the outside world. The council had long ago set the guidance that once a denizen of La Magie departed and chose a life free of magic, they must give up their ties and use of magic. I've never questioned it much. My father brought him so many things over the years, but now it's worth examining the matter from a fresh perspective.

I let my vision go lazy and unfocused., recalling that something on the counter had caught my attention. That purple folder had runes circles around an old protection symbol. But what did the runes spell out? I guess I just didn't pay enough attention, but I know there was a name. This was no folder of shop receipts or ledgers. It belonged to a student; it belongs to her. I am as certain of it as of anything I had ever been, and I can't tell you why. I just know.

I force the imagery of the counter to come into sharper focus, pushing all of the force of my energy, my magic, to the folder. Thank the Nine Worlds for a photographic memory. I narrow my gaze to the name written on the folder. There it is! Ember Wright. That's her name. "Ha!" I laugh. "I knew it started with a M, kind of...

I can't believe I finally know her name. This calls for a celebration! Instead I'm hit with another wave of sadness, averting my eyes from the corner of the room that once housed Father's workspace. He enjoyed working in the same space as me, watching the spark of understanding come to life as I learned my craft. I practically lived for that look in his eyes. It was the only time I felt any connection to my father. He may have been emotionally vacant, but his passion for the work survived; that's how I could make him see me beyond his memories of my mother. He'd remark on how much I looked like her, saying quietly and wistfully, "So like my Lena. She lives on in you."

As absent as my father had been, at least I have that to hold onto–his pride in my accomplishments. This very pride has driven me to accomplish as much as I have, ascending to the highest levels of the Maker's Guild, revolutionizing inventions and making a fortune of my own. I've done all this in my father's memory because I know he would've been proud of me. I just wish I could hear him say it.

"I miss you, Dad." I whisper the words through the growing lump in my throat, my voice thick. I take a deep breath and shake my head as if I can ward off all the feelings my memories have inspired. "So much for ghosts." My mind returns to Mr. Whitley and his most recent custom order, the rose-colored lenses. I can't focus enough to sing anything awake today, not with these thoughts whirling around in my brain. My mind returns again and again to the connections, the questions, the girl.

Grabbing my coat, I move toward the door. This mystery won't wait.

4
killing time
Whit

I light the candles lining the spell-casting circle on the floor. Its obsidian lines protect from psychic attack with a wider ring of clear quartz amplifying the magic. Painstakingly cut and shaped crystalline formations fit into routed grooves I carved into the floors so many years ago. There was little magic to be found in les Dormeur, but I was determined to find every bit available to me.

It had been the work of more than a year to covertly procure these crystals for my summoning circle. My now-departed friend and only confidant, Merrick, went to great lengths to provide them. We were two men who'd lost everything and everyone we'd ever loved in an instant, though the circumstances surrounding that loss had been vastly different. My heart breaks when I think of Meri and the son he'd left behind. I miss the clandestine meetings that maintained our friendship over the years. Even now, in this space so many years later, gratitude swells within me and I blink away tears. The ability to tell someone, especially a friend, about my situation preserved my sanity, even as I was trapped in les Dormeur.

Meri and I solidified our friendship during our apprenticeship in the Maker's Guild. We became so close that I'd been the attendant at his vows ceremony. Meri and Lena had an undeniable connection, so much so that she'd forgone taking her Orders with the Priory of the Vala. I'd secretly envied them, so fearless in their pursuit of love. But that was years ago and I have work to do. "Trips down memory lane aren't going to get this Geasa Droma Draíochta spell woven..."

I clear my mind and focus my thoughts, reaching deep within. The familiar swell of power grows in the center of my chest. Mystical energy tingles within me, making me feel more alive. As much as that power might be restricted in the mundane world, I'm still capable of summoning up enough to bind her powers, though the magic I wove around Ember dissipates more quickly with each passing day. This is the third time I've had to bind her abilities this month—nearly every week now. Will my influence wane as she nears the age of majority? Eighteen is only the age of adulthood here in les Dormeur, not Elysia. Maybe because we live in this realm rather than our own, we are bound to their rules.

Sitting on my meditation cushion, I shift my weight, buckwheat hulls inside crunching together. The crackle distracts and irritates me as I try to silence my mind. But my body complains too much to sit on the unpadded wood floor. Looking down at my photos of Ember, I narrow my focus to her. I can't wait until all this hiding in plain sight ends! It'll be a relief to go home and feel real power again. But underneath my desire to return home lurks an inescapable fear of what I'll find. How will it play out when it finally happens? No use dwelling on it, but my chest tightens and my pulse quickens at the thought of having to admit the truth. As I look at her photos, a flash of memory overtakes my thoughts. I'm kneeling down to kiss the palms of a five-year-old Ember. She imitates the gesture, professing her love for me. My heart squeezes again at the image repeating in my mind. And once again, I redirect my thoughts.

"Oh, for the love of the Nine Worlds, she'll either accept it or she won't, she'll forgive you, or she won't. Worrying isn't getting her powers any closer to being bound, is it?" I chide myself once again.

Reaching down, I sprinkle Dragon's Blood, Copal, and Nag Champa onto the hot charcoal tablet beside me. With a crow feather, I waft the fragrant smoke around the space. Finally the space feels ready. I open my mouth, and my tenor voice emits a melody of my own making. Each practitioner's song invokes their magic if they're gifted in the art of Ariamancy, a complementary branch of the magical practice to Thaumaturgy. My voice, clear and strong, explores the resonance between the notes, bending the pitch to catalyze the energy building within me.

Thin gold lines on my summoning circle's final border begin to glow, now hot to the touch. Adding the real gold had been costly, but it paid off with the power it helps me achieve. The natural energy conductor has given me access to more magic. My voice rises and falls as I intone my Spirit Song. The magic in my voice causes the crystals' jagged points along the eight compass points to vibrate. The crystals emit a pulsing luminescent glow, highlighting the swirling energy within their crystalline structure as they cast shadows into the circle. They sing in sympathetic resonance with my voice, taking on the same vibrational frequency as my unique magic, a task that becomes easier with every spell casting. We've developed a relationship. They know me, my voice, my energy. The magic I can scrape together soothes me, slowing my breathing and clearing my head.

The smell of ozone fills my nostrils. The smell of magic reminds me of home, making me long for the people I've left behind. The mystery of my disappearance, unsolved. I hope in the end, they can all forgive me. Especially Ember.

I force my thoughts to order themselves into logical progressions. There's an odd echoing sensation in my ears, and my voice trails off, the final notes of my personal song of conjuring fading away. It takes a few moments longer to fade from my inner ears, my Hearing ears. I rub the back of my neck and up into my temples.

The gift of clairaudience had not presented itself within me at the usual age of 13-15. I'd been well into my apprenticeship with the Makers Guild when they began manifesting. For all their tardiness, though, they integrated so seamlessly into my other senses that I may as well have had them from birth. As a novitiate, I hadn't endured the usual tedious exercises to hone my gift. Words like gifted and prodigy were used. Though I'd never wanted the gift, living here in les Dormeur, so far removed from home, draíochta, the mystery of it, feels like a piece of my soul is missing. Hearing anything within the protective power summoning circle makes me feel whole again.

Here I am, still and quiet, Listening with my inner Hearing, waiting for the guidance to come through.

> ... The reckoning draws near, and the gift manifests
> daily...

The words are spare and straight to the point. The act of Listening is something I've never understood. It's different here than in la Magie. Still, my lack of understanding has done nothing to deter my belief in my gift. It's a quiet conviction that manifests into my knowledge, as though it had always been a part of my understanding. The gift varies from person to person with varying degrees of success. I never doubt the Knowing. I know what I heard is the truth—and for the second time that week, I set about binding my daughter's gifts.

I can't afford for her to have any breakthrough Visions or guidance being whispered in her ears. Thank the nine... that she was too young to remember her abilities as they began manifesting within her. They came early. While proper magic was much more difficult to perform here, the gift itself was less affected. She would go on and on as a child about pictures that appeared in her mind, the things she heard, the voice that whispered answers to unasked questions to her like an invisible friend. How could her gifts manifest at such a young age, without even living in the magical cities?

She would be powerful as she grew into her powers, making them all the more difficult to contain until the time was right to free them. Squeezing my eyes together tightly, I try to focus on my task. Everything depends upon it.

5

burning skies

Ember

I go right instead of left when I reach the intersection. "Why am I even doing this? There'll be hell to pay for being late for dinner. Ugh, some things just can't wait." I turn my scooter toward the abandoned mental institution, with its water tower looming above the city.

Thanks to Whit, my helmet feels like a lead weight, squishing my ratted hair into a flat mess as my headphones and new goggles compete for space. Siouxsie and the Banshees suit my mood for this ride, and the music is loud enough to hear over the noise of the road and the wind. As I get closer to the mental hospital, the streets are deserted as far as I can see.

Now that I'm completely alone, I can sing along. I love the way that singing feels, the way the notes expand in my throat and then my mind, but something is missing, like trying to solve a riddle with only half the information needed. So many times I'd wished I could sing. When I was young, one of my foster fathers was a singer in the church choir. I tried to join and was tactfully told, "Your talents are best utilized where they shine the brightest." It took me months to realize that I was tone deaf and not really welcome in their choir.

"You have so many talents, Ember. Is it necessary to do everything?" and "Jack of all trades, master of none." And of course the absolute worst: "You have so much potential."

I could never express that my need to sing always felt like a compulsion, but Whit always got so weird when he heard me singing, like my voice set his nerves on fire or something. So, all that discouragement pushed me to pursue other talents.

"Man, what is it with all the odd images and memories today?!" I mutter to no one. "Those images that popped into my head when I was about to pick up Ms. Regana's shawl were so strange. It really felt like I was seeing her as a younger woman in some Loom Room. Great, I'm talking to myself again, trying to work it out. And now, riding toward the old deserted mental asylum. What the hell?"

Perfectly ordinary little bungalows and ranch houses sit unperturbed by the structures that give the city's residents discomfort, or a serious case of the "heebie-jeebies," as everyone says. I always thought they were just being superstitious, but I can't deny that something is off about this place.

As I get closer, the houses become more run down. A weathered orange brick water tower looms overhead, rising far above the tree line. Curious about the building, I found out it was once the largest asylum in the state, but it had previously been a quarantine facility for people afflicted with tuberculosis.

The streets stretch and curve before me, deciduous trees forming a canopy above my head. Gathering storm clouds look ready to explode into rain as I approach the hospital. I've never been this close. For all the time I've spent gazing up at the institution, I've never actually been here. Laughter escapes my lips as I look from side to side, "Finally, I made it. Hope they don't decide to keep me here."

Clouds overhead continue to darken, but when the institution's main building comes into view, I pull into the parking lot. Hastily I park the scooter, take off my helmet, and grab my book bag. I begin to remove the goggles but hesitate, remembering the way they showed me the iridescent aura that hovered around Whit. Maybe they'll show me something here, too.

I'm surprised, but not really, to find graffiti scrawled on some of the surfaces of the building. Blackened windows highlight the spiderweb cracks etched in other windows. It's larger than my school and surrounded by other smaller buildings equally run down. Patchy grass and a dandelion-peppered lawn underfoot complete the dilapidated vibe. But there's something else. An odd awareness plays at the edge of my consciousness. It certainly isn't the first time, but it's stronger now, buzzing my senses like an alarm.

I squint at the building, narrowing my eyes to tiny slits like I can trick the building into thinking I'm not looking at it. I want it to reveal all its secrets. I lift my goggles, then put them back in place, lift them and replace them again. There's something slightly off about the scene. My vision seems clearer when I have the goggles on than when I take them off, like what I'm seeing is partly transparent when I have them on. Even when I remove the goggles, I can sense the place's wrongness, but with them on, there's a sort of ghost image that is way more than my imagination. I close my eyes hard and squinch them up, the afterimage still casting a shadow on the blackness of my eyelids. Opening my eyes, the superimposed quality of the asylum is still there. "Clearly, you are losing your shit. And you really should just go home, probably late for dinner already..." I mumble to myself.

I know I should feel creeped out walking around the deserted grounds with everything I'm seeing, but I don't. Absently I put my hand into my bag, my fingers seeking the woolen yarn of the hat I'm knitting. Simply touching cashmere yarn shouldn't make me feel better, but it does. My most profound thoughts and realizations usually come as I knit.

As I round the corner of the building, I spy a bench in what would've been a courtyard. Walking to it, I sit down. Staring at the deserted building, I pull the hat out of my bag, wrap the inky yarn once around the ring finger, under the middle, and a double loop around the index finger of my left hand, just like I always do. With needles in hand, I begin knitting. In a pause between songs on my mixtape, I hear the subtle clicking of the needles. The familiar voice of Morrissey melodically ignites a pang of loneliness within me as "There Is A Light That Never Goes Out" plays. Yearning for that feeling fills me, wanting to be seen and loved for who I am. Somehow, a song expressing the true belonging of finding a home within another makes me feel sadder than the loneliest of songs.

As I pass one loop through another, one loop through another, one loop through another, the familiar calming rhythm of knitting clears my mind. I become rhythm and feelings. In the distance, the crack of lightning shakes my reverie, and the scent of ozone fills my nose, the familiar smell of rain. It's coming, but I can't leave.

A low rumbling begins to sound overhead, audible even over the music. It won't be long now. It's going to be a wet ride home. Just want to finish this round and then I'll go face the music. Again the rumbling begins, and I quicken the pace of my work. Finishing the round, I place little blue foam caps on the ends of the knitting needles, looking up from the project just in time to see a crack of lightning blaze across the darkening sky.

As electrical energy surges across the sky in its momentary light show, the scene before my eyes changes from a crumbling brick building to something else for just an instant, rising high above the hospital's ghost image, lingering like a projection. My stomach lurches, my breath catches in my throat, my feeling is confirmed: there is a secret here.

A towering building rises high enough that I can't see it all without looking upward, but before I can, it disappears, the afterimage burned into my mind's eye. It looks like nothing in this unremarkable city and everything like a building in my imaginary city. I blink hard, but all I can see now is the moldering structure that's always been there. I blink again, but it's no use. It's not coming back.

The first drops of rain fall. The loud rumble of thunder sounds again. I stuff the knitting back into my bag, running toward my scooter.

Strapping my bag to the luggage rack, I grab the helmet and shove it on my head. The scooter hums to life and I make for home, hoping to beat the worst of the oncoming storm. But those first few drops give way to a torrent that leaves me soaked to the skin within seconds.

I stand dripping at the back door of the Bradshaw home, setting my wet canvas bag down and taking my boots off. They make squishing sounds as I shift my weight from one foot to the other. From around the corner, Mrs. B walks into the little mudroom. "Well, you're really bringing the mud to this mudroom, aren't you, Ember? Why are you late? If you had come straight home from that junk shop, you would've beaten this rain."

A truthful answer will cause more questions and get me into more trouble, so I say, "I'm sorry, I had a rough day at school and I was riding around." This is true to a point, I think—omitting the part about the asylum isn't going to hurt anyone.

"Well, while you were out joyriding, you missed dinner. There are leftovers in the fridge if you're hungry." She begins to walk away. "Just don't make a mess."

6
happy house

Ember

I gasp, awakening from the nightmare. It's here again. Will it ever stop? My jaw is locked, teeth clenched tightly, pain radiating to my temples, nails clenched tightly into my palms. Crescent moon shapes appear on my hands, etched in red. Small droplets of sweat trickle down into my hair. This dream haunts me as far back as I can remember.

The landscape of the dream is familiar. I have been there hundreds of times, the spires of a familiar yet unknown city, modern to the point of futuristic. Lush green hills in the backdrop contrast sharply with high buildings.

In the way of dreams, I find myself with my mother—beautiful, sweet, and still alive. Her voice is high, sweet, and clear as she intones a melody whose words I can't make out. It's only in the real world that I'm trapped away from you, she says, half singing, half speaking. But in our dream world, I can always talk to you. I lie with my head in her lap, her hands brushing over my hair, saying it again and again: I wish I could be with you. Sadness colors her voice as she repeats the words. Maybe someday we'll find each other. Again, her voice rings out in a hypnotic timbre. It all feels so real.

As my mother pets my head, there's a transformation happening, unbeknownst to me. Her hand slows and hovers around my forehead until her fingers find the iridescent white marks surrounding my hairline. That's always when the physical sensations begin, alerting me of the change. It's dangerous. She begins to press on the white spots, first softly, then firmly, then so hard that her fingers are a focused point of searing pain.

With an extreme effort of will, I jerk my head away, something that's easier now than when I was a small child. Turning to face her, I'm horrified to find a faceless woman. The contours are all there, but not the features—a vaguely nose-shaped bump but no definition. Her mouth is now a sucking hole, her eyes black, empty, vacuous, threatening to consume more of her face.

This nightmare woman reaches for me, desperate to take something. All the while, I sleep, locked into a contest of wills with an unknown foe, this villain blotting out the memory of my mother's lovely face with this monstrous parody of features. I'm trapped in a small room as she tries to get her hands on me, her hunger palpable. Slowly, one labored step after another, the villain edges closer, her hands outstretched, locked in a wordless struggle for dominance. Her hunger intensifies, the dream harder and harder to shake, the headache getting worse.

As usual, the struggle jars me awake, just as the woman is about to overpower me. But for the first time, I remember my mother's face, at least the dream version of her, anyway. It's layered in my memory over the monstrous face I usually remember. It feels like she's pushing for something, testing me. What does she want? Whatever it is, it's locked tightly within, and it feels like giving in will leave me a hollow husk. Oh hell, this is a dream I'm talking about, not a real woman, not my real mother either; she's a nightmare.

I lay there, my breath ragged and quick. Sitting up, I look out of the bedroom window. A full moon, just like always. So much for going to bed early. Everything is as it should be in my room: posters of The Cure and Siouxsie and the Banshees stare down at me from the bright white walls glowing in the moonlight. The posters and a few of my own cityscape drawings are the few things that reflect my taste or interests. How is this city so beautiful, but whenever I'm there, it turns into a nightmare? My fingers fidget, working the silken edge of the velvety Velluxe blanket as the headache pounds my temples.

"Great, only a half hour 'til my alarm goes off. No point in trying to go back to sleep." I'm too unsettled, and that will last all day. This is the worst possible day for my head to be in a daze. I have that stupid test today in geometry, and I really need to do well on it. I sigh. There's no getting around it.

But having this first remembered glimpse of my dream mother, I'm anxious to commit her memory to paper. I sit up in bed and grab my sketch pad and charcoal. My hands fly in broad strokes as the charcoal marks the white paper, the lines of her face and her eyes undeniably like mine. Though I draw furiously to recapture every detail, the woman's image is indelibly burned in my mind's eye. There will be no unseeing it.

I have no memories of my mother and am desperate to know more about her. Whit will rarely discuss her, saying, "It's better to focus on the future than reminisce about the past. No amount of wishing or wanting can change things." I've basically given up.

The pink rays of the rising sun replace the moonlight. I pull the covers over my head, not wanting to face the day. Groaning, I pull the covers back down again. Might as well get up now and beat the rush to the shower. An hour of makeup and hairstyling and another half an hour of dressing, and I'll be able to face the world.

I open the small closet that also holds Mrs. Bradshaw's off-season wardrobe. My fingers push the hangers to the left until I find one of my favorite outfits. Thank goodness the days are finally warm enough to wear it. I started with an old corset I found at Whit's and hand-sewed scraps of cool fabric and lace onto it. I call it Post-Punk Patchwork, paired with a full lace skirt and crinoline underneath. I layer on silver jewelry pieces, including an ancient Egyptian ankh, a dragon pin, a rhinestone choker, and a cartouche that hangs suspended on a long chain: a gift from Whit that spells out my name in Egyptian hieroglyphics. I twist my nose ring around so the flattish part of my homemade ring is on the inside of my nose and pull on some fishnets, followed by my Docs. Finally, I grab the lightweight wool scarf I designed and knit a few years ago. It's absurdly long, reaching mid-calf in front and back after being looped around my neck, the length inspired by the Fourth Doctor in the Doctor Who lineup. Sci-fi television and movies are my not-so-secret obsession, something I picked up from a foster father.

"Off to face the Borg drones," I mutter to myself, referencing the automaton characters I saw on Star Trek the night before. I take the stairs quickly, running late as usual. Even before I reach the kitchen, I hear Mrs. B. humming to herself, bright and cheerful, a flurry of activity. The middle-aged woman busies herself, opening and closing the carved honey oak cabinets in her country kitchen, then walking the circuit between the sink, the almond-colored double door refrigerator, and the stove. She wears a chambray dress cinched at the waist by a matching oversized belt. Her short frosted hair feathers away from her face. Like chambray, she's the poster child for average.

Even in her haste, I know she'll never miss an opportunity to remind me. "Ember, black is such an off-putting color. So—morbid. Maybe if you wore something bright and cheery you'd have an easier time making friends. I think you'd look pretty in pink..."

My foster brother, Eric, echoes her sentiments. "Going to a Halloween party after school, Ember?"

I stick out my tongue and mouth the word Jackanapes at him, satisfied that my antiquated insult will stump him." Really, Eric? Shouldn't you be at sportsball practice? Batting your football or something?" Mixing up the sports will infuriate him.

"You two, could you at least try to get along?" Mrs. Bradshaw chides, exasperated.

"Sorry, Mrs. B," I mumble.

Eric looks smug as he whispers, "Home court advantage. You lose. Or should I say 'you loser?'"

"Blunderbuss."

Mrs. Bradshaw shoots a look over her shoulder at us. "Enough," she says, her tone finishing the argument.

Sitting in my first-hour art class, I bring the image of my dream mother back to mind, hoping that analyzing it again might yield a clue. I have no idea what my mother actually looked like, only this dream version.

If I pull some tarot cards about it, I'll get the three of swords, but I've been getting the Tower card lately. Fingers crossed, the predicted upheaval, chaos, and destruction visualized by the tower's collapse have not happened—yet.

I refocus my mind, putting my pencil on the paper. "Maybe drawing her again, differently, will give me a new perspective," I mumble to myself, sketching out the shape of the woman in short strokes.

Predictably, my day flies by as I live in my head. My daze is all-encompassing as I think and rethink my nightmare. I walk through the hall between fifth and sixth-hour classes, row after row of tan lockers set into old brick walls stretching out before me. I've only been going through the motions today, still caught up in the dream. It's so simple but feels so real. Maybe I'll tell Whit about the dreams. Maybe he'll know something. I mean, he knows about everything else...

Walking down the hall, my thoughts far away, a familiar arm wraps itself through mine, and Nico pulls me to her. I can see the concern on her face.

"What's wrong, babe? You're dazed."

"I've got the morbs, that's all." We round a corner, and she pulls me into the girl's bathroom before I can say anything more. There's only one other person there, but unfortunately, it's Jane-the-big-mouth-Martin standing at the mirror, applying lip gloss to her full lips. Everything about her is exaggerated in its proportions. Large, heavily mascaraed eyes peer out from behind translucent peach glasses, the many bangle bracelets tinkling with each move of her hand. Her tightly fitting Guess overalls are worn over a white sleeveless turtleneck, accentuating her petite figure.

"Why so glum, chum?" Nico asks.

I look in Jane's direction as I answer her question. "Nothing. I just didn't sleep well last night." I know that Nico figures out that I'm reluctant to talk in front of Jane, who is doing little to disguise her interest in our conversation.

Nico walks toward the mirror, saying, "Listen, Elton Jane, why don't you give the lip gloss a rest and mind your own business?"

I stifle a laugh at Nico's clever jibe. I don't usually condone making fun of people with glasses, but I'll make an exception for Jane.

Jane's mouth drops open and she shoves her gloss into her overall front pocket, leaving in a huff. Nico returns her attention to me. "Now that Big Mouth Martin is gone, what's wrong? Did you have the dream again?"

She's the only person I've told about the nightmare. "Yeah, I did, but I actually remembered the woman's face this time when I woke up. It's the first time that's happened. I drew her in Art Class this morning."

A look passes over her face. I'm afraid to ask, but I risk it anyway. "What is it?"

"Oh, I just hate that you have nightmares about your mother that are so messed up. It's bad enough that you don't have any memories of her, but then to have some phantom baddie of a mother show up to haunt your dreams? It sucks."

"Um, yeah, it does. But I'm more concerned that I didn't do well on my test this morning. I'm used to the stupid dream," I reply. "That and things were tense this morning at the Bradshaws. I can't wait until I'm eighteen and can move out. Being roommates with you will be awesome!"

"Can't wait, babe. I've already started looking at places. Now come on! We'd better get to class before we're late."

After we walk into the hall, I hear my name called over the intercom.

"December Wright, please report to the office."

My stomach gives an unexpected jolt at hearing my full name. I groan and roll my eyes. The intercom's hum and crackle make the school's secretary sound like she's speaking through a tin can, calling the entire school's attention to me. Turning back in the direction I've come from, the halls one after another look the same, creating a never-ending corridor.

… guarded words heard in a dream
a secret no one speaks
is there a light in the dark
or is it a fire to burn away the secret
leaving only ashes in my hands…

There they are again—song lyrics. Unbidden, as always, getting stuck in my head like a feedback loop, driving me crazy. I do my best to ignore them. Distracting myself as I walk, I note every detail of the hall, obstinately focusing my thoughts on the thin rectangular bricks sandwiched between rows of scratched lockers, but it's not helping.

"Jennifer Slater, please report to the office." The abrupt voice and buzz from the speaker startle me out of my thoughts.

"S'cuse me!" The voice comes out of nowhere as a girl nearly plows into me in her rush to the office. She has an almost identical hairstyle to half the other girls in this school: permed hair, long layers in the back with a shorter top and sides. She has the usual giant curled bangs and sides hair sprayed out to look like wings. "More of the Lowest Common Denominator styles for all of the normal girls in this school," I mumble before realizing I've said it. But Jennifer hears me. Slowing, she replies, "What's your problem anyway, freak? Jeez, you're so weird."

"What was your first clue?" I ask in answer to her insult. She just scoffs in return and picks up her pace. Why should I care if people live their entire lives in the mediocrity they seem to enjoy? Damned if I know and damned if I'm not tired of trying to figure it out.

Finally, the poured concrete floor transitions to green-flecked tiles at the office entrance. I open the door quietly with my head down. I'm greeted by the whirr of the ditto machine and the smell of ink on paper as a teacher cranks out copies of something. I note the musky perfume of the school secretary. There's a small bank of windows behind her desk, offering a much-needed airing out of the accumulated stale smells that winter's locked windows caused. Only momentarily do I look up from the floor tiles.

"You called me, Mrs. Reid?" My voice is only slightly more than a whisper; no need to draw more attention to myself than necessary.

"Oh, sure, Ember. Somebody turned your watch into the Lost and Found," Mrs. Reid says distractedly, trying to do at least three things at once. The slight woman is friendly enough unless you're in trouble. Her thick, wavy, blonde hair is cut at precise angles, swinging gracefully forward just below her chin. She leans forward to retrieve a watch and holds it up for me in one fluid, graceful motion.

She smiles, holding the watch in her outstretched hand. "Something wrong, dear?"

Automatically, I look down at my wrist to double-check that mine is on my wrist. My all-black Swatch watch is where it should be, "Aaahh, there must be some kind of mistake, Mrs. Reid. I haven't lost my watch."

"I don't know, Ember. It looks like something you would wear," Mrs. Reid replies. She turns the intricately fashioned timepiece over to look at the underside. "It has your name engraved on the back. If it's not yours, I can't imagine whose it would be, so there you go."

Slowly, with timid fingers, I reach for the watch I've never seen, let alone touched, before. What I can see of the timepiece is beautiful. It does seem like something I would wear.

In truth, I rarely look at my watch because I have an uncanny sense of time. I only bought it because I got a gift certificate for a store in the mall. Honestly, it fails to make me feel like the cool urban people featured in the magazine ads. I feel more like an underprivileged kid who's spent too much money in a prestige brand department store—a kid that the loss prevention staff follow with suspicion.

This watch is different from the fashion piece on my wrist. As I turn it over, my fingers find nooks that seem made for them. I'm again dumbstruck to see my name delicately etched onto the back.

My heart flutters as I gasp in surprise, realizing only then that I'd been holding my breath. The gasp is inspired not by the etched name but by the hand that had done the etching. There is no doubt that at the bottom of the plate is the maker's mark. Three Arrows made this watch for me because he wanted, somehow, to reach out to me, to know me. This is no secretive order Whit made. This is Three Arrows, himself, thinking of me.

My heart pounding loudly in my chest, I hear the blood rushing in my ears for several long seconds before I realize I'm still standing there, mute. Looking up, Mrs. Reid notices me staring at the watch. "Ember, is there something wrong?" There's a puzzled look on her face.

"Oh, right—sorry, Mrs. Reid, sorry to bother you, but did you see who dropped the watch by the Lost and Found?" This question burns on my lips, the answer holding so many possibilities for me—hopefully.

"Sure, dear. It was Molly Christina Larsen," she says with a shrug.

I head to the door, offering a quick thank you to Mrs. Reid. Finding Molly is now my first priority. I glance down quickly at the watch's face, seeing three minutes left until the bell sounds for the last period. Molly is a sophomore, cute and sweet and easy to approach.

I nearly knock into a small clique of popular senior girls as I rush toward the sophomore classroom halls. "Watch it, freak," one says. Another chimes in. "Undertaker's convention after school today, Ember?"

My face tingles, and I flush scarlet with embarrassment. If I had a less important thing to do, it might bother me more than it does today. As it is, I barely have time to mumble apologies while passing them.

How did Molly find the watch? Did she see him? Three Arrows, or the guy the arrows on all his creations represented, has been at my school, knows about me, and is interested in who I am.

Seeing Molly out of the corner of my eye, I stop abruptly, unexpectedly skidding at the sight of her. I've nearly passed right by her, not more than a hundred feet beyond the senior girls. I didn't expect to find her in this hall with all the junior and senior classrooms. "Molly Christina!"

With my voice much louder than usual, I nearly pant to catch my breath, my feet again skidding to a halt just in front of her, drawing way too much attention to myself. Molly's face blanches in surprise at my voice. With her blonde french braids on either side of her head, she's got a quasi-Swiss Miss vibe, her overly large blue eyes showing surprise.

"Sorry! Didn't mean to startle you." Hopefully this girl can shed some light on the mystery. "Molly Christina, did you find this watch and turn it into the 'Lost and Found'? Where did you find it? Did you see anybody that doesn't go to school here? When did you find this?" I force the words out of near-breathless lungs.

Molly looks at me hesitantly. "Yeah, I was by the front door, coming back from lunch. I looked up, and a guy stood there, kind of weird-looking." She flinches slightly at having called him weird-looking but continues her story. "He was just standing there, out of nowhere, holding the watch and looking at me, so I asked him if he needed something. He held the watch out for me to take and told me he thought someone must've lost it and wondered if I could take it to the Lost and Found."

"Did he say anything else? Does he go to school here? What did he look like?" I'd like to ask her about a hundred more questions, but our time is limited and she probably already thinks I'm a total weirdo, so I ask only the most pressing.

"No," Molly begins slowly, as though she's genuinely thinking about the questions. "He didn't say that much, and I don't think he goes to this school. He looked a bit older—maybe two or three years?"

Molly is momentarily lost in thought again, trying to recall every detail. Finally, she stammers, "You know, h—he... he kind of reminded me of you, a little bit. Maybe." It's apparent Molly doesn't want to be rude by pointing out the obvious differences between me and everyone else, yet she wants to give all the information she has to offer.

This last bit is all it takes to ignite my hopes.

"Thank you so much, Molly Christina!" I say, moving away toward the school's side entrance. With no regard for the fact that I'm about to cut my sixth-hour class, my hands hit the dull brass bar on the old wooden door, and I rush to the side parking lot.

Fortunately, I scored a good parking spot this morning, out of sight of the office window. I'm sure I won't make it through an entire class with this watch in my hand and this knowledge in my brain. I head toward the Vespa, intending to go straight away to Whit's place, wondering what, if anything, he'll have to say about this.

As I scoot toward the shop, I notice the streets in that direction are remarkably clear. Thoughts buzz: Whit probably doesn't know about the watch or the visit from Three Arrows. How can he? If it was Whit's intention that I have this strange watch, he'd have given it to me a few days ago with the goggles. If I tell Whit about the watch, he'll be suspicious and prying about it. He's always been so dodgy about me meeting Three Arrows.

"Man, I have got to find out his name or come up with a better one for him..." I stop at a red light, my mind wrapped up in this mystery.

Not really noticing the gassy smell of the engine as it waits to be shifted into gear or the music coming through the headphones sitting on my ears, I turn right onto a side street that redirects me from the shop to a small, secluded park. I need time to think. I've been so preoccupied with the watch's delivery that I haven't had the chance to look at it, study it, see what it can tell me about its maker.

I pull the scooter into the parking lot and angle into the first spot available. I absently move through the shut-off procedure, quickly lifting and rocking the scooter back, engaging the double-legged kickstand from underneath the floorboard, and throwing the keys into my book bag. I unhook my helmet and hang it on the loop near the seat. Then I pull my goggles up so they sit on the top of my head, though I'm prepared to look through them at the watch, hoping they alter my perception again like at the mental institution.

All the while, my mind burns with possibilities too far-fetched to be true.

Making my way down a grassy slope, I walk quickly, grateful as I reach the small mound of grass under the tree—my tree. I've spent so much time here over the years. Sitting under its large canopy of leaves in the summer, the tree shields me from the hot sun. Sometimes I think about whatever problem is currently troubling me. Other times I foolishly contemplate what my life might have been like if my parents were still alive—what it must be like to have a mother who loves you unconditionally and a protective father threatening mock violence toward any boy brave enough to come calling on you.

These thoughts always lead to trouble. I can barely wrap my head around the idea of unconditional love. The closest thing I have is Whit. I couldn't love him more if he were my family, but I always feel like he's holding something back. It's as though he loves me at great cost to himself, almost grudgingly. It's just his way.

Sitting down, I pull my knees to my chest, untie my boots, put them off to the side, and repeat the motion with my socks. Contentedly, I stretch out my feet, wiggling them, black toenails and all, in green blades of grass. I pull the watch out of my pocket and, for the first time, really look at it. There are three different-sized faces, stacked one atop of another, overlapping. I hesitantly touch my finger to one of the faces partially obscured by another. Slightly startled, my finger recoils as the face I'd touched rotates into the top position, covering the other faces. I graze the other two faces with my fingertips and watch them turn and replace one another.

The first face is obvious in its function, displaying hours, minutes, and seconds. A second and larger face has detailed paintings of the various moon phases, with one long arm pointing to its current phase. This face has a dial around it that can be moved and aligned to any of the moon's phases, though I can't imagine what the additional dial is for.

The final face is the most peculiar: a series of concentric circles surrounding the center, divided into twelve segments, each displaying the character for one of the solar system's planets. Five arms topped with circles instead of arrows hover over small symbols I don't recognize in the inner ring. It's weird, though, that one of the characters looks like the old-timey ℞ drugstore symbol. One of the disks hovers over the sign for the planet Mercury. The center circle is also divided into segments, displaying Norse runes, but I have no clue why they're there. That dial seems to move separately–half a turn to the right, a complete turn to the left, and then a quarter turn further.

I can turn some of the other dials but decide not to, as I don't want to break them. This final face leaves me vexed. I'm going to have to show this to Whit after all, so he can explain it.

Frustrated, I pull my headphones down around my neck. My new mixtape is distracting me from focusing on what I'm feeling. I sit for a minute, my senses on edge. Then realizing I only took my earphones off and the once full voice singing is now small and tinny, filtered through the tiny speakers, I click the stop button on my Walkman.

I try to refocus my thoughts on the watch. Staring blankly at it, my eyes go lazy, and I begin to see the soaring spires of a building. Like I'm looking through a telescope, a landscape appears, a lush, sweeping vista filled with an eclectic mix of people all dressed in all manner of clothing. The buildings' styles are unlike anything in this city. Where is this city and why is it always living inside my head? It's not even real.

Reflexively, I reach into my book bag and grab my sketch pad and pencils. I guess I need to draw yet another scenic landscape of my imaginary city. Maybe that will help me to understand.

That's it! I have to meet Three Arrows, or at least get Whit to tell me his name. Anything! So I can at least, I don't know, try looking him up in the phone book or something stupid like that.

"Oh good, Ember, spy on him. Stalker much?"

But still, I have to try.

8

mother tongue

Kenyon

"It's you!" The words escape my lips with breathless exhalation. All the air in my lungs feels like it's been sucked away. "It has to be you. I see your shine."

"I—I can't believe it's you. There's something about you that calls to me." Here I stand, talking to myself, stuttering and stumbling over the words, in shock at the sight of her. I'd glimpsed her at Mr. Whitley's shop the other day, but it had been at a distance. I'm so close to her now that I'm surprised she doesn't hear me.

How is this even possible? I'd almost begun to believe she was a figment of my imagination, but here she is, every bit of what I imagined she'd be. I almost wanted her to be a dream, a fleeting thought conjured in my loneliness. It would've made her absence almost bearable. Yet I always knew she was somewhere, just out of my reach.

Beyond the fact that she looks nearly the same as she did then, I can feel her. Her presence is a siren song I couldn't resist even if I tried. The sight of her nearly erases all thoughts of anyone or anything that isn't her. There were so many restless nights and unrequited feelings. There was inevitable emptiness with such failure, but now it's gone instantly.

Sitting there under that giant oak tree, she is drawing something, the watch I made for her held loosely in her left hand as she sketches with her right, her book propped awkwardly on her crossed legs. What is she drawing?

I'm such a stalker for sneaking up on her in the park like this, especially since I tracked her down at her school and sent that girl with the watch like a calling card. But none of that matters. Finally she's here, in front of me. My heart is beating so hard that I hear the blood pumping in my ears. Please, by all the Nine Worlds, let her see me, know me, feel me the way I feel her.

"Here goes..." I say under my breath as I walk toward her. I cross the distance in fewer steps than anticipated and find myself in front of her. I shift my body to block the sun from her, and she looks up, shielding her eyes from the sun that still shines around my body. I take a deep breath.

"Ember Wright?"

9

mesmerism

Ember

"Ember Wright?" The rough, gravelly edge of his voice surprises me, his query half question and half statement. "It's you. I can't believe it."

I look up, rotating my head skyward from the sketch I've been working on. I'd been alerted to him initially by the way he was blocking out the sun. But as I look up, it still shines brightly around him, creating a halo around his head.

Startled out of my reverie, I'm unable to stifle a gasp. I generally feel most people's approach, but I didn't sense his.

My eyes widen and connect with his, large and stormy blue, rimmed in smudged shadows of faded kohl. A dark, well-arched brow frames his eyes. I feel my face flush as a smile crosses his face, accompanied by a small dimple in his cheek. I sit wordlessly, sketchbook forgotten in my lap and my long black dress spread on the ground.

Though he is a stranger, he feels so familiar. Unexplainable alarm bells ring in my head, warning me of something dangerous. Before I can think more about it or respond, he extends his hand to me. His shirt and coat sleeve rise higher onto his arm, revealing faint bluish-white luminescent lines etched into his skin. They don't look like any tattoos I've ever seen, pulsing ever so slightly as he moves his hand closer to me.

I suppress an initial desire to recoil from his hand. The lines remind me of the spots around my temples that I try every day to forget, but then I realize that if he has these marks, he might be able to tell me about mine.

Slowly, I raise my hand to meet his, my mind racing for something to say. As I move closer, my fingers prickle, anticipation growing as my hand nears his. My initial reaction to the designs on his skin falls away as I look at him.

My hand reaches his, and I feel every nerve ending. His fingers slide against mine over my palm to wrap around my wrist. The luminous lines on his skin react as we touch. Uncrossing my legs to stand, my sketchbook falls from my lap, and I feel unsteady as I get to my feet. My vision focuses on him as the rest of the world falls away, and my whole body flushes with warmth, my blood rushing harder.

I stumble slightly. He reacts quickly, his free hand shooting out to brace me, his hands brushing my bare skin, causing all the hair on my arms and the back of my neck to stand on end.

He stands several inches above me, longish, raven black hair falling in varying lengths around his strong jaw and contrasting his pale skin. A breeze blows lightly around us, revealing an undercut of closely shorn sides. Black pants, black shirt, and the most amazing pair of pointy-toe Docs, also black. He wears a lightweight vintage black leather car coat—the coat I had recently noticed missing from the shop. Looking at him, I understand why Molly made the comparison between us. We complement one another. Well.

There is something different in the way the sunlight shines on him. There's something oddly familiar about how the light pulses slightly around him.

I look back into his stormy eyes, and my thoughts fall away. The intensity of our eye contact is the only thing in this moment.

"Three Arrows." It's a statement rather than a question. Because I know. I feel it. I feel his presence in a way that until now had been unfathomable.

"What?" he asks me—confusion passing over his face.

"Three Arrows," I repeat. "The mark you leave on your creations. It's stupid, but I don't know your name. Whit won't tell me, so I started calling you by your maker's mark."

"Oh," he laughs as realization dawns on him. "He's never told you. I wonder why?"

"No, he's always refused to tell me," I reply, my stomach flipping backward and then forward. "So what is it?" I ask, feeling off-kilter by his nearness, feeling stupid that I don't know his name.

"What?"

"Your name?"

"Oh! Right. It's Kenyon McQuiston." He seems as lost in the weirdness of the moment as I am.

"So, why sign your work with arrows instead of your name?" Our questioning is quickly becoming banter.

"Well, the three arrows are a part of my family's heraldic crest, and it's what my forefather and foremother named the house they built, the house I grew up in. My workshop is there. Plus, it has fewer characters to etch than my full name."

"Checks out," I reply to his statement. "Plus, wow, you have your own heraldry. Fancy!" I tease, trying to break the tension.

"Um, yeah, my family has roots."

His demeanor changes slightly. "Sorry for the awkwardness of seeking you out this way, but I had to." There's a hint of vulnerability in his voice. "I realize it's a bit inappropriate, but I recently dropped off some devices at Mr. Whitley's shop. The items he requested this time piqued my curiosity about him and his special orders. The goggles were an unusual request for an old man living where he does. Living the life he's..."

"What do you mean?"

"Well, they were a tipoff. Obviously, they're not Mr. Whitley's style."

My hand absently moves to touch the goggles I've pushed up to the top of my head, causing me to feel silly and obvious. "That's not the question I was asking. What do you mean about Whit living the life..."

"They suit you," he continues as if I haven't clarified my question.

"Whit was unusually agitated when I was there the other day, hurrying through our transaction. Which is definitely not like him. Usually he's happy to talk endlessly about what's going on in la Ma—" But he cuts himself off mid-word, shifting to, "—to talk endlessly about all I'm 'tinkering with,' as he put it. But I was late to drop off the items to him. His rush to conclude our business was a clue that there was something he didn't want me to know about. So, what was the harm in going back and waiting in an unseen location to satisfy my curiosity? So I waited."

I thrill at the idea that he'd made the connection, too. It had not escaped his attention that all those creations had been for me. All the pieces fit together, pointing in my direction! Here he stands, perfect, and wanting to know more about me. The intensity of my immediate feelings for this stranger almost scares me.

"How did you know it was me? How do you know my name?"

"I noticed your name on a folder in the shop when I was dropping off the driving goggles. Your name is unusual."

"Tell me about it," I grumble without meaning to.

"I didn't give it much thought then, but when I thought back on it, I realized it must belong to you. So when I headed back to the shop, you were just arriving. I knew immediately that you were the employee Mr. Whitley is getting stuff for—the one that loves my inventions so much."

"I totally needed that folder at school that day, too," I blurt out, sudden embarrassment flushing crimson across my cheeks at my stupid outburst. A low chuckle escapes his lips.

"Well, for what it's worth, I'm happy you left it for me to see. I had to know who you were, to meet you, and know why I feel so drawn to you," he says, catching me off guard with his directness. It's everything I am feeling but would never be brave enough to say.

I look down at my fingers which are picking at my cuticles nervously. I've inched closer without noticing. But his directness makes me feel bold, and I let out a small laugh. "I guess it's safe to say I'm also drawn to you. I've been steadily moving toward you without even real-izing it."

But before I can say anything else to embarrass myself even more, he begins again. "Why are you here? Why is Whit here?"

"What does that mean? Where else would we be?" I ask a bit teas-ingly. Something about him pushes me to say everything in my mind without filtering it.

A cautious look overtakes his face, and he seems to be deliberating what he should say next. "It's just that there is something slightly off about him. I mean, he's not from this city originally. And I'd be willing to bet that the same is true for you. I can't feel you the way I can feel Whit, but it makes no sense..."

"What are you talking about?" I take a step backward, my voice quieting. His appraisal feels oddly hurtful, though I'm pretty sure he didn't mean it to be. Squinting at him suspiciously, the full afternoon sun shining from behind prevents me from seeing his face clearly. I take another step back onto the soft grass, feeling it compress beneath my bare feet that peek out beneath my skirts. This shift puts me further under my tree, and Kenyon steps closer as well.

"No! I'm sorry, I didn't mean anything by that," he fumbles. "I only meant that—"

But I can't hear him anymore. His words fall away, and everything slows to a near standstill. My vision blurs at the edges, my senses on fire as they jump into overdrive. Kenyon's face is frozen in a mask of turmoil as I look at him, but a buzzing sound like a feedback loop has captured my consciousness. It hurts. My eardrums ring painfully. My hands shoot to cover my ears, but it's no good. The noise is coming from within. Finally, expanding out of the buzzing white noise, I hear the words.

> ... guarded words heard in a dream
> a secret no one speaks
> is there a light in the dark
> or is it a fire to burn away the secret
> leaving only ashes in my hands...

Song lyrics. Now? Really?!

The chorus plays out with agonizing slowness, time hanging suspended in the balance. When the world finally rights itself and the song fades away, my vision clouds over, fading to white. Panic squeezes my heart like the grip of a vice—my clenched jaw locks. I try to open my mouth to cry out for help, to scream, but nothing happens. My heart beats so fast, I fear it might explode. My vision is now completely white. I can't see or hear anything.

I'm standing here blind, deaf, and mute.

My eyes shoot in every direction, trying to make sense of the white overtaking my vision. Finally, a line of red unfurls across my mind's eye: a graceful silken ribbon drifts, caught in a breeze, fluttering as it cuts a path through my field of white, until it begins to grow, and as it does, any grace there was in the movements is now gone. It collides with the ground and pools into a puddle, becoming liquid, its edges uneven and jagged.

Lightning blazing in the night sky replaces the dominating white and red colors, creating an eerie imitation of daylight. At that moment, I see Whit. There is no question in my mind: Whit is in danger!

Then it's gone. The bottom drops out of my stomach as a wave of nausea hits me. A chill runs through my body, and I can't breathe. Whatever this was, it was real and felt like the world crashing in on itself.

Without warning, everything returns to normal. I can see and hear again. Time recommences as though nothing happened. Where I had been unaware of my feet and legs, I now felt like someone turned up the dial on gravity, pulling me with an inescapable force. My knees buckle, and I fall. A croaking sound escapes my lips, and Kenyon steps forward to catch me. "Ember, did you just have a Vision? The way your eyes went white, I've heard that happens when a Vala receives the Völuspa! Is that what happened?"

How could he know? But all I can think about is Whit. I know he's in danger.

Standing there with my heart pounding, feeling the blood coursing through my chest, I'm struck with doubt and fear that I imagined it all. Or what if my instincts aren't right? What if everything is fine and that weird Vision thing is nothing?

The feelings of panic are undeniable, though. When I open my mouth, all I can manage is one word.

"Whit!"

10
a strange day

Kenyon

I've never seen a Vala amid völuspa; few outside the Priory have. I have heard about it, but I was too young when my mother died to remember her that way. So I'm completely unprepared for what is happening. Her skin changes from the lovely flush of shyness to an alarming pallor, and she falters as the mists of the Vision recede from her eyes and her knees give way. Fortunately, I'm close enough to catch her, and even through my alarm, I can't ignore the zing of electricity as I touch her. Does that make me a cad? I'm afraid it probably does.

"Are you ok? Can you stand?" I ask.

"Yes," she whispers. Removing her hand, Ember stands on her own, regaining her balance.

"No, I—I mean, I'm ok, and I don't think Whit is. I can't explain it, but I don't think he's ok."

"You had a Vision. No need to explain. Let's go!"

Ember roughly shoves her bare feet into her boots as she grabs her socks, stowing them into her book bag. Without a glance in my direction, she runs toward her scooter. I easily keep pace, my long legs covering the same distance with fewer strides.

She throws her hand back for mine, not that I'd need it to keep up, but it somehow feels natural to do, like she needs reassurance that I'm still here.

Extending my senses, though there is little of la Magie here, I can tune into her at least. I can try to glean something from the frenetic rhythm of her heart and her erratic energy. As we reach her scooter, Ember grabs her helmet, pulls it roughly over her head, then turns the key in the ignition and kicks the starter. Without invitation or hesitation, I take my place and wrap my arms around her.

Nausea settles into the pit of my stomach, the feelings rolling off of Ember setting my senses alight. Whatever she'd seen in the Völuspa is urgent and imminent. I'm suddenly afraid for Mr. Whitley.

The shop isn't far from the park, but it feels like every stop sign is against us. We cover the distance between the park and the shop at record speed. Finally, we round the corner and fly past the shop toward the parking lot, going too fast, but she manages to turn and park without crashing. Pulling her helmet off as she runs toward the building and stumbles over loose gravel, she curses at the sidewalk before righting herself and pushing into the shop. Ember does a double-take, confusion evident on her face as we catch a fleeting sight of a disappearing person standing over Mr. Whitley. Then her attention focuses on his prone form lying lifeless on the floor.

Terror radiates off Ember in waves as a strangled cry escapes her lips and her glassy eyes brim with tears. Had he suffered a heart attack? He is almost fifty, after all. Whatever the case, I see her standing there in shock and know I need to take control.

Ember drops to her knees at Whit's side and recoils as she spies the little white marks around his forehead, four on each side of his temples, highlighting his graying hair. The iridescent and shimmering marks disappear into thick tufts of his hair. Her reaction to the spots feels extreme, making me wonder if she's seen magical marks before this. Why are these marks so jarring to her?

"This just happened! There may yet be time enough..." I mumble the words but let them drop off as I position myself above Whit's head.

Reaching into my pocket, I draw out a handful of crystals. They're beautiful, cut into shimmering facets, with points on either end, each of the sides with an etched rune. "What are you doing?" She demands. "We need to call an ambulance!"

"Ember, the doctors of this world cannot help him. This attack was energetic."

"What are you talking about?!"

"Ember, there is no time for this!" Panic colors my voice as well. If I don't start soon, it will be too late. "Can you please just trust me?"

She nods her assent slowly.

Thank the Nine Worlds I carry these with me, I think, wondering if I possess the necessary skill to perform this kind of magic. I pray I can do this! Especially here in les Dormeur.

Arranging the double-terminated crystals along the length of his body, finishing with a halo around his head, I position myself. Extending my hands, palms jutting forward to cup Whit's head, my fingertips make contact with the throbbing white spots at his temples. The energy radiating from them feels malignant.

Taking a step backward, Ember mutters, "I don't understa—" But her protests die upon her lips as I shoot her a dire look.

I fill my lungs with a deep breath and magic builds within me, accompanied by the crystals' hum and vibration. I extend my auric field to join with Mr. Whitley's. As the intensity grows, the magic embedded in the skin of my arms comes to life, the tattoos pulsing and glowing, intensifying my draíochta. I breathe a small sigh of relief.

Magic gathers, and I close my eyes, finding the quiet place as Father taught me so many years ago. Within the silence, the voices of my ancestors speak to me in whispers, sending their voices in an invitation to join them and wield the energy to save this man. As their voices reach a crescendo, I begin to hum. Low vibrations rumbling deep in my throat grow louder and louder. The first notes escape my lips, fluid and resonate, awakening the crystals to catalyze their magic. They hum and vibrate in tune with me. But this is difficult. Given the lack of magic here, maintaining this much energy demands all my concentration. My father's lessons will now save his best friend, but one deviant thought and it will all slip away.

Glowing crystals shine with light as pure as the sound they sing. The iridescent marks on Whit's temples pulse and glow in time with the melody I weave.

Now in my own solitary world, I've created a circuit, sending energy through the crystals, back to me, and then to Mr. Whitley. Each rune-strengthened crystal increases my focus and stamina. All the stones quickly align with each other and to Mr. Whitley's energy as I move my hands swiftly, making healing and protective runes over him.

An unexpected memory seizes me. I'm a small boy, looking at my mother lying at the bottom of the stairs. Father weeping over her body as he tries to perform the same healing ritual I'm performing—Not now! I reprimand myself, refocusing my thoughts and energy. Bad memories can wait for another time, I think, forcing my voice to form the notes to concentrate the energy. I silently implore my ancestors to lend me their clarity, begging to be released from the grip of memory.

My voice fills the room, transitioning from melody to words of power sung rather than spoken, threading from my mind to my voice. Magic glints shimmer, hanging in the air like dust motes caught in sunlight. The long intertwining lines and runic symbols of magic in my tattoos shine brightly, increasing the depth of the draíochta I wield.

The energy intensifies, coursing through me to the old man. Energetically inflicted wounds are the worst to heal. Only a very powerful will could inflict the wounds that left these shimmering marks seething with the hatred that motivated them.

But who could have it in for Whit, with his harmless shop and doting affection for the girl?

Stop. You must focus on this task if you're going to save him.

Even if I can keep Mr. Whitley from dying, I will still have to take him to an experienced healer. Mr. Whitley's body demands the energy from me, silently fighting to live, to make it back from the other side. My renewed focus is rewarded with twitches in his extremities. A promising sign, but from the corner of my eye, I see and sense Ember's fear, her hand clasped over her mouth to stifle a cry that had already escaped.

Tremors run through his hands, and I give one final push. I don't know how long I can maintain this level of energy. The magic is waning, and I'm desperate to hold on. Whit's closed eyelids flutter slightly—another good sign—though he'll still have to be moved as quickly as possible to a healer. Little by little, the energy recedes as Whit regains a fragile grip on consciousness.

I edge back from Whit's head to find Ember staring at me in disbelief, her face pale and drawn. Her breaths are short, almost panting. I don't think she's aware of magic—yet she is clearly magical. Just looking at Ember and Mr. Whitley, they're obviously from Elysia. Why, then, are they living here? The reason must be profound. While I sense power in both of them, their magic seems different from one another's. Whit's magic feels repressed, while Ember's seems bound, waiting to be freed.

My thoughts are interrupted by groans that signal Whit's return to consciousness. The old man's eyes flutter open as he takes stock of the situation, realization dawning in his gaze as it passes from me to Ember.

"I see you didn't need me to make an introduction for you after all, Little Rose?" His voice is rough as a croaking chuckle escapes. "I never could deny you much of anything, anyway, could I?"

There is more here than meets the eye as I stand mutely trying to figure out their relationship, waiting for Mr. Whitley to take charge.

11

stars are stars

Ember

"Well, Kenyon, I guess we'd better get to Elysia; I'll need to see a healer. I'm guessing you two scared away the attacker when you crashed through the door—though I suspect they'll be back soon to finish the job."

Whit takes charge of the situation as though nothing has happened, as though there aren't a million questions to answer. He orders his thoughts much sooner than I would think possible. Again the flash of the stranger appears in my mind's eye. But before I can voice my question, Whit says, "Kenyon, do you have the energy to take us to Elysia? I'm so out of practice, and expediency is critical. But I don't want to ask more of you than you have to give."

"I'll manage it," he replies, sounding hesitant.

"What the hell are you guys talking about?" I demand. "Is this magic, and where's Elysia? California? It sounds like California. And for that matter—"

But I don't get the chance to finish as Whit motions for me to come closer, silencing my rapid-fire questioning. "I'll explain everything as soon as possible. But this is neither the time nor the place."

I nod my consent, grumbling at his promise of an explanation, hating how petulant I sound, yet standing next to him without further protest.

Snapping my thoughts to attention, Whit says, "I know, Little Rose, how disturbing all this must be. I've shielded you from all this for so long. Alas, my ability to do so wanes." His ragged voice gasps for breath. My own breath feels erratic at the thought of how fragile he is. His condition is better, but he's weak and unable to hide it. The look of urgency on his face warns me of his concern about what comes next, and the questions grow exponentially in my mind.

"Let's just get out of here," I say, mustering more courage than I feel. I head toward the front door of the shop, saying, "We'll get you to a healer—or whatever it is we need—to make you well again." The words feel foreign in my mouth. A healer seems different than a doctor. It's only a fleeting thought because Whit grabs my hand, saying, "Not that way." Placing his hands on my shoulders, he turns me to face the always-locked door of his office. "This way, then, "Whit says, pointing to the tiny back room in the back of the shop. I put my arm around Whits' back to help him to his private room.

"Sooo, I'm finally going to see your 'Secrets Room' after all these years," I quip nervously, referring to it by the name I'd given it long ago. This is his domain. I've only glimpsed the room in passing when Whit disappeared behind the heavy oak door.

Every flat surface in the office holds a collection of quartz crystals, tiny and large, fat and thin. Turning my head to look around the room, I take it all in: hundreds of crystals— seriously, hundreds of them. One in particular catches my attention. It's flat on the bottom with a naturally faceted, wicked-looking peak. Many of the crystals have what looks like a seed embedded in them, so it doesn't seem like an imperfection. Around the largest crystals stands a multitude of smaller ones. I reach out my hand and lay my fingers on the point. The crystal is warm to the touch, almost hot, and it makes my insides jump as small currents of energy pass through me. I don't bother saying anything. What would even be the point? There are already so many questions on the table that remain unanswered.

On the floor is a round, thickly tufted oriental rug, and a small writing desk is at the far end of the narrow room. Only a pad of paper and a fountain pen sit on its surface, all meticulously tidy—a stark departure from the other side of the door. A drawing I made as a little girl and a photograph of me hang on the wall. I had to be about seven at the time, looking precociously at the camera. The square photo with rounded corners has faded to a sepia tone, though it had only been from the late 1970s. The unexpected sight makes my heart swell.

I wonder: what are we doing in this room? We need to get out of here! Whit interrupts my thoughts, saying. "Kenyon, help me move this rug, please."

"Ah, so this is where the added draìochta came from," he says aloud, more an observation spoken to himself.

"Yes, this is the room where I weave the Geasa Droma Draíochta enchantments around Ember," Whit says in response to Kenyon's observation. A dark look of understanding passes over Kenyon's face. Whit looks somehow both chagrined and contrite.

"The what!?" I demand. I don't particularly appreciate feeling left out of the conversation, and I like it even less when I'm spoken about, like I'm not even here. And I especially don't like the sound of this Geisha Domo Arigatou enchantment or whatever they said. I know I got it wrong, but these words make about as much sense together as those.

Yet again, I want to question what Whit's talking about, but I know it won't get me anywhere. Kenyon pulls the rug toward the writing desk. Hiding underneath is an inlaid multi-ringed circle of cut semi-precious stones surrounded by gold. I recognize different Norse runes set in the compass directions. My mouth falls open and then closes, then opens and closes again, working wordlessly, not even knowing where to begin. But before I can say anything, Whit ushers me into the center of the circle.

"Uh—Whit, is this a summoning circle?" I ask, finally overcoming my speechlessness. I mean, I'm positive it is, but what's it doing here, belonging to Whit? Is he a witch? No, men aren't witches. They're wizards, or warlocks, or...

"Mr. Whitley, I don't know who pursues you, though you're clearly in great danger. Wouldn't it be better to send Ember to a safer location?" Kenyon asks.

I'm incensed at his words. "No!" I shout. But the panicky feeling growing in me forces me to ask, "How are we going to escape?!"

"Ember, not now!" Whit's abruptness catches me off guard. It's the first time he's spoken to me so harshly. I'm not sure I like this new secret-keeping-snappy-Whit, but that will also have to wait. His fear sends mine skyrocketing; I have no idea what we are running from, how we will get away, or where we are going. Elysia, I guess–wherever that is.

Standing in the confines of the circle, Kenyon reaches into his pocket and pulls something out. Lifting his hand, he reveals a slim, round device. Arching onto my tiptoes to get a closer look, I'm surprised to see what looks like a fancy makeup compact. Kenyon lowers his hand a bit so I can get a better look at the outer casing, dull copper with a darker patina around the edge of the opening. Kenyon angles it further, flipping the lid on its hinge with a flick of his thumb, revealing a face within. It reminds me of my goggles. I can tell he made both devices.

There are eight symbols made of lines, half-circles, and dots, like a compass, but not exactly. The device catches Whit's attention as well. "What do you have there, son?" he asks.

"A portable Vegvísir, sir." He looks toward me. "A contained tesseract."

His swapping out one word for another, neither of which I knew the meaning of, does nothing for me. Seeing my confusion, he continues. "It accesses the intra-dimensional space between two locations. Then it finds the correct frequency to activate the quantum entanglement between the particles of two places. Once the link forms, it activates the tesseract within the vegvísir. Travel is nearly instantaneous." He pauses. "Once the parameters are locked in," he adds as an afterthought.

"A Veg-Va-*What?*" I ask, my mind muddled. His explanation sounds more like science or sci-fi than magic.

"It translates to Way-finder, Ember," Whit interjects. But directing his further thoughts toward Kenyon, he says, "Remarkable! In the time that I've been gone, someone managed to compress it into a handheld device!" Though he seems exhilarated by this, I see Whit's energy ebbing away again.

Before I can ask more questions about the device, the shop's front door bells rattletrap to life again. Someone's coming in the front door!!

Kenyon's hands move around his device like he's pulling strings I can't see. As he does, thin white lines of light spring to life, encasing us in the summoning circle. They pulsate in time with the light his arm tattoos give off. I'm fixated, openly staring at them. That's when my own spots begin to pulsate. It's creepy, but it makes me feel weirdly connected at least.

Kenyon's fingers are flying, turning the dials of his vegvisir. With each turn, a line of glowing energy appears before us. A large square glows in mid-air. Another turn, another bar, extends toward us. Quick, decisive strokes of Kenyon's hand make me think he's making calculations on the fly. Three sides of a cube surround us now, behind and on either side. Instead of finishing the last line of the cube, more lines come to life, forming a second smaller cube in front of us but further away. He connects it to our polygon with the elongated lines he's creating. Finally, he completes the cube's final side to contain us, which seems like an odd geometric shape. Frankly, it doesn't look natural or like it should exist. And I get it—I'm no genius at geometry, but this looks like two geometric shapes cobbled together. I doubt anything will happen, but I feel energy building within the contained space. It's working. I still don't know what it's doing, but I'll find out soon.

Kenyon breathes a sigh of relief after he completes the complex manipulations.

"Uh, now what?" I ask. It seems like he's done a lot of work and nothing has really happened.

But before anyone can answer, I hear someone tearing through the shop, knocking antiques over as they approach us. Glass shatters. My heart beats double time again and my skin feels clammy with sweat. "Better hurry, Kenyon!" Whit says. Kenyon begins humming, softly at first, then progressing to fully-fledged notes. The melody is at odds with the destruction coming from the next room. Sweat gathers on his forehead and trickles down the side of his face. The enclosed cube-shaped generates heat within it. I feel the electric energy building.

There's more than one person out in the shop, and the sounds are getting closer and closer to the door. I'll hyperventilate if my breaths come any faster. My heart beats so hard it almost hurts, and I'm dripping with sweat. The heat of this little room and the energy the cubes generate intensify everything. Before anything else can go wrong, the distant smaller cube flashes a brilliant starburst of white light and rushes toward us. As the smaller cube envelopes the larger, it feels like we're hurtling through space. There's darkness all around. Traveling inside the larger of the two cuboidal light box thingies feels like riding a roller coaster and falling off a building.

The last thing I see is the large door to Whit's room opening and a woman's shoe peeking through the widening gap. Then it all falls away.

I close my eyes, pressure building in my ears, my limbs heavy. I hope the dizzying sensation will end as quickly as it began. Thankfully, it lasts only a moment, and my ears finally pop. I feel lighter, like I'm floating just above the ground. Raising my hands to my ears, I push them closed, open, closed, and open, trying to release the remaining pressure. They shift, and I let out a breath I didn't realize I was holding. Opening my eyes, I can't stifle the gasp that escapes my mouth as my senses take everything in.

There are stars as far as the eye can see in the night sky. Obviously, I'm a bit startled by the fact that it's suddenly nighttime. It was late afternoon when we left the shop. I look down at my Swatch to find the arms going haywire. Quickly looking away, I'm afraid my already faltering grasp on reality is gone completely. I look around me, gaping at the multitudes of trees surrounding us. They're tall and old. I've never seen this place in any of my Visions or dreams. Turning around as I stare up at the trees, I gasp again. Shock, recognition, and realization hit me. This is the building from my imaginary city.

Whit draws in a long breath, filling his lungs. Relief washes over his face as his shoulders relax from their usually tense position. He turns to face Kenyon, saying, "Thank you. You have done me a great service that I can never hope to repay. Your father would be so proud of the man you've become." He pauses and places an affectionate hand on Kenyon's cheek. He continues, "You should return to your home now. If we are lucky, we can hide your involvement in this."

"I don't think so, sir," Kenyon says solemnly.

"Very well. Ember, please follow me. Try not to talk too much. This is a Temple, and it is full of rules you don't yet know."

His statement of the obvious irritates me, so I reply, "Oh, I'm Umble-Come-Stumble on that, Whit." And I use all my powers of sarcasm and my newly discovered archaic vocab to tell him I understand. Mostly because it seems to annoy him.

But he only gives me a pointed look. "I promise you before this day is done, you will understand everything that has happened." He turns away from the oak grove and walks toward the massive building with even taller spires.

•••

"She's here! The blood can never be fooled, and I feel hers as surely as I feel my own," she utters aloud, though it's not a conscious decision. "I knew it was close enough to her birthday for it to work. He could only keep her from me for so long. Making such a bold move when he's at his weakest did the trick. My beloved daughter returns home, and now we can be together the way it was meant to be." The Prioress of the Vala may have been speaking only to herself, but she isn't the only one to hear.

"I'm sorry, Prioress. What did you say?" Sister Annon's large brown eyes look puzzled as she gazes at the Prioress Phaedra. But she quickly looks away, not wanting to be reprimanded by Sister Ordonna, the Prioress' most trusted Devotee Laureate.

"Oh, nothing. I was talking to myself. It's a bad habit, really..."

But the Prioress continues as though she hadn't been disturbed, unbothered by the women sitting before her, as though they weren't patiently waiting for her edicts.

"What to do next? Shall I visit her in Onirique? No, that's best saved for another more opportune time. Perhaps the direct approach is best for this situation..."

Turning abruptly, she looks toward her Devotees, saying, "Go now. I have much to do if I'm to be ready to greet the Beloved One, who shall finally join me in her rightful place of honor."

Without another word, she turns and leaves the room.

12
i'm set free

Whit

My vitality wanes. I knew my words to Ember had been harsh and, even worse, belittling. It pains me to make her feel small, knowing she already struggles with those feelings. Let the hurting start now, I guess. Everything I will say tonight will hurt. I don't want her barrage of questions setting the chain of events into motion before I'm strong enough to deal with it.

The Priory of the Draíodóir are the most skilled and powerful healers. They train for years. Their experience and clairaudient intuitive gifts make them the best. I am now dependent upon their largess for my life. Without further healing, I doubt I will make it beyond this night, but it's unnerving to be on this side. I'd never appreciated the sheer terror some of the souls I'd laid hands on to heal must've been experiencing. My years of healing caused me to take the ability for granted.

We walk in silence, each of us lost to our thoughts. I'm almost numb, thinking of what's to come, facing it all, facing her demand for answers. Facing him, I know he's still here. I can feel him. This will be difficult.

My relief at finally being home, feeling the magic coursing through my body, almost feels like a drug. But my ease is tempered by the reality of our situation. Of all the possible outcomes, I never imagined I'd be the prodigal son, returning in desperate need of healing.

"Whit, are you going to be ok?" Ember asks me.

"I think so. But it's much more complicated than being ok, Little Rose," I try and fail to disguise the heavy sadness in my voice. Ember doesn't reply. My vague answer likely raises more questions.

Approaching the vast doors of the Temple, Ember's eyes widen, taking in the circular glass doors complemented by carved runes. I follow Ember's movements as she looks skyward until her sight lands on two of the structure's corners. Atop one corner's spire stands a statue of a woman. She holds a tall staff at arm's length, and a golden cord wraps around and down her body. She's an imposing figure meant to evoke a sense of mystery within the viewer. I wonder if Ember feels it. I imagine it calling to her; it's in her blood, after all. The statue's plaited hair hangs down her back, over the centuries-old gown and mantle garb of the Vala. On the other corner, a statue of a man holds a Celtic harp, his hand resting upon its golden strings. Having been away from it so long, I almost feel like seeing it for the first time with her, only I know everything about this place, its history, its purpose, and its secrets—at least I used to, anyway.

We're mere feet from the Temple, and something inside me shifts. The time to lament all that I have done or had not done for Ember has long since passed. It's time to be strong for her, stronger than I've ever known how to be. There was never going to be an easy homecoming. Still, my heart aches from both the attack as well as the anxiety building within me. Not only will I break Ember's heart, but I must also face Phaedra. She's become so powerful, and I'm sure she orchestrated my attack. All these years, and she still hungers for what she lacks over what she has.

My heart races as I imagine Ember confronting the truth, knowing I'll be the cause of the heartbreak that will inevitably stretch across her face. As I imagine how difficult it will be, a self-indulgent moment of weakness overtakes me. I never asked for this future, never wanted the gift of clairaudience, to be one of the Draíodóir. But it had come to me, nonetheless. Yet the overwhelming relief that blooms in my heart is undeniable. To breathe the air of home, surrounded by my beloved oak grove behind the Temple, is truly a homecoming.

But my private reverie of disparate thoughts ends with Ember's sharp inhalation of breath as she sees details she's doodled when she wasn't aware I was looking. How unnerving it must be to see her own drawings come to life.

How many of The Draíodóir will I recognize? How many will remember me? Passing through the double doors, I nearly lose my footing. Ember and Kenyon catch me under each elbow, finally crossing the threshold of my former home.

The entryway is vast, with soaring archways demarcating the space, but Ember's attention is diverted by a small meowing black cat that saunters up next to her. It has only one eye and is very talkative, its tail twitching. Two more cats hang around the entry, both of them black. The one-eyed cat is now rubbing itself against her leg. Men notice us and abandon their various tasks to attend to me.

"I, Adair Whitley Wright, hereby request asylum from The Priory of the Draíodóir for myself and my two companions. Furthermore, I request healing." I speak the words in a stiff, formal manner; my voice betrays how frail and faltering I am.

Ember's head turns to look at me as I use my full name, one she's not familiar with. She's visibly startled by the revelation.

I sense him before seeing him, and my heart races as he says, "It can't be...Addi, is that you?" It's him. "Addi, you've come home! It's been so long. Where have you been?"

It's my old friend, my once dear companion, Brother Aaric Aumont. My forbidden love. He looks older now, his close-cut beard mostly grey with silver streaking his temples. But he's still my Ari. A silver oak leaf, the badge of the Prior, is pinned to his tan over robes. My heart twists at seeing the mark of authority worn by him, a twinge of jealousy as well as guilt for him having to assume the responsibility.

"Ari." His name escapes my lips in a whisper, without permission. I knew he'd be here; he's a loyal and dedicated man, his devotion to the Priory unquestioning. But I guess I hoped I wouldn't see him in this condition, the after-effects of her attack still emblazoned upon my skin. The pain lingers at my temples, pulsing malignant magic meant to steal my power and my life from me. I knew the iridescent markings still glowed faintly, having seen the phenomenon almost eighteen years ago.

"Addi?" The question turns demanding.

"Yes, Ari, it's me," is the most I can manage. The weight of all the unspoken questions yet to come hangs between us. It takes only a moment to see the hurt and betrayal in his eyes. My heart breaks all over again, fluttering wildly. I'm unsure if it's a palpitation due to my weakened condition or excitement at seeing him. Despite the hurt look lingering in his eyes, he steps closer, drawing me to him in the most intimate of embraces. I can almost feel Ember's eyes widen in surprise. She's never seen me be so affectionate and familiar with another person. There's more tenderness in our embrace than Ember would guess me capable of. I can only hope I get the chance to show her a true vision of the man I am.

"Addi, you—you, well, you look just terrible! What's become of you?" Ari asks, referring to me by my old nickname. Hearing it makes me feel like I've come home. A crowd clusters around us, drawn by curious concern about the commotion.

"In due course, my dear Ari, I require healing, my Brother. I promise you the answers you seek. All of them," I add meaningfully.

"I owe them to Ember as well," I continue, sneaking a furtive glance at Ember as I say the words, certain my guilt is plain to see.

"Of course, all in due time," Ari agrees reassuringly.

Ari turns his attention to the tangle of Brothers surrounding us. "Brother Hans, please call the strongest of our healers into the Medicamentous Room. We'll be healing one of our own, our beloved."

The last words spoken by Ari inspire sudden hushed and stifled conversations.

"Please, I must know that we three have the asylum of The Draíodóir!" I plead in an alarmed voice.

"Of course," Ari answers automatically, confusion in his voice. "Though I don't understand why you need it. You've come home, my Brother." At these last words, Ari puts his arm underneath mine to support me as they guide me away. Energy surges between us.

I sense Ember's apprehension even at a distance. Seeing the look on her face, I ask, "Brother Aaric, is there somewhere my companions, Ember and Kenyon, can wait where they won't be disturbed?"

"Of course, Addi. Brother Imanu, please see Kenyon and Ember to my private library. Discreetly. I do not want them disturbed, as I assume their presence here will draw unwanted attention?" He phrases it as a question, but everyone is clear on the answer, so I just nod, offering no further explanation. Ari presses on. "We'll get the whole story once we've done the necessary healing. Thank you, Brother Imanu," Ari finishes, speaking with the authority of a man used to having his directives followed.

"Thank you, dear Brothers," I mumble, relaxing a bit. I let myself be led to the healing room, secure in knowing that both Ember and Kenyon will be safe.

In the growing distance, I hear Brother Imanu break away from the larger group, saying, "This way, please." And I resign myself to what I know will be the second most difficult day of my life.

black celebration

Ember

Stepping forward, Brother Imanu gestures with his hand. His hair is worn in an afro, neat, and close to the scalp. He's wearing long dark robes, as all the Priory does. And though I know that I'm awake, it feels impossible and surreal. It's one part exciting. I mean, magic's real, and I finally met Kenyon, yet it's devastating. Whit's a liar. Or rather, Addi, I guess. The hollow feeling in my stomach tells me that what remains of my world is about to shatter. The shoes echoing on the concrete floor are the only sounds punctuating the silence.

"In here, please." The stoic man opens the door.

The door latches closed with a quiet thk. The silence is worse than the sound of the footfalls we left behind. At least I could focus on them.

I nearly gasp as I enter the impossibly large room, so expansive, so tall that I'm sure it must be two stories high. Bookshelves line every wall, climbing to the extra tall ceiling. Library ladders are latched to metal bars attached just below the ceiling. A well-worn reclining chair made of molded plywood and leather with a matching ottoman sits near the corner of the room. I imagine this is where Brother Aaric sits to relax. The chair does look comfortable, But as much as I long for comfort, there is only one. So, I settle for the black leather cube-shaped chairs on either side of a matching couch. They face a wall made of so many windows it seems all glass. The night sky is visible; the stars twinkle so brightly here. It weirds me out. How are they so much brighter?

I look back at Kenyon, and his face reflects my tension and apprehension. Who could blame him? He's taken a chance to seek me out, to explore the connection we both feel. And really, can I stop here and say, swoon, sigh, weak in the knees, and all the adjectives? He makes me feel all the things. Yeah, I know my life seems to be going to hell in the proverbial hand basket right now. But damn, this guy is hot and, for some reason, looks at me like he thinks I'm hot, too.

Anyway, he finds me to give me this rad watch, and all of a sudden, he has to save Whit's life. Now here we stand, and I know that all my questions will only weigh on him. I know he knows at least some of the answers. But as much as I want answers, they are not his to give. It's Whit who needs to answer for what is happening here, so I decided to let him off the hook. I walk to him, pushing my way into his arms. Kenyon lets out a long breath like he's been holding it, waiting for the other shoe to drop.

"Ok, I am officially batty-fang, after all that, and kinda feel like I'm losing my mind. Is this—is this real?" I ask hesitantly, feeling foolish.

"Yes, Ember. But I don't know much more than you." He says. "And what does batty-fang mean?

"Oh, right, it means thrashed, damaged until unusable. And I assume we'll find out what kind of skilamalink is goin' on here, and soon!"

"Skilamalink?" He asks, and he's obviously stifling a chuckle, holding me at arm's length so he can look into my eyes.

"Sorry, I guess that's the problem with using antiquated phrases. It means secret or shady. I was getting into too much trouble with my foster families for using swears. So I started learning old Victorian insults. They cracked me up, so I started using them."

"You are such a wonderful weirdo," he says, wrapping me into another hug.

After a minute, I pull away from him. I don't want it to get weird. I walk back and forth, crossing the room over and over. My hands brutally pick at my ragged cuticles. "I mean, I've always known that I was different, but this is ridiculous," I say, words followed by a mirthless laugh meant to be light, but isn't.

"I'm so confused. I'm afraid for Whit, but I'm also upset. He's been lying to me, obviously! I thought his last name was Whitley. How many other things has he been lying to me about?" I ask, talking to myself again.

I replay those song lyrics as well as Whit's healing in my mind, trying to make sense of it: how my vibrations aligned with Kenyon's melodic chorus, engaging my consciousness in the process, how energy hummed around me, in my brain, in my body, like a second heartbeat. And my spots! You know, the spots around my hairline, creepy, iridescent, and unexplainable? Yeah, those, they pulsed during that healing. Weirder still, it seemed to be in time with both the melody Kenyon was intoning and also with Whit's brand-spankin' new spots. Awesome, now we have weird matching spots. Secrets and scars now lay between us, uniting us and threatening to tear us apart. Flashes of memory, all the times that some person's unspoken truth or song lyrics popped into my mind. They were warning of what was to come, and now this Vision of danger makes sense.

With a gasp, I whisper to myself, "I'm magic! It's not just Whit and Kenyon; it's me, too." Realization hits me; I'd never been just an ordinary girl, and the strange feelings and alienation I felt were clues. And Whit knew it! How is this even a thing? I might be unobservant sometimes, but that is the only explanation for what is happening here.

Betrayal courses over me like a wave, pulling me into an undertow of realization and doubt; I've been so stupid. How could I not see what he'd been hiding in plain sight? And this is just the start. What else was he hiding? Bad things never happen alone; they roam in packs, waiting to destroy your world.

"Ugh, I give up!" Forcing my hands to drop to my sides, my nervous attack on my cuticles will draw blood soon if I'm not careful.

Walking again toward a bookcase, I notice leather-bound books of various ages in different states of repair. I read their titles, happy for a distraction. But it does nothing for the nausea in the pit of my stomach. So I let my mind wander, wondering what the Book of Hours or the Book of Days could be about. Looking up, I spot more intriguing books. A Definitive Guide to Alchemy by Sir John Dee is familiar, but I can't place it. Continuing my stall tactic, I read more titles, The Esoteric and Whimsical Writings of Finnias J. McCoy and Mastering the Inbetween Spaces by Asedor the Clever. But it's Advanced Ariamancy by Eloni Amaru that catches my attention. There are like a thousand books in here. One shelf lower, I see a collection of identical spines, all bearing the same title, Collected Prophecies of the Draìodóir. This collection strikes a sense of fear. Something about these books doesn't sit well. Even more foreboding added to what I'm already feeling doesn't do me any good, so I give up on my feeble distraction technique.

My gaze returns to Kenyon. I walk to him without a word. He wraps me easily into his embrace. My head feels like it's going to explode. One question following another, contradicting another. I try my best to silence them for the moment, just reveling in this embrace, wanting to get lost in this moment. He's familiar in a way that I can't explain. It feels like a homecoming. And believe me, I get it; this makes no sense, but there it is—he feels somehow like home. He lightly strokes the small of my back, a gesture meant to be comforting, and it is, but it's a lot more than that. And if I stay like this, I'll likely do something stupid like try to kiss him. Wanting to avoid an awkward rebuff, I pull away, only to have him squeeze me closer to him for a long moment before letting me go.

He grabs my hand before I get too far away, entwining our fingers together. When I hugged him last, he might've been just reciprocating, trying to comfort me in this situation. This contact, though, he's chosen. The fluttering butterflies in my stomach attempt to slam dance at his gesture.

Giving my hand a little tug, he leads me to a couch by the window wall. He tucks me into the crook of his arm as we sit. It seems he wants to be near me as much as I want him to be, so I settle in.

While I want to live forever in the comfort of his embrace, my anxiety builds again as my mind wanders. I've never known Whit to be a liar, but clearly, he is. Hell, Whit isn't even his real name. Not counting that it's his middle name, that doesn't count. He'd gone by that name to deceive. As if it wasn't enough that he spent my whole life lying to me, his upcoming truthing time causes me dread. And I can't help but notice; the lies all involve me. I mean, I'm not saying I'm the center of the universe, but it's pretty clear that I'm a part of his mess. The once fluttery feeling in my stomach is gone. Now my stomach feels leaden, my head dizzy at implications I can't ignore.

Kenyon's fingers slide along my cheek as I cry embarrassingly fat, round tears. I feel like I'm betraying myself somehow. Feeling anything else would be better—anger, confusion, or outrage. I try to reason that it's understandable that I'm crying, but I dislike it—even in private. Tears always feel like weakness in the face of things I can't do anything about. It's wasted emotion that changes nothing.

> ...guarded words heard in a dream
> a secret no one speaks
> is there a light in the dark
> or a fire to burn away the secret
> leaving only ashes in my hands...

And then, of course, there it is—that stupid song playing itself again for me in that familiar, annoying way. Realization dawns—and honestly, I feel kinda dumb for not realizing it sooner. The song lyrics are a part of some kind of magical ability. It seems like a super indirect way of having a premonition, though.

I pull away from Kenyon, turning my body around to face him, wanting to focus my thoughts. "So, this might sound crazy or stupid, but—for as long as I can remember, I've gotten songs stuck in my head, but not like a normal person does. When it happens to me, it's like it takes over my entire consciousness until finally something ends up happening that makes it seem like it was a premonition. I researched in the library and found something called Stuck Song Syndrome, but it's not exactly the same. Now I think it might be some sort of prophetic ability."

"Ember, I definitely think it is. It sounds a bit like clairaudience or an unexpected variation. Perhaps having your magic bound caused it to manifest this way."

"Really? My magic is bound?"

"Yes, that is what Whit was telling me earlier. You know the Geisha Domo Arigatou enchantment, as you called it. It's a power-binding spell. He's been locking you up tight. Or at least, he thought he was, but you are of the blood. Your draíochta—the magic in your blood, bone, body, and every cell within you—is strong. Even through his bindings I feel your magic, but it's weak, muffled. Maybe this is your clairaudient gift expressing itself the only way it can, though the gift of Hearing is a mark of the Draíodóir, the domain of men. It isn't unheard of for women to have the gift. There are historical examples. But usually, women have the gift of clairvoyance. They are Vala, the Sighted Ones."

"What do you mean, the magic lives in my blood? I mean, if it lives in my blood, I'm sure I'd have been magic-ing up all kinds of trouble long before now, even with Whit's binding."

"Draíochta or magic is a part of who we are, Ember. Specifically, it lives in our mitochondrial DNA, converting food into energy in non-magical people, but in us, it also produces our draíochta. Our magic is weaker in les Dormeur, yet we can sense it in one another, or more precisely, sense the absence of it no matter where we are."

"What are La Magie and les Dormeur?" I interrupt.

"It's shorthand of sorts. We're la Magie, meaning the magic, and the rest of the non-magical world is called les Dormeur. It means the sleepers, but we usually call the people the Ordinaries. I've always sensed the magic in Whit, and I could detect a faint trace of your draíochta, but not enough to figure all of this out. Can you sense it in me?"

I feel my cheeks flush crimson, which brings a smile to Kenyon's lips. "I don't know—I mean—I feel something…" Can I continue this conversation without feeling like a moron? "I feel something when I'm near you, but I don't know if I have the words to explain it. Sometimes I kinda feel it in my friend Nico, too." His face startles at Nico's name, but I continue hesitantly. "You feel like home." I feel stupid for saying it out loud. The nearest thing I've felt to this is with Whit when he lets his guard down, but that feeling is nothing compared to this.

Before I lose my nerve to sheer embarrassment, as I'm so not used to chatting up hot guys, I ask, "When you first walked up to me in the park, after you said my name, you mumbled something like, 'It's you, I can't believe it.' What did you mean by that?"

"I—" Kenyon starts. There is a quiet knock at the door. Brother Imanu lets himself in, and Kenyon is quickly on his feet. I'm thankful we had not been mid-embrace, but my gratitude transforms into irritation. The Brother's reappearance cut off what Kenyon had been about to say. This had better be good news about Whit, I think.

"Is Whit okay?" I demand.

"Yes, Brother Addi will make a full recovery." His use of Whit's bizarro world nickname surprises me, yet that's what he calls him. That's his name, after all. Before anything more is said, Whit rounds the corner. He still looks pale, with bags under his eyes and a bit of stooped posture, but he's OK. I rush over to him, forgetting myself and my anger. I throw my arms around his neck. Hugging him so tightly, I can feel his breathing.

He squeezes me, uncomfortable at the contact. I never hug Whit, but this seems like an exception. Pulling away from the embrace, he says, "So, I suppose I have a bit of explaining to do, then."

"Ya think?" I reply, surprised at how level I've kept my tone. I must be in full-on shock now. "There are so many questions that I don't even know where to begin."

"Well, if you can wait a few minutes longer, The Brothers have called for an assemblage so that I may tell my story—*our* story. They've granted us asylum for the time being. Based on what I tell them, They will decide what course of action to take."

"I am sorry you must hear the truth of your life's story with a group of strangers. This is not how I would've chosen to tell you," Whit finishes. The bottom of my stomach hits the floor. So I might be at the center of this drama after all.

Before I can respond, there's a tentative knock on the door. My frustration grows with every interruption; they always happen whenever I'm about to get some answers, first with Kenyon, and now Whit. I try to regain the tiny shred of composure I'd managed to scrape together but feel it slipping away. Then I try consoling myself. It won't be much longer until I know everything—or at least as much as everybody else in the damned room, for once. Still, a hint of bitterness creeps in at the edges.

14
anywhere out of the
world

Ember

We follow Brother Imanu down a small hallway, its warm gray walls strangely menacing. Maybe it's just me, but seriously, everything about this place feels menacing. I keep looking down at my non-magical watch, and, yep, it's still malfunctioning. Not like time matters at this point. Oh, duh! I bet that watch that Kenyon made for me works here. But then I realize it's in my book bag, which is still at the shop, forgotten in the haste of our flight. What I wouldn't give for my walkman, though, for the escape that music brings or my Tarot cards. Whatever. I'm just glad we're finally getting on with this—no more waiting.

Hard as I try to avoid it, my mind can't stay away from everything that's gone down today. I feel it down to my bones, the truth I've been avoiding. I'm a secret in a secret world. Is that a double negative? I never thought I'd miss my stupid foster family with their stupid house and rules. Almost makes me miss sitting down to do homework and fighting for tv time.

But my lamentations come to an abrupt end as we stop in front of the Assemblage Room. I walk straight into Kenyon's back. Will there ever be a time I'm not going to feel stupid and embarrassed?

Kenyon turns to face me with a hint of a smile, putting me more at ease. He wraps me into an undercover one-armed embrace, placing a quick peck on my forehead, then releasing me so quickly that nobody around us seems the wiser. But the sensation is electric. A hint of a smile tugs at my lips.

As the procession begins again, we enter the room. Chairs are formed in a semicircle, with several tiers sinking a few feet below the previous one. It reminds me of an old-fashioned college lecture hall.

Brother Imanu ushers us to the center of the front row. The leaden feeling in my stomach is back, knowing Whit will soon take the stage. I can't imagine him being comfortable doing this, but there's a lot I don't know about him. Perhaps he's a born performer. How easily these cynical thoughts creep into my mind! All eyes will be on me as he tells his tale of woe. My skin crawls and I swallow hard, a prickling sensation in my throat, tears threatening to come soon.

Without warning, Brother Aaric walks to the front of the room, addressing his fellow Draíodóir. "Brothers, thank you for joining me at this very late hour and with little notice. Your patience is great, and I ask for your further indulgence. As I understand it, we have before us a solemn choice to make that will, I'm sure, forever alter the future of our great order. So, I ask that you use your gifts to Hear the truth— and moreover, to Hear the proper course of action that should be taken."

Something about how Brother Aaric asks the Brothers to hear the truth in Whit's story sets me on edge. While it's established that he's a liar, I don't like the immediate mistrust. But then I remember just how many lies he seems to have told, so yeah, I think we could do with some of their magical superpowers of "hearing," or whatever.

Again, he pauses; the pauses never end with this guy. For the love of all things, man, please get on with it.

"Today has brought the return of one who has been lost to us, whose presence has been dearly missed by myself and others among you. He comes before us to share his story and his reasons for leaving us those many years ago."

With only a glance between the two men, Whit slowly stands up from his chair next to me, trading places with Brother Aaric. Brother Ari is sitting next to me. Can he use his Hearing superpowers to hear my thoughts or guess my feelings? Clearly, I'm a part of Whit's absence from this world.

"Thank you for receiving me, my once and former Brothers. It is gratifying to see some familiar faces remain within The Priory. Let me get straight to why we are here and why I left."

"Seventeen years ago, I left my quarters to perform my assigned rounds of The Temple; In a small remote room, I came upon a baby, abandoned and near death." Palpable shock travels around the room. However, it's only me who gasps in surprise at his statement. My eyes lock with Whit's, and I understand immediately. The truth of my realization is mirrored in Whit's eyes. So many unspoken emotions tangle in our shared gaze. "Though I thought she was dead, I found the faintest heartbeat keeping her alive."

He looks at me again, and his eyes soften, "She had been laid out in the middle of a temporary power raising circle, drawn hastily with chalk. I don't believe that the intent had been to kill her. Still, the iridescent marks at her temples were lingering after-effects of a powerful ritual. I believe that the ritual used was the ancient and forbidden act of Confractio Anima in an attempt to appropriate her draíochta, her power." He adds the last bit lamely, for my benefit. Whit thinks I don't know the words of this world, but I know that one, and I'm learning. Fast.

From the gallery of onlookers comes the question, "Why on earth would anyone try to steal the power of an infant?"

"The child was born of lies and deception; born of two, who had forsworn personal connections and the creation of familial bonds: her father, a Draíodóir, and her mother, a Vala, both liars. I believe her mother hadn't intended to become pregnant, but I suspect that as the fetus grew, so did the mother's powers. Ember possesses a tremendous amount of draíocht and both gifts of the Oracle. Perhaps in desperation to retain that power, her mother tried to siphon some of them for herself."

Someone yells out, "Who's the mother?" And Whit looks surprised. I guess he's not used to being interrupted.

He pauses before answering as though it will make any difference to me. What can he say to destroy my world any more than he already has?

"He seems to steel himself and says, "Sister Phaedra Rule. She is Ember's mother."

The murmurs of outrage are terse and hushed. Angry and disbelieving voices whisper words like "Preposterous" and "The Prioress?"

But Whit continues without letting more questions or doubt slip into his narrative. "The failed attempt left her near death, her spirit's essence ebbing away, mingled with traces of the person who'd tried to rip away her gifts. The baby I found that day is obviously Ember Wright."

Out of the corner of my eye, I see Kenyon's head turn to look at me. He takes my hand, squeezing it. If Confractio Anima means what I think it means, which duh, of course, it does, the words even sound like Spirit Shattering. And apparently, my mother already did that job long ago. I'm damaged goods. Spirit shattered. And what about my name? My memory plays back to the moment I discovered his real name, Adair Whitley Wright. It's the same last name. It's the same last name! What does this mean? Is—Is he my father?

I look to Whit, and as if he can read my mind, he nods, his eyes filled with unshed tears. I look away. The tears that had threatened previously at the corners of my eyes have made their triumphant return, burning as they fall.

I feel so vulnerable and exposed sitting here, heat flushing my cheeks. I want to run as far away as I can, away from Whit's betrayal. While I want to run, I'm too stunned, too nauseous to move. The truth hits me in waves, one crashing down after another, confronting me. Whit is actually my father! This is impossible; how could he do this to me?! Why didn't he raise me, love me enough to be a father to me? Surely I deserve one, don't I?

Adrenaline floods my heart, making it pound faster, making even its rhythmic beating painful. Panic quickly follows. I don't want any of this to be true. Nausea rises again, and I taste bile in the back of my throat. I push down the feeling, hoping I won't be sick.

I was born of deception, my birth a betrayal. My thoughts come fast and whisper to me: I am a lie. My whole life is a lie. It's always been a lie. If Whit had loved me enough to be a father to me, I wouldn't have had all the crappy foster situations. Is the faceless woman I've so often seen in my dreams my mother? I mean, clearly, my father isn't dead, so who's to say she is?

The room is silent, and I feel every eye on me. Worst of all, I feel Whit looking at me, but I can't meet his gaze in return. Looking at the floor in front of me, I wish I could magic myself out of the room. I wish

I could blink my eyes and be a million miles from this place—or at the very least, blink and make the tears disappear.

I roughly wipe my face with my palms and then sleeves, smearing mascara in the process. An unnerving sensation overtakes my senses, like I'm falling into a dark pit, the darkness ready to consume me.

My erratic breathing comes in shallow gasps, making me light-headed. Finally, I'm moved to action. I jump out of my chair, feeling small and stupid. In a split-second decision, I run as fast as I can, yet the door seems miles away.

If I can find a secluded spot, maybe I can calm down and figure out what to do. I mean, I got this; I'm a foster kid, and I'm used to taking care of myself and mistrusting parental figures. But I can't clear my mind with all these jerks surrounding me.

I run, turning corner after corner until I find a small room near the end of a darkened hallway. The light filtering in from the hallway through the ornate, leaded cut glass is enough to see my way to a low, overstuffed chair. Throwing myself into it, I cover my face with my hands, sobs bursting free, wracking my chest. My breath comes in ragged fits. "What the fuck am I supposed to do with this?" I asked myself and the room. A sudden bark of laughter escapes my lips. All that work to stop swearing, and it just slips right out. But one word is not enough to capture the maelstrom that brews inside me. In a harsh growl, taut with tension, I spit, "Rotten—lying—Sonofa Ratbag! What the WHAT just happened to my entire life in there?" I stop, forcing a deep breath into my lungs.

"Ugh, Zounderkite," I yell, slapping my palm to my forehead, "I can't even believe I bought all his lies." My volume rises in a crescendo of quasi-cursing. But the distraction of Victorian expletives is short-lived. My mind frolics through now hurtful memories of the years I spent looking up to Whit, the years I spent wishing he was my dad. "Ha! Wish granted, I guess."

15
giving ground

Ember

Honestly, I have no idea how long I've been sitting here when the creak of the door announces a visitor. A thin sliver of light turns into a wedge before receding into darkness. A long sigh of exasperation escapes my lungs before I can stop it. I don't feel ready to talk to anyone, but it seems there's no escaping it. Looking up, I see Kenyon standing there, leaning on the door he just closed, his eyes looking sadly at me. It's the last thing I want to see. Seeing pity in strangers' eyes is nothing new to me; teachers and new foster parents look at me that way. It always makes me feel so small, reduced to my history, to what has happened to me rather than who I am.

"Come in." I stand as he walks the small room in a few long strides. Immediately I'm in his arms, his hold tight and protective. I let myself feel the moment of safety he offers. My tears come again, and I bury my head in the crook between his neck and shoulder, rough sobs wracking my body.

Again, I sense that I'm falling. It feels like falling into a bottomless pit, the light from the top fading quickly, the darkness encroaching around me, leaving me utterly alone, even as I stand in his embrace.

Kenyon's face is inscrutable. His arms wrap me tighter before he releases me, though he keeps a hold on my hands. He's a near stranger, and the care I feel from him is a light shining into my heart—light I want to see, to feel, to be the light itself. To be so full of light that it emanates from me—but all I feel is this growing darkness.

I wearily swipe at the tears covering my face, knowing the mascara trails on my cheeks look ridiculous. Kenyon moves his hand to wipe my face with his thumb. I feel so hollow and bereft of hope, but in him I find the light I've been longing for.

Without forethought, my lips meet his with an intensity that scares me. My desire for his light makes me reach for it. This isn't the gentle first kiss I would've dreamed of receiving in the park only hours before, though that seems like a lifetime ago. This is a desperate kiss, an attempt to save myself from darkness.

Kenyon's soft lips are yielding, his passion growing to meet mine. The scratch of his stubble rubbing on my face has an oddly sobering effect on me, demanding I be present in the moment and not lost in my darkness.

Though my kiss is desperate, I feel something different in his: the true depth of his feelings. At this, my stomach fills with a fluttering sensation. I don't understand how or why, but I feel his unspoken feelings as clearly as my own. I lose myself in the kiss, wanting to be good enough for him, to deserve the complex emotions he feels for me and that I inexplicably feel for him. This goes way beyond the fact that he is super hot. I feel something for him that makes no sense; I mean, I've known him for less than 24 hours. Fleetingly, I wonder if he can feel the fire that erupts deep within me because I can feel it in him. The longing I feel for him makes every other feeling of desire I've felt pale in comparison.

He seems to sense my emotions and presses further into me, deepening our kiss. Kenyon's closeness compounds the heat I feel, magnifying it to an unfamiliar fire. I've never been this close to another person, sharing something more, sharing something so fragile.

Kenyon gently pulls himself from me. He continues holding me tightly, though, our bodies so close together, our foreheads together. I feel his breath. The heat between us is inescapable. I lift my head again, and his lips move again to mine. This is the gentle and sweet first kiss I've dreamed of.

Almost as quickly as it began, it ends. Kenyon gently pulls himself away from me, regret evident in his eyes. This closeness is unnerving, yet I feel utterly safe.

"We need to go back." I know he's right. If we're gone much longer, more people will come searching. And that's the last thing I need.

"They stopped once you left the room out of respect for you," Kenyon says hesitantly. He seems unsure how this last bit of news will go over.

"Please—tell me that's not true!" I reply, dread in my voice. "Now I have to go back and have them all watch me walk into the room, the sad little girl who couldn't take it and had to run away."

The light filtering in through the window shines on Kenyon. He shakes his head, a lock of black hair falling forward, contrasting his pale skin. He's quick to reassure me. "It's not like that. Nobody is judging you for being upset. You have every right to be."

Without speaking, Kenyon wraps my hand in his, leading me back to the Assemblage Room. Retracing our steps, rounding corner after corner, I hadn't realized how far I had run, making me wonder vaguely how Kenyon had even found me. Before I can ask, we turn the corner and we're back.

There's a heaviness in my chest, dread rising, threatening to over-flow. It's like he can feel it through my skin. Kenyon releases my hand and wraps his arm around my shoulder, tightening his protective hold on me.

As we descend the stairs, most of the Draíodóir sit silently, looking directly ahead. Only a few dare look at us as we enter, and I'm grateful for this small mercy.

As Ember and Kenyon take their seats, Brother Aaric Aumont stands up, tactfully giving no indication that anything has happened. Ember lets out a long sigh of seemingly momentary relief. He walks the short distance to the center of the room while I stand hovering at the edge of the stage.

Ari turns to face the assembled. "Brother Adair has more he wishes to impart regarding the events that drew him away from us. And those who've returned him to us." His manner is so formal that it doesn't suit him. He was always easygoing, quick with a smile or a laugh, but that was almost eighteen years ago. The weight of unexpected leadership has pulled his shoulders into a slump, etching lines around his mouth and forehead.

"So once again, The Priory of the Draíodóir cedes the floor to him, that he may conclude his thoughts." He walks away, and I feel more than ever that I am on trial. It hurts to feel the weight of their suspicion added to the sorrow I see in Ember, the betrayal I see in her eyes. But in for a penny, in for a pound, I suppose. The worst part is finished; the rest are just coffin nails.

I begin again, knowing everything I have to say is semantics. I'm relieved not to interact with Ember just yet. I'm a coward, and I hate myself for it. I could have told her years ago, made her life easier. At least she would've known why it's been so difficult for her to fit in. But that time is long past, and now it's time for the truth. In this very moment, I could lose her.

But I press forward, clearing my throat. My voice is thick as I begin. "As I indicated, my daughter—" I stumble over the word, knowing it's the first time I've called her that, and I see her blanch at the word. Again, I clear my throat, amending my word choice to her name instead. "Ember is the child I found in that room, the product of two oracles and herself dually gifted.

"Given that I found her in such a state, I realized I must remove her from Elysia, raise her away from magic, and hide her from a mother who would try to take her powers. However, the weakening of our draíochta in les Dormeur is so pervasive that I dared not try to conceal both of us, making it impossible for me to raise her. So, I used all of my energy to bind hers. I performed the Geasa Droma Draíochta enchantment for many years to bind her magic. It could not be allowed to manifest. Even so, premonitions have broken through. They continue to manifest more fully as she reaches the age of maturity and consent."

"Seeking safety in subterfuge, I stood at the sidelines, moving her from one foster family to another, all while trying to teach her basic tenets of magic without raising any power. Despite all my efforts, her mother has continually attempted to locate her, confirming that my instinct to hide her was the proper course of action."

Ember's mouth falls open, a strangled gasp escaping her mouth, her hands trembling.

"I cannot regret the actions I've undertaken to keep her safe, or further, that brought her into this world. If I'd not broken my vows, this beautiful child, my daughter, would not be sitting here. And through it all, she has been a gift to me," I finish, trying to impart the love I've never shown in our daily lives into this one statement, as though it could somehow redeem me or my choices. All I have is hope that she can, in time, forgive me.

On impulse, I look directly at her, speaking only to her. "I'm so sorry, and please know that I have always loved you. And though I know I do not deserve your forgiveness, I pray one day you'll find it in your heart to grant it." I hear another gasp escape Ember and face the Draíodóir. "I will answer any questions now."

Brother Ari is the first to speak. "You have betrayed all who sit in this room, Brother Addi. However, by the pain evident in your voice and the guidance I hear with my gift, it's clear you took the only avenue you felt was available to you. Who is to say what the proper choice would've been?" He looks around the room for any comments but is met with stoney-faced silence.

"Brother Addi, you who were to be our leader, our guide, our most beloved, I cannot pretend the betrayal of your vows and subsequent departure does not cut us deeply. I am but a pale second choice to lead The Priory to the future you might have heralded. It broke my heart seventeen years ago when you disappeared." His voice breaks. Taking a deep breath, he continues. "My heart breaks even more for this poor child."

I see Ember bristle at his assessment and sentiments. Just when I think she might raise and tell him off, I see Kenyon grip her hand more tightly, causing her to look down at their entwined fingers. I again find myself thankful for his presence.

Brother Ari presses on, "Long has she suffered for your trespasses! You stood by and let ordinary mortals raise your daughter, away from her birthplace and birthright, her ability to harness her draíochta! You have denied her the knowledge, skill, and wisdom foundational to her identity!

"Whether or not she is a dually gifted oracle seems to make little difference. Her delayed entrance into la Magie and lack of training make her abilities nearly irrelevant. So much has been denied her; can she ever realize her true potential?"

Before he can continue, he's interrupted by a woman's voice, silencing the Draíodóir. "We believe she can. Furthermore, if left unprotected and untrained, she will flounder and be at risk to forces that would corrupt her gifts." The voice echoes in a tone so commanding, it brooks no argument.

All of the Priory turn their heads in unison to find the speaker emerging from a concealed door. She strides confidently into the room, leading a small retinue of Sisters. Everyone stands in surprise at the entrance of the uninvited company of women.

Her golden skin glows; she wears the magical tattoos favored by those who wish to dedicate the fullness of their lives to their Gift. They shine with their otherworldly luminous blue light. Wide-set eyes blaze beneath cropped graying hair. My former counterpart, the intended Prioress of the Vala, Sister Vadoma Palgrave, graces us with her presence. The faintest hint of a Romani accent in her voice distinguishes her from others. When our eyes meet, hers shine.

I cannot stop the words. "My dear friend, Sister Vadoma Palgrave."

The women are uniformly dressed, unchanged in all these years, in blue woolen dresses with structured semi-circular seams under the bust, layered over red underskirts. Woven crimson cowl necklines are framed by oversized woven shawls pinned at the shoulder, entrenched in enchantments and process. The threads catch the light, metallic shimmers intertwined with the iridescent glow of magic woven throughout. Drop spindles hang from belts slung low to one side. Memories flood my senses. I'm home, and yet somehow in a foreign land.

17

kingdom's coming

Ember

Those shawls— they're so strange! Why are there iridescent spots and lines on them? They're woven into the fabric, reminding me of the marks on my face.

I guess magic leaves a mark. My spots, Whit's brand-spankin' new spots, the tattoos Kenyon wears on his arms, and now these shawls, I don't have to ask if it's true. I know it is.

These women are of the Priory of the Vala. There hasn't been much talk about them, but who else could they be? It's not like they could be anyone else. What other pack of women would be hiding in the meeting rooms of a Temple?

These women all know my mother, or the woman that gave birth to me and then tried to rob me. They're her people. One of these women could be her! My pulse quickens at the thought, but I quickly dismiss it. Surely Whit would've reacted if he'd seen her, if Phaedra had entered the room. How do the women know we are here?

Murmurs of shock and disbelief ripple through The Priory as Sister Vadoma makes her way through, a small group of the Vala following behind.

Then my mouth drops open. Standing there, amongst the women, is Ms. Ragana and, even worse still, my best friend, Nico Jones. How is this possible? Is everyone in my life lying to me, betraying me?

I manage to find my tongue to speak through the sudden unshed tears in the corners of my eyes. "Nico, I don't understand. What are you doing here?"

She walks forward from the group and looks me straight in the eyes. "I'm so sorry, Ember. I hated lying to you, but necessity dictated my secrecy. Otherwise, I never would've."

"But why? I thought you were my friend!" I nearly yell.

Sister Vadoma steps forward to answer. "Young Nico is a Novitiate to the Vala, and we needed to protect you. So, I sent Nico to befriend you and keep her eyes on you."

Looking past the Sister, I direct another question to Nico. "So I was an assignment for you?! Thanks, I needed one more person in my life to lie and betray me." Her eyes look glassy, like she's fighting tears, too. Looking from her to Whit, I see he's surprised to see Nico, too.

"No, Ember. I may have been sent to befriend you, but our friendship is real!"

"As if..." The bitterness in my reply is palpable. "Skullduggery!" My accusation in our shared language hits home as Nico looks at me, but I turn my face away, looking anywhere but in her direction.

Again, Sister Vadoma steps in. "This subject must be tabled for the moment. There are more urgent matters before us." She looks pointedly at the Sisters around her. "We, of The Priory of the Vala, stand before you to give witness to the truth of the matters spoken today. Long have we watched the events of these poor souls in silence, but we can hold our silence no longer, for all has transpired as it has been foreseen. Our efforts move forward in the service of survival, spinning our yarns and weaving on the looms of the Norn."

Ms. Ragana walks forward and my heart sinks to the floor. She carries my oversized artist's portfolio. This will be the moment of truth, proof I somehow knew of this world, that I'm magic and see things that are hidden.

Sister Vadoma clears her throat. "Sister Zola, please come forth and bear witness to all you've observed in your time as the teacher of Ember in les Dormeur."

Ms. Ragana looks at me with clear eyes. "I'm sorry, Ember, but this is necessary." She turns then to the entire gathering. "I have seen Ember amid the Völuspa, her eyes misty white, half in and half out of Onirique, seeing the past. She has drawn many aspects of our world. Even through the binding spells that Brother Addi has performed over the years, she has never been far from la Magie."

Unzipping the portfolio, she pulls out large and small pieces of paper: sketches and finished assignments alike, all comprised of some part of this world.

I hear murmurs yet again. Seriously, for being Oracles, these people are easily surprised. They seem to know nothing.

"You said you had proof of her gifts..." Brother Aaric demands.

"Indeed, I do—although not as much as I soon will," this last remark is rather cryptic for my liking.

"Sister Zola, please bear witness," Sister Vadoma says, tilting her head at Ms. Ragana.

Looking up at me through thick black lashes, her usual mischievous expression is nowhere to be found. Sister Zola, as we're apparently calling her now, you know, as it's her actual name, continues to pull out pieces of my art. As she does, I notice a small black tattoo on the inside of her left wrist, far enough up that I'd never seen it at school. The Sisters' woolen gown shows the tattoo freely. I wonder at its meaning, if it's a symbol of the Vala or something special to her. I assume it's the latter. It's not like Oracle societies have logos.

Her tattoo is different from the iridescent markings that both Kenyon and Sister Vadoma wear. But my momentary distraction is gone as her hand continues its progress. The Sisters have moved a table from the side of the room near us. She lays my art out to be seen by all. Arriving in Elysia the way we did, via an improbable-looking geometric hypercube and magic, I didn't have the chance to see any of the surrounding buildings other than the Temple, which I recognized right away. I can only assume that I've drawn other buildings from the city.

Sister Zola revealing my art in front of all these strangers feels like an indictment against me rather than proof of Sister Vadoma's statements and my abilities. But to be fair, being teased too many times by fellow art students about my subject matter, I've become private about my work.

Undeterred by the dread clouding my face, Sister Zola sets the portfolio down on the table. An eternity seems to pass as I watch the Sister arrange various assignments dating back to my Freshman year of high school. Shocked gasps and excited murmurs sound through the group.

As I look at city scenes drawn from imagination—or so I thought, I want to gather them up and protect my privacy and pride. The city that haunted my dreams for years turned out to be real. The random drawings and doodles all confirm I'd been drawn to this city.

However, the most shocking drawing seems to be from the other morning, after awakening from my recurring nightmare. It was such a surprise to actually see the nightmare mother's face and retain it after waking up.

I knew it was coming but dreaded it most. This woman has to be my actual mother. The last time I had the dream, I remembered more than I ever had, and it was creepier than ever. I don't know for sure, but I know it's her. The fearful reactions my body experienced in sleep ignite again and seem inescapable. It tightens my chest, knots my veins, my blood pumping erratically. I pick at my cuticles again, wedging a fingernail under the half-moon skin that borders the nail, then pulling it.

An unexpected stab of pain jolts my awareness to my fingertip. A bright red drop of blood stands out at the edge. I'm amazed at how quickly blood accumulates, threatening to fall to the floor. My finger twitches, nearly of its own accord, toward the edge of my shirt to stop the bleeding. But my attention refocuses on the commotion and the tension building in the room.

A few claim Sister Zola has influenced me to draw this woman. The crowd is alight with astonishment. Honestly, I can't fully comprehend why it matters so much that I'd drawn her, but before I can ask the question, Sister Zola's voice cuts through the many conversations among the assembly, "You see, even with her unrealized gifts bound, she still sees la Magie. She has a blood memory connection." My art teacher stands revealing the truth of my secret insights. I feel stripped bare for all of the Draíodóir and Vala to behold, for them to judge my credibility.

I turn to Kenyon. "I don't think I can take much more of this." Moved by my pleading, Kenyon gathers me into a protective hug. It also feels a bit like being claimed by virtue of this public embrace.

"Can't you see this is too much for her? Yesterday she was just a regular teenage girl. Today her reality has been ripped away, discovering she was nearly murdered by her mother and betrayed by her father. Not to mention the city in her dreams turns out to be real. It's like she's stared too long at the sun and turned to find her reality burned away." Kenyon's eyes flash during his tirade.

Why does it have to be so hard, so awful? Wasn't my magical world supposed to be an escape from the unhappy reality of my everyday life? The imagined life stolen from me is not supposed to be the life I'm running from.

My body convulses as all these realizations hit me, as the protective and repressive wisps of magic that obscured Elysia spin away from me. Magic cocooned me most of my life, blurring my Vision and guarding me with ignorance. Now it's ebbing away, leaving me. The impression of slipping gives way to a forceful, ripping-away sensation. The more the magic unravels from me, the stronger my convulsions.

I'm only dimly aware of Kenyon's panicked attempts to still my spasm-wracked body. I want to scream in protest as I feel myself being taken from his faltering embrace.

A great rush of energy surrounds my body, encompassing every part of me—above and below—inside and out. My brain floods me with images, my mind overtaken by voices. In an incomprehensible blur, memories that aren't mine play unbidden, flooding my mind until I can no longer distinguish what's mine and what's not, waging war for my consciousness until the memories and the voices win the battle, over-taking my awareness. We're one now.

The images are violent in their speed, aggressive in their truth. I would run from them if I could, but there's no escape as they flood my mind's eye. Whispering voices hiss, though I can't make out what they are saying. There are too many.

Too fast! Too fast, the images and voices come too fast, spinning out of control. Too many voices to make sense of! They're out of synch, each saying something different, something urgent. The pitch and intensity growing, my ears ringing in the din. It's too much to bear!

Until it's all black.

The pressure in my temples makes my blood throb, and for the second time in twenty-four hours, there's a pulsing sensation in the scars around my hairline. Whispering voices permeate my mind; there are too many to distinguish what's being said. Their voices create a hissing sound. Single words "–Investiture, Initiation, Ignorance–" slip through the din of what seems like a hundred voices. As the voices die away, a final voice speaks so quietly, little more than a whisper. "Survival" and "True Voice…"

The blackness disappears when I open my eyes. I'm surrounded by an expanse of white as I lay on the ground. Looking at my outstretched arm under my head, I see several drops of blood pooling under my finger. Bloody red is the only color I see. I can't distinguish where the ground ends and where the rest of this strange place begins. My breaths come quick and shallow as my heart beats faster and panic escalates. Am I losing my mind?

Getting up, I look around. A hazy mist gradually develops, obscuring my vision. Within it, a woman coalesces, ancient and wizened, bone visible in parts of her face. Faintly glowing bluish-white lines run from the tips of her fingers and up the length of her arms. Behind her, other figures are developing, wisps of fog clinging to them like suggestions of clothes. They are part bone and part flesh, but not in a zombie, brain-eating way. More like they are becoming less human as the generations pass. They are somehow beautiful and also terrifying.

Without meaning to, I take a step toward the first woman. Norse runes appear on the side of her face, pulsing with power, causing my spots to do the same. The tattoos are long, elegant sweeping lines branching off into designs and more sigils than I can identify. Power radiates from her in waves, an electrical quality to the sensation. The tattoos look similar to Kenyon's but are much more powerful.

The first woman looks at me impassively as I take her in. I startle as voices come together, an unearthly echoing tone speaking in near unison, saying "Disir" and "Ancestor witches" and "Grandmothers." Their communication is alien in its spareness. The statements resonate in my blood, in my bones, and in my heart. The sensation is visceral as they answer my unasked question. I feel the truth in my body, the way it pulls toward them, seeking the magical light radiating from their manifested bodies. An undeniable connection links me with them. These are my Grandmothers from generations ago.

"Blood of our blood, bone of our bone..." As they say the words, I reflexively look at my finger where I'd torn my cuticle off, darkening the expanse of white. I can feel the blood in my body calling to them.

"Blood calls us."

"Even such a small amount?" I ask.

"Your blood—our bones. Our blood—your body, all one. All made of stars," her face expressionless as she says it. I feel a sweeping sensation in every part of me. There are emotional, physical, and spiritual bonds connecting us.

I long to be near them, but their presence is intimidating, so I stay put.

"Now, truth revealed—gifts claimed," the deep voice reverberates in the din.

"Deceived..." Comes another disembodied voice, hissing.

"A lifelong companion..." another intones, and I realize they're stringing one sentiment together a few words at a time.

"Now ripped away..." Yet another voice proclaims.

"Veil lifted." It's like some kind of call-and-response game, Truthing Edition.

"Gifts—reclaimed. Eyes open—See."

"Listen to Hear."

"Truth Known."

"Bound no longer."

"Gifts bound now awaken," the first Grandmother says—a statement of fact.

"I don't understand. How are you going to free my powers?"

The Grandmother replies, "You will."

I balk internally at her vague words. How's that even going to work?

"Trials await." She pauses as though letting it sink in.

"Do I have a choice about these trials? What if I'm not ready?" I feel like a petulant child asking this question, but I can also hear the quaver in my voice.

"Choice is always yours. Determiners possess free will," the Grandmother says. "Forget all you've remembered, live life of Sleepers, or face challenges. Use eyes that See, ears that Hear, your gifts can guide. Live as Waking Dreamer." Her countenance is radiant, her words confusing in their brevity.

"No, I'm sorry, that's not what I meant. I don't want to go back to the world of the normals; I've never fit in there, if that's what you meant. But I'm just not sure that I'm ready to face a trial. I mean, I'm not exactly at my best..."

"Seldom are we ready. But gifts unexplored await—deep connections close at hand."

"But—" I begin.

"Connection unfolds in time," she says, and it's clear the topic is finished.

Even as the Grandmother speaks, an image of Kenyon comes to mind. Is there some weird mystical connection between us? There is something that intrigues yet frightens me in ways that have nothing and everything to do with him. My brow furrows at that paradox, as well as the Grandmother's unwillingness to explain any further.

Instead, I give voice to a question I hadn't realized I wanted to ask. "What is a True Voice? I heard one of you say something about finding my True Voice."

"True Voice is Spirit—full force of will and being." She pauses, giving me a moment to process the gravity of her statement. "Choices not easy, but yours to make."

"What choice? Are you talking about a new choice or the other thing about going back to the normal world?" These women seem to speak in Yoda-level riddles.

The Grandmother does not hear my questions or, more likely, doesn't care. As the edges of Onirique start to blur, color seeps in, muddying everything. One last statement echoes in my ears. "Our gift..."

The whiteness of Onirique entirely dissipates; I guess that's what this place is called. I mean, that's what the Sister called it. The Vision changes and I find myself standing in the mouth of a cave. An uncontrollable compulsion to enter overwhelms me. And I assume this is the initiation I heard one of the Ancestors speak of, though it seems obvious if you ask me. I mean, here I am at the mouth of a cave, and those Grandmothers are all Yoda-ing it up.

I realize I'm stalling, standing here picking at my cuticles again and using sarcasm to mask my fear. But it's my last defense mechanism. And I know I'm going to walk into the cave and face whatever fresh hell awaits me.

Another stab of pain at my fingertips alerts me to a second cuticle casualty, sacrificed at the altar of my nerves. I look down and see a drop of blood. I shake my finger and see it hit the ground. This drop of blood acts as a catalyst for the Vision or situation or whatever this is to begin. No more stalling, I guess.

Rough walls glisten in the dim light of the moon. A corridor leads to a larger opening, where the light is even brighter. It seems unnatural. Then it occurs to me that laws of physics don't apply here.

There is a puddle of moonlight on the floor in the next opening. Guess that's how it's lit; maybe the cave has a skylight? In the middle of the light, there's a pedestal with a box on top. I can't look away from it. My stomach quivers and my feet itch to move forward. I feel its pull with every part of my body. Whatever is in that box is mine. It feels like me.

My eyes zero in and I realize this is no trick of light. The box is illuminated from within. Hesitantly, I push one foot forward. A light shines on me, and a mist begins to swirl around the tunnel. From out of the darkness, a voice rings out. "FREAK!"

The single word is an assault, even in my Visions. Emerging from the mist, I see kids from school, their voices taunting before they're even fully materialized. The teasing voices echo into the cavernous space, bouncing off rough walls.

"FREAK!"

"LOSER!"

The words hit me, making my heart lurch and tighten. My peers can't really be here. Can they? I want to run away. I look down at my feet, but I can't move them. Then the many foster parents I've had swirl into view. As they solidify into a corporeal state, they scold me about what I'd done to get kicked out of their homes. "Maybe if you could've just been a normal teenager," says one foster mother.

"Why do you have to look like a devil worshiper?" Asks another, disappointment written all over her face.

"Lying is never a way to earn trust, Ember," a foster father chides. Their voices form a chorus, louder and louder.

I remind myself that these people can't really be here, but their words cut me nonetheless. Every fear I've ever had about myself is trotted out into the light, every secret truth about my own failings revealed. My face heats in shame and guilt. It feels so cruel to experience these emotional land-mines on top of everything else that's happened today.

One last figure coalesces in the mist, and of course, it's Whit. He looks me in the eye and says in his matter-of-fact manner, "After everything I've given up for you, you're such a disappointment. You fail me constantly. I've tried so hard to give you the knowledge to help yourself, but you were too busy wallowing in self-pity." He spits. "Every choice you make is the wrong one; how can you ever expect to succeed at anything?" He shakes his head in resignation. "You are not worth my time, you foolish girl. You waste time making mediocre art. All your craft projects will never amount to anything." His final words feel like a knife in my heart.

Isn't it bad enough that he's lied to me all these years? Now he's leading the chant. Escalating voices begin a chorus of words that regales me with my own insecurities, both acknowledged and secret. Their faces are contorted masks of disdain as the mists swirl around them. The din of their insults increases and decreases to let through the most hurtful words loud and clear.

"Strange..."

"Unworthy..."

"Weirdo..."

"Unoriginal..."

"Nobody wants you..."

"Unloveable..."

"Imposter..."

All my fears, all my failings, in a cacophony of voices. They run together, telling me I'm not enough and too much all at the same time. They slam into my heart like an oncoming storm.

"Ember, you don't even believe in yourself; how do you expect us to?" Whit's final demeaning insult makes my hands shake. "I never wanted children."

Now I'm certain. These are all the things I hate about myself, things I fear are true.

And, of course, one final insult to injury, a loop of song lyrics joins in the chaos of noise in my mind. It's more than I can bear. Death by a thou-

sand cuts, my worst fears realized. I'm being examined under a microscope and coming up pitifully short.

Something in me snaps. The weight of everyone's opinions finally breaks me. But instead of covering my ears and curling up in a ball, a different emotion rises within me. Apoplectic, my rage burns me from the inside out. I no longer care what any of these people think of me. There's no room left in me. I'm too full of grief, full of anger, the words boring a hole through my chest, all the way to what's left of my heart.

Everything I have ever known about myself or the world has been ripped away, leaving me with nothing. There's no room left for the petty grievances of classmates or failed foster parents or even Whit. Especially from Whit. I have no room for his lies or anything else. My mother tried to steal my powers, and my father stood by and watched as others raised me with no love and half measures of tolerance. I feel like everyone in my life has taken turns thieving little bits of my soul away. All the now hollowed-out places in me fill with sorrow, and I finally understand what's truly wrong.

It's not all of the superficial crap they say about me. It's my willingness to blindly accept their accusations as truth, allowing them to belittle and take pieces of me.

In rage and rejection, I push their voices out of my mind. Gathering myself to my full height, I muster all the power and determination I can find and command, "NO! No more. You're not real and mean nothing to me." That at least stops the cacophony of voices. But it's not enough. I need to stop them once and for all. "You have no power! I REJECT your lies!" I stare wordlessly at the mute ghosts. It's only when the truth of my words settles in the blood, bone, and every cell of my body do I see these specters for what they are.

I see through all of them; they were paper tigers all along.

I look left and then right. The once-solid forms of people are nearly gone. But rather than fading away completely, they change their shapes and wear my face. All the figures look at me with an uncanny likeness to me, visions of a younger me. There's 12-year-old Ember that hated herself for not fitting in. The 14-year-old envious of her classmates, wishing to look like them, to be them. 15-year-old Ember who wonders whether her life is worth living, contemplating its end. 16-year-old Ember who secretly wishes for a surprise Sweet 16 birthday party, full of friends she doesn't have. Even a nearly current version of me who resigns herself to an unhappy life, tells herself it's better to accept unhappiness than hope for some sort of high school miracle to change her life.

Looking at them, I have a weird urge to thank them. They endured a lot but kept on going. The lessons I learned in those incarnations became me. Before I can say another word, they all look at me and, in a resonant and unnatural voice, say, "We are of you. You were always enough. The power inside you is yours to give away or keep." As I look at them, they're so real, like I could reach out and touch them. Staring at me with eerie eyes of understanding, their gaze acts as a catalyst. In unison, we say, "Self-inflicted wounds." It's then that I realize these are not just visages of me. They are me! All these Embers are living manifestations of past selves.

Then they're gone. In the space of a heartbeat, they all disappear, taking with them most of the mist they're made of, leaving me with the knowledge that my own fear is my biggest enemy. It's the worst betrayal of all. No matter what Whit or my mother or anyone else has done to me, all of it pales in comparison to my willingness to betray myself.

In that moment, we are all healed. All the Embers inside me feel whole. The magic of this cave has brought me the ability to touch the consciousness of my younger selves. My whole life healed, not forgotten, the lessons and experiences are still there. They just don't hurt so much anymore.

This flash of insight lasts for only a moment. Still, it changes me profoundly. All of my mental and emotional processes are moving at lightning speed. I don't think I would've come to those realizations in the real world.

The light radiating from the box at the end of the tunnel is all I can see now, casting light and shadows onto the cave walls. A rattling grows until the partially opened lid flies off violently and clatters to the floor.

Once the lid is gone, the light gets even brighter, and slowly, I walk toward it.

Rhythmic heartbeats echo off the walls and thrum in time with my heart. My blood is whooshing with the heartbeat.

It grows louder with each step I take, commanding all my attention. As I draw nearer, I see a heart rising out of the box. Rays of light blind me, but I can't look away or alter my path. I'm pulled inexorably toward *it by a force that connects us. Somehow, I know this is my heart, or maybe it's a bright shiny fearless new heart. Whatever the case, I know it's mine.*

I nearly run the rest of the way down the narrow corridor. I need to merge what remains of my battered heart with this marvel shining at me from the end of the hall.

Shooting spires of light into the darkness, the rays grow brighter still. Somehow my eyes adjust, learning to see. Where fear might've been, I feel only yearning. For the first time, I feel complete. I really believe that I'm enough, just as I am.

Extending my hands, I reach out. But before I can touch it and examine it, the heart launches itself toward me. The thud of its impact slams me back as it connects with me. It bores inside of me, my chest cracks open to welcome it. I open my mouth to scream, but all I can hear is the heartbeat.

Momentary pain radiates through my chest as my insides shift to make room, and its beating replaces the heart that sat within my chest before. Again, I'm keenly aware of the feeling of blood coursing through my veins, pulsating as magic travels to the furthest reaches of my body. I feel it deep within; it's actually all I can feel. This heart is magic, my magic, overwhelming every sense and permeating my body, filling up all the once hollow space left by the ghosts.

Every sense, every thought, every experience I've ever had is now filtered through this new heart. I'm reborn unto myself. My skin tingles and feels hot as the light dances upon it, burning away all the fear and doubt that once existed, etching patterns upon my skin, beginning at my fingers and traveling up the length of my arms until they join the light shining from my chest. My eyes flutter, blinking at the sudden appearance of the light tattoos. The patterns last for only a moment before they recede back into my body. As they do, the all-encompassing light shines more brightly than before. It blinds me as I become the light.

Again I find myself in the white room, my senses reeling. I look down at my chest and see a starburst pattern etched in light over my heart. It's the same magical light as my forehead spots, but this is beautiful, reminding me of my own power.

The intensity of the Vision fades quickly, but I do not question that it has happened. There is no doubt in me that it was real. It has become a part of me, my body first, and then my mind. This is something that I must feel to understand. Every part of me has shifted to accommodate this new magic. This was an Initiation. My body confirms this as I hear the thought in my mind. Finally, understanding it's the gift of clairaudience. The song lyrics that always got stuck in my head had been my gift breaking through the binding magic Whit used to hide me. The Sight is an active part of me now, too. This Vision broke the bindings placed upon me as a child.

A shimmering haze appears, and this time as the white mist coalesces, only the one Grandmother is standing there. The swirling fog recedes. She looks mostly corporeal, except for an iridescent shimmer about her, surrounding and emanating from her. It pulses like a heartbeat. She is a living incarnation of magic.

"It was a test and an initiation." Said the Grandmother answering the question I was about to ask.

"A Test? Well, did I pass?" The sarcastic retort is out of my mouth before I can stop it. Habit, I guess.

"Initiation requires confrontation of fear to receive gifts." And with that, the woman fades away.

"Wait!" I yell, as though yelling loudly enough will cause the spirit to return.

"NO!" I have so many questions. I try to fight, but it's no use. The colors of the "real" world continue to flood the edges of Onirique, the white world of nothingness colorized. The void of that world and its Vision are gone. Slowly I return to full consciousness.

I open my eyes slowly to relieved faces all around me.

18
all my colours

Ember

I blink several times to focus. Kenyon lets out a massive sigh of relief as he gathers me in a hug. As he holds my head in his hand, our cheeks touch, and I feel his growing stubble on my cheek. His lips brush against my ear, whispering, "Don't scare me like that."

Before I can reply, he helps me stand. My knees feel shaky, probably the lingering after-effects of the Vision or of having Kenyon so close to me. I don't know, but our surroundings pull me back to the situation. I can't face talking to Whit yet. I'm just not ready.

"It's been a long night, and I believe we've heard enough. Brothers, let us sleep on these matters and listen for guidance." Brother Aaric pauses, finally saying, "I think it would be wise to keep your presence here quiet—at least until we come to some decisions about our next course of actio—"

He's interrupted as a sound rings in the quiet room, alerting us to the presence of someone at the door. And suddenly, there's a suspicious absence of the Vala. Which makes me wonder why they need to get out in such a hurry. Before my mind can linger on the question, I feel it, a strange cold sensation settling into my bones. Shuddering cold trickles down my spine, and I suspect that this day is about to deliver its final blow. Through my exhaustion, I steel myself for whatever's coming.

A woman opens the door slowly, and it feels like normal time has been suspended. Finally, there she stands—terrible in all her power.

My mother.

I know it instantly; I feel it immediately. This visceral sensation requires no confirmation from anyone.

The room is electric. My perceptions are much stronger than before, and my senses are on full alert. The hair on my arms stands up. Power rolls off the woman, my mother. I recoil without meaning to. When Whit began speaking of my mother, it was in the abstract, but coming face to face with the woman is startling. My eyes widen, I blink rapidly, and my jaw drops open.

She's short. Shorter than I would've expected. Hearing everybody talk about her, I thought she would be six feet tall, but she's maybe just over five feet. Yet she's not small, her presence dominating the room as she walks in, followed by a small retinue radiating the same power, only to a much lesser degree. Her skin glows with magic.

Seeing her, my balance falters. She has a face so like mine, it catches me off guard. She was a concept before this; it had never occurred to me that I might look like her. Until today, I hadn't given any thought to the possibility of coming face to face with the mother I believed dead until a few hours ago.

I don't know how I feel about the fact that I look like her. She is several inches shorter, which surprises me, having always considered myself too short. We both have inky dark hair and dark almond-shaped eyes. Only her eyes hold a shrewd, calculating expression, appraising all she surveys. Well, I guess there's no doubt about whether she's my mother... I think darkly. And I vaguely wonder why the Brothers were so doubtful of my parentage. I mean, I look just like her.

The unnatural feeling of power rolling off her fills me with dread. My whole body tightens, and I cross my arms, hugging my waist.

As the Prioress enters the room, my senses spring to life. I feel her movements like they are my own. I can also feel the eyes of all the men in the room stealing furtive glances at her, their eyes darting back and forth in a grotesque parody of my life.

"Prioress, it is an unexpected pleasure to see you. I was not aware that you were in The Temple." Brother Aaric bows his head in deference. It's apparent the two leaders of their orders were not well-matched.

But the words seem like nothing more than an unwanted distraction for Phaedra. She turns to thoroughly look at me, though her eyes have never actually left me.

"You've come home to me!" Phaedra says, stepping forward, reaching for my hands. Instinctively, I step backward, though she manages to graze my hand with her fingers. Though she only touched me briefly, the electricity running up my fingers to my forearm makes my stomach lurch. Drawing my hand back, I recoil.

"Your reaction tells me that your father has filled your head and heart with lies about me. He stole you away from me in his guilt, determined to make me suffer for my part in his disgrace." She turns her hateful gaze toward Whit. The look lasts only a moment, but it's enough.

Returning her eyes to me, Phaedra continues. "My child, I am so relieved you are safe and have finally returned to me. I've tried all these years to find you. But your spiteful father hid you too well." She pauses ever so slightly. "Though he did not hide nearly so well..." Her tone changes from over-the-top sweet to vengeful, an overt acknowledgment of her involvement in Whit's attack.

"What about these, then?" The words fly out of my mouth before I can even give them a second thought as I sweep my bangs to the side, revealing the eight pale and shimmering marks that pulsate. They began throbbing the minute Phaedra entered the room.

"I don't know how you got those, my darling. It's certainly evidence of the magic used upon you. Perhaps as your father was binding your powers, or in his efforts to hide you away, he fumbled and left these as a constant reminder of his mistakes. Though they are evidence that magic was used upon you, it wasn't by me."

At this, Whits mouth falls open, working wordlessly in outrage. "That's a lie!" Whit counters, finally managing to speak. I jump in surprise; I've never heard Whit raise his voice, undeniable anger making the three words seethe.

Brother Aaric awkwardly clears his throat. "This seems neither the time nor place to have this discussion. The Draíodóir is hosting our former Brother and his companions, and they are under our protection," he says pointedly. "Perhaps, if they agree, a meeting between you could be arranged tomorrow. However, the Draíodóir are engaged in a private function, apart from the concerns of the Vala. Your attendance was neither requested nor required," Brother Aaric concludes.

"Well, by all means, then. Please, don't let me disturb The Priory of the Draíodóir." She turns her face toward me. "Once they've concluded their business with you, I'd very much like an opportunity to tell you the truth."

She turns quickly on her heels and heads toward the door. "I look forward to seeing you again. We have unfinished business." Without another word, she turns to the door and leaves, followed by her entourage.

I surprise myself by being the first to speak, "Man, rough day to be me! I guess keeping a low profile is kinda out of the question now." My voice is thick with the irony of timing and the dark humor that comes to one in such times of world-shaking strife.

"Indeed," Brother Aaric concurs, no irony in his words. "We will furnish you with accommodations for the night and reconvene after we've taken rest to decide our next course of action."

He looks around the room at his Brothers, saying, "My brothers, I would ask you to spend some time in meditation to Hear the correct course of action for The Priory." Without a word, he leads The Brotherhood the Draíodóir out of The Assemblage Room.

I continue to feel an uneasy undercurrent of shock as we walk through The Temple, following Brother Imanu again. We move through one hallway after another, each looking the same. How far into the Temple are we? How long do we need to walk? I want to lie down. Not that I think I could actually fall asleep, but maybe I could not think about everything circling around my brain for a minute.

Brother Imanu stops at a nondescript door. "Miss Wright." He gestures to the two entries further down the hall. "Mr. McQuiston. Brother Adair." He pauses and says, "Someone will wake you in the morning before we are ready to reconvene." With a final nod of his head, he walks away.

I feel my senses expanding, reaching out almost of their own accord, to feel everything and everyone near to me. I've tried to perform that exact thing so many times before, but now the act works. I feel the energy and actions happening around me. A small creature approaches. I look down to see my one-eyed cat friend from earlier rounding the corner and mewing to be pet. Bending down, I oblige and am greeted with a loud purr. It's a perfectly timed distraction, allowing me to avoid facing Whit. I don't know what to say to him; I'm still too angry.

"Ember, listen—"Whit begins, grabbing my hand and pulling me to stand. But I cut him off as I rip my hand out of his, saying, "What the fu—"

"December! Language!"

"Really, Whit? After everything you've said and done, my language is the issue?"

He lowers his head. "Right, a force of habit, sorry."

"I'm not sure I have anything to say to you right now, Whit. I don't have words strong enough to tell how—how F'ed up this is. Just leave me alone. I can't..." But I don't finish. Instead, I hurry into the room, slamming the door. I feel so weak and pathetic. I wonder how we're ever going to be ok again.

Standing with my back to the door, I hear Kenyon say, "I'll check on her in a bit, sir." Kenyon is clearly trying to reassure him, but his words sound tentative, unsure.

"Thank you, Kenyon. I don't think it would go over so well if I try." Then there is only quiet.

19
the light

Kenyon

I wait a half hour; even that long is a test of strength. I knock on the door, but I inch the door open before she responds.

"Ok, if I come in?" I whisper.

"A bit late to ask now, don'tcha think?" Ember waves me in. Her tone is flirty but unsure, standing there toweling her hair. The sight of Ember stripped down to a tank top and leggings makes me want to make her mine.

"You've got good timing. Any earlier, and you'd have come when I was in the shower." She finger combs her inky hair.

"Well, that would've been just terrible," I say suggestively.

Crimson spreads across her cheeks, down her neck, and onto her exposed chest. In that blush, I see an iridescent starburst pattern emerging from under her tank top, covering her heart. I'm practically mesmerized by this evidence of a profound magical encounter. Still, I don't want her to think I'm staring at her chest with such rapt attention. Obviously—I mean, she's beautiful, and looking at her like this, my desire is obvious. She's so lovely, innocent, and vulnerable; I want to both protect and corrupt her at the same time.

Ember interrupts my thoughts. "I—I don't—"

"I'm sorry, that wasn't—"

"No, it's ok, you just caught me off guard..."

Surely she knew I'd come to check on her. After that kiss, how could I not? I've kissed a lot of girls, but I've never felt anything like that. It felt like she was touching things inside me I didn't know existed.

I tentatively push further into the room, and I hear the door shut behind me. Ember's face and chest go pink, our mutual attraction undeniable. Without hesitation, I cross the room and sweep her into my arms. This time, it's me seeking her lips as I kiss her. I can't stand to see how much pain she's in, knowing that I can do nothing to fix it. I've never wanted anything so much, knowing that I am helpless to do anything. I don't know her or the situation well enough to even guess the right course of action. But I do know that I'm drawn to her in ways I don't understand, and that scares me.

I pull away from our embrace, looking deeply into her eyes. She puts her hand on my face, a tender gesture that only highlights my confusion. "I don't know what it is between us, but I've never felt anything like this. None of the why matters right now, though. I'm here, and you won't face any of this alone." I put as much conviction into my voice as I can manage. I need to make her feel how strongly I feel for her. It doesn't matter that we only met twenty-four hours before. I feel like I've known her my whole life. I know that my track record with women isn't exactly stellar, but I feel so differently about Ember, like the emptiness is gone when I'm with her. But I can't say that now. I'm sure it would totally freak her out.

I move my face to her, lightly grazing my lips against hers. She's quick to return the kiss. And I'm grateful. I feel like I'm out on a limb here. I walked into her room without an invitation, embracing her without asking. But there's a connection here, and we both feel it.

Finally, I force myself away from her. "You need to get some sleep. I'm sure this has been one of the worst days of your life. I can't actually imagine one worse, to be honest. Sleep will help." I lead her by the hand to the twin bed in the corner of the barren room, its dove-gray walls free of decoration. The bed is neatly made with a woven blanket. I wonder if the Sisters are responsible for them. It makes sense with all the weaving they do.

"Please! Stay with me..." Her response is pleading, and she moves toward the bed, her hand still wrapped in mine.

It's too much for me to refuse. She looks so lost, so alone. If the situation was different, I would've suggested it. But as things stand, I couldn't. I'll admit, though, it's what I wanted, coming to her room.

But I have to be careful. My unexpected feelings for Ember could make it easy to get lost in her and go too far. For her, anyway. Taking things all the way would be a mistake, especially here in the Temple.

Turning on the bedside light, Ember sits down, making room for me as she pats the space next to her. So I sit next to her on the narrow bed, wondering what I should do, what she expects. Before I can contemplate too much, Ember grasps my hand and pulls me down next to her. She wraps her leg around mine, arm curling around my stomach and her head on my shoulder. Well, I guess that answers that question. We fit together perfectly. So I lay my head on hers, kissing her crown.

Our breathing is in sync, but it's stilted and staggering. The urge to kiss her again is overwhelming. But before I can make an attempt to do so, she shifts, looking up at my face.

"Today was the worst day of my life, but it was also the best. You were there."

And that's all it takes; I move my lips to hers and kiss her.

just like honey

Ember

"Today was the worst day of my life, but it was also the best. You were there." I'm sure if he'd been looking at me before I said it, I would've lost my nerve. I can't always find the right words to express my feelings. Does he think I'm lame?

There's an intensity in his eyes that I've never seen. This feels different than the other times we've looked at each other. The intensity of today makes me feel out on a ledge, with only him to seek for guidance and support. So I kiss him again.

It doesn't take long for our tentative kiss to escalate. Turning onto his side, he pushes me onto mine, and his arm slips around my waist, drawing my body closer to his.

His hands run the length of my back and waist. Moving his hand to cup my face, he breaks our kiss. The intensity is too much. If we don't stop, there will be no stopping. I'm full of unknown feelings. My skin tingles everywhere our bodies touch, and I want to kiss him again, no matter the consequences.

Pulling his head back, he says, "Ember, I—we have to stop."

"I know, but you make me feel reckless."

"You make me wish for things I've never dreamed for myself. I've known you for twenty-four hours, but you feel like everything I've ever wanted but was afraid to wish for. That scares me a bit."

My stomach flips like I'm on a rollercoaster, and I swoon at his words. They're perfect. For all the opportunities he seems to have, he seems lonely. Maybe I'm taking wild stabs in the dark, but there's a forlorn look in his eyes. His words sound hopeful, but there's hesitance.

I decide not to worry about it right now. I don't have any room for new problems. It's enough that he's here with me. I feel safe in his arms in a way I never have, so I let it all go as his warm arms surround me, and I drift off to sleep.

I wake up for the millionth time, and I feel terrible. Fitful dreams. Plus, this bed is seriously awful. It's super hard, and the pillow is too thick. But each time, Kenyon's here, wrapped around me in some fashion.

There's a quiet, insistent knock on the door. I panic briefly, then lunge toward the door as Kenyon heads for the bathroom. Opening the door enough to see who's knocking, I prepare to tell whomever it is to go away.

But it is not one of the Draíodóir, as I expected. One of Sister Phaedra's minions stands outside my door. It's easier to call her "Sister Phaedra" than my mother. I'm not ready to acknowledge our relationship. Or rather, her relationship with me, I guess.

The tall Sister with a lithe body and light brown skin waits, impatiently tapping her foot. Thick wavy hair cascades down her back and her blue eyes are striking. A large piece of polished amber hanging around her neck compliments her blue woolen gown. She's so beautiful that I stand a moment too long gawking at her.

In my stunned silence, the Sister takes the opportunity to speak, "I am here on behalf of The Prioress. She has requested that I bring you forthwith to meet with her. I'll wait here while you—compose yourself." Her curtness leaves no room for a dissenting opinion.

"What if I do not desire to meet with her?" I don't like bullies.

"It would be in your best interest to meet with The Prioress," Her clipped tone is demanding.

"Fine. But I'm supposed to meet with the Draíodóir soon. I don't want to be late." I want her to know that the Brothers will be looking for me should I come up missing. I mean, we all know how we got here in the first place, and I wouldn't assume Sister Phaedra's intentions are good.

Pulling my head back through the door, I turn to find Kenyon next to me, his face full of undisguised concern.

"You cannot go! It isn't safe!"

"It doesn't seem that I have much choice. I'm pretty sure the Prioress' minion will drag me there if I decline the invitation. Plus, you know I'm going, and if I'm not back soon, tell Whit that I'm with Phaedra. I need to hear what she has to say. I'll be okay," I finish, trying to sound braver than I am.

"I still don't like it."

Slipping clothes on over the leggings and tank top I slept in, I head toward the door, hoping that taking this chance is fearless, not foolish. There's no way I couldn't meet with her; I need to hear what she has to say. I mean, Whit has proven himself a lying liar about—well everything, I need to listen to her side of the story. Plus, maybe I can find out about the dreams– if that's her visiting me, or if they are just weird, recurring dreams.

With my hand reaching for the doorknob, Kenyon's arm shoots out, pulling me into a brief but passionate kiss. He releases me as unexpectedly as he'd embraced me, urging, "Please, be careful." With that, he turns and, in a few long strides, is back in the bathroom. Another demanding knock on the door. I open, step through, and shut the door behind me.

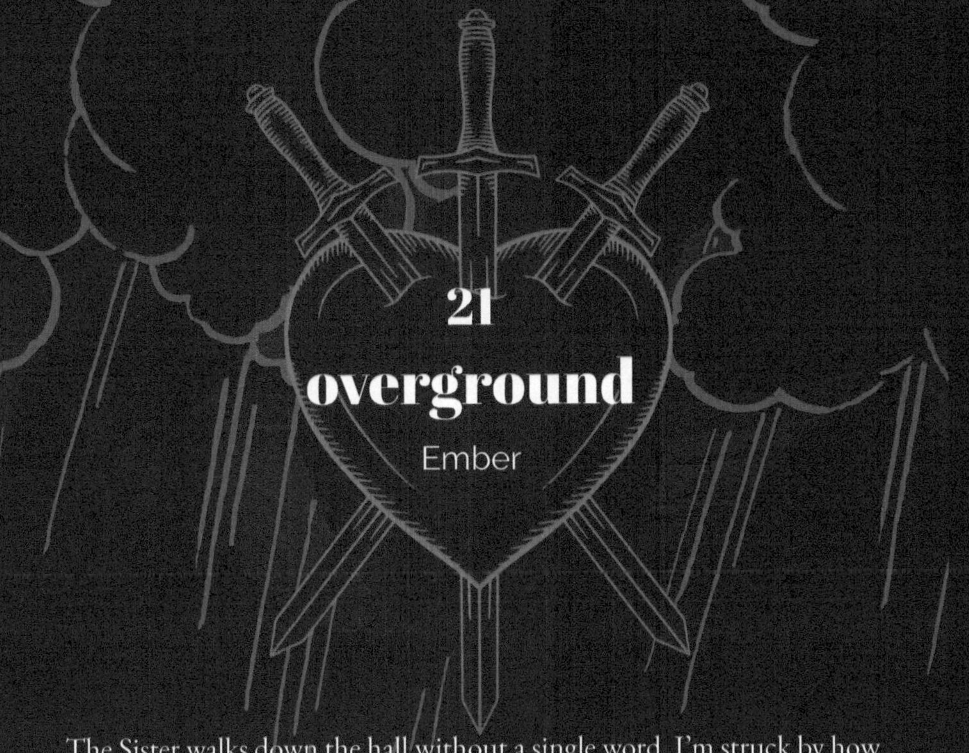

21
overground

Ember

The Sister walks down the hall without a single word. I'm struck by how rude Phaedra's Sisters are compared to the kindly other Sisters I'd met. Even their energy is different. It must be all the evil.

We walk first through the dimly-lit wing that the Draíodóir call home, through The Temple's central vestibule, and into another dimly lit wing that I'm guessing belongs to The Vala.

In all the lack of conversation with the minion, I notice the Temple's design. Hallways diverge from the main corridor seamlessly, without detracting from its stark beauty. I can't figure out how many rooms are in the multi-floored Temple, but it seems like a lot. We travel at a brisk pace to the end of one hallway, turn, then walk to the end of another. At the very end of that hall, The Sister halts, knocking on the last door. Immediately, the door opens.

As we enter, I see a young woman sitting with Sister Phaedra; she looks drawn and pale. Standing up, she genuflects to her Prioress and walks toward the door. Her gait is unsteady, and I wonder what is wrong with her.

"Sister Miranda, please help out dear Sister Sasha to her quarters. She requires rest and revitalization." Sister Phaedra is full of energy, unnaturally so, especially for this early in the morning.

"Certainly, Prioress." Sister Miranda replies, putting an arm under the ailing Sister and helping her to the door. The Sister who'd escorted me makes a subordinate's brief half-bow and withdraws, leaving me alone with Phaedra. I feel totally creeped out. There is something not quite right going on here, and it has my Spidey Senses tingling.

I've been trying to prepare myself for this moment. I knew we'd be alone. I'd have to stare into those eyes, wondering what I might find. Will there be any recognition—any love—for me? How could there be? Stupid, Ember, stupid!

"Please, my darling, sit." Phaedra greets me as though everything in the world is right and normal, like I've always been her darling, not raised by strangers as an outcast.

"Look at you, so dramatic, dressed in all black. What do they call that style in your world? Whatever it is, it suits you."

"Is that really what you called me here to talk about? Besides, it's not for you to like or dislike."

She clucks her tongue. "So dramatic, indeed. But please, save the histrionics; I know drama. It's a trait you've inherited from me." Her words belittle me. They're meant to.

"Now, down to business. I'm sure you have many questions to ask, filled as you are with Brother Adair's lies. Shall we discuss the truth?"

I have to stifle the scoff that nearly escapes my lips. I mean, I know Whit has lied to me all my life, but I suspect she's going to accuse him of something very different. Clearly, this woman has beef with Whit. Plus, it's super weird to hear Whit called Brother Adair or Addi. And while her accusations make me bristle, I remind myself to shove the defensive feelings for Whit away. He doesn't deserve the benefit of the doubt anymore. Again, see the lying liar's decisions in the life I've been forced to live.

Plus, it won't serve me to jump into accusations against Phaedra and ruin this one chance I have. Distracted, I begin picking at my nails, and a small stab of pain reminds me not to touch the scab on my cuticle from yesterday. I really do need to give up that habit. Dropping my hands to my sides, I walk stiffly to the chair set uncomfortably close to Phaedra.

Sitting down and acting on instinct, I launch into the questions I'd most wanted to ask, and most dread knowing the answers.

"I just have two questions. You've acknowledged that you're my mother. Did you really try to steal my powers? And have you been visiting my dreams?" I hadn't meant to be quite so direct. "Aren't you afraid that acknowledging me will threaten your position?" I add spontaneously.

"That's three questions, but I'll allow it. I applaud your directness, another quality you inherited from me, obviously," She replies proudly. "But the answers are a bit more complicated than a simple yes or no. You are young, with not much life experience and even less knowledge of our ways, the ways of draíocht. So I don't expect you to fully comprehend its nuances."

Her "complicated" answer might as well be an admission, and I balk at the idea that I don't understand "their ways." I think I know enough to know what she'd done is wrong. And I long to say so, but just as I'm about to unleash the accusation, she begins again.

"I'm not sure why I seduced Brother Addi. I suppose it was a challenge to me; I was so young and full of admiration for him. He was a bit of a mentor to me; he was so brilliant in his gift. It was moving to hear him speak of Prophecies he'd heard. I had a bit of hero worship for him."

She pauses briefly, as though pondering it herself, "At the time, the two Oracle societies worked closely together. An experienced Brother would work with a novitiate Sister and vice versa. As we worked together, he was kind. His praise and encouragement were like a soothing antidote to all my insecurities and the pain from my childhood."

A new tone of darkness colors her voice. "I never felt good enough —all the love that I didn't feel from my own father and his wife, my stepmother. Consumed as they were with their own lives and concerns, they only ever noticed me when I did something wrong. I was a pariah, a burden, not a daughter to be cherished. I was an afterthought if thought of at all."

Her eyes narrow. "My real mother's absence was a topic of which we were not allowed to speak. She left us. We weren't enough. So she ran off one night, never to be heard from again." There's a far-off look in Phaedra's eyes now, like she's reliving the pain. Her bottom lip trembles slightly, and I can hardly look away. I marvel at the likenesses between us as I sit for the first time alone with my mother, a woman I thought to be dead.

Staring into the darkness of her eyes, I see the pain twist itself into cruelty. How much of Phaedra's story is true? How much is her perception colored by years of hurt feelings and perceived injustices? How much actually matters?

"Everything I ever loved has been taken from me, taken or left me. Fate is always trying to break me into submission. But I never did—I never broke."

"I tried to join the Vala as a novitiate. Seeking the sanctuary of The Temple, I knew I would be loved and accepted here. I felt the camaraderie every time I visited. All the Sisters always seemed so at peace, talking and laughing, and there's so much power! Sister Vadoma refused my petition to join, citing the weakness of my Völuspa. But I'm not a trained monkey able to perform on command!"

Her voice is hard now. "I am extremely adept in all manifesting practices using my draíochta. However, my gift of prophecy was late to develop. So I had to wait. Three miserable years trying to develop my abilities. All that spinning and weaving with no instruction from the very people meant to teach me. All the while, Holier than Thou, Sister Vadoma continued to refuse my petition."

"I pleaded, telling her of my developing gift and my dire need to escape a family. She still refused, saying a troubled home life wasn't a ticket in the Vala. I swore I'd show her what power truly looks like—" She halts her monologue abruptly, without explanation. She sounds so angry that I worry for Sister Vadoma's safety. "In desperation, I employed extraordinary measures to enhance my gift. And finally, I was able to join The Vala."

My stomach tightens at her mention of power. According to her, she's Captain Awesome at manifesting with magic. Why would she need so much more power? How does that impact the ability to have Visions anyway? I make a note to ask Sister Vadoma if I have a chance. But she answers my question.

"I need power for myself, to never be at the mercy of another. I will forge my own destiny. Never again will anyone reject me! More power equals more choice. Destiny has never been a friend to me. So when I could finally join, my Völuspa was still weak. I hoped working with the talented Sisters and Brother Addi would teach me some tricks to enhance my abilities. Or I would never be able to fulfill my dream of rising in ranks of leadership within the Vala." She pauses. I'm about to ask a question, but again, she beats me to the punch.

"The more time I spent with Addi, developing my gift, the more my admiration for him grew. He was so talented, able to induce a trance state and tune into the voice of guidance almost on command. Such mastery is appealing. Well, I began to have more than platonic feelings for him, unattainable and handsome in those days. I'd lay awake trying to think of ways to involve myself in his life—scheming ways to impress him. Make him need me the way I needed him, a task made more difficult given all these ridiculous vows of chastity. Further complicating the matter, Addi's affections seemed to lie in Brother Aaric's direction."

At this, my stomach flips uncomfortably, and I feel my face flush with embarrassment. Not only is this more information than I've ever wanted to know about her desires, but it also confirms my growing suspicions about Whit. Thinking of this woman, this stranger, lying awake at night obsessing about Whit, is gross. And not just because they're my parents. Her scheming and manipulations are gross. She wanted to steal his power.

Phaedra, oblivious to my discomfort and fidgeting, continues, wholly engrossed in her story. She seems relieved to confide in me, like I'm a Confessor.

"So, of course, I found little ways of endearing myself until finally, one day I was so full of heat and need, I could stand it no longer! We were alone in the private library. He was standing close to me, looking over my shoulder, and—I turned and kissed him. Oh, he tried to turn me down. After all, we'd pledged ourselves to our gifts and the furtherance of them; indulgence in physical love would muddy our senses—but I persisted. I knew he would relent. I kissed him again, pushing my hands into his robes this time. My hands roamed his body, tracing his outlines, and I found he needed me as much as I needed him. I felt the fire burning him, tormenting him, as we continued our forbidden kiss. And, well, let's just say I took care of his needs."

Her tone transitioned from confession to confiding, like a girl confiding naughty secrets to her best friend. And still, Phaedra doesn't notice me recoiling in aversion. I'm not sure anybody should learn the details of their conception.

I want to tell her to stop, that I don't need to know this, but my tongue is frozen in disbelief. An image of Whit and Phaedra, limbs entwined in their forbidden carnal embrace, springs to life in my mind's eye, compounding my horror. My stomach convulsing, I mutter to myself, "Gag me..."

"Oh, grow up," Phaedra retorts. "You're not a child; stop acting like one! People have sex! Seiðr once involved sexual components; it's utterly ridiculous that we take vows of chastity, anyway."

She resumes her story, but her voice takes a snide, menacing tone. "As we shared our embrace, I could feel his power, like his gift of prophecy was a tangible thing living within him. It flared to life during our encounter, and I swear it had its own pulse beating its own rhythm. It was so powerful I felt like I would walk away with enhanced powers from our experience. Instead, I walked away pregnant. But of course, I didn't know that at the time.

"I felt your gifts developing within me and foolishly believed I had been gifted with enhanced powers from my encounter with Addi. My Völuspa was as strong as that of Sister Vadoma. Consequently, I made some well-timed and profoundly important revelations in those first few months. My dream of a leadership position with the Vala was within my reach. And I moved quickly up the ranks of leadership, to be sure. But as I said, destiny has never been a friend to me."

"It didn't take me long to puzzle out the enhanced gifts I experienced belonged to you—betrayal on top of betrayal. But, for the first time in so many years, I didn't have to worry my gift wasn't strong enough. I shared your gifts with you, and given that you were a fetus in my womb, I was entitled to use them. They came from me, after all. However, with this came the realization that I would lose these new abilities when you were born. What part of that was even remotely fair?" She looked as though she expected me to answer her question, sympathize with her at the injustice of it all.

"As I created and sustained you in my womb, I began to love you. You are a part of me, and I knew I'd never been alone again. I thought if I could rise high enough within the Vala, I could find a way to keep you with me, raise you in the ways of the Völuspa. We would make an unstoppable team.

My dreams took shape as your small body grew, along with our gifts. I would need to retain some of your abilities if my plan was to succeed. I couldn't—wouldn't lose those gifts, left again with nothing by someone I love so much. How many times was destiny going to leave me holding the bag? The idea of having to supplement my gifts after you were born left me bereft, empty."

"I began to implement my plan. Hiding the truth of my pregnancy from the Priory was so difficult! I wove several kinds of magic and glamors together to camouflage you, both physically and energetically. Even sinking to the depths of employing the glamors produced by Elves to conceal my growing belly. They are adept at concealing their true nature, so their charms also hid the nature of my condition."

My jaw drops open at this, and I blurt out, "What?! Elves are real?"

"Of course they are, though they are not creatures I suggest you become involved with. They are cunning beyond most people's ability to comprehend. As I was saying, by the strength of my Völuspa and the faint echos of clairaudience I'd never experienced, I sensed you would possess both gifts. Tell me, do you experience both gifts of the Oracle?".

Her abrupt question startles me; her manner keeps me off balance. "Umm, yeah, I guess I do. Though Whit bound my gifts for so long, I mostly experienced clairaudience, not the Sight. Though right before we came here, I did have a Vision, I mean Völuspa." And the minute I confess the truth to her, I know I've made a mistake. I don't know why, but it feels like I shouldn't tell her anything.

"I knew it would be so! I felt them." Her voice is self-satisfied with her correct assumption of my gifts. But the direction of her story changes abruptly. "I didn't like lying to the other Sisters, but I didn't want to leave, and I knew they would make me. That was an unacceptable outcome, so I had no choice. I was so young and scared. After all, who had I really hurt? Nobody. One indiscretion. Surely they'd forgive me, but Addi had different ideas. I could not hide my pregnancy from him. Blood calls to blood. He saw through my enchantments and threatened to expose us both, saying he couldn't continue in the Draíodóir, knowing he'd betrayed his vows. He was weak!" Disgust rings in Phaedra's voice on the last word. "Couldn't live with the consequences of his actions. However, he was incapable of exposing me. I was fastidious in the magic I used to hide you. Your growing powers were adding to my own. Pity he was so bound up in the rules and laws that serve no one."

"So, when it was finally time to give birth, I left The Temple on an 'errand' for the former Prioress. I went to a midwife disguised as a peasant woman. Once I'd had you, I sneaked you back into The Temple. You were so quiet, almost as though you sensed the need for our secrecy."

"I had to devise a plan to bring you into the Vala without being caught. I toyed with the idea of saying you'd been abandoned, but I wanted to be involved in your upbringing. I couldn't risk that you'd be sent to an orphanage. I loved you too much for that."

"I was deathly tired; you had not been an easy delivery. The midwife told me so."

This final statement surprises me. Who tells their child that kind of information, like a baby had some say in the matter?

Unaffected by the emotions crossing my face, Phaedra forges ahead, "The minute you left my body, I felt the loss of your gifts. I felt gutted." She sounds so defeated.

"During my pregnancy, I began researching ways to retain the abilities you brought into my life. I knew using the Furta Spiritus method only temporarily enhances our capabilities, using the draíochta taken from another person. That wasn't going to be enough. I needed to permanently retain some of your draíochta.

"I couldn't return to using Amplicon to enhance my abilities, and finding people willing to sacrifice a portion of their draíochta is untenable. So this plan had to work."

"What's Amplicon?" I ask, interrupting her.

"It's energy taken from the quartz crystals that transmit the energy of the Ley Lines. Once the piezoelectric energy is harvested from the crystals, it can be ingested to increase the users' ability to channel greater amounts of magic. But prolonged use erodes the mitochondrial DNA's ability to convert raw magic to draíochta."

"Wait, you used to use that stuff?" I asked, shocked at her easy admission of having used it before.

"As I said, I had to go to great lengths to earn my spot in the Vala Priory. It's quite a rush when used, and the magic you can wield is phenomenal, but I don't recommend you use it."

"You don't need to worry about that!" I say. But then ask another question, "How much of your draíochta did you lose using that stuff?" But as soon as the words are out, I know they were a mistake.

"No need to worry about that little girl; I've forgotten more about magic than you'll ever know." The venom in her voice makes my heart race. I can't wait to get out of here.

"As I was saying, after coming up empty-handed, I began searching through ancient tomes for anything that might help me to retain some of your gifts. You had more gifts than you could possibly need. And I deserve some."

I'm utterly dumbfounded by her logic, that she feels entitled to my abilities. It's so flawed and selfish. Her belief runs counter to my grief as she speaks her truth, exposing every frayed emotion and yearning to belong. Feeling like I'd been flayed open, exposed, I want to cover my ears to block out her words and rock myself to soothe my jagged nerves. I'm suddenly afraid I might cry the unshed tears of so many years, weeping for the lost childhood denied to me, wishing for the happiness that eludes me. In seconds an alternate timeline of what my life could've been, should've been, plays out in my mind's eye. If my mother hadn't been a power-hungry maniac and my father hadn't been a liar, that is. But as quickly as the Vision played out, it's gone.

"So, I finally decided that I would try an old ritual. Confractio Anima. It's ancient, but I hoped it would be the answer to my problem. It looked quite promising. I didn't know if it would work for the gift of prophecy, but it was my only chance. I hoped that maybe because we had a blood connection, I could borrow some of your abilities and find a home for them within my body. That they wouldn't be temporary."

"Borrow my powers!?" I balk. But I don't know why. It's not like I didn't realize what she'd done. I knew. But hearing her speak of it so freely feels like tiny daggers piercing my heart.

"We've been over this. Your outrage or piety is wasted upon me. Why shouldn't I benefit from giving you life? After all, I made you; your gifts are a part of me, as much as they are you." She pauses, her face weirdly serene given what she's speaking of. "You were just a baby. After all, we are of the same DNA and blood—practically the same person. The magic that lives in your blood is directly from me. It is always passed from the mother to the child. It should've been easy enough to wrest a portion of your gifts. You were only hours old. Then after the ritual, I would present you as an abandoned baby."

But she's repeating herself. These are facts already established, as she's said. It's like she's still trying to work out what went wrong.

"As I've said, I was exhausted from your difficult delivery. But I didn't have the luxury of time to rest before the ritual, so I centered myself before your crown chakra, still soft, and called your powers to me, blood to blood. However, I think I must have performed some part of the ritual incorrectly in my exhaustion.

Your powers resisted me. They refused to present themselves. I tried harder, but it was no good; you were growing paler and more still by the moment. So I left the room to get help. I couldn't exactly go running through the Temple with a faltering newborn. When I returned, you were gone. I believe your power called to the like power in your father, blood of his blood and all that. It was a most unexpected turn of events.

"I went in search of Addi. I was certain he had you. Slowly, I dragged my tired body down the halls of the Draíodóir until I arrived at his room. But he was gone. He had stolen you away in the night before I'd had a chance to make sure you got the healing you needed. But what could I do? What choice did I have? It's not like I could run to the Prioress and tell her he'd taken you, so I kept my secrets. I hid them well and began to search for you in Onirique."

My mouth opens slightly. I can only guess that I'm wearing a confused look on my face because she starts describing Onirique.

"Onirique, it's the Dreaming, the Spirit Plane or Otherworld, the plane where our spirit dreams at night but where the adept can travel to in their waking hours to manifest the most powerful of spells. The energy there works differently, faster. It's not bound by the limitations of the waking world."

While I had known some of that, it was interesting to hear her explanation of the place.

Phaedra stops briefly, trying to read my reaction. I keep my face inscrutable while Phaedra continues with renewed gusto, "So, now that you've returned to me, you can join me. You can take your rightful place at my side, be my second in command! Under my guidance, you could soar. I could hone those gifts to be things you can't even imagine!"

She's looking at me, but I don't think she's seeing me. She sees a

Vision of her new, perfect world. Her eyes are hungry. The fire in them is glowing and covetous, full of schemes.

Stunned by this idea, it takes me a minute—and a few false starts, my dry mouth working wordlessly—to say anything, sputtering, opening, and closing. I still my thoughts and take several long seconds to compose myself. Breathing deeply, I try not to have a panic attack. I force my face into a mask of neutrality. "I'll take it under advisement." I retort.

I can't think straight. The tale that Phaedra has woven together makes me feel like I might be sick. I need to get out of this sequestered little room!

"Of course, I realize you need time to digest all this new information, so you are free to leave now." She summarily dismisses me, adding, "I just wanted you to hear the truth."

I don't hesitate for a second, getting up in an ungainly movement and lurching to the door. It's all I can do not to run.

This is a lot to process; I need to talk to Whit—a wall came down around that thought; Whit isn't Whit anymore, he's Addi now, and I don't know if I can trust him anymore. Maybe I can share this with Kenyon. I mean, he already knows most of the story. What's a little more?

22

the tinderbox (of a heart)

Ember

After leaving Phaedra, I'm in serious need of some time and space for myself. There is no way I can process any of this while I'm with Kenyon. Maybe sitting under one of the giant oak trees behind the Temple will help. Walking down one hall that turns into another and then another, I wonder, How many rooms do these people need? They all look so similar. Disoriented and wandering the halls, I'm growing impatient to find an exit. Any exit to the outside will do. I'd be happy to walk around the stupid building if I had to; just let me out.

"Everything Phaedra told me was so awful!" Aannnd, my habit of talking to myself is alive and well, keeping me company as I puzzle out my conversation with my mother. Nope, still can't do it; she's still Phaedra, not my mother. "Ha! I hear the truth! No wonder I talk to myself all the damn time!"

But it's all too much! How much can I handle in one day!? "Too much! So, Whit is now Addi and my father on top of that, who's lied to me all my life. My mother is alive, just like in the dreams I've had as long as I can remember, and wants to make me her protege but only after giving some of my gifts to her. What could possibly go wrong?"

With no idea where I am anymore, an uneasy feeling grows inside my chest. It's tightening, and there's a cloying warmth building around me.

I turn another corner and walk down a dead-end hallway, "How many times am I going to have to backtrack to get out of this place?"

My mind rummages through the images of my recurring nightmare as I try to escape this place. Lingering on the first part of the dream, on the sweet version of Phaedra, my breathing calms. Unexpected warmth spreads in my chest.

"Could there be some part of her that's good? I mean, who knows what my life could've been if she had gotten to a healer instead of Whit finding me and taking me away? Maybe seeing me almost die could've changed her. What if being a real mother could've brought out her better nature? There is no way to know what that future would've been like. But she's still alive, and nobody is beyond redemption, right? Maybe now that I'm here, no longer hidden, her maternal instincts will kick in. Maybe I can help her to be a better person." Liking this idea, I say, "All she ever seemed to want was to be loved and accepted. That's all I've ever wanted, too. Maybe we can find that together." Yet I know hope can be a dangerous thing.

After having backtracked down two more hallways, I see a door that looks promising. Breaking into a jog, I reach out my hand to open the knob before I'd even reached the door. It turns easily, opening to reveal a small, deserted room.

But I only make it a few feet into the room, skidding to an almost comical halt, leaving skid marks on the dusty floor. There's a hearty layer of dust on everything.

Though I'm barely standing inside the threshold, the sensation is immediate. A strangled cry escapes my lips, and my stomach lurches. I'm being attacked! There's an intense, burning ache at the crown of my head like it's on fire, like someone is stabbing my head with a red-hot poker.

Doubling over in agony, my stomach seizes from ongoing pain. Lifting my head, I half expect to see an attacker unleashing a fresh torrent of pain at my head. My vision is all spotty, and I feel like I'm going to puke. But I can't stay like this forever, obviously.

Blinking my eyes rapidly to clear my wonky vision, I finally lift only my eyes, searching the room. The space is empty except for a few forgotten boxes. But the effort required to even lift my eyes to examine the room sends me reeling. More exploration of the room is out of the question.

My stomach launches another angry volley, and there's no stopping the bile that escapes my mouth and hits the floor. Throat burning and head aching, I know I won't last long here. I'm going to pass out.

A small voice speaks in the back of my mind. This is the room. It happened here. Phaedra attacked me here! It's my clairaudient gift, telling me that my mother had taken me here, as a newborn, to rip my powers from me. The room feels haunted and violent. There's an imprint on the space that never went away. This visceral sensation attacked me like the memory that lingered in the room. I need no confirmation: I know this was the room.

And any hope or illusions I entertained about second chances for Mommy Dearest are gone. The way this room feels informs me what she did to me is beyond anything a person should ever do to another, no matter what they have to gain.

I struggle to stand up straight, with bile rising again in my throat; I stand there, hunched over in pain. I can't endure the energy vortex and have to force myself out of the room. My hand still on the door handle, I pull myself out and shut the door in one fell swoop, landing myself on the floor for my efforts.

Rising to my feet, I'm trying to run before I'm even upright, turning back the way I'd come, launching into a run. I turn corner after corner, desperate to escape. Finally, I see the sun shining through the round doors we first entered through. I burst through, adrenaline coursing through my veins, my heart racing.

Running past the trees as fast as I can, a sob wrenches free from my mouth. My body finally releases the tide of emotion that I'd been stifling all morning. The sobs are coming full force now, growing more insistent as I run, only half taking in my surroundings in flashes and blurs.

The wooded area outside the Temple transitions to sidewalks. Colorful buildings lining the streets of Elysia whizz by, but I don't really notice them or the people going about their business. They're a blur of colors and bodies. I pass people walking dogs, an arching sky bridge between two buildings, people eating al fresco along a boulevard. They're behaving like today is just another day because, for them, it is.

I'm the one on this street whose world has been torn apart. But it's still early; maybe one of these people will have their hearts broken, too.

I feel like I've run five miles, a stitch in my side stabbing. I don't know how far or how long I'd run, but the Temple is no longer visible as the river comes into view. Shades of pink break through the lavender twilight as the morning sun rises between two buildings in the distance. The strange magical city landscape is still a blur, and I barely notice the tall buildings. The pain of the stitch in my side is a welcome distraction from psychic pain. An echo of the attack in that desolate room reverberates inside me.

Endorphins flood my body and mind bringing new awareness. I've faced three devastating situations in the last two days, and I've run from each of them: first, Whit's story, then Phaedra's drama, and now, that room.

There's a set of carved stone steps between two buildings, and I take them two at a time. My pace slows as my body screams in protest. My sobs begin to slow, too.

Yet, I am still running...

Awareness continues to dawn like an epiphany disguised as a metaphor—running from all the betrayal is relinquishing control of my life. The longer I run from the pain, the longer I'm at its mercy. How many times am I going to run away from my life instead of confronting it? All the things I've run from happened in the past. They don't have the power to hurt me beyond what I give them. It's the lesson from the cave again. Seems I'm destined to live that out in my real life, too, but I can't run anymore, metaphorically or physically. This has to stop.

I slow my pace to an awkward walk as my body adjusts. Blood rushing through my heart beats too fast, my feet throb, and the rising sun shines in my eyes.

I have no idea how to get back to the Temple. Not that I'm ready to go back yet, but still. I'm at the riverfront or the harbor...maybe it's a wharf? The river is deep here, its sides contained by thick corrugated metal seawalls. Shipping crates of varying sizes hang in the air, waiting to be lowered to docked ships. Around me is a warehouse district. It's all industry and function, no scenic vistas here, but there are very few ships in the port. I see a few off in the distance. What are they carrying? There's so much I don't know about this world and its culture.

In the corner of a doorway, I see a derelict-looking man sleeping. I guess no place is immune to a homeless population. Grateful for the mostly deserted wharf, I keep walking.

I've always known there was something more to my relationship with Whit. I mean, why else would he stick around? And while I'm super pissed at him for all the lies, I know we'll get through this. I don't know what that looks like yet, but I know it's possible. He's been pretty straightforward with me since we got here. With Phaedra, on the other hand, there's a lot she's not saying. Her assertion that I owe her for birthing me and that I should join the Vala is nothing more than an invitation for manipulation. Plus there's the whole justifying of nearly murderizing me. Unbelievable.

Just thinking about all this causes awareness of the magic inside me. My senses prick, and my inner alarm sounds that something's not right. Somebody's watching. Energy radiates from my heart, through the center of my body, to my extremities. A buzzing sensation runs along my arms and my hands tingle. Energy rolls off me in waves, and for the first time, I'm entirely unfettered; my magic is free.

What a strange sensation! That something I hadn't known I possessed until yesterday should feel like such a natural part of me now. When did that happen?

As I wander around the dock, looking out at the river, a shimmering aura surrounds me. I can practically see it! It feels incredible, like I can do anything. If only I knew how to do anything, that is. I want to learn everything, and I wonder if all the stuff Whit made me read is some sort of foundation for learning to use magic. I hope so. Otherwise, I'm just a super well-read history nerd. But who will teach me? Whatever, I'll figure it out. It never occurred to me that I might actually like magic in all the craziness of the past few days. That it would feel so good. But what does my crazy, messed up life look like now?!

Oh my God! The Bradshaws! They are going to kill me for not phoning to let them know I wasn't going to be home, or for that matter, that I wasn't dead. It's only been what, like, thirty-six hours or something. I'm sure they'll kick me out for this, too.

But wait, who says I have to go back? I mean, I'm home now, aren't I?

But before I get too far into worrying about everything, I focus again on the sleeping man in the doorway. He's turning over and shifting, trying to get more comfortable. Lifting his head, he looks around. He's looking for something. His eyes stop at me, appraising me.

I should get out of here, only I have to walk by him to go back. He's still looking at me. And the closer I get, the more I see hunger in his eyes. I really don't want to deal with this guy's crap today. I mean, seriously, when will this shitty day max out? What's the threshold?

His narrowed eyes shine from their hollow sockets and I can feel them all over my body as he takes me in. His long stringy hair and tattered, dirty clothes tell me he's been homeless for a while. I kinda feel bad for him, but any sympathy I might feel is quickly banished as he stands up and walks toward me. There's no avoiding this now. I could run, but that would reveal my fear and only make this worse. Crossing my arms in front of me, I instinctively hide my heart, my vulnerabilities. Like that will actually work. But it's too late.

Rubbing my arms, I suddenly feel the chill of the morning air. All the heat I generated from the run is gone. Seeing an opening between the two buildings, I feel a surge of hope. Adrenaline surges through my blood, and I walk faster toward my escape.

I'm about to turn the corner, and there he is. The man has caught up to me with stealthy and alarming speed.

"Where ya headed to, miss?"

"I'm all good, thanks."

"Pretty young girl like you, all alone on the streets, doesn't seem safe. Maybe you need an escort?" His hot breath touches my ear as he walks too close to me. I shudder.

His skin is sallow, his cheeks hollow. And don't even get me started on his teeth, much less his breath. This guy is death's head upon a mopstick!

"No, really, I'm fine. Leave me alone." I stand up straight. "Listen, whatever it is you want, I don't have it!"

"Sure 'bout that, are ya?" He asks.

"Look, I don't have any money." I breathe only through my mouth as the smell of the man wafts toward me, but I swear I can taste it.

"Ya have power! So much draíochta! It's all there, free-flowing, ready for the taking." His gaze is fierce and greedy as he moves closer. "I'll be taking some of that now!"

His palm glows with a dingy gray light as it lurches out and grabs me around my arm hard. His fingers dig into my bicep, dirty fingernails pressing further into my arm. Gross! I can only pray they don't break the skin. I might need penicillin to fight that level of nasty.

Thankfully, my instincts and the self-defense classes I took last year kick in, and my hand shoots out at him. My surprise counterattack catches him off guard, and I wrench my arm free of him.

"What in thunderation is it about me that makes everyone want to steal my powers!?" I mutter to myself, stepping away from him. I'm going to have to run. Just as I'm about to take off, there he is again. My breathing is ragged as possible outcomes flash through my mind. And adrenalin floods my body for what feels like the hundredth time today. Realization hits along with that adrenalin; even this vagrant has more magical chops than me. And I've got exactly zero chance of using magic to defend myself.

"Great! I'm really going to have to fight this Todger!" I mutter under my breath. Running through the easiest moves I know to get out of a jam, I choose the quickest and dirtiest of them. I square my shoulders to face him.

Using all the strength I can muster, I throw my forearm to his neck. A savage scream tears free from my throat as my forearm connects with his Adam's apple. Man, does that ever hurt! But my attack is successful; a guttural choking sound escapes his mouth as he falls to the ground. His hands fly up to protect his throat from further attack.

Lying on the ground, wheezing sounds coming from him, I turn to run from the wharf and see Whit coming at me at a dead run. His glowing hands gesture wildly through the air in front of him, creating glittering light and symbols. He's spell-casting!

He's not looking at me; he's running toward the man I felled moments ago. As Whit approaches the thief, he hurriedly gets to his feet, sprinting away, hands still protecting his neck.

Whit doesn't give further chase, bending over, winded and panting. A faint glow lingers around his palms.

"Thought...I would...have to rescue you..." Righting himself and catching his breath, he continues, "Obviously, you don't have full command of magic yet. But you did just fine on your own."

He sighs, "I'm so relieved he didn't hurt you, Ember. All I had to do was back you up after you did the heavy lifting. I'm impressed with your ability to defend yourself."

"Whatever. That guy was a chump. I've been a foster kid, like, my whole life. I know how to take care of myself. Have to, don't I?" Yet my bravado doesn't match the way I feel. I guess I'm doing the whole "fake it 'till you make it" thing on this one.

Noticing Whit is still slightly out of breath, I ask, "You gonna make it there, old man?" I'll be mad at him later; right now, I'm just grateful that he's here.

"Yes, I think so. Apparently, years spent arranging vintage furniture and jewelry are not quite the workout I would've hoped." He replies, trying to normalize the situation between us, and I can't really blame him.

"Well, that is shocking information," I joke, carrying the feeling forward. What a relief to feel the ease and familiarity of our usual banter.

"I appreciate that you followed me. I could have been in real trouble there." I pause, gathering my thoughts. How much do I say now?

"But, I'm still super pissed at you, Whit!" I say, walking up to him and wrapping my arms around him. Apparently, my actions are as confusing as my feelings are conflicted.

He wraps his arms tightly around me. "You'll never know how sorry I am." His whispered words are so direct it surprises me.

Not wanting to delve too far into that subject at the moment, I pull away. "How did you know where to find me, anyway?"

"I was outside walking in the oak grove when you ran out of the Temple...or rather, I saw a streak of black whirring by. I'd never seen you run like that. I thought something might have happened. And clearly something happened. Are you ok?"

"Yeah, I'm fine. I mean, that sucked a lot! But I'm ok. He never got what he wanted."

"Thank the Nine Worlds for that."

"So wait, you were running behind me that entire time?" I ask.

"I was. Though I was some distance behind you, having difficulty keeping up with you."

"That's crazy. I was running as fast as I could. How did you keep me in sight?"

"You aren't exactly easy to miss. All I had to do was look for the blur of black." He chuckles slightly.

"Right. Well, thanks. I appreciate that you—that you were looking out for me. Look—I have to tell you, I'm at odds with my feelings. Now that I've seen firsthand how cunning Phaedra is, I understand why you felt like you had to get me away from that place. That Temple. But, it doesn't excuse every other decision and deception, and I'm still super pissed at you."

"I know you are, and you have every right to be, Ember. I did what I had to, not seeing another viable choice. However, I know my actions after we were out of immediate danger hurt you. I accept the consequences of my actions."

He gestures with his hand to start walking away from the wharf when he suddenly turns to me. "What do you mean you've seen firsthand concerning Phaedra, and what caused you to run from the Temple like that?" He asks.

"Early this morning, one of Phaedra's minions came to my door, saying she wanted to meet with me. Kenyon was—" I stop abruptly, not wanting to be in trouble, but defiance rises in me. "Kenyon wasn't keen on me going." I finish my thought, half daring Whit to comment on my choices today, of all days. He instead casts a glance at me, silently disapproving. I shrug it off and continue. "But I thought that the meeting would be brief due to the meeting with the Draíodóir—Oh, did I miss that?" I ask, half hoping that I have.

"They can't really have it with the both of us gone, can they?" he answers as we set out toward the Temple.

"So, I met with Phaedra, and she told me her side of the story. And I'll never be able to scrub my mind clean after the images she unleashed on my brain. But honestly, she sounds like a petty child. And her grip on reality seems questionable at best. She actually thinks I'll join her and usher in some bright shiny future–one in which she's using me for my abilities, or worse, trying to steal them from me again. How can she possibly think that?"

"I don't know, Ember. Phaedra is very complicated, as we all are at times But with her—it's like she's a prisoner of her memories. She operates as though she can assuage past pain with present actions."

"Hmm. Doesn't seem to be working out for her."

"Seemingly, no. But, nothing is ever quite as simple as a black-and-white assessment of a situation. Let me tell you about when I first got to know her, and maybe it will help you understand her a bit more."

I don't quite nod, but Whit can tell I'm listening.

"About a year before you were born, I was in line to be the next Prior of the Draíodóir. Which put me in charge of an ongoing revitalization effort. Over the years, our roles in society had become less important. It was decided that we needed to hone our gifts to make our organization more relevant. To that end, the Draíodóir spent time with members of the Vala, thinking we might enhance all our abili—"

"Yes, I know all about that. Phaedra told me how you worked together, and then she seduced you. Etc.etc." I say, interrupting him.

"Yes, well, I spent a lot of time with her before our—encounter. I knew that she was developing inappropriate feelings for me. She idealized me, held me in very high esteem, largely because I was the next 'Leader of the Listeners,' as she called me. But I was always professional with her."

"Until you weren't." I blurt out before I can stop myself.

"As I said, it's not that simple. We spent a lot of time together, and she often talked about her childhood, regaling me with stories of injustices she experienced. She needed constant approval. Honestly, it was all a bit exhausting."

He looks at me like I might react to his last statement, and I give him the go-on-hand gesture.

"It was nearly time for me to begin working with another Sister, and Phaedra began to lash out in anger. Her moods became volatile, demanding assurances that I wouldn't abandon our friendship. At one point, she threatened to end her life if I didn't maintain our relationship. However, in her mind, she made more of that relationship than it had been in reality."

"Geez! So she really threatened to kill herself?"

"She did, and I would sometimes see marks on her arms, like scratches or cuts that I'm certain were self-inflicted."

"Did you tell anyone?"

"I thought about it and intended to, but didn't. She is an incredibly manipulative woman, Ember. She has a way of twisting every situation to suit her."

"That checks out; I got some glimpses of that when we were talking. And can I just tell you that this is all super awkward for me? Thinking about you and her having sex. It's not great..."

"Well, I understand that, but it's all relevant to your question. I believe that your mother—"

"Don't call her that," I reply sharply. My stomach churns at the thought.

"What?"

"She's not my mother. She gave birth to me and tried to steal my powers; that's not something mothers generally do." Heat floods my face.

"Ok, Ember. I'm sorry. I should've been thoughtful in my word choice."

"I shouldn't have snapped at you. Please go on."

As we leave the industrial district, we approach a little park with lots of trees. Sunlight filters through the high foliage, creating a dappled lighting effect on the ground. I want to lose myself in the sight, find a nice big tree like mine at home and just sit for a minute, gathering my wits. But Whit begins speaking again.

"I don't have many answers regarding Phaedra and her choices. Had I known..." He shakes his head, dismissing the thought. "Well...I would've handled things differently."

There's a faltering quality to his demeanor, but I can't make room for that right now. It's hard to see him struggle; I want to tell him it'll be ok and that I forgive him, but I can't. I won't lose the chance to get answers from a man who's evaded my questions at every turn. Plus, I need to hold him accountable. That second part is more complicated.

"I can only answer for myself. The choices I made once everything happened. I've hurt more people than you know, but my greatest regret is hurting you. I've always done as much as I could to help you feel loved, to be happy as you could be, considering our circumstances."

"That's a bit of a stretch, don't ya think?" The words fly out of my mouth before I can ponder their impact.

Whit's face shows the hurt my words cause. The unvarnished truth of my feelings hits him like a slap to the face. Seeing him process that hurt, I say, "I'm sorry, Whit, I didn't mean to hurt your feelings. It's just, I always wanted to live with you when I was a kid, and I always felt like if you loved me, you would've let me. So I just assumed you didn't like me enough to let me live with you. That it was only out of obligation that you kept me around. You know, the whole 'Godfather' thing." I'm not sure my words offer any comfort.

"Ember, I stayed because I am your father, but more importantly, I stayed because I love you!" He says it so easily, it leaves no room for doubt. But still, the words cut me a bit. When he speaks, my breath hitches and hiccups as I stifle the emotions welling within me. I have to wait for it to recede before I can talk.

"It's all too much! My head is killing me. Between meeting with Phaedra, finding my near-death room, and that Zounderkite's attack to steal my draíochta, or whatever, and now this. I'm getting a serious headache."

"Wait! You found the room?" Whit asks, again startled by my revelations.

"Yeah, I was going to get to that part next. I met with Phaedra. I just wanted to get out of that stupid Temple and walk around the grounds or something. But I got lost, so I was basically wandering around. I thought I had finally found an exit at the end of a long hall."

"I know the room of which you speak." His tone sounds ominous.

"So, I ran to it, and as soon as I opened the door, it felt like I was being attacked! It was overwhelming. Every part of my body reacted; my head felt like it was going to split open. I ended up retching up bile on the floor. It was all I could do to get out of the room. I felt frozen in place, but when I finally could, I ran. I was completely unaware of where I was going; I just needed to get out. And then, I found myself on this wharf, and that Ratbag attacked me." I rushed the details to get through the story, not wanting to relive it again so soon.

"So, Ember, what did you call that vagrant? A Zounderkite? A Ratbag? Are these colorful metaphors from your Victorian Vulgar Tongue book?."

"Yeah, you know, Ninnyhammer and thunderation and like that. Don't you remember I was reading that book of Victorian cursing? Figured it was better to use those than actual swears." I'm sick of being scolded.

And I'm grateful for the subject change; I'm so done with recounting my sucky morning. As we continue to walk, large trees shade us from the bright morning sun. Birds chirp back and forth to one another.

Approaching a bench, Whit motions to sit down and talk. Seizing on this rare occasion of his openness, I accept his invitation and take a seat.

He sits nearer to me than usual, putting his arm around me. We're both super awkward about it. This move is at odds with my experiences with him. But I guess this is the new Whit, or Addi.

Before I can say anything, my senses come to life. My toes twitch, and all the nerves running along my spine jump to attention. His consciousness is somehow expanding and touching mine, the edges of my awareness becoming fuzzy.

There's tightness in Whit's heart; I know this because I feel it in my own chest. Memories, only minutes old, play in my mind's eye as I experience them from his perspective. His heartache at knowing I'd been alone in that room is now my heartache, too.

I see myself as he did the other day when he gave me the goggles. I feel the burst of happiness that erupted within him at my joy. Feeling his affection and looking at myself through his memories shows me a very different picture of myself than I could have imagined. He saw me with so much love it makes my heart swell. But it also inspires melancholy for what our relationship could've been.

They come faster and faster, turning into impressions rather than fully-fledged remembrances. His sadness, like his happiness, touches me unexpectedly, softening my anger. Seeing flashes of myself in rapid-fire succession, It's like a wheel of memories. I glimpse myself, feeling the glut of emotions he'd held back every day for so many years. Finally giving way to an overwhelming sense of regret, remorse floods my senses like a tidal wave. The dam breaks, and tears roll down his cheeks in our shared consciousness. I feel them rolling down mine as well.

Our connection is a one-way closed circuit; I don't let my boundaries drop for him. I accept Whit's invitation into his mind, but I guard the edges of my memories. I'm not ready to share my experiences yet, plus I don't know how to choose what he sees. But I feel his acceptance of my boundaries and his willingness to be open with me. I'm amazed at this new instantaneous form of communication. The wonder I feel at it makes him smile. Until we get to a memory I'm not prepared for, "Please don't die! Please don't die! Please don't die!" As he runs, he whispers the words over and over.

I see him perform a healing ritual before he begins talking to the baby that was me again. "Oh, my sweet girl. Please don't die!"

He pauses, taking a deep breath. "I never intended to create you, but looking at you now is so surreal. You are a part of me, and I'm in awe to see your little body. But I sense your spirit is not settled within you. How could it be after what happened? Naming you is the only way to ground you. Even in this I will fail you, with no time to do it properly, but I will give you everything that I have." He exhales, and the expression of sadness on his face forces the unshed tear that had been lurking to stream down my face.

"But there is no time for pessimistic thoughts," he says to himself, but it's almost like he's saying the words to me as well. "I have a child to protect; she is my only focus now." The words he speaks have unexpected power in them, and a chill races up my spine.

Taking in a breath, I see him focusing his energy. He breathes out slowly, and I swear I can see tiny motes of dust and magical energy swirling around him. Taking another deep breath, he begins, "I name you December Roisin," each syllable with power so ingrained, it causes the hairs on my arms to stand on end. He presses his lips to my forehead, where the marks are still pulsating. They cause the ones on my head to pulse in time. "You are the ending and beginning of a new chapter, my little rose. You are my virtue lost and now regained."

Whit knows what I've seen. The tears are streaming down his cheeks, too, as he wordlessly tells me that my future and whatever part he might play in it is entirely up to me. He'll spend his whole life trying to make amends to me if necessary. I know I may never be able to reconcile all my feelings about his choices, but for now, it's enough to have him here, waiting for me, as he'd always been, in his own way. It won't be easy, but I can see forgiveness in his future.

Technically, the Crystal Cave is open to all citizens, but visiting alone in the dead of night is sanctioned. The colossal crystal formations jutting from the cave walls and leading deep into the heart of the cavern have a regenerative effect.

The Lemurian Seed crystals, known as the Keepers of Memory, were carried by their ancestors from Atlantis and Lemuria, the twin cities, creating new magical cities at all the power centers on Earth. Thus, the Commonwealth of Atlaria was born. The Crystals contain the knowledge of past generations, and having stored so much wisdom, they developed an ambient consciousness. When placed in the crystal caverns, they imbue the existing crystal matrix. They conduct and amplify the Ley Lines' energy, radiating it throughout, activating the draíochta within each person's mitochondrial DNA. They touch nearly every facet of life in the realms of la Magie.

But thoughts of their history are not what Sister Phaedra, Prioress of the Vala, considers as she enters the cave under cover of darkness. It is only safe to journey at night if she wants to get anything done.

Her body responds to the power radiating from the crystals. Walking through the mouth of the cave, the power buffets her in waves. The deeper into the cave she journeys, the stronger the power becomes. She allows the crystals' energy to fill all the empty places, their power acting as a soothing balm to comfort, chasing away the memories that relentlessly haunt her. Dizzy in her stupor, she continues into the cavern until she reaches her desired location deep within.

She walks in a large circle, dripping blood onto the packed dirt earth, its smaller outcroppings of crystal clusters breaking through. She must befriend these crystals, merge her energy with them, use the most potent magic she possesses: her blood, her sacrifice.

When she feels full of magic and has completed the bloodletting, she hums in a low, quiet voice, infusing it with subtle hints of magic. Little by little, she raises the volume, weaving the thread of her magic within her lovely voice. Her blood moves in synchronous time with her aria, the *droplets connecting to one another, forming a solid circle. A perfect summoning circle, though there will be no summoning this evening. Just friends getting to know each other, her and the power of the city.*

More and more, she infuses her song with magic until she reaches her capacity to expel it. But it's enough; all around her, the smaller crystal clusters sing louder and louder. If she can just push them a little harder, a bit further, she could really begin the process. She could start to entrain the crystals, make them bend to her will. But it would be foolish to push them too quickly. She has time yet.

Gradually she lets her voice trail off; she will return again.

24
rocket ship

Whit

Whit
~~Addi~~
Whit

Clearly, I've got some things to figure out. Having been Whit for the last seventeen years makes my life as Addi feel like a lifetime ago. Well, I guess it was. When Ari calls me by that name, I feel like I've come home. But that's the least of my problems at the moment. Dismissing my thoughts, I extend my arm in a gesture to begin our journey back to the Temple.

As we walk, the towers of the city center loom overhead and stark spires soar on the horizon. There's been so much new construction in the time I've been gone. I would never have imagined the city would encroach so close to the Crystal Cave, where the wealthiest and most powerful now live and conduct their business.

Nearer to where we stand, the buildings are older and smaller but no less grand in their details. It's been so long since I've been here, it feels like visiting a new city. I suppose it is a new city. I'm taking a circuitous route to spend more time with Ember. I want her to see something of our home in a positive light, not only through the filter of betrayal and heartbreak.

"Whit, I have some questions," Ember says, seizing the opportunity to question me further about Elysia.

"I thought you might."

"So, what was that? That thing you did where I was able to experience your thoughts and feelings. It was like remembering your memories. Did you just Vulcan Mind Meld me?"

"Yeah, I guess I kind of did. Only it's called Erindring. It means remembrance, in Norwegian, I believe. It's exactly as you describe it, though. We can open our consciousness to one another if we choose and share our experiences. If the other person accepts the connection, that is. As you know, it's quite a revealing experience."

"About that, Erin—Erindring—whatever you called it, why does every magical thing in this world have a foreign-sounding name?" Ember is walking more slowly now, carefully studying the buildings we pass.

"The etymology of Erindring and many other terms that have been vexing for you are usually of Gaelic or Norse. That's the lineage of the Draíodóir and the Vala, respectively. But, other aspects of magic have terminology hailing from other cultures. You're hearing more of these terms because we're currently dealing with these Oracle societies. Soon, you'll hear other foreign-sounding words as you are exposed to more of the city. Still, the terminology for magical things remains of the Ancients."

"Ok, speaking of lineage and the city, I don't understand why sometimes I could see glimpses of Elysia and other times, not so much. Plus, none of the non-magical people can see it. What's up with that? I mean, how is this entire city hidden by a mental hospital? Plus, what makes this place magical? "She pauses but quickly continues, her questions stumbling out rapid-fire. "If we are magical here, are we still if we leave here? Where exactly is Elysia, anyway? I don't understand where it is geographically with the non-magical city. Is it a city within a city?"

I raise my hands to stop her questioning. "I'll answer as many questions as you can ask, but one at a time, please."

"Is it in California?" She repeats her joke from when she'd first heard the name. "Elysia sounds like a city in California."

"Those are mostly good questions," I say, raising an eyebrow at the last one. "Only people descended from magical ancestry of the Twin Cities, Atlantis, and Lemuria can see magical cities."

"What?!" Ember interrupts again. "That's unbelievable! I always felt like Atlantis was real!"

"Indeed—"

"There are more?"

"Of course, there are. Many, in fact. There are the thirteen Capital Cities, like The Hanging Gardens of Babylon, Akrotiri, Kitezh, Zerzura, etc. Then there are smaller magical cities, and everywhere there are large convergences of Ley Lines. Every city is unique and often feels similar in spirit to the non-magical community they are tethered to. They are always hidden, though, with the possible exception of Acadia and New Orleans. Any legendary cities that human explorers cannot find are home to la Magie. As I mentioned, this city is built upon the earth's Ley Lines, the energy grid of the planet, exuding powerful psychic, electrical, and magnetic energies. Intersections of these lines intensify the effect: the more intersections, the more powerful the magic is. Caves with enormous crystals grow at intersection points that magnify and transmit magic through the cities. It's stronger here but does not leave us when we leave the city. Ley Lines encircle the world, so our magic is always with us. Though it is greatly diminished when we are not in one of the magical cities."

"But why do the magical cities have to be hidden?"

"As les Dormeur expanded, it became necessary to conceal our existence. For several reasons, chief among them was the rise of intolerance and mistrust. Once persecutions began, our options were limited. By the time they were burning the poor souls deemed witches, we had long since hidden ourselves. A combination of charmed spatial displacement and compression creates a slightly different dimension and conceals Elysia. The dimensional difference allows the two realities to exist in the same space. The Honourable Guild of the Arcane maintains the boundaries."

"That is some Doctor Who-level stuff there. But if we have magic, they can't hurt us, can they? Can't we just magic ourselves out of a jam?"

"To a certain extent, instantaneous spellwork has its limitations,

Ember. It's not exactly abracadabra, the way it's portrayed by the mundane humans."

"What about the magic you were doing at the guy who attacked me? I mean, I assume that's what you were doing, making all those hand gestures as you ran at him."

"Well, obviously, I'm a bit out of practice with spell work. Other than power binding and obfuscation, that is," I say, clearing my throat uncomfortably.

"Um, yeah—So what was it that you did when you attacked him?" She prods me again.

"Oh, right. I was using runes. Think about the various books and texts you read over the years; recently, I asked you to learn about Norse Runes. I wanted to begin preparing you for our return home." The word home slips from my mouth so easily, and I see her blanch at it. She hasn't come to terms with this place as home. I should be more thoughtful.

"I used some of those runes to defend you. With that type of magic, practice matters. It's been so long since I've used Runes that I could only scare him a bit. You already frightened him with your physical defense."

Starting down a new path of inquiry, Ember asks me, "So what about back in the shop with the Veg-va-sir." She speaks the word slowly.

"Some of our most powerful magic is produced in rituals and rites to influence outcomes. But there are also magically imbued devices that utilize both magic and technology, like the Vegvisir. It is a complex combination of math, magic, quantum entanglement, and harmonic resonances. It's very precise and indeed magical, but it is a device that shortcuts the otherwise necessary rituals. As a side note, I hadn't seen a pocket-sized Vegvisir until Kenyon pulled that one out. I suspect he may have been involved in its invention."

"What are they normally like?" she asks. I suspect my mention of Kenyon has piqued her interest.

"They are old, immense permanent structures centrally located in all the cities of la Magie. They form an interconnected web allowing instant travel." I answer.

Changing the subject, I gesture my hand toward the approaching street market. "Let's take a detour and walk through le Labyrinthe de

Magie up here on your right. We can get something to eat as we walk back to the Temple. I suspect you haven't had breakfast, and it would be good for you to see more of Elysia than just the Temple."

"Sounds great, but don't we have to meet with Brother Aaric?"

"They're not going to help us, Ember. This meeting is little more than a formality. And to be fair, I knew they would not. But the Draíodóir would be hard-pressed to deny anyone temporary shelter. My request for asylum allowed time for my healing and safety for you, so let them wait. You are the only person I care about at the moment."

The frankness of my sentiments catches Ember off guard, her jaw dropping open a bit. She turns her head to look at me. "Good, cuz, I'm starving!"

this is the day

Ember

In the distance, colorful banners attached to tents flutter in the breeze. A riot of color and sound becomes clearer and my empty stomach growls for food and flips in excitement at seeing what this fair has to offer. Of course, I don't have any money, so I'm not quite sure how that's going to work out, but I'm hoping Whit has a plan. He did suggest this, after all.

Our pace quickens as we approach the market. Whit seizes the silence to make an observation. "I've had a theory for some time now. The magical cities are spelled to repel the Ordinaries, which is probably why you encounter problems with the non-magical folks. The magic within you is likely off-putting to them."

"Well, ain't that a kick in the head. So you're telling me no matter how much I behaved or tried to fit in, which obviously I didn't, I would never have?"

"Likely not, Ember. But the effort was worthwhile. Imagine how much worse it would've been had you not tried."

To his statement, I make an observation of my own, "You know, It's hard not to notice that your entire demeanor has changed since we got here."

"Oh?"

"Um, yeah. I'm not really used to you being—being this direct about anything. My whole life, it's been riddles cloaked in cryptic secrecy. Now all of a sudden, you're Captain Direct with an honest answer and a new name? What am I supposed to call you, anyway? Is it Addi now?"

So my observation may have gone a bit off the rails there, encompassing a few more things. But I'm uncomfortable, and there is no way I can start calling him dad. The thought is so foreign I can't even give voice to it.

"You may call me whatever you're comfortable calling me. I've been Whit for many years now. I suppose with our return, I'll have to get used to hearing both."

"So it's your intention to stay?"

"I had always planned to stay once you knew the truth of who I was and of your origins. I've dearly missed la Magie. There is no escaping your destiny now, Ember. You will face Phaedra again, of that I am certain." I take note that Captain Cryptic is alive and well within him.

"But, it's not right this minute. C'mon, let's check out the street market!" I say, trying to avoid the unavoidable in favor of breakfast.

"It's been so long since I've been to a street market. The food is always so good." He grabs my arm, pulling me toward the causeway. I've never seen this much excitement in him. It's super odd, but I like it.

A painted wooden sign hangs beneath an intricate cast-iron archway marking the entrance. Tents of every color are heavily ornamented with all manner of items. "Welcome to Le Labyrinthe de Magie. Everything you never dreamed you wanted is here for the asking," Whit says, but the smell of food is too close to ignore, drawing us forward like cartoon characters floating nose-first attached to the aromas.

There's no point in pretending that I'm not going to stop by at least a few tents on the way to eat. There's a tent, paper star lanterns floating under its ceiling, selling origami cubes, balls, birds, and animals. Unable to stop myself, I pick up a round folded ball and immediately find myself in trouble, as the hand of a wizened Asian woman shoots out, retrieving the treasure. The woman looks at me through narrowed eyes, suspicion creasing her already-lined, golden-brown face.

"Oh! I'm so sorry! I just got excited to see your beautiful origami. I've always found it fascinating." I ramble. I guess I should've figured the rules might be different here.

At my apology, the woman's face relaxes, and without a word, she pulls at the edge of the paper ball. I gasp in delight as the sphere opens to reveal a delicately folded crane. Holding it in her hand, she gently blows on it, and the crane takes flight. It glides through the air, leaving a trail of golden glitter in its wake and returning to her hand. I cannot contain my delight as I bounce on the balls of my feet, clapping my hands. And then I promptly feel like a dork. What am I? 12?

I look at Whit, who says, "I promise you we can return and fully explore the market once we're done at the Temple. We can purchase as many trinkets as you'd like." His statement elicits a scowl from the woman as she turns her back and walks away.

"I'll also need to free up the bulk of my financial assets now that we're back. They don't exactly accept American dollars and coins here. I need to reach out to my brother as well..."

He's talking to himself, not me. But that doesn't stop me from interrupting his thoughts, "Wait, you have family here? And what kind of money do they take here, anyway?" I ask, addressing both parts of his statement, trying to gain as much info as possible.

"Of course I do, or rather we do. My parents are gone now, but I have a brother, Théo. He's a few years older than me, married with adult children."

"Will I get to meet them? Do they know about me?"

"I've managed to keep in touch with Théo on and off over the years. He knows about you, and I'm sure his wife also does. But I'm unsure about their children."

"Will I get to meet them?" I ask again.

"If you'd like. But I think it best that we wait until the situation we face has passed—"

"Whit, where will we go if the Draíodóir aren't going to help us?" I ask, worried about what comes next.

"Initially, I thought we would take up residence in my family's home, but Kenyon has graciously offered to let us stay in his home. Phaedra knows the location of both Kenyon's and my family's homes, but his house will be more protected. I do not believe she would be so brazen as to show up there. So I've decided that we will take him up on his offer."

"But we can still stay at your family's home—if we need to? It's just—things aren't exactly clear between—" Thankfully, he interrupts me, laying a hand on my shoulder. "Certainly, if it comes to it. I guess —just keep me posted?" I'm pretty sure he's figured out what's going on.

"Finally!" I groan, tired from all the walking, my stomach rumbling loudly as we approach all the food smells.

And then I see them! My whole body works in unison to achieve my goal; I pull on Whit's arm, drawing him toward a booth as I exclaim, "Whit! Tacos! Can we please get tacos?"

"Sure, Ember, we can get tacos for breakfast." He replies with an eyebrow raised. It's a far cry from his usual breakfast of tea and porridge, but if I see tacos, I eat tacos.

As we enter the stall, my senses work overtime, taking everything in. All around me are small painted skulls and paper mache skeletons posed as people would be. A couple holding each other like they're dancing and two Frida Kahlo figures sitting holding hands, their hearts outside their bodies connected by a single vein. As I pass them, they begin dancing and interacting with one another in rudimentary jerky motions. My jaw drops open in surprise, and Whit gently pushes it closed, saying, "There are all manner of new things for you to delight in, but first, food." He shifts me to the counter to order.

There's a variety of tacos to choose from, and none of them look anything like what Mrs. Bradshaw serves. I do my best to guess what I might like and place an order. And, of course, Whit orders like a pro, like he eats tacos every other night.

"Ya might've helped me out there with ordering!" I say, glowering at him.

"Why? You did just fine with your order. They're tacos, Ember, not a life or death decision."

And he's right. I'm pretty sure I'll like them no matter what. My theory is about to be tested as the curvy brown-skinned woman behind the counter asks, "Vanadium or coins today, sir?" and Whit responds, "Vanadium."

"Three Joules, please," she replies as she hands our order to him. A smile lights her face as she says, "¡Muchas gracias!" Whit gives her something palm-sized and black, almost like a really thick metal credit card.

"So, what about money? What is used here? What is Vanadium?" I ask as I tear into my taco. I'm right; this taco is nothing like any taco I've ever eaten.

"It's a bit more complex in la Magie than in les Domeur. Without getting into an overview of la Magie's socio-economic workings, some people use gold and copper coins. They're called Aurum and Aeris. But, most people use energy called piezoelectricity, collected from crystals compressed by a piezoelectrometer. The energy joules are compressed in a vanadium battery, often called a Vana for short."

"Ok, that was so not what I was expecting. But why would you have to get into socio-political stuff to explain the money?"

"People talk about money and power as separate but related things in les Domeur. In la Magie, they are interchangeable. But because this world utilizes the energy of crystals for magic, they also became currency in their own right. As such, the city's dependence upon them is beyond measure. There is growing concern about the mass crystal harvesting currently happening. Stolen crystals flood the underground markets in the form of Amplicon. It's a drug of sorts that temporarily but significantly increases the amount of magic a body's mitochondrial DNA can wield. A similar form of this energy can be harvested from people as well. But it's perilous—"

"Wait! Is that what Phaedra and that bum were tryin' to do to me?" I demand as I interrupt Whit.

"In a sense. They were attempting furta spiritus, which takes magical energy from other humans rather than ingesting Amplicon. It's safer for the user but obviously not for the person being robbed. Amplicon can damage the user's mitochondrial DNA, over time diminishing their ability to use magic."

"Yeah, Phaedra told me about Amplicon, at least a little bit. Did you know she used to use it?"

"Told you, did she?"

"She did. She said she used it to boost her ability to have Visions, so she could make it into the Vala. Did you know?"

"I suspected. She was always so worried about her abilities. I think that her—our entanglement was an attempt to obtain some of my draíochta—"

"Oh, it was. She thought she'd done it, too," I interrupt.

"Yes, well, as I suspected. Anyway, not long after, she had more confidence than ever. She was also completely unconcerned with our friendship. I think she mistook your growing powers as newly acquired abilities."

"Yep, that's what she told me. But I don't want to talk about her anymore. Besides, I'm still not seeing the political aspect you were talking about."

"Because the crystals are such an inherent part of this city, the guilds that govern the city have definitive views on how they should be managed. That's where it gets political."

And I know Whit doesn't want to get into the inner workings of Atlaria. I'm all for that. There's enough stuff to learn without all that mess. Before I can tell him I agree, he changes the subject completely, asking, "How's your taco, Ember?"

A small laugh escapes as I answer his question with my own. "What is this little green herb on my taco, Whit?"

"It's called cilantro. It's typically not my favorite part of Mexican food. It tastes a bit soapy to me."

"I like it. I see what you mean about the soapy thing, but that doesn't bother me. This might be the best taco I've ever had! It's a far cry from the tacos they serve for school lunch or at the Bradsha—OH! The Bradshaws! I've been gone so long, I'm sure Mrs. B is furious. I mean, I know you are planning on staying here in Elysia, but it's rude to just disappear on them. I'm even sure they'd miss me, but—"

"I've contacted them already. Please don't worry. And no, you're not going back to stay with them."

"Definitely not!" I echo his sentiments. "I was kind of wondering about that earlier today before that fopdoodle attacked me."

"Fopdoodle?"

"Yeah, it means idiot."

"Alright, finish your taco and we'll head back to the Temple and face the music."

We walk as we eat, and there are about twenty-five booths I want to stop at. At Loranan & L'yari Elfen Charms, I watch a woman's hair change from brown to lavender. I think of Nico and her ever-changing hair color and realize she was never wearing wigs at all. The palm of a hand with an all-seeing eye in the middle is painted onto a placard, hanging above the entrance of a tent. It seems like your average palm reader until the eye slowly closes and reopens. I swear, it's looking right at me!

The paths leading through the booths have no discernible pattern. There's a tent with herbs hanging bundled, both dried and fresh, filling the air with all the smells, followed by a booth with fire blazing around fat-bottomed iron pots. I tug Whit's sleeve. "It's so witchy! I mean, cauldrons! Doesn't get any witchier than that."

"Yes, I suppose it is pretty "witchy." I know he's humoring me, but I don't care; it's all very exciting. Much better than dreary Oracle Societies.

"You know, this is more what I had in mind when I imagined a magical world. Not all this attacking and power-stealing business I've seen so far. I'm so over it!"

Nearing the edge of the market, I see a man standing in the middle of the walkway, looking like he's playing an instrument, but I can't hear anything. As I get closer, I see he's surrounded by a transparent bubble. The instrument looks like nothing I've ever seen, like a small acoustic guitar body with a black box attached where the strings should be. Little keys protrude from the box and a crank handle juts out the end of the body. I turn to Whit with what I'm sure is a confused look.

"It's a Bobleverden, a bubble world. If you step into the sphere of the bubble, you'll be able to hear the music, and the man is playing a hurdy-gurdy."

I have to work to stifle a laugh as the Donovan song plays in my head. "Wait! What the what? How is a bubble world a thing?"

"As I said, there will be many new things for you to delight in; this world is full of as much wonder as corruption. Sadly, you've seen more of the latter, but I promise it's no—"

The rest of his thought is cut off as I step through the bubble. His voice is replaced by the music of the hurdy-gurdy, which also sounds like nothing I've heard before. It's like someone smashed some bagpipes, a pipe organ, and a guitar together inside a droning machine. OK, I know that sounds a bit odd, but so is this instrument, all rigged up to a custom belt thing to support the instrument. The man sways as he cranks the handle, long tendrils escaping the braid he wears under a top hat. A faded jean jacket covers his white puffy collar poet shirt, and a woolen kilt and tall boots complete the look. Honestly, the guy is kinda hot.

"We really should get back; I'm sure Kenyon is wondering what's happened to us by now." Whit pulls me out of the spell the hurdy-gurdy guy has spun.

"Shit!" I say under my breath, as Whit gently pulls me out of the bubble. I'm sure Kenyon is mad at me for being gone so long.

birdmad girl

Ember

Pushing the door open, Kenyon steps toward me, sweeping me into a fierce embrace, whispering, "Where were you? I was so worried!"

"I'm sorry. I didn't mean to worry you. After I met with Phaedra, I was too upset to come back here; I needed to get some air. She—what she said, was so messed up delusional, so out of touch with anything resembling reality."

As Kenyon holds me, I could stay here for at least an hour. But I don't think I can get into everything while he's hugging me. So I gently push away from him and explain everything: the meeting, the running, the attempted magic heist, and finally, hanging out with Whit.

"You do seem to have a knack for finding trouble, don't you?"

That was not the response I was expecting. "Wait, you're not mad? I thought you'd get all overprotective or something," I blurt out in my surprise.

"Do you want me to?" He asks. "Because I can." His hands ball themselves into fists as he speaks. "The fire I feel defies logic. I haven't known you long enough to feel this strongly, but I do."

"No, it won't help anything. Besides, it's all over now, and I made it through."

"Exactly. You're standing here, and you're fine. Never mind that your absence and my worrying may or may not cause me to never let you out of my sight again. Kidding, I'm kidding. Kind of."

I can't stop the nervous giggle that slips out of my mouth, mortified that my body can even produce that sound, but I digress. I know what I need to say, and I'm dreading it.

"Listen, I want to tell you how much I appreciate everything you've done for Whit and me. But I think you might want to run away from me right now. None of this is your problem, and trust me, it's not trouble you want! I'm not trouble you want." Insecurities fall out of my mouth, left and right, leaving me vulnerable. The entire time I'm telling him this, in my heart, I'm pleading for him not to go.

"Why would you say that?" he demands, his eyes misty. "It's your choice to make, Ember. But let me ask you one thing. Do you want me to go? Or do you feel like you should send me away because of the impending 'trouble' you mentioned?" A wave of turbulent emotion breaks across his face, and I swoon just a little bit inside, my knees weak. "Or is it that—you just don't really like me—like that?" He looks pensive and embarrassed as he asks his final question.

"Oh my God, no! I'm totally into you!" I exclaim before I can stop myself. I would've chosen a much cooler way to tell him than blurting it out like that. A low chuckle escapes his lips, and I feel blood rushing to my face as my cheeks burn crimson. Before embarrassment can take control, he reaches for me and wraps me in his arms, saying, "Good, because I'm totally into you, too." He chuckles again, but this time I feel the rumbling in his chest, and I go all swoony again. My heart swells in size to accommodate the new feelings growing there. Grinch style. You know, when he hears all the Whos in Whoville singing, even though he stole Christmas. That's me with the growing heart.

"After everything that happened this morning, though, I'm not sure it's enough. I'm certain that Phaedra will come after me!" I interrupt and realize I'm almost making a case for him to leave, and I really should stop now.

Disentangling the top half of his body, Kenyon looks into my eyes. "It doesn't matter," he whispers, lowering his face to meet mine, his lips brushing lightly over mine. Into his kiss, I say, "Ok..."

We're lost in a sweet and tender kiss as he wraps his arms tighter around my waist, lifting me slightly off my feet. My arms snake their way up to his chest and around his neck. The intensity of our kiss escalates until knocking on the door breaks our perfect moment. I jump in startled surprise, disengaging from our kiss.

Opening the door, I'm not surprised to see Whit. Without greeting, he launches into his thoughts. "I knew that they were not going to help us, but it burns me nonetheless," he declares, his face flush with stifled anger. "They have grown weak under the Aaric's leadership." He looks conflicted. "Seems like the Draíodóir have become irrelevant, little more than glorified healers."

"I'm sorry, Whit, I'm sorry for you that you were right."

"I know," Whit says ruefully. "Que sera sera, I guess. Are you two ready to go? Are we—"

"Yes, let's head to Kenyon's house," I quickly interject in answer to his mostly unspoken query.

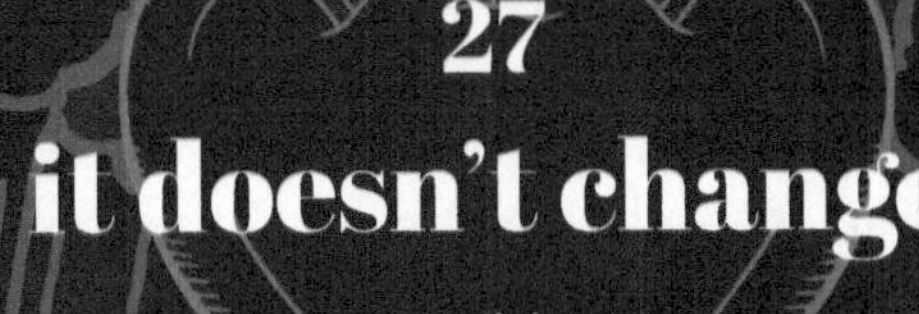

27

it doesn't change

Whit

Stepping forward, Kenyon takes the lead and walks out into the hall, where we encounter Brother Aaric. His eyes lock with mine, ignoring Ember and Kenyon.

"Addi, you have to know how sorry I am." His voice is low, meant for my ears alone, as he entwines his arm around mine and pulls me away.

"I know that you are doing what you feel is best for the Draíodóir, but I feel you are failing to grasp the enormity of the situation at hand." My anger with Aaric is at odds with my happiness at being so near to him.

Electricity dances along my skin everywhere our bodies touch, just like always. Blinking my eyes hard, I wrest myself free of the physical sensations threatening to derail my thoughts. "However, I understand your reticence to get involved." I know the hurt and disappointment I feel show in my expression, but I can do nothing about that.

I feel Ember's eyes watching me, her concern and confusion at what's happening.

"Addi," Aaric implores, "You've finally come home. Don't let this be the end. I know that you will not rejoin the Draíodóir, and we are the poorer for it, but don't—don't let this be the end of us." The fervor in Aaric's words surprises me. Does he know what they mean to me?

"The bonds of our friendship were always stronger than we could acknowledge. I believe, or at least I hope they can withstand this, too," Aaric says, confusing the situation again.

Turning my head away, I feel even more conflicted. Catching sight of Ember again, I can't help but think of my desperate hope that she forgives my betrayal. How can I expect forgiveness if I cannot give it to my oldest friend? Overwhelmed by emotions, my mind and heart act in unison; my thoughts pour out without forethought or editing. "I am the one who ran away, leaving behind my life and our friendship without so much as a word. I am the one who betrayed my vows with another, a woman I didn't even love. Aaric—of course I forgive you."

Feeling lighter, my emotions are freer for laying down the burden of anger and years of repressed fear. "Though, honestly, I should be asking for your forgiveness. I've betrayed our friendship. When I had my encounter with Phaedra, it was not her that I was thinking of, not her that I wanted to touch and be touched by. But I was afraid."

This is it. This is my chance to say everything I've wanted to tell him for the past seventeen years, all the things I regret.

"I was afraid that what I felt for you was different than it was 'supposed' to be due to our vows. But I was also afraid you didn't feel the same about me. Constantly telling myself, I imagined your affections for me as more than you intended. Even as Phaedra manipulated the situation, moving us toward our encounter, I was more vulnerable than I should've been. In my desire and unrequited feelings for you, I came undone. It's no excuse, just an explanation. After it happened, I could barely look at you. The enormity of what I had done overcame me. It was too late when I finally realized I had not imagined our feelings. There was no looking back."

"So that explains what happened. All those years ago, I knew something had changed between us..."

I interrupt before Ari can finish. "This is no excuse. I betrayed my vows and you, what was unspoken between us. And it is the latter that hurts most all these years later."

I pause, feeling the lump building in my throat, but force myself to continue before I lose the nerve. "I could have sent word to you about what happened. But my shame was too great." I confess and feel my face flush pink. "I couldn't face you."

The time for apologizing has ended, so I move my free hand toward Ari, placing it on his cheek. The sensation of electricity and attraction mingles and overwhelms me again.

Never have I spoken so freely of my feelings, but I'm tired of pretending. I'm no longer a member of the Draíodóir. Emboldened by this new sense of freedom, I move my hand along Ari's cheek toward the back of his head. He's standing mere inches away, our faces close. This has to be the time.

I move in closer, my mouth near Ari's ear, and I work up the courage to say what I've longed to, all these years. "I love you, and I always have." The admission comes easily to me. Standing so near him, taking him in, I realize it's as true today as ever.

But I had forgotten how being so near to Ari set my senses alight. How his smell, the essential oils he used, a mix of citrusy balsam fir with clove and amber intoxicates me. Drawing in a long breath, my body hums. Feeling magic again is exhilarating, combined with the electricity that thrums between us— it heightens my already alert senses. I wait impatiently for Aaric's reply.

His body tenses in surprise, his mouth dropping open. "I hear you, but what am I—" But I don't let him finish, brushing my lips against his. Acting on impulse, it's something I've yearned to do, and there will not be a better opportunity. After all these years, I have to take the risk. My boldness is rewarded. After a moment's hesitation, his lips move against mine. It's everything I've hoped for, except for the audience. But I can't worry about that right now. This is my first kiss with the man I've loved for so long.

The kiss is tender, all the love I feel encapsulated into one heart-breakingly sweet moment, acknowledging the years of loss and separation. It could quickly escalate, but I can't push Aaric. He is still bound by his vows.

I want to hope for a new beginning, but I know this is likely a good-bye: our first and last kiss.

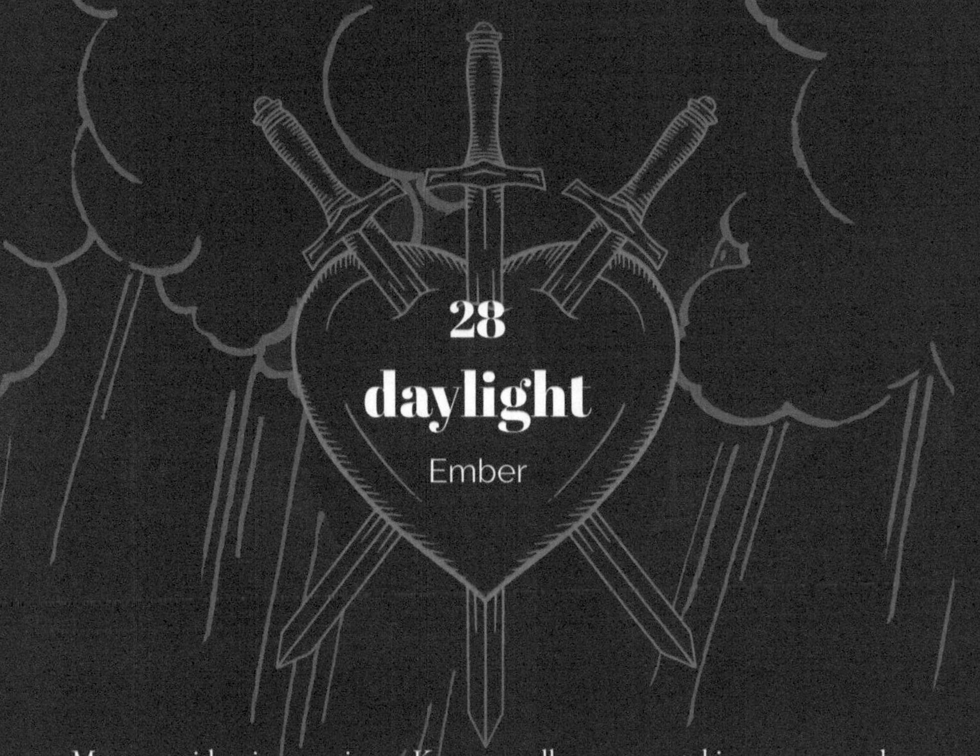

28
daylight

Ember

My eyes widen in surprise as Kenyon pulls my arm, taking me around the corner to give the men privacy.

"This day has been full of surprises," I quip under my breath, my surprise mingling with happiness for Whit. "I think it's great that—" but my thoughts are cut short as Kenyon's lips find mine. It lasts only moments as Kenyon pulls away, saying, "I want to be clear about something, Ember. I was going to say this earlier but got—distracted. I don't expect, well, what I mean is that you're going to be staying at my home, and I have no expectations..."

Standing on tiptoes, I place a small kiss on the hollow of his neck below his ear. "I appreciate that."

His arms encircle my waist. Before Kenyon gets any further, Whit rounds the corner. "Thank you for giving me a moment alone with Brother Aaric. We had some, um—unfinished business."

"That's cool," I say, trying to sound as nonchalant as possible. "Whit, I'm—I'm happy for you. That you have someone, I mean," I blurt as we walk toward the door. "But why did you never date or get involved in the non-magical world? All that time, were you going to... what's the name—ah, the Blue Moon Social Club? You know, the gay bar?" I ask, no longer able to quell my curiosity.

"Who says I didn't date?"

"Oh, I guess there really was a lot I didn't know about your life..."

"Oh, Ember, I never dated because I had my hands full trying to keep you safe, in a home, out of trouble, and most of all, non-magical." He says, ticking his fingers, counting off his tasks. "It was nearly a second job." He pokes me in the arm as a broad smile crosses his normally serious face.

Opening one of the double doors, he takes a deep breath, sunlight illuminating his face, looking like a free man after so many years of imprisonment.

"Let's get to my house and get you guys settled so we can discuss what comes next," Kenyon says, ushering us to a waiting car.

"Tomorrow, Sister Vadoma will join us to teach you some basics of spinning and weaving. I believe she hopes to glean some knowledge of Phaedra's intentions," Whit says matter-of-factly, but it feels like a lot of pressure to perform my first time at the spindle.

Walking down the high marble steps, my mouth drops open as I see a man whizzing by, seated in the middle of a single large wheel rotating around him. Everywhere I look, mechanized marvels of transportation challenge my understanding. Some look like futuristic concept cars seen only in sci-fi movies while others are vintage cars, all featuring a similar modification. But I get really excited when I see scooters like mine, all modded up.

Looking at the sky, I see airships. "Umm, wow! This is unbelievable. It's—it's like something out of Bladerunner or Tron!

"So, when I took off after my run-ins this morning—" embarrassed as I acknowledge my fight or flight response to what happened "—was all this goin' on?" I gesture to the scene in front of us. "Did I just somehow miss all of it?"

"Yes and no, Ember. Given the time of day and the area you were in, there probably weren't many things to see. But as I promised, there are many wonders in this world for you to experience." Whit sounds wistful and full of love for his home.

"Um, I gotta tell ya, it's been a pretty mixed bag so far," I say before I can stop myself. "But I definitely look forward to learning how to do some magic!"

Whit opens his mouth to speak but seems to think better of it, closing it as we reach the bottom of the stairs. Walking to the edge of the street, Kenyon motions to a vintage car that nearly takes my breath away. I love, love, love fancy British cars, "Whoa! What kind of car is this?" I run a finger along its curved planes.

A svelte woman emerges from the right side of the car. Her formal demeanor suggests she's older but doesn't look it.

"This is Ms. Samara Zandi, assistant extraordinaire."

She's beautiful, wearing a tailored suit, tall with dark skin and a long graceful neck. There is the barest hint of where her hairline would be if she weren't bald.

"Wait, wasn't she your father's assistant?" Whit asks.

"Yes, she agreed to stay after my father died. She's an invaluable help, friend, confidant, and wrangler of my life and schedule. Zandi is the only family I have. I'd be lost without her," Kenyon says, affection in his voice.

In a subtle British accent, she says, "You are too kind, Sir," clearly uncomfortable with praise. I guess it's safe to say that I love British cars and accents.

"Really, Zandi? Still with the Sir? You gotta let that drop. Anyway, this is, well, what should I call you now?" He asks, looking at Whit.

"I'm still Ember Wright. Whole life changed, but the same name."

"I believe I'll be keeping my moniker, Whit, though I have no issue with being called Adair or Addi either."

"Fair enough. Zandi, these are my friends, Ember Wright and Adair 'Whit' Wright. Ember is new to our world and Adair has recently returned. They'll be staying with me for some time. Additionally, we need to strengthen my wards around the house and grounds. There's some potential nefarious behavior."

"Oh?" She raises a single eyebrow, Spock style, as she looks toward me and Whit.

"Oh, no! Not by my guests. By another, against them."

"I see. Yes, Sir," she says as Kenyon rolls his eyes.

"In answer to your original question, it's a 1959 Jaguar MK2 in cypress green, with a few modifications to make it compatible with our road system, of course," she says with assured accuracy.

"It belonged to my father. It was his pride and joy, once," Kenyon interjects with a mix of melancholy and pride. "It's the only car I have large enough to accommodate all three of us plus Zandi.

"Well, it's definitely a sweet ride!" I walk around to the front of the car and notice a significant modification in front. A rounded glass dome juts out from the grill. Within it, there's an electrode-looking object with a long quartz crystal at its center. Tiny strands of electricity shoot out from the center of the crystal like small lightning strikes.

"Woah! What is this?"

"It's a type of plasma ball with a Tesla coil. The crystal inside this glass vacuum dome collects magical energy and converts it to plasma gasses. The plasma filaments you see are part of the process which powers the car. This system powers the vehicles and the entire city," Kenyon answers.

"You mean like the plasma they use in Star Trek to power the warp engines? Is it a plasma injector?" I ask excitedly, letting my true nerd colors show. I'm unclear where the line between fact and fiction resides in this new fantastical world.

"Something like that," Whit interjects. I realize a bit too late that Kenyon isn't familiar with my pop culture references. Of course he isn't.

"But, I've seen something like this in les Dormeur." This is the first time I've used their term for the non-magical world, and I feel like a poser.

"The plasma ball was invented by Nikola Tesla, who was of la Magie. After he invented the plasma ball, he hoped to adapt it for the Ordinaries to use, realizing that energy was, and would continue to be, a big problem for them. Unfortunately, this invention didn't translate into much more than a novelty. Nikola was largely exploited rather than acknowledged for the genius he was. It was tragic. He gave it all up for nothing." Whit shakes his head. "It's why citizens of la Magie are encouraged not to intermingle with the Ordinaries. There are now stiff penalties for sharing our technology with them."

"But what about all of the inventions that Kenyon brought to your shop? Could he have gotten in trouble for those?" I ask, my stomach lurching at the thought.

"That's somewhat different. The inventions I brought to you were for you and Whit, and you are both from Elysia, even if you didn't know it. So truly, I was not bringing magical items to the Ordinaries." Kenyon interjects in answer to my question. "But, I do appreciate your concern."

Zandi moves to open a door, but Kenyon calls to her, "I've got this," opening the back door for me. Whit opens the door to the front seat, saying, "I'll sit upfront. I'm ready to get a good long look at my city," a note of genuine excitement sounding in his voice.

Ducking my head as I get into the car, I quickly shift my eyes toward Kenyon as he moves to the other side and enters. After Whit seats himself, Zandi pulls away from the Temple. The car is completely silent.

Unable to stop myself, I look back toward the Temple as it recedes behind us. Feeling the weight of one chapter of my life closing, albeit a short one, as another begins, my mind is unsettled. Though I'm distracted, I refocus as buildings familiar to me come into view, the buildings I've drawn. My mouth falls open in my surprise; there are so many I recognize that it's getting a bit creepy.

"I cannot believe how much of this city is familiar to me!"

"Oh, I know," Whit replies. "There were many times I worried my binding spells were becoming less effective on you. I can't help but wonder if the increase in premonitions you're experiencing is because your eighteenth birthday approaches. I surmise you had the warning Vision in the park because I was so near death, and my draíochta was weak. But it seems your awareness of all things magical was escalating, even before that incident."

As Whit returns his attention to observing the city, leaving me to stew in my swirl of inner turmoil, Kenyon grabs my hand and places a whisper of a kiss on my cheek. My stomach flutters at the sensation, and I realize there is so much I don't know about him. I wonder if the closeness I feel with him is more a product of the situation we just lived through than anything. But I dismiss the thought, remembering how drawn I'd always been to his creations. That means something, right?

Dominating buildings crowd the city's center, covered in reflective solar panels and alien-looking structures, and finally transition to a more residential area. The roads are smaller, and homes rather than buildings whizz by outside my window. It's a mixed-up mess of ultra-modern rectilinear angled houses next to rustic European-looking structures. Everywhere I look, it's green grass, plants and trees shading the houses. Dogwoods with wild pink flowers contrast with the lavender blooms of lilac trees. I roll down my window, my nose greedy for the sweet floral scents that permeate the air. It's idyllic; it looks so perfect, and I can't fathom what it would've been like to grow up here. I have to chase away the bitterness that threatens to overtake my feelings at the thought.

I realize we're at Kenyon's home as we turn into a hidden driveway. It's tucked away behind landscaping that provides privacy without being obvious. Rounding the curved driveway, a sprawling house comes into view, and my eyes widen again at the sight.

It looks like it's four stories in some places. It's a wonder of modern architecture, both modern and ornate, made of tightly joined cut gray stones. A prominent central chimney intersects the house perpendicular to a series of flat roofs and cantilever balconies seeming to hang in mid-air, creating the most dramatic interplay of angles I've ever seen. There's even a wall made entirely of glass.

"Now, this is a house I never saw in any of my Visions."

"Welcome to Three Arrows," Kenyon says, capturing my attention with the name. I laugh at hearing it spoken by him. He looks at me questioningly.

"It's what I used to call you, remember?" I say quickly, to keep him from thinking I'm laughing at him. "Whit would never tell me your name, so I called you by your maker's mark, Three Arrows. I called you that in the park."

"Oh, yeah, I had almost forgotten that," he says, and I see the tension leave his shoulders. "It was named by my fore-elders. They commissioned its building and named it after the three arrows on our family's crest. It's a bit more original than calling it McQuiston Manor, I guess."

"It's amazing! But I feel like I've seen something like this before, like in les Dormeur."

"You probably have. The architect of this house was Frank Lloyd Wright. He has also designed several famous homes and buildings in les Dormeur, including one very similar to this, called Falling Water. He worked here in Elysia for a time."

"How did that happen?" I ask.

"He worked in the different cities of the Commonwealth, but, I suspect, he felt his genius needed to be appreciated by a larger audience. He left la Magie and began building for the Ordinaries. He did achieve great fame for his designs. Unfortunately for him, though, his structures often leaked without magic, and the cantilevered roofs and balconies that defined his style often sagged," Whit explains.

"Ooh, burn!" I say before I can stop myself. "But how do you know all that, Whit?" I ask.

"My parents were well acquainted with him, so I was always interested in his architecture in les Dormeur."

"He was also friendly with my fore-elders before he left. Fortunately, my roofs don't leak or sag," Kenyon says.

"I'd forgotten how truly breathtaking your home is! Have you kept the interior the same as well?" Whit asks.

"For the most part. I didn't realize you were so familiar with the house, Whit. I remember you and Father as good friends. Did you also know my mother well?"

"I did. We were all excellent friends. Your father and I took our primary education together as well as our Guild Apprenticeships."

"What's that about? What are these Guilds?"

"They are part educational intuition and part professional association. Our education is general until we are thirteen or so. Once our magic manifests, we learn spellwork and the Language of Allthings. After completing our final year of primaries, we become a novitiate to one of the Guilds until we find the craft that suits us. After the apprenticeship, we take our Orders, pledge our career to that Guild, and begin our adult life. You may change professions, but you must go through an apprenticeship again," Whit answers. "For example, my Listening ability manifested later than most. I was nearly through my two-year apprenticeship with the Guild of Innovation. I finished and then went on to apprentice with the Priory of the Draìodóir. Once my three years passed, I took my orders."

"You mean you planned to be something else?"

"Yes, I have a decent understanding of mechanics and engineering. I had planned to be one of the Makers. But my fate was woven into a different path. I'll tell you a secret," he says, nearly whispering. "I never gave up my tinkering; I had a tiny inventor's corner in my quarters in the Temple. It's of no consequence now, having long since broken my vows." He finishes with a mirthless laugh.

"Let's get settled in. That's been quite enough re-living of the past in the last few days," Whit says, ending the discussion about his youth.

His words inspire a mix of feelings in me, and I have so many questions about everything.

I'm working on a case of "I-can't-take-anymore-level-of-exhaustion." Sighing, I follow Kenyon, walking toward a nearly hidden door at the side of the house.

As Kenyon approaches the door, it slides open for him without prompting. Leading us through, we round a corner and enter an open living space. As Whit enters the room, he exclaims, "You've redecorated!"

"Yeah, too many memories attached to the old furniture, plus the Prairie style is too stuffy for me."

The woodwork seems original to the design, but it's stained dark. The furniture is more industrial-looking, has an asymmetrical organic design, and has rough surfaces. Angular molded plywood lounge chairs sit opposite an asymmetrical charcoal-colored couch. Between the chairs sits a cool little footstool that looks like a giant wooden chess piece.

The whole house is Bauhaus meets Brutalist. I only know this stuff because I ran across a book about the Bauhaus movement, and being a fan of the *band* Bauhaus, I was intrigued. It started me on a phase of studying architecture and furniture design.

Leaded glass windows are held in place with shapes that look suspiciously like runes. I wonder if they are for protection. Whatever the case, they let in lots of natural light and a view of the manicured yard. The large-scale potted plants everywhere also help integrate the interior and exterior views.

Thick tufted rugs cover the hardwood floors, and clusters of uniquely shaped hanging lights like Chinese lanterns illuminate the space. As Kenyon shows us to our rooms, I feel awkward. There's nothing for us to do to settle in; it's not like I brought anything with me. I mean, what am I going to do here, sit and meditate or take a nap?

"If you'd like to freshen up, we can come back together in the great room and plan how to move forward from here," Kenyon says, as he takes a step into the room and steals a quick kiss from me, and then exits just as quickly, leaving me alone.

Out of habit, I let my body fall onto the bed before realizing I should be more careful in Kenyon's pristine house. I don't want to think, ponder, contemplate, ruminate, speculate, meditate, or muse about my situation. So I get up again and wander around the spacious room, going to one of the two leaded glass casement windows. I look down and see the river running through his yard. "Wow, this place must've cost a fortune!" I mumble to myself. Everything here is custom-made.

Stepping into the attached bathroom, I'm intrigued. A huge old clawfoot tub sits against the far wall with a complex faucet system Like nothing I've ever seen. The floor is covered in tiny hexagonal white tiles with black grout. A large mirror figures prominently in the room, and I feel dread over what I know the mirror will show me. Wow! I am seriously batty-fang! I think, chiding myself. My normally perfect makeup is gone, and my tear-stained cheeks are doing me zero favors. My hair is a wreck; sleep-induced cowlicks have asserted their dominance.

"Uhh! How very. I can't believe how hellacious I look. Someone could've at least told me." Perhaps I could use some time to freshen up after all. Walking to the tub, I'm hoping it's less complicated than it looks. That's when I notice an enclosed shower stall around the corner. "Now, all I'll need are all my toiletries, makeup, and fresh clothes. I wonder if Mrs. B would be kind enough to just send those along to me."

29
somewhere

Kenyon

Sitting outside together, we're alone for the first time since the craziness started. I rarely use this patio, as I never bring dates here. But I like the way she looks sitting here in my home. A fire crackles in the concrete table fireplace, lighting Ember's features in a warm glow. Above us, the sky blooms in shades of purple, violet, and pink, swirling together in striations. A thousand stars burst open above us as the final moments of twilight fade into darkness. The sound of the river is an ambient sound-track filling the awkward spaces between us. And suddenly I have no idea what to say to her. I've never been good in silence; it's part of why I've got the Casanova reputation. I fill silence with action. Kissing will always end uncomfortable silences, turning tension into something plea-surable. But that's not what I want with Ember– well, not just that.

"This is amazing! Actually, it's kind of perfect," she says, breaking the quiet, and I'm grateful. But this small talk won't be enough. My mind cannot stop calculating the imminent danger her mother poses. Phaedra is a manipulative woman with a lot of political power as the Prioress of the Vala. No matter how many lessons they try to squeeze in, it won't be enough to make Ember adept at wielding magic.

As if she's reading my mind, Ember says, "No matter how many weaving lessons or Visions I have, it will not be enough to stop Phaedra. I'm uneducated in magic, and what's worse, this feels like cramming for a test at school where there's no chance of passing. Whatever, I guess. I can't change what has happened or what I know is coming. She can try to steal my gifts, even kill me, but I will never willingly give her my power."

A shiver runs up my back as the echo of power reverberates through the room. This untrained novice has imbued her words with power, real power. It seems that along with her gift of Clairaudience, she also inherited the Truthsayers ability of VoceInvocare. It takes years to develop normally, but like all things Ember, she can manifest power without even realizing it.

I say nothing of it to her, opting instead for, "I believe you and in you." This is not the time or place for long-winded explanations of Force of Will, Manifestation, and Vocal Resonance. This is a date, after all.

Clearing my thoughts, I pick up one of the Lightening Bugs I've recently completed. Drawing a rune in the air above it to bring it to life, I watch as tiny gossamer metal wings begin beating furiously and take flight. Activating the lead bugs triggers a group of them to follow. They light up the night sky, and Ember's surprised reaction is priceless.

"I thought perhaps a bit of light," I say, gesturing.

"They're amazing. I can't believe you made them. Well, I mean, of course I can believe it. I've seen your creations and they're always incredible."

But I don't want to talk about my inventions. Without another word, I lean toward her, and my lips meet hers. Moving my arms to encircle her, my hands rest on the small of her back, drawing her closer.

Again I feel the pull to take this further, and again, I know it's not the right thing to do. Finally breaking the kiss, I bury my face in her neck and kiss her smooth skin. Her body goes limp as she arches her neck, allowing me greater access. My hand cradles the back of her head and I whisper, "Tell me if you want me to stop." My breathing is heavy.

She turns her face saying, "I don't want you to stop, but I'm not ready to—to go any further than this." Her words are quiet and shy, "I'm not ready for that yet."

"I understand," I say, trying to sound reassuring, but I also have to be honest. "I mean—I want to be with you, but what I feel for you is—" I pause, searching for the right words. "Well, it's unexpected. You make me feel things I'm not used to feeling, and it scares me a bit."

And I know I've got to tell her. I can't feel these things for her and not tell her what that means. I've dated so many girls. I've never felt anything close to our chemistry. But I don't want her to get the wrong impression and I don't want to scare her away. This is not just chemistry I feel with her. As inexperienced as she obviously is, knowing how many women I've dated will not work in my favor. No, that can all wait.

"Wow! You really know how to make a girl swoon."

Before she has a chance to say anything else, I draw my lips up the length of her neck, and she shudders, wrapping her arms around me tightly. She pulls me in in a smooth motion, and we lie back on the couch.

Kissing at a fevered pitch, our energy merges and envelopes us into our own private world. It's not quite the total intimacy of sharing Erindring, but it's akin to the experience. Even as I feel the complexity of her feelings, I know she senses mine as well as my hesitancy and confusion about them. With the stars twinkling above and the crickets chirping around us, everything about this moment feels right, especially as Ember takes control of our embrace. Something in her releases and she kisses me with an intensity I hadn't expected. This girl is full of surprises. I can't seem to keep my feelings from becoming entangled with her, or around her, or about her, I guess. Shit, that doesn't even make sense.

The last few days and my recently rediscovered memories from childhood are all we've shared, yet, the feelings crowding my heart stretch it beyond its limits. I can't make sense of it all. But now is not the time to share my cognitive dissonance or my somewhat questionable dating choices. Ember has broken down my walls, and my fear of potentially being hurt, but all that can wait.

I do my best to shut down my brain and throw myself into the physical sensations her touch brings me. My hand moves the length of her body, finding her waist again, gripping it tightly. Rolling onto my back, I shift her on top, and I feel understanding dawn in her. She's in control. That simple move inspires an unexpected fresh wave of desire in her, and kissing this way is sweet torture. As she's already stated, this can only go so far.

Without warning, she pulls us out of this magical cocoon, suspended in time, and jettisons us back to reality.

"Um, I should get to bed," she says awkwardly. "I'm kinda tired. But —you could walk me to my room and kiss me goodnight."

Was our accidentally sleeping together in the Temple a mistake? Did it create a heightened sense of intimacy that can't be sustained?

That night in the Temple, the inherent limitations were unspoken. Now we're in my home, with only the limits we place upon ourselves. It would be easy to go too far, feeling the way we do. It's definitely something to contemplate, I think, as I try to subdue my body's response to our activities long enough to walk Ember to her room.

"I suppose I can manage that," I reply. And with that, our date ends.

30
dressed in black

Ember

His kiss at my bedroom door makes me seriously reconsider ending our date. But I know it's the right choice. Everything felt safer in the Temple. It could only go so far then, but the training wheels are off here. Plus, he's like way more experienced than me, obviously, and it makes me feel inept and stupid. And I've known him for like a day? So no first-date, virginity-losing plans tonight, thank you.

Watching Kenyon walk away, I shut my door before he's out of sight. His room is at the end of the hall, and Whit's is at the opposite end. No reason for that observation, just saying. But I refuse to dwell on Kenyon or his room, where it's located, or what it looks like. I've got a lot of other life-threatening matters to overthink.

What is Phaedra's endgame here? She had to know that attacking Whit wouldn't help her cause, unless she thought she could win me over with her sparkling personality. Who could resist? That's sarcasm, in case you missed it.

Shaking my head, I decide I'm not figuring that out tonight. I walk to the adjoining bathroom and see several glass vials and jars on the counter; I'm guessing this is Zandi's handiwork– labels affixed to the potions written in a unique practiced script. These are custom-made toiletries. Are they infused with magic? Opening them one by one, I inhale their scents, and delicate notes of amber and honey overtake my

senses. Then I brush my teeth, wash my face, and follow with mois-
turizer.

Opening the closet door to hang my clothes, I find an assortment of
new clothes waiting for me, very modern in their silhouettes, even sculptural at times. I get a thrill looking at them. Most are black, but both a
stunning Prussian blue dress and a forest green number surprise me. But
honestly, as breathtaking as they are, I'm afraid I'd wreck them the very
first time I wore them.

Who purchased the clothes for me? Everything I could need is here
—skirts and dresses, pants and tops, even under stuff and socks. The
tailoring on these garments is impressive, and a moment of self-doubt
creeps in as I look down at my own custom creations. Forcing my
thoughts in a different direction, I dismiss them. These were obviously
made by a professional tailor, and I'm a self-taught teenager. These are
aspirational pieces, not yardsticks to measure myself against.

I grab a pair of structured, wide-legged capris, their seamed
construction tapering at the bottom. They're the coolest pants I've ever
seen. I don't really wear pants, but I'll wear these. Who knows what
craziness tomorrow will bring? Moving hangers back and forth, I find a
rad short-sleeved top with a high structured collar that stands up off the
shoulders to pair with the pants. Holding them up, they look like they
might be too big for me, but I'm sure I've got at least one safety pin in
my current outfit.

When I try them on, I'm startled as the once too-big pants begin to
shrink, fitting themselves to my body. They look made for me. The same
thing happens as I put on the tunic-length shirt. Gasping in delight as I
see my reflection in the mirror, I notice a selection of makeup off to the
side. He thought of everything.

The cosmetics are also hand-made. Removing the lid from a tin of
powder, it smells of roses. Not the overwhelming variety, but like the
high-end cosmetics my former foster mother two families back used.

A memory surfaces at the familiar scents. I'd gotten into the
woman's makeup, and I'd gotten in a lot of trouble for it. My chest
constricts as the memory floods my mind. The lecture about respect for
other people's possessions and privacy I received had been grueling. This
unwelcome memory is the last thing I want to think about.

With great determination, I redirect my attention back to the cosmetics. Picking up a thin brush and dipping it into a pot of inky black eyeliner, I draw a perfect cat eye line on my top eyelid. It's the most amazing eyeliner I've ever put on, and I suspect the makeup is spelled as well. I've never drawn a line that precise, ever. Yep, spelled.

I could spend the next hour trying on the new clothes and kinda wanted to. But I also want to thank Kenyon for his thoughtful gifts. So, stealth mission it is, sneaking down to his room and hoping he's still awake.

"Turnabout is fair play," I whisper, trying to muster my courage for what I want to do. Coming to the end of the hall, I say to myself, "This is it..." Simultaneously, I knock on Kenyon's door and open it. And like the night before but in reverse, I ask, "Ok if I come in?"

"A little late to ask now," he replies, echoing my response from the previous evening.

Hurriedly, I run forward to his bed, where he sits reading. Hopping onto it, I disrupt his calm, saying, "Thank you! I can't believe you were able to arrange to have amazing clothes and cosmetics delivered. Pretty sneaky..." My words are cut off, and I'm suddenly kissing him, both of his arms wrapped tightly around me. My heart beats faster, a shudder runs through my body, and my arms wrap around him in return.

His arms tighten around me, and again we're lying together. Only this time, we're in bed, and his body is half on top of mine. The weight is both unexpected and welcomed. Every cell in my body buzzes with energy, and I feel more alive than I ever have before.

Without warning, I feel Kenyon pulling his energy away from me, and I wonder what I've done wrong. Is he mad that I barged into his room and got him all worked up again? I pull my head back to look into his eyes and ask, "What is it? Did I upset you?" I'm nervous to hear his answer.

"No!" He barks out a laugh. "What would make you think that?"

"I don't know, you suddenly pulled back, and I was afraid you were mad at me for coming in uninvited. And if you really want to know the truth. I'm a pent-up mess of inexperience and insecurities masquerading as a girl." The admission is more than I planned to say. "Aaaand, now I feel stupid—" But I quickly clap my hand over my mouth to prevent any more humiliation.

He just laughs again. "Not to worry, Luv, you're fine." Wrapping his arms around me, he lays back on his pillow. My head lands on his bare chest, and the sound of his heartbeat captures my attention. We lie there silently, and the sound begins to lull me into a hazy, sleepy feeling, and I know I should get up and go to my own room. I'm not sure this is the precedence I want to set on my first night here. But it's so warm in Kenyon's bed, and he's all cuddly...

•••

The route Phaedra takes from the Temple to the Crystal Cave is quiet this time of night. She did not anticipate being seen by anybody, her path circuitous by necessity. She can't risk being seen.

Entering the forbidden space, a chill runs through her, reminding her how much she loves this natural wonder, how much she loves and longs for that power to live in her. She can't be too greedy; the crystals have memory and their own consciousness. The full extent of their awareness can't be known. If she pushes them too hard, they will reject her, possibly even harm her.

"Just a moment of pain," she murmurs to herself, poking all four fingertips and thumb with the blade of the sgian-dubh strapped to her leg. The blood flows freely, drops falling to the ground, threading themselves together, forming a circle as she completes her circuit. Placing her own enchanted crystals within the summoning circle cast of her blood aids her efforts. She will entrain these powerful crystal conduits of magic to serve her.

Lowering herself in the middle of the circle, she sits and opens her mouth, letting her voice sound. Innocuous at first, she's just here to be in their presence. But slowly, she lets her magic thread through the melody. A counterpoint to the overarching song, her true power is in her voice.

Her song is achingly beautiful. Of love and loss, heartache and isolation, unspoken but offered within the notes, she sings.

The Lemurian Seed Crystals that populate the room begin to respond. They're humming her song back to her in voices higher than the most accomplished soprano or opera singer.

Letting the notes of her song trail off, she's happy. This is tremendous progress, more than she had hoped, even. She could use this new power to enact her plan. She has a visit to make.

31
all night long

Ember

The imagery is unfamiliar, but after a few seconds, I realize it's Kenyon's room. I'm still lying in bed with him, and Phaedra stands at the foot of the bed. My heart beats double-time as I watch her watching me. She seems to be appraising the scene before her. Looking to my left, I see Kenyon still sleeping, but I can't feel him. I reach out to shake him, praying I can wake him and that he'll know what to do, but it's no good. Either he sleeps like the dead, or maybe this isn't really happening.

Looking back to Phaedra, I demand, "What have you done to him? How did you get here?"

"I've done nothing to him, child. And more importantly, where is here? Are you sleeping with this young man? Has Whit taught you no morals?!" Her questions drip with intrigue and hypocritical reproach, as though I'm accountable to her. Before I can say anything, she speaks again.

"You're hidden from me no longer, sweetheart. I sense you, blood of my blood." She holds up her finger to reveal a cut, bleeding freely. "Foolish girl, I'm not actually here. I'm walking in my astral form in Onirique. You really should recognize this; it's not like it's the first time we've been here...though I will say, it's the first time I've visited you when you've had a visitor in your bed." Her tone is still judgmental and scolding.

"What do you want, Phaedra?" I demand.

"Don't call me that. I'm your mother. Show some respect!"

"Ha! As if! You're no mother to me. Now, what do you want? Wait, I don't care about anything you have to say. Just go away."

"So, now that you have a protector, you're brave. Ready to stand up to me? Just yesterday, it was run, run, run," she accuses. "Do you honestly think they can stand up to me?"

"I don't need or want to involve anyone else in your twisted plans. If it's me that you want, leave them out of this!"

"As you wish," she replies. "Though it's extremely ironic that you should end up with him—her son. No matter, this is not the first time I've dealt with a meddling McQuiston getting between me and I want."

"What is that supposed to mean?" I demand, trying to keep the building panic from my voice. My heart clenches in my chest.

"It doesn't matter right now," she says, capitalizing on my fear, weaponizing it.

"It doesn't matter?!" I ask, repeating her words back to her, trying to turn the tide. "You know, by your own admission, you're not all that powerful, are you?" My defiance multiplies and rises, emboldening me.

"I told you that my gifts were slow to develop, not that I lacked in magic. So you see, little girl, I'm not so weak as you may believe." She begins to fade away, and the not-so-subtle threat is not lost on me.

My whole body is tense and rigid, jaw clenched as I lay there watching my evil mother fade, the ghost that has haunted my dreams for as long as I can remember. I'm cold, and a sheen of sweat clings to my body, making me uncomfortable. I try to speak, but I'm between sleeping and waking. The words come out unintelligible, mumbled, and muttered.

Slowly, I become aware that Kenyon is shaking me. It seems like half of forever before I can open my eyes. When I do, hot tears stream out the sides of my eyes and into my ears, my breath unsteady and hard.

"Phaedra was in my dream. She knew I was with you. She said something strange, though. That it was ironic I should end up with you–but I don't know what it meant. And there was definitely an implied threat toward you," I confide, not wanting to repeat her unsettling words.

"I'm not afraid of her," Kenyon replies, his chin jutting out as indignation shadows his features.

"I think I'm going to have to ask Whit about what she said. Maybe he'll have some idea."

"Good idea," Kenyon responds.

Trying to breathe deeply, to calm myself down before I get up and talk to Whit, I feel the tension rolling off Kenyon; I think he's trying to quell his anger with his deep breathing. Reaching for me, he closes his eyes and wraps his arms around me. But my heart still beats too wildly, adrenaline making me antsy, and I can't hold still. I need answers.

"I'm going to wake up Whit," I say resolutely, hoping he doesn't feel rejected as I free myself. But I don't have a choice. I need to move.

Thankfully, Whit is a light sleeper and it's easy to wake him. After filling him in, I'm grateful he doesn't ask much about why I was in Kenyon's room. But the furrow between his brows and the way he rubs his chin tells me that he's troubled by what's happened.

"And you say it was like she was in the room with you, not in a dreamscape of Onirique?" Whit asks, double-checking the information.

"It felt like she was in the room. But I guess her vanishing ability means she was walking in Onirique. I always get paralyzed when she shows up in my dreams like that—"

"Wait, you've seen her in your dreams? Was it like this?"

"Yeah, I guess I never mentioned it, but I've had this recurring nightmare as long as I can remember. It always feels like it did tonight, not quite real and not quite a dream, either, but I'm always paralyzed as they happen. I usually wake up all stiff with my teeth clenched and a super nasty headache."

"I see," he replies.

I decide he wants me to continue. "Phaedra knew that Kenyon was there and seemed to think that he was the reason that I was resisting her. There was an implied threat toward Kenyon, too. She said this wasn't the first time she'd faced a meddling McQuiston."

Kenyon's face darkens. The frustration radiating off him is palpable. "How dare she invade my home! And then, to threaten us! I will not stand for this!"

Looking in his direction, I say, "I'm sorry." My voice is small and quiet.

"What are you sorry for? None of this is your fault," he says, his anger bleeding away.

"I'm the one who brought her into your life, so it's totally my fault."

"Apparently, she and Whit were in our lives from before I can even remember, so this is not your fault," he replies with determination. Turning his attention to Whit, he asks, "Do you know what she was speaking of?"

"I don't, but I certainly intend to find out. I can't really say any more than that for now," he replies. "But I want the two of you to take care in your precautions. As evidenced by her attack upon me, she is desperate. She's been accessing Ember through Onirique all these years. Now that your magic is unbound and you're here, you're more vulnerable than ever to her attacks in the Spirit Realm. Who knows the lengths she will go to at this point?"

"I find that particularly unsettling! Not because I'm afraid of her, but somehow, I feel like I've been waiting for this to happen all my life," Kenyon says, his face stormy and unsettled.

"What do you mean?" I ask.

"I can't put my finger on it, but her implicit threat touches a memory somewhere buried deep inside." Kenyon furrows his brow.

My heart plummets at the thought that I'm connected to something that brings Kenyon distress. Though Phaedra's only my mother biologically, I can't help feeling that I'm paying the price for that tenuous connection yet again.

"Well, we are not going to solve any mysteries tonight. Let's all go back to sleep," Kenyon says.

"You've got your meeting with Sister Vadoma tomorrow, and I'll have time to investigate then. Perhaps the light of day will cast out the shadows obscuring what she has conceived in darkness," Whit says.

"Sooo, not at all cryptic there, Whit. Is that just habit, now?" I tease. I can't help myself. Plus, it lightens the mood a bit as both Kenyon and Whit laugh.

"Alright, alright, point taken," Whit answers, putting his hands up in a gesture of surrender.

We all start moving toward the upstairs bedrooms, Whit going first, and Kenyon holds my hand walking deliberately slower. Whit reaches his room first.

Pulling me into a tight embrace, he kisses the top of my head, whispering, "If you don't want to sleep alone, you can come sleep in my bed. I can watch over you."

"Thank you, I'd like that." I feel guilty that my presence in his life endangers Kenyon, yet he wants to protect me.

I feel unbelievably lucky in all my bad luck. And though I didn't expect Phaedra to visit me again, I breathe a sigh of relief when I awaken the next morning and realize that she didn't.

gathering dust

Ember

Aaaand, I overslept. Or maybe they decided I needed to sleep in after the night terror. I don't think they bothered to tell Sister Vadoma about a later start time because I hear Whit talking to her as I near the kitchen.

"I guess she's going to have to wait a bit longer because I'm definitely going to need to eat breakfast before today's trauma begins..." I mutter.

I round the corner from the great room to the kitchen. Ducking around the corner, I grab a banana and rummage through the pantry. Aha—a handful of nuts.

From around the corner, I can hear what they're talking about now. Whit's recounting last night's incident. "And those are the words she used, exactly?" the Sister asks in response.

"Those are the words that Ember recounted last night after waking me. After returning to bed, I began to think of my last interactions with Phaedra. Just before—our encounter, a few of us would get together here at Three Arrows. It began as a social club but soon escalated with lofty ideals and thoughts of changing our world. How to conquer corruption, that sort of youthful idealism." He pauses. "It came to an abrupt halt when Lena—Magðalena, Kenyon's mother..." But before I hear anything more, I decide it's probably wrong to keep listening. I clear my throat, uncomfortable that innocently overhearing their conversation has become eavesdropping.

Walking up to join them mid-conversation, Sister Vadoma says, "I knew Lena well. Before she decided the direction of her future, whether to join the Vala or pledge vows of convenance with Merrick, I was her mentor. I was dumbfounded when I heard of her death, so sad for the family. And—now, well, I think I see where you're heading with that train of thought. I guess anything is possible, and there is no easy way to ascertain the truth."

"Unless—the timing would be about right..." But Sister Vadoma's thoughts trail off like she's speaking more to herself than anyone in the room.

"I may have an idea. But I cannot discuss it just yet. Let's talk after Ember's lesson," she finishes.

"I thank you for your attention to this matter," Whit says in acceptance.

With that, Sister Vadoma turns to me, placing her hand on my back. She gives me a gentle nudge toward the stairs, saying, "We are fortunate this day. Kenyon's mother, Magðalena, was, in her youth, an apprentice to the Vala. She was a gifted seeress but chose not to pledge her talents to the Priory. She fell in love with her future husband, Merrick, and struggled with the decision." Pausing at the door, she gestures for me to enter a large room with a complex loom hanging from the ceiling. I mean, I think it's a loom, but I wouldn't know how to use it if I had to.

"At one point in our history, she wouldn't have faced that choice. The Vala or Vǫlur, as they were known, were typically older women without familial bonds who were followed by an entourage of young women. As our cities hid themselves from the Ordinaries, solitary practitioners mobilized in central locations. Their followers became novitiates. To ensure freedom from familial entanglement, vows of chastity were instituted. Though Lena declined to join the Vala, she had the right to use her gifts, so I helped her build this sanctuary, complete with its loom and spinning tools. I don't know where her spindle went, though."

"Thank you for sharing that, Sister, but I don't understand what weaving has to do with seeing the future? I mean, I wondered if that's a loom. It looks like a loom, so I assumed it is."

Making a settle-down gesture with her hands, she continues. "Novitiates start in the spinning and weaving room. Our hands must learn to perform the art so completely that our mind is free to enter a trance state while still performing the task—"

"Oh! That sometimes happens to me when I'm knitting. I'll get so relaxed, I just zone out and even doze off sometimes," I interrupt.

"Excellent! You are familiar with the trance, though that does not include falling asleep. Once the pupil attains this state, we begin teaching the art Seiðr or Fate magic. Seiðr literally translates to cord, string, snare. Through it, we endeavor to understand the course of fate and bring about change. We symbolically weave new events into being as we assert our will. To do this, we—" But before Sister Vadoma can complete her explanation, there's a knock on the door.

The Sister's brow furrows in consternation at being disturbed. Letting out a heavy sigh, she mutters, "Yes, come in."

The door slowly opens, and Kenyon stands covered in a thin sheen of sweat, wearing fitted workout clothes. It is all I can do not to leer at him lustfully.

"Can I help you, Kenyon? I was just explaining to Ember the basics of Seiðr. As I left instructions with Whit that I preferred not to be disturbed, I assume this must be important." Her voice is frosty.

"Yes, I'm very sorry! I was out taking a run and lost track of time. But I knew you were probably spinning or weaving today, and I thought Ember might need a distaff and spindle. I realize you might have brought one for her, but I wasn't sure. I went through my mother's things and found hers."

Kenyon trusting me to use something so precious makes my heart sing. Without consulting the Sister, I walk to and out the door and around the corner, pulling Kenyon with me.

Putting my arms around his neck, I kiss him, my lips brushing against his in a sweet kiss. Hesitantly, I pull away from him and whisper, "Thank you. It means so much to me that you would let me use your mother's instruments. Are you sure you want me to use them?"

"They're yours as long as you need them. And if they suit you, keep them," he replies.

"I couldn't take something so precious."

"Honesty, these things are meant to be used. They are normally handed down through the mother's side, from seer to seer. Obviously, I have no sisters and no female cousins. From what I understand, my mother was a gifted seer, so maybe there's still some of her juju in these things," he says with a small laugh. "It's stupid for them to sit unused and forgotten, gathering dust. You can just take this old yarn off the spindle. It must be from the last time my mother did any spinning."

"Wow! How about if I use them today, and we can see how they work for me. Sister Vadoma may have thoughts about that. But I'm honored. Thank you," I concede as I pull him into another kiss but force myself to disengage as I hear the Sister clear her throat.

Kenyon gives her a sheepish look over his shoulder. He pulls away from me and looks at the Sister. "Thank you for letting me steal her away for a minute."

Her face softens. "Look at you; you've become such a handsome young man. You are a near-perfect blend of your parents."

"That's what they tell me." He pushes a dampened curl back from his face.

"Thank you for bringing your mother's spinning tools. They will help facilitate Visions that will lead us to the truth behind these troubling circumstances.

She looks in my direction and says, "Shall we then?" She holds her hand out to me. As the Sister closes the door behind us, I examine the tools. The Sister starts the lesson by explaining those tools in their practical and ritual aspects.

"The seiðstafr or distaff, the tool you're holding in your left hand, is a device that holds combed fibers ready to be spun."

Turning it at different angles, I examine it. It looks like a long metal bar with a swirly orb attached. Even though this thing hasn't been used in many years, I feel magic radiating off it. There's a patina-darkened wooden handle covered in carved runes, including the Vegvisir. As I realize what I'm looking at, I turn my eyes to the Sister, saying, "Why is there a Vegvisir on this distaff? There was also one on Kenyon's traveling device thingy."

"There is also one on the spindle. It's sigil magic, Ember. The Rune helps to guide us in the right direction. I assume you feel the power emanating from the tools you hold?"

"Yes," I answer in a brilliant show of my intelligence and wit.

But she continues on, unphased. "When we are ready to begin spinning, the drop spindle comes into play."

Picking it up, I look more closely at the spindle. A smooth palm-sized stone disk of lapis lazuli feels heavy. It's a deep blue color with gold veins running along its surface. Piercing its center, there's a twelve-inch wooden rod about a pencil's diameter, three inches on one side of the rod, ending in a hook, and nine on the other. Like the distaff, there are runes on it that radiate magic. Wrapped around the wooden rod is a swath of dark grey yarn that's softer than anything I've ever felt. My fingers tingle with an unfamiliar sensation as I touch it, almost a feeling of foreboding.

"The distaff is held upright in the crook of the arm, opposite from the spindle." Before Sister Vadoma can continue, I interrupt her with a question.

"Where is Seiðr from?" When the Sister gives me a stern look, I realize my mistake, "Oh, I'm sorry. I didn't mean to interrupt you. I'm just—I guess—I just want to know more about all this before I go having any more crazy Visions and stuff," I say, hoping to gain understanding, but instead revealing more of my concern about what's happening.

"Ah, I forget how new everything is to you. Seiðr is a type of Norse magic for telling and forging the future."

"But I'm American," I reply stupidly, mortified as I feel the heat of embarrassment climbing up my cheeks.

"Nations are a construct of the Ordinaries. Their territorial boundaries make no difference to us in la Magie. Spirit's connection to home and heritage needs no lines on a map to direct its way."

Steering the conversation back to the lesson, she says, "The practice Seiðr today is not as it was practiced by our ancient Norse ancestors. It evolved as we did. But modern Vala wield too much political power. Too much focus upon what *will be* instead of what *is* robs us of life."

"Now, I think we ought to properly resume the lesson. Spinning is a great metaphor to represent manifesting reality." My head is starting to spin.

"The act of transformation occurs as we spin loose fibers into yarn. It represents formlessness into form, the magic of creation. We focus our intention, taking substance in hand and creating form. Focus, Substance, Form. Magic manifested. It is the same for Vision or spell-work; the basics remain the same."

Can she see the impatience to start spinning? Her lesson appeals to the knitter in me as I push the flat Lapis disk along the length of my thigh.

"That's it, Ember! That's exactly the movement to get the spindle spinning and turn the fiber into yarn. You're a natural."

"Cool! Not to be impatient or sassy, but are we gonna start soon, and should I pull this yarn off the spindle? Kenyon thinks it's the last yarn his mother spun before she died." I lightly touch the yarn, feeling like some kind of magical voyeur.

"I understand that you are eager to begin, but there is just a bit more to know before starting. We spin to incite Visions and weave to catalyze our future realities. It is our best chance to interact with the Norn."

"Is it possible to have Visions while knitting?" I interrupt again. I'm not usually this rude, but every time she starts talking, it causes more questions.

"I suppose so, though I am unaware of any who employ knitting as their modality for Visions. Why do you ask?"

"Well, just before my life imploded and we came to Elysia, I was knitting, and I saw Elysia beyond what I'd seen in my dreams and nightmares. I zoned out, and while I was near the mental institution in les Dormeur, I saw it for real while knitting."

"By necessity, our ancestors had to spin wool into yarn and weave cloth to make their clothes. The Visions came during these activities. It seems you entered into a near trance state and a brief flash of a Vision came to you," the Sister answers.

"So, can't I just knit then?" I ask, suspecting the answer will be no.

"I believe you were drawn to knitting because the craft of fiber is in your lineage. Even the binding of your powers could not prevent the pull of the craft. But you are here now, and the Vala have a long and rich tradition of spinning and weaving. It would be a shame for you not to learn these acts. It is your magical inheritance."

Crossing the room, she stands before a built-in cabinet, pulls a fuzzy woolen mass from a drawer, and secures it to the distaff. "You may sit or stand, though sitting is easier."

So I sit in a chair and wonder if Lena McQuiston used this, too.

"So hold the distaff between your legs, just above the knees," She says, moving my legs apart and the distaff into place.

"We'll attach a lead to the spindle." She pulls a fuzzy fat length of wool from the mass and attaches it to a loop from the old yarn.

"Stabilize the lead with your hand. Now push the disk along your leg to spin the spindle with the other." The Sister arranges my hands in the appropriate positions. "We work this way until the trance is upon us that we may See."

"So we're just gonna attach it to the yarn that Kenyon's mother spun?" I ask, trepidation in my voice as my stomach lurches.

"We are fortunate beyond measure that Kenyon brought us such a gift! I cannot be sure, but I suspect a connection exists between Lena and Kenyon and Phaedra's veiled threat last night. Connecting your yarn to Lena's might provide insight into her last Visions. I think this is key to understanding connections previously hidden. I know it's daunting, but there is no better way to obtain such a potentially powerful Völuspá."

"So, no pressure or anything, then..."

"None whatsoever, Ember. You cannot control the Vision you have," the Sister says.

Still feeling intimidated, my shoulders slump as I continue to fidget with the spindle, jeopardizing the join between Lena's old yarn and the new wool roving.

"Who are the Norn?" I ask, half curious, half stalling.

"The Norns are the beings that measure and regulate fate to implement the destiny of all beings. They are the masters of Seiðr, weaving the fates of all of us. Each of us is a string on their loom."

"They are three, and their names literally mean the aspect of time they govern. As with the Language of Allthings, the word is the essence of the thing it Names, a True Name if you will. Perhaps you might think of them as an avatar of the Name. They have the ability to construct the content of time. Urðr means "The Past," Verðandi means "What Is Presently Coming into Being," and finally, Skuld means "What Shall Be." They are the Past, Present, and Future and live near a well named Urðarbrunnr, the "Well of Fate," which lies beneath Yggdrasil, the World Tree at the center of the Otherworld. It holds the Nine Worlds in its branches and roots."

"So, with that, we are ready. Let us begin," The Sister says, chanting in a deeper voice than I would've imagined possible. Placing the stone disk against my thigh, I push the spindle down my leg. The motion forces the spindle to twist the attached wool roving. The die is cast, and my Vision will be linked to the yarn Kenyon's mother spun eighteen years ago. I feel the weight of it, like an incoming wave of foreboding that pulls me into an undertow.

"The Vision wasn't completely clear. It's kinda like looking at people through a fog. But I know I saw something awful! It's unspeakable! Did you know?" I demand.

"Did you know this would happen?" I demand again, impatiently. "Is this why you wanted me to use Lena's yarn?" My stomach twists in knots at the thought of being manipulated by the Sister.

"No, though I did suspect there would be something difficult, but worth seeing, and I confess, I hoped you'd see the truth of events," the Sister calmly replies, irritating me even more.

"How could you? It's beyond cruel! How could you hope for me to see her death?"

"I hoped for you to see the truth, child, not what that truth would be. Has there ever been a situation where you were better off not knowing the truth?" Sister Vadoma asks, but the question is rhetorical, and she continues undeterred. "It is what has gone before. There is no changing it. However, you can change how you respond to the future. Let the truth of what happened inform your decisions." She pauses. The hesitation feels like foreboding.

"Ember, I'm sorry to do this, but I need to see what you saw," she says with a mix of compassion and steely determination. The change in her demeanor startles me as much as the words she says. "I have to ask you to journey once more into Onirique, this time taking my consciousness with you, that I may know the truth. Everything depends upon it, Child."

"What!? I can't, "I say, feeling gutted. But I quickly find my resistance. "My birth started with manipulation and deception, and now I find that everyone I've ever cared about has been hurt by my very existence! I can never make any of that right. And now you want me to relive this horror?"

"I will be with you. You have the strength to face this. There is something you have yet to see in this; I am certain of it. There are always nuances to events that remain unseen that can be glimpsed in a return to the Vision."

Without another word, Sister Vadoma walks to me, placing her hands at the base of my skull, splaying her fingers out. "We'll do this together. We will share Erindring, and I will clear the Vision, that you may see the full truth, not a half Vision filled with questions and assumptions."

Then Sister Vadoma instructs me to begin spinning again, and the edges of my consciousness connect with the Sisters. Instinctively I know I have to let my guard down, and my thoughts and awareness merge with hers; I hear the Sister in my head. And yes, it's totally like a Vulcan mind-meld, she says, parroting my exact words back to me.

"Relax, child, it makes it an easier melding of our two minds." As the connection between us deepens, I hear the Sister thinking, Yes, child, it is an intimate experience. So let us focus on the Vision you had, that I do not intrude upon your thoughts and feelings any more than necessary.

Right... I think in the Sister's direction. This is so weird.

Start spinning again, the Sister instructs.

•••

·

My Vision shifts from seeing my hands on the roving and spindle, now viewing them through the Sister's perception. Our conscious minds are one, and everything is white again. We are in Onirique.

The Vision is much clearer than before. Looking to my left, I see Sister Vadoma standing next to me. We're still in Kenyon's home, standing in an entryway, but the interior furnishing and decor look entirely different. Somewhere deep in the house, a small child wails.

A woman with icy blue eyes and a crown of raven-colored curls rounds the corner of the second level. Her trim figure is outlined by the dressing gown that conforms to her shape. She nearly flies down the long stairs, opening the door without asking who's there. It's Phaedra, because really, who else would it be? But she's youthful, not much older than me. This other woman, I've come to realize, is Magðalena McQuiston, as she looks just like Kenyon.

"Phaedra, please come. Follow me upstairs if you like. I was tending to Kenyon; his Nanny has run an errand for me. But we can chat while I tuck Kenyon into bed for his nap," she says, turning toward the stairs.

My heartbeat quickens as I hear the door shut behind Phaedra. It only gets worse from here. Phaedra follows Lena, and her face looks curious. "What do you want to talk to me about, Lena?" Her expression shifts, and she seems nervous now as she looks around furtively, the barest hint of a quaver in her voice.

"I know you're pregnant, Phaedra." The words are so abrupt, it's an accusation. Phaedra's mouth works wordlessly, shocked by Lena's state-ment. "H—How?" She finally manages.

Lena finally gives up on settling Kenyon in his crib, picking him up. "Come, let's go downstairs," she says, passing by Phaedra. "We can discuss it properly in the great room." Turning out the light with a swish of her finger, she leaves Phaedra in the dark. Spurred into action, Phaedra follows Lena, who puts Kenyon on the floor to walk by himself. His chubby fingers grip Lena's as he steadies himself. He pulls his hand away to walk on his own, bouncing his hands up and down like he's celebrating his accomplishment. I can't help but smile at his happiness.

Catching up, Phaedra grabs Lena by the shoulder, spinning her around so they face one another. "This can't exactly wait. I'm in a serious mess, and I don't know what to do."

"Phaedra, I cannot tell you how distressing it was. I was already deeply unsettled, with a feeling of foreboding hanging over me, so I decided to spin. And when the Völuspa came, I saw you, pregnant, very pregnant. Then my Vision changed to one of you attempting to steal the girl's powers." Lena stood there, silently demanding answers.

"I can't speak to what you saw in the future; maybe your abilities have faded due to not being an active member of the Vala. And while it is true that I am pregnant, I would never harm my own child," she replies indignantly.

"Beyond the fact that I know what I saw to be the true future, I am also left to wonder how it is that you find yourself pregnant? You've sworn vows of chastity, have you not?"

"What are my vows to you, anyway?"

"Those vows are the very thing that kept me from joining the Vala. I took that oath seriously, obviously more seriously than you. I had to choose between my gift and my love of Merrick. But here you are, breaking your sacred vow as if it were nothing!"

"You know it hasn't always been this way. In the days of our ancestors, the Vala were not required to take this oath."

"We live in the here and now, Phaedra. You took the vow, and you broke it. I cannot remain silent." There's sadness in her voice that I hadn't noticed the first time I'd seen the Vision. I look to Sister Vadoma, who motions with her head to pay attention to what's happening.

Phaedra reaches for Lena again, and it's suddenly like slow motion. Ghostly figures emerge from nowhere before Phaedra can even touch Lena. There are men and women, all shapes and sizes. Some even look inhuman. Crowding onto the small landing at the top of the stairs, they watch with mournful faces as the women argue. The ghostly figures speak to one another in a low murmur. Again, I look to the Sister and ask, "Are these Ancestors?"

"I believe they are. Yours and Kenyon's!" she answers, never looking away from the translucent figures. Their murmurings turn urgent. "No harm!" and another, "Spare children!" and finally, "No More!" The voices resonate, booming, many of them speaking in unison.

"They speak with VoceInvocare: Words of Power, spoken with the full force of their determination," Sister Vadoma murmurs.

Without any perceptible movement, the Ancestors surround Kenyon and Phaedra. One of the beings places a hand over her womb, then another, and still another. With their combined will, they pull something out of her body. A glowing orb shining with opalescent light, the sphere is agitated and spasming, cradled in the Ancestors' hands.

With a nudge, Sister Vadoma directs my attention to Kenyon. Around him, three of his Ancestors pull something out of him, the same kind of glowing orb. The apparitions stand around them, now cradled within their protective circle.

My heart lurches. With sudden clarity, I realize that our ancestors pulled the consciousness of my fetal self and little Kenyon from our bodies.

"Children protected!" The figure says, looking directly at me. The bottom falls out of my stomach, and Sister Vadoma floods my senses with warm protectiveness, softening everything.

The ancestors create a bubble around themselves, cocooning the orbs. I watch, awestruck, as our two souls come together in a large ball of glowing light. But there isn't much time to dwell on it. As their consciousness merges, my attention is drawn back to the scene of Phaedra and Lena. I want to tap into my fetal spirit's experience of merging with Kenyon rather than see what's about to happen, but I can't.

Phaedra pleads, "Please! Just give me a chance to figure out what I'm going to do! You'll take everything from me! Have some compassion instead of being so judgmental!" Phaedra's panicking voice gets louder with every word she speaks.

Lena begins to turn and go down the stairs when Phaedra grabs for her shoulder again. Before she reaches it, though, Lena jerks away, trying to avoid any further physical interactions with Phaedra. But her motion is an overreaction, causing her to lose her balance.

She falls backward down the steep stairway, her head thudding loudly on each step it hits. Phaedra's mouth drops open as she lunges forward, trying to stop the fall, but she hesitates a moment too long.

"Lena! Oh my God! I'm so sorry!" She yells as she runs down the stairs. When she reaches the bottom, she places her fingers on Lena's neck.

Breathing a sigh of relief, it's evident that Lena is alive. "What am I supposed to do now? Oh, Rémy, I wish you were here; you'd know what to do!" She mutters to herself.

"Maybe I'll just let the Fates decide. Both our destinies brought us to this moment; they will decide whether she lives or dies," she says as she flees.

The last thing I see is the protective bubble. It bursts as Phaedra runs away, pulling my orb away from Kenyon's, leaving a confused and frightened boy standing at the top of the steps looking down at his mother, surrounded by his ancestors, spirit reentering his body.

My Vision is white again. I can no longer feel Sister Vadoma. I guess our connection has ended. I'm alone in the white place again, wondering if this will be another meeting with my ancestors.

The reverberating echoes of a voice I remember from my last encounter speak to me, but this time no ethereal bodies accompany them.

Their droning voices finally speak. "Heart's fire shines light upon the hidden."

"Why am I here? And who are you?" I ask as wisps of mist become women materializing before me.

"We are Disir."

"Just like the Grandmothers. So what exactly does that mean, anyway?"

"Kindred spirits of Fate, traversing boundaries—life—death. We protected you."

"Guard you no longer," another says

"Grown—will face trials," they intone in unison, their voices a chorus of reverberation.

"Um, so thanks for letting me know, I guess. I mean, I kinda figured there's something else that Phaedra's planning. She doesn't seem the type to just give up." I pause but impulsively add, "So what am I supposed to do?" I mean, it can't hurt to ask, right?

"Powerful gift you have...."

The Disir are next-level cryptic, but they fade away before I can ask them any more questions. Feeling a sharp tug at my navel, my spirit travels through Onirique at dizzying speed. I can't see it, but I feel it. My skin prickles and my breathing is shallow, like wind blowing in my face, making it difficult to breathe, until finally, I fall to my knees, feeling like

I might actually vomit. So I hug my legs to my chest until I catch my breath.

When I finally feel some semblance of my wits return, I get to my feet to find I'm standing under a giant tree in front of three women—well, an approximation of women, as if sculpted by someone who's never actually seen women. They are unnaturally tall with faces that are too angular. Standing side by side, they each hold a section of a seemingly never-ending yarn. It has bumps and splits, textured in places and smooth in others. Each of them examines the area they hold in their hands like it's the most consequential thing ever. They don't seem to know or care that I'm standing here.

And all of my reading about Norse mythology pays off as I realize I'm standing at the foot of the enormous World Tree Yggdrasil and The Norn. As I do, the woman standing in the middle, Verdandi, the present, looks up and regards me, finally asking, "Why do you entreat us?" Her voice croaks, sounding like it's used little, if ever.

"I don't know," I admit timidly.

"Then why come?" The question feels like a demand, cutting to the heart of my fears and uncertainty.

"Why?" I ask, finally finding the one word to sum up my feelings.

"Explain," the three say in unison.

"Why? Why go through all this song and dance and let people question you, or try to weave a new destiny for themselves, or beg you for what they want if their fate is already written? Why bother? Why even make yourselves known to us mortals?" My question is full of defiance, and I feel the awesome weight of their terrible presence, the trouble these beings could make for me. I'm pretty sure they could think me dead if I anger them too much. But the question burns within me nonetheless, demanding to be answered.

"You speak as though you are removed from the outcome," retorts the woman who stands to the right, the Norn who oversees the future, Skuld.

"Actions matter," Skuld reprimands, followed by Urd, the past, who says, "Actions make no difference; the past is past has passed."

I can't shake the image of them as bickering sisters. Finally, Verdandi raises her hand. The other two are silent, looking at me with thoughtful gazes, asking in unison, "If you believe destiny fixed, why question?"

"Because—I could be wrong."

"A glimmer of wisdom shines," Says Verdandi.

"A flawed understanding of fate," offers Urd.

"We are the Masters of Fate, the weavers of the web, but the string we spin is made of your nature," Verdandi interjects. "Your nature meets its inextricable fate as decided by your nature. An infinite loop. Thereby your fate is written by you."

"No more questions will we answer," Urd says in a tone that brings no argument.

"Search yourself; answers reside within," Skuld says, her tone telling me there will be no negotiations to this end.

"A gift, I will give you," Verdandi says, surprising me. "A boon for the glimmer of wisdom shown this day." She pauses and bows her head slightly, lowering her eyes and gathering herself. When she looks back at me, there are no words to express what I see in her eyes. They bore into my soul through my eyes and there, in hers, is everything and nothing all at once. The whole of time lives in her gaze, encapsulated in a moment. I'm desperate to look away, but I cannot. I'm trapped in her sight. Without breaking our contact, she says, "To understand this moment without the trappings of future or past is powerful. Within the span of a breath you may harness the ability to change your fate..."

As she completes her thought, everything about the place dissolves. The World Tree becomes transparent, as do the three giant women.

As my view of the Onirique fades away, my world shifts back into view. My vision clear, now looking at Sister Vadoma in Lena's spinning room, I'm home.

33

a sullen sky

Kenyon

"You haunt my every thought, day and night. I cannot escape what has begun again…" The urgently whispered words trail off as I turn the corner to find Whit and Brother Aaric sitting in the great room. But before I can process any of what I've heard, Ember and Sister Vadoma enter the room.

"Ember, Sister Vadoma, you're finished," Whit says, shifting his body awkwardly, trying to drop Aaric's hand without being noticed. "That was somewhat faster than I had imagined, but then I've never been privy to the arts of the Vala."

Sister Vadoma takes the lead, saying, "I see we are fortuitous, again this day, for we are all together. I'm glad you're here, Brother Aaric. Today I began teaching Ember the art of spinning in hopes of achieving a Völuspa. She was successful beyond my imaginings." Ember seems irritated at her praise, but I never had any doubt. There is something about her. It defies reason or explanation, but she possesses a potent, yet latent, ability to wield power. Once trained, she'll be formidable. Her power draws me to her, but I can never tell her that. I fear she would assume I want that power for myself when all I want is to be near her shine.

But my thoughts are interrupted as the Sister begins speaking again. "Kenyon interrupted our lesson as we were beginning, bearing an invaluable gift. He brought us the distaff and spindle of his mother. On the spindle was a generous length of yarn spun by Lena many years ago. Seizing the opportunity, I directed Ember to connect her fiber to that yarn and begin spinning."

"A bold move, Sister," Whit interjects.

"Indeed, inspiration struck as the threads of destiny aligned. In doing so, Ember forged a connection to the Völuspa that the yarn manifested and the final moments of the spinner's life."

Whit draws in a sharp breath and, in a low voice, says, "'Tis true. I hear the truth in her words."

I study the pattern woven into the rug as the Sister speaks. Standing still, the words play themselves again in my mind. Holding my breath, I close my eyes for a moment waiting for the sting, waiting for despair to consume my heart. But it's lodged in my chest, refusing to move, leaving me unsteady. I'm not at all ready for the next revelation to crash into me because I know, beyond all doubt, the worst is yet to come.

"She was able to achieve this because her spirit was there as well. Phaedra, pregnant with Ember, was summoned here and confronted by Lena, who knew she was with child. An argument ensued, and Lena fell down the stairs."

"No offense to Ember is intended here, but how can you be sure of what happened back then, much less begin to assign blame to Sister Phaedra? This child is a novice and inexperienced at navigating Onirique. It would be easy for her to misinterpret the Prophecy," Aaric interrupts, his voice doubtful.

"Because the memory of the previous Völuspa was embedded in the yarn. And as I mentioned, Ember's fetal spirit was there when the incident occurred. The Vision presented an opportunity to access the prophecy and its related events. I linked my consciousness with Ember's, and she brought us both back to the Vision. She is a gifted seer, though as you point out, she is a novice and needs training. This is where my expertise came in useful, as I am no novice."

"I've never heard of such a thing!" Aaric exclaims.

"Pardon me for saying so, but the Draíodóir are not privy to the intricacies of Völuspá," the Sister replies in a curt but polite voice.

"By all means, please continue." Aaric's tone is equally curt.

"I saw the events unfold before my eyes. Phaedra tried to grab Lena's shoulder as they argued, and Lena lost her balance as she flinched away.

She overcorrected and fell down the flight of stairs. Phaedra bears no responsibility for this except that she chose to leave. She said she would 'let the Fates intercede to decide what would happen next' and fled the scene—"

"She did what!?" I demand, my emotions finally dislodging from my chest, making room for outrage. My outburst startles Ember, but I can't worry about that right now. My heart feels too big for my body as it beats faster and faster.

Sister Vadoma begins again, her calm demeanor unflappable in the face of possible confrontation. "The yarn you brought us yielded a gift more profound than I could've imagined. I instructed Ember to continue spinning that skein of yarn—"

"Yeah, I got that the first time. But what I'm trying to clarify is that Phaedra is basically to blame!"

"As I said, she is culpable but not the cause of the incident," the Sister repeats.

"Incident!? My mother died! And it was Phaedra's fault. She could have saved her!"

As though I said nothing, the Sister continues. "There is one more thing we need to impart. Phaedra called out to someone in her distress, someone named Rémy. I have long wondered if she's involved in a romantic entanglement, and so it seems she is. Or at least was—though I suspect the affair continues even now."

In a brief pause between Sister Vadoma's thoughts, I interrupt her musings about the intrigue surrounding Temple politics.

"You'll have to pardon me if I have no interest in the inner workings of the Vala. What I really want to know is what you intend to do with this knowledge? This implicates her negligence in my mother's death, at the very least!"

Sister Vadoma ponders momentarily, saying, "I think we should bring these discoveries to the Convocation of Esteemed Equals. It may not yield action to our cause, but it's a start."

"Good! She must be punished for her duplicity," Whit replies.

Scoffing at Whit's misguided notion that anything could come of this, I turn my attention away from the others. "Ember, could you please come with me?" Not waiting for an answer, I grab her hand and lead her from the great room up the stairs to the fourth floor.

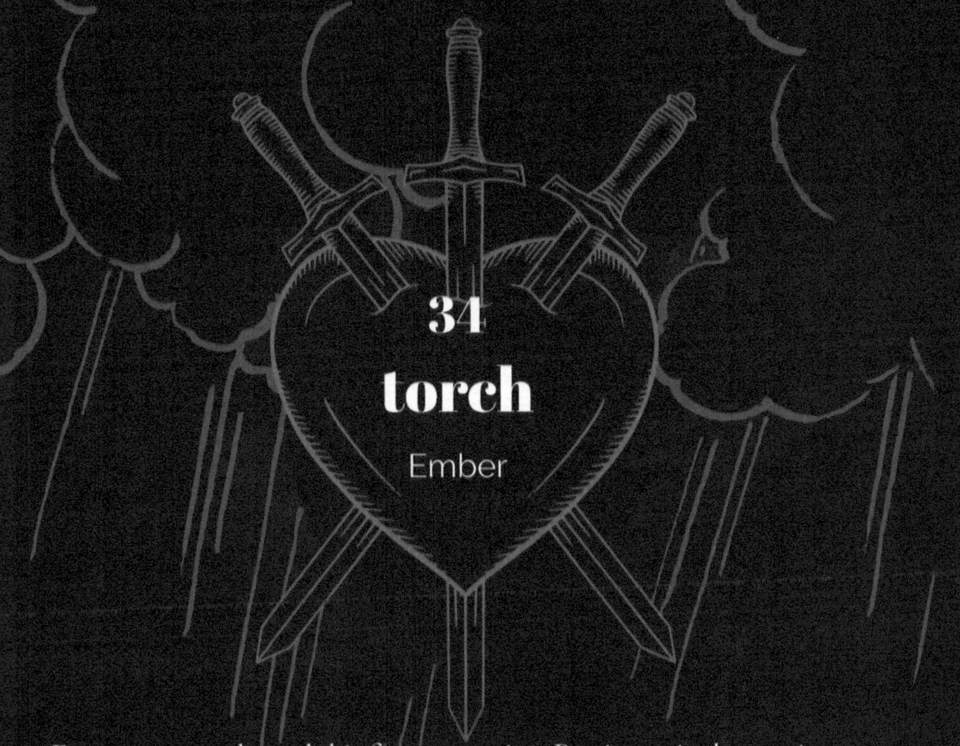

34

torch

Ember

Energy courses through his fingers to mine. Putting a single emotion to it is impossible; it's too complex, too mixed up. Opening his door, he leads us through his room, passing the tidy bed and dressers to the door leading to the large balcony.

Closing the door behind him, he puts a finger to his mouth for silence. Pulling a small glass bead from his pocket, he makes a series of complicated hand gestures above it. It begins to grow, going from the size of a grape to a grapefruit in just a few seconds, then placing it on the couch that faces the river. Within seconds the bubble engulfs the sofa.

Once Kenyon is satisfied that it's ready, he takes my hand again, walking to the edge of the opalescent dome. Holding his palm to the fragile-looking structure, he pushes, and his hand passes through. Stepping forward into the bubble, he pulls me into his private domain.

"No one can hear us within the sphere."

"OK," I reply, wondering what Kenyon could tell me that would require such privacy.

But before he can begin, I can't stop myself from blurting out my feelings in a rush. "Kenyon, I'm so sorry. I can't believe you had to hear all that from Sister Vadoma and that yet again, I'm at the center of more problems in your life. But there is more to the story that I need to tell you. The Sister saw it with me. Actually, I only saw it because of her.

She helped clear the Vision, and then I saw everything. I couldn't see it well when I first saw it. It was kind of foggy."

But instead of saying anything, he steps in my direction and wraps his arms around my waist, kissing me. Desperation that reminds me of my own, yesterday in the Temple, emanates from his body. I let my thoughts fall away, returning his kiss.

The edges of my senses are touched by Kenyon's, reaching out to me to share consciousness. Pulling away, I say, "I want to share something from my Vision with you, but I also don't want you to see what happened to your mother that day. It happens before that."

"Focus on what you want to show me, and I won't push to see anything beyond it," he says, kissing my neck. A low moan escapes my lips, and I move my face toward him, our lips meeting again. His mind touches mine again. This time, I open to him, trying to focus on the moment when the Disir materialized, skipping everything he already knows.

But I'm completely distracted by the overwhelming emotions ruling him and his feelings for me—his need to not be alone.

I hear Kenyon telling me, "No matter what, none of this is your fault." And it's the weirdest thing; I experience him saying the words while feeling them as though they're my own.

"No matter what you show me, none of this has anything to do with your choices. I could never blame you for what your mother has done."

I try to wrap his senses in mine like I'm hugging him, but I can't linger on what he's telling me. I'll lose my train of thought, and I need to show him what I've seen. Focusing my thoughts tightly, I push the image toward him.

Surrounding us, the Disir pull our spirits from our tiny bodies and put them together, protecting them. Kenyon's surprise is undisguised as we watch them form a bubble around us, cocooning our spirits from the realities of what was happening.

Forcing the Vision to fade away quickly, at this point, not wanting Kenyon to witness any more, I feel his awareness of this, along with terrible sadness at what he knows will come next. Feeling Kenyon's presence in my mind pulling away, a nervous tension builds in me as our minds separate.

"Ember, don't you see? The connection we feel for one another was destined to be before you were even born. Our ancestors, or the Disir or whatever, brought us together to protect us. Now they have brought us together again so that we can protect one another. This Vision is the answer to the question that has lain within me, the question of why I feel so safe with you. Why I'm so drawn to you. Why you feel like home."

My heart swells and my brain floods with relief as my nervous tension ebbs away. Far from being put off by how we'd been brought together, he sees it as our fate.

The desperation in his kiss turns to sweetness as he kisses me again. Arms around my waist, he presses on me and I pull him down, his nearness causing every nerve in my body to feel suddenly more alive. My blood pulses through my body, and my heartbeat quickens. I want this moment to last longer than I know it can.

Propping himself up on his arm, he looks into my eyes. "I want you to stay here with me. You'll have your own room and everything, but I don't want you to leave. I want to wake up knowing I'll see you in the morning. I want to kiss you goodnight. Whit can stay too."

"Ummm—I haven't actually thought about where I plan to live. Everything has been so focused on what Phaedra is doing or will do."

"Just think about it. I'll talk to Whit later and extend my invitation to him as well." He kisses me again but stops, saying, "I'm not sure I can continue like that and not want to lose myself in you. And I suspect the Sister, Brother and Whit are wondering what's become of us. I'm certain they intend to take these revelations to the Convocation today, for all the good it will do." His face darkens cynically.

"What do you mean? I thought you would be happy that we're reporting her."

"I would be, if I thought it would amount to anything. You'll see. There's a lot of corruption in this city and in the Commonwealth. I believe it either begins with or should end with the Primus Inter Pares, the First Among Equals, Remigius Châstellain." Kenyon's disgust is so evident there's no need to ask how he feels about the man.

"Everybody knows he's dirty, but nobody can prove it. I suppose you don't become the Headman of the Honourable Guild of the Arcane if you're an open book."

Kenyon's very formal in pronouncing all the titles and Guild names. It strikes me as odd, but before I can ask, he continues. "But it's the whole lot of them really, and their corruption and inability to come to a consensus and enact meaningful reform, that is the most disheartening." He stands and pulls me up, giving me a final peck on the cheek.

Placing his hand on the glass dome as he had done when we entered, it pops like a soap bubble. Looking toward the couch, I see a tiny glass sphere sitting there. Kenyon scoops it into his hand and puts it back in his pocket. Grabbing my hand, he leads me back toward the others.

• • •

Time passes slowly as she waits impatiently for darkness to fall so she can enter the Crystal Cave. The monotony of leadership is far more tedious than she would've guessed. Still, her ability to access and harness power isn't possible without the position. Someday soon, it will all pay off. She will need to move on with her plans more quickly. With every passing day, her daughter gains more strength and comfort in this world, bettering her chances of standing up for herself, of claiming her powers as her own.

Once Ember discovers that Phaedra can claim her powers, they will be impossible to wrest from her. I've got to get these crystals entrained more quickly, she thinks. Why are they so stubborn? I've given them my blood. I've sung to them. What else will it take to win the rest of them over? The paltry amount that sing with me is insufficient to ensure my success. I need that foolish girl to let go of her powers. I need her Sight!

Frustration blooms within Phaedra's chest as she walks the perimeter of the Crystal Cave, her blood falling to the floor yet again. Its viscosity changes as it hits the ground, transforming from fluid to gelatinous. It's thick and imbued with her will, smelling of iron and maleficium. Each drop of blood that falls from her body connects to the previous. They undulate and quiver with a life force all their own until becoming a single line of blood, her summoning circle—the most powerful of summoning circles.

Opening her mouth, a high note emanates from her throat, and her soprano voice carries. It fills the giant space to its high, crystal-encrusted ceiling. Innumerable Lemurian Seed Crystals embedded within the quartz magnify the magic into the city. And now, in this space, they magnify her high, lilting voice as well, the sound and light bouncing on faceted surfaces. She is breathless, radiant upon hearing her voice align with the singing crystals.

Slowly she sharpens her will, infusing it into her melody. The pitch shifts slightly, and her voice falters to a flat note. She quickly modifies her pitch, hoping the slight variance won't affect her ability to synchronize the powerful magic these crystals wield to her biorhythm. Refocusing, she let more of her intention seep into her voice. Breathing into her diaphragm and closing her eyes, her voice sounds with intention and determination. Drawing upon the power already entrained crystals offer, her pitch is true and the sweetness of her voice multiplies. Finally, more crystals vibrate in sympathetic rhythm, like a string vibrating in tandem with others, her power growing.

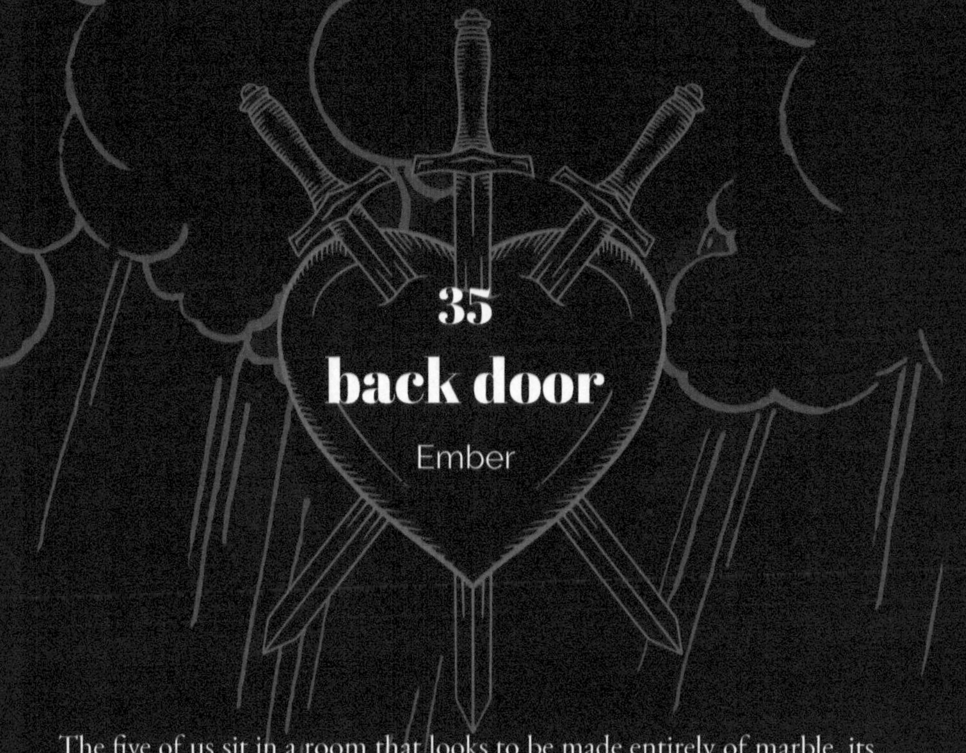

35
back door

Ember

The five of us sit in a room that looks to be made entirely of marble, its domed ceiling made of glass held in place by mullions that look like runes. The shapes repeat in the high stone arches that line the walls, rising to the glass ceiling's edges, all carved with runes. Trying to take in every detail of the room, I lean over to Whit. "Is this entire building made of Marble?"

"Actually, it's Quartz. It was built ages ago of quartz to magnify the room's energy and magical dealings. This quartz is spelled, so it echoes and reverberates strangely when exposed to lies. That's the thought, anyway." Whit answers.

"Oh, thanks—" But my thoughts are cut short as members of the Convocation of Esteemed Equals enter the room. Sister Vadoma rises, and we follow. As they seat themselves, they gesture for us to take our seats.

A distinguished-looking man sits at the center of the table. He pounds his gavel once, saying, "I call to order this session of the Convocation of Esteemed Equals. Let the record show that five of the thirteen members are in attendance. I am Justiciar Remigius Châstellain, Starosta of the Vede Mecum of Allthings, Headman of the Honourable Guild of the Arcane and Primus Inter Pares of this Convocation."

This guy has a big title with a lot of words. I want to believe he's playing up the importance of his role, but the power that emanates from him tells me that my hope is futile. His vestiary choices give credibility to his stature as well. I'd bet money his tricked-out charcoal suit is custom-made. It's somehow both conservative and flamboyant at the same time, a feat I would have never thought possible.

"Also in attendance are: the Venerable Magister, Idris Pritchett, Luminary Innovator, and Headman of the Honourable Guild of Innovation."

At the announcement of this man, I see both Whit and Kenyon shift uncomfortably. The Magister inclines his head toward Kenyon, who does the same in return. I'll have to ask him about all that business later. Idris Pritchett is very proper, living his best Victorian-mad-scientist life in his brown and tan windowpane plaid suit with a yellow ochre tie over a stiff standup collar shirt. Actually, this suit is Whit's jam, too, come to think of it. Anyway, his bushy white mustache ends with handlebar styling, and the deep lines on his face make him look stern.

"Also, Venerable Magister, Pan Ling OuYang, Wěiyuán of the wu Oneiromancers and Headmistress of the Honourable Guild of Liminal Space." The woman's eyes narrow on me, and I feel like I'm being examined. There's no evidence she's leaning one way or the other.

She's a tan-skinned woman with black hair shot through with dramatic streaks of white at her temples. I can't tell her age. Her hair is pulled tightly into a headdress that's all flowers, tassels, and pointy sticks that could double as weapons, and it's all kinds of amazing. A bracelet of tiny human skulls that looks made of bone encircles her wrist. She's wearing a sleeveless red qipao dress embroidered with golden dragons. But, rather than regular slits on the sides, they travel up to the top of her waist and reveal form-fitting black leather pants underneath.

Remigius Châstellain drones on with another introduction. "Venerable Magister and Tempestarii Denma Beridze, Master of the Storm Callers and Headmistress of the Honourable Guild of Stewards."

This woman seems distracted, even disinterested in being here. I can't fathom whether that's good or bad for our cause. Her hair is pulled back in a low ponytail so tight I wonder if she has a constant headache. She's wearing a suit of fitted pants and a slim-fitting woolen asymmetrically cut suit coat, like a futuristic Amelia Earheart.

"And finally, Venerable Magister Vesta Parker, Forewoman of the

Alliance of Pragmatists, Quidnuncs, and Morality Guardians, and Headmistress of the Honourable Guild of Future Destiny."

I see Whit shift again, and I can only guess that the Morality Police lady just introduced might have a thing or two to say about all of this. Her cold blue eyes narrow as she examines Whit, and then she looks at me with pursed lips and gives a perfunctory smile. She wears a tailored white silk jacket with a giant integrated bow that covers her entire chest, and her perfect white blonde hair is swept back into a low bun.

"Now, formalities and introductions are out of the way; as I understand it, this meeting brings the Honorable Sister Vadoma Palgrave of the Vala before us. What is it that we can do for you, Sister?"

"I am grateful the Convocation has agreed to see us on such short notice. Thank you."

"It is not every day that we are visited by a diverse and accomplished group such as yourselves. We assume the urgency with which you have approached us aligns with the nature of what you bring before us?"

A soft-spoken older man offers, "We are pleased to see the beloved first son of Innovation, Kenyon McQuiston." All eyes turn to Idris Pritchett, his white hair bound into a ponytail at the base of his head, though his bald pate shines like it's been polished. His pale pink-tinged skin makes him look perpetually sunburned.

"Yes, Magister Pritchett," the Sister replies, allowing no time for any more formalities or niceties. "I believe we have uncovered the true nature and character of a member of the Vala. She is, I believe, corrupt and quietly influencing our members to gain power for her own glory and not that of the Priory."

"This hardly sounds like a matter to be adjudicated by this Council. Rather more a matter of internal politics within the Vala. Or at most, to be taken up with the Headmistress of Liminal Space. They are, after all, the Guild that oversees the Priory of the Vala and all Oracle Societies. Beyond that, these things have a way of righting themselves over time. This Convocation hasn't the right nor the will to intercede in matters of internal politics," says the Justiciar Châstellain, firmly, as if this settles it.

Before Sister Vadoma can respond, the Headmistress of Liminal Space, Pan Ling OuYang, raises a long slender finger, saying, "Let's hear them out, Rémy. I am the Mistress of Liminal Space, so it is within my purview to know of such matters. Besides, we are all here now, and surely the Sister had reason to come to the Convocation rather than to me directly." The implied warning in her tone does not go unnoticed by me or anyone else in the room.

"We are grateful for latitude, Headmistress OuYang. We bring this matter before the Convocation rather than the Guild of Liminal Space due to the nature of the evidence we present."

I'm stuck on the use of the nickname Rémy for Remigius, and I work to stifle my gasp. I lean over to whisper to Whit, "Do you think it's the same Rémy from my Vision of Phaedra?"

"Who is disrupting this Council Meeting? Have you something more important to speak of, girl?" Magister Pritchett askes with a pointed look in my direction.

At this point, Whit stands up and says, "My sincere apologies to the Convocation. I am Adair Whitley Wright, and I have been away from Elysia for many years, protecting my daughter from one who would steal her gifts of clairvoyance and clairaudience. She has only just returned to the city and has many questions. She is also not familiar with the etiquette of such a meeting as this."

"But I assume she has basic manners and knows that interrupting is rude. Moving beyond this lack of decorum, your absence has not gone unnoticed. The last I knew, you were bound for the Priory of the Draíodóir when you left the Guild of Innovation. How do you find yourself with a daughter?" Magister Pritchett peers over his old-fashioned oval wire-rimmed spectacles.

"I think it best that we focus specifically on why we are here, though admittedly, my story does intersect. But those details will be revealed as the story unfolds," Whit replies.

"This Council is not accustomed to being denied the details of any story, Mr. Wright," Headmistress OuYang says, making it clear that this woman is not often told no.

"Yes, Headmistress OuYang. But telling my tale does, in fact, play in the larger truth we're here to tell. I would never want to waste the time of an esteemed group such as yourselves with repetition," Whit says, his flattery attempting to placate the formality-driven fustilarians.

Her face relaxes slightly, and she says, "Proceed with the facts you wish to share."

Sister Vadoma stands. "As I said, we have evidence of corruption within the Temple. We need your guidance to come to a resolution about this matter." She pauses briefly, looking in Majester Pritchett's direction. "As you mentioned, Majester Pritchett, Adair Wright did pledge his gifts to the Priory of the Draíodóir, which he served for many years. In fact, it was widely held throughout the Temple that he was destined to become the next Prior. Fate had other plans for the accomplished Listener, though. He was seduced by a member of the Vala with ill intent. She conceived a child from that union and kept her pregnancy a secret. When the child was born, she tried to use a Confractio Anima ritual to steal the infant's gift. That child is Ember Wright, who sits before you now, and her mother is Phaedra Rule, Prioress of the Vala. Furthermore, evidence of that ritual remains written on her skin. This young woman bears the marks of malevolent magic."

The Sister motions for me to join her in front of the Convocation; I'm not sure about this anymore. I'm deeply uncomfortable with what's going to happen next, but I stand and walk to her. Without a word, the Sister pulls my hair back to reveal the iridescent spots I've spent most of my life trying to hide.

They are silent, their eyes wide at this revelation. My stomach jolts at their reactions, which is stupid. It's not like I didn't know it was going to happen. I never thought I'd be so glad to have strangers reacting to those stupid spots like this, but if it helps prove how evil Phaedra is, good! The Convocation stand and more closely examines my skin.

"Ember was, with some assistance, able to achieve full Völuspa, witnessing Phaedra's treachery and involvement in the death of Lena McQuiston," Sister Vadoma offers.

"How did she come to have this Völuspa?" Wĕiyuán OuYang asks suspiciously. "For an untrained to achieve such a thing is uncommon. Its timing is particularly convenient given her upcoming Investiture of the Sacred Spindle ceremony."

"This situation came to us, not the other way around. I stand before you to bear witness to the events as they have unfolded before me. I am fully cognizant of the weight of the accusations I must levy. We were gifted with a length of yarn, the last yarn spun by Lena McQuiston, the yarn responsible for the Vision regarding Phaedra." The Sister is calm and assertive in her reply.

"How is that possible?"

"Once spun by a Vala, the Völuspa is forever etched within the fibers of the yarn. As the yarn revealed, the Vision pertained to Phaedra and her pregnancy. Ember was in utero when these events took place; thus, she could see the aftermath of that yarn's revelations. That Vision revealed that Phaedra was culpable in the untimely death of Magðalena McQuiston."

This time there are gasps about the room. A low murmuring begins.

"This is a grave allegation, Sister Vadoma," Magister Vesta Parker says.

"I'm aware of that, Majester. And if you give me a bit of latitude, I'll explain the circumstances that brought me to this accusation. Prioress Phaedra is not directly responsible for Lena's death, though she was present and could have saved her." The Sister then looks in my direction, knowing she will shock me with what she's about to say. "—Furthermore, what is not well known, is that Lena was herself pregnant." I sneak a quick peek at Kenyon. His lips are drawn in a thin line and his eyes look hard. He knew his mother was pregnant.

The Sister pauses as the shock of her statement takes hold and lets the outrage murmurs die.

"So you see, Phaedra is culpable in the death of Lena through her negligence, impacting the potential life of a second McQuiston child and nearly ending the life of her own child with the aforementioned ritual. These trespasses merit investigation by the Council and potential removal from the Vala."

"This is preposterous!" Justiciar Châstellain interjections. "You have many accusations and precious little proof. Are we to believe this outrageous tale? The evidence is beyond ridiculous, supported by only the markings on this young woman's face, the word of an apostate Draíodóir, and a questionable Vision trapped in yarn for eighteen years. Only to be miraculously rediscovered by a long lost daughter, clearly under the sway of the disgraced Draíodóir?"

He visibly stills himself, taking deep breaths before continuing. "What would you have us do? Put the Prioress on trial, accused of Maleficium, and exile her from la Magie based upon this tenuous evidence? Your Order wields much political power, and this sounds more like sour grapes on your part, Sister Vadoma. It is well known that you were slated to be the next Prioress of the Vala and were beaten out by Sister Phaedra—who is the most well-loved Prioress of your Order, in many years."

I look at the faces of the Convocation, and it seems not all of them love Phaedra, particularly Wěiyuán OuYang. Her face looks like she's eaten something sour and can't wait to spit it out.

Magister Parker speaks. "I must confess that I also find the evidence a bit lacking. Though I do find your accusation of Prioress Phaedra's usage of the Confractio Anima ritual disturbing. The addiction to Amplicon and the equally disturbing Spiritus Confractio ritual-driven theft of people's draíochta is a blight upon this city. Any allegations pertaining to such activities demand serious consideration. In my estimation, you are a luminary within your Order, and I do not doubt you believe wholeheartedly in the evidence you bring before us today. But, as my fellow Council members indicated, this nebulous information is insufficient to implicate the Prioress. The epidemic this Commonwealth faces is deeply rooted and must be stopped. If the accusation has merit, I would encourage you to find more substantive proof for this Convocation."

"Yours is an arcane art, as is my own, and we've long served our communities. However, the amount and quality of Völuspa have been, shall we say, lacking," Wěiyuán OuYang offers. "Even more evidence that there is something wrong within the Order. It has lacked in every way due to her leadership."

"We bring you evidence that this corruption is potentially linked with this lack of Vision, and you want to dismiss our concerns as an internal matter," Sister Vadoma asserts, her irritation with the bureaucracy competing with her attempts to remain respectful.

"We simply need more proof. And no offense is intended here. But a memory stored in nearly twenty-year-old yarn and the Vision of a novice, new to our world and ways, are not compelling enough evidence," Denma Beridze adds.

Idris Pritchett chimes in with a rebuke for Kenyon. "On a personal note, Mr. McQuiston, I am saddened to see you, a first son of the Guild Innovation here, supporting such allegations. This calls into question your judgment and associations. I urge you to distance yourself from this matter and return to innovation rather than intrigue."

I feel Kenyon stiffen next to me at his words, and his energy bristles with irritation. He slips his arm around my shoulder in defiance of the Magister's comments, saying, "I'll take that under advisement." It's hard to miss the sarcasm in his voice. It also reminds me of the words I spoke to Phaedra, the ones meant to tell her I had no such intention in mind.

"We have complete confidence in your abilities, Sister Vadoma, to resolve this issue if indeed there is one. Please inform us of any noteworthy developments that we should be aware of at our regular open Convocation forums," Justiciar Châstellain says, interrupting the growing ire between the two Makers and abruptly ending the meeting. Picking up his gavel, he bangs it three times, saying, "So Mote It Be, this Convocation is adjourned." Out of the corner of my eye, I see a satisfied smirk on the face of Justiciar Châstellain as he dismisses us.

Walking over to Sister Vadoma, I whisper, "Do you think Remigius Châstellain may be the same Rémy that Phaedra called out to in our Vision? I mean, that was like almost eighteen years ago."

"I believe so, yes. His adamance about Phaedra's innocence and his attempt to turn this into an accusation against me makes me suspect there is more to this story. Perhaps he is involved in whatever Phaedra's larger plan entails," the Sister answers quietly.

"So what now?" I ask as we walk out of the grand building. "Clearly, the Convocation of Esteemed Equals is useless—"

"Ember!" Whit protests, "They are not useless, and the Governors of this community deserve our respect. They are very deliberate in their dealings and are not quickly moved to action. That is wise."

"Whatever you say, Whit. But they seem like a bunch of throttlebottoms to me," I reply

"Throttlebottoms?" Kenyon asks, looking at me quizzically.

"It's Ember's obsession with Victorian insults and profanities. Let me see. Throttlebottom means something like a futile or inept person in public office?" Whit says, answering for me.

I put my finger to my nose and tap, saying, "On the nose, there, Whit. How did you know?"

"Oh, I looked into your Dictionary of the Vulgar Tongue, if for no other reason than to understand what in thunderation you are saying," he replies.

I giggle at his use of thunderation. Kenyon shakes his head and says, "She has a point. You've been gone a long time, Addi, and you've not seen the corruption that has taken hold in our city, infecting even our most trusted leaders."

Sister Vadoma joins in, adding, "The appointment of Châstellain and his obsession with his Necessaritarian Initiative and its 'Less is More' mantra to restrict magic use has let many aspects of this city fall into disarray. With our new understanding of his potential entanglement with Phaedra, I am even more dubious about his or the Council's willingness to help us."

My stomach twists at the Sister's agreement; somehow, I'd hoped my assessment would be wrong. "What do you mean his whole 'Less Is More' thing?",

It's Kenyon who answers me. "It's a bit involved, but basically, Justiciar Châstellain proposed that the use of magic should be extremely limited on a day-to-day basis. Mundane tasks done manually without magic, that sort of thing. Save magic for magical workings, thereby making the city more equitable. But people of lower socioeconomic standings are the ones who would suffer most in this mandate. Their lives are more mundane than magical; the lack of magical intervention would make their daily lives exponentially more difficult. Furthermore, he is not forthcoming about who decides the particulars of his doctrine. I mean, how much power do the deciders wield? It's extremely problematic at best. Elitism disguised as Egalitarianism."

"Seriously?! That's wack."

But Kenyon is single-minded. "We cannot let her get away with this!" His hands ball into fists at his side, his knuckles turning white in anger. "I knew they would be useless. They have been since Châstellain's appointment!"

"I must return to the Temple; if my suspicions are correct, Sister Phaedra will have been informed by the Justiciar of our meeting. I do not know if she was aware of my involvement in this matter before this, but I'm certain she is now," the Sister says.

"I'll join you, Sister," Brother Aaric says. Before he departs, he looks at Whit, saying quietly, "Think about it, would you?"

"I will," Whit replies, his face flushed.

"Thunderation!" I exclaim, "I forgot my new purse under my chair. You guys keep going. I'll just run back and get it."

"Not a chance! I'll go with you," Kenyon says. I don't care enough to fight him on this.

Turning, we head back to the Hall of Wisdom and Acknowledgement and enter. It's so quiet, and I'm glad the soft rubber soles of my Docs don't make noise. Walking down the hallway of doors leading to the main chamber, we hear the voice of Rémy Châstellain.

"Ugh, this is the last thing I need right now," he mutters.

Kenyon puts out his arm to stop me and pulls me toward a small alcove where we'll be hidden. I can still hear the sounds coming through the door that sits ajar. A quiet click of something being opened is followed by a serene voice. "Welcome to the Oculus Network; how may we serve you?"

He takes a deep, audible breath and says, "The Prioress, Sister Phaedra of the Vala." He pauses and then resumes speaking. "Phaedra, we need to speak urgently. Do you have the time and privacy for a conversation?"

"Give me just a moment," She replies, her voice quieter than his. After a brief pause, she says, "Rémy, How did I get so lucky to hear from you in the middle of the day?" Her voice drips with sweetness.

"Listen, I've just concluded a meeting of the Convocation, where we heard several accusations about you. Credible accusations."

"Who?! Who is accusing me of what?" She demands.

"Sister Vadoma was the primary accuser, accompanied by Prior Aaric, Kenyon McQuiston, Adair Wright, and most importantly, your daughter, Ember Wright. Apparently, she was in the midst of a Spinning lesson, and the Sister had the bright idea to connect new fibers to some old yarn that Lena McQuiston spun just before her death, or some such nonsense. Suffice it to say, your daughter had a Vision of everything that happened the day Lena died. Also, they are bringing the failed attempt to steal her powers as a transgression for which you should be held accountable. I've told you a hundred times that your plans were unlikely to succeed. Please tell me you have a better plan to deal with these new allegations. There is only so much that I can do to cover for you." His voice is terse, rife with tension.

"I promise you that I have the situation well in hand. I have a plan to end her interference and give me greater control of the Crystals. I know I can make this right. I'll have enough power for us to rule the city, the

Ley Lines will be ours to command, and then the entire Commonwealth of Atlaria! We'll be unstoppable, and then we can finally be together, out in the open. My vows and your wife, a forgotten bad dream," she finishes.

"Let's not get ahead of ourselves; we have much to do before we can realize your ultimate plan. But I, too, dream of a day when we no longer have to hide our feelings, my love," he replies with an artificial sweetness.

"Amplicon usage is escalating, as is dependence upon magic for every little thing. We must reinforce the "Less is More" campaign at every opportunity. I see no other way to save the magic from depletion; we must put an end to this accusation against you. It will be difficult for you to represent the cause if you're credibly accused of performing Confractio Anima. Much less on your daughter!"

"Rémy, I was young and dumb; surely you won't hold my past mistakes against me. will you?"

"No, of course, my darling, I will not, but the public is another matter. It would be better for our cause if these allegations don't receive broader attention."

"When will we have the chance to be together again? I miss you," Phaedra says, changing the subject, her sentiments punctuated by lust.

"Soon. I'll need to see you, discuss some formal business, and then we can have our private encounter. I'll be in touch soon," he says, and the small click sounds again, ending the call.

He sighs. "What am I going to do about her?"

Once again, we hear the click. Who will he call next? A panicky feeling blooms in my chest at the thought of being caught here. Then comes the sound of high-heeled shoes clicking on the tiled floor.

They are approaching quickly, and I want to make a run for it. Feeling my anxiety, Kenyon puts his arm around my waist to steady me. Before the woman reaches the office, I hear her mutter an expletive, and then the sound of her heels recedes into the distance.

Kenyon tugs my waist, pulling me back the way we came. "Come on, I know a different way to the Great Hall."

36
don't fall

Ember

Nearing Kenyon's Jaguar again, we see Whit leaning against the car, looking tired, as Zandi waits behind the wheel. Once we're within speaking distance, we fill him in on what we heard.

"What now, Whit?" I ask.

"Well, I don't know what Aaric and Vadoma plan to do when they return to the Temple, but Phaedra is definitely aware of our discovery. If she hadn't already been planning something, she is now," Whit answers. "So, I believe our main focus should be keeping you safe and teaching you the principles of spellwork and protective runes for a start."

"That's great, Whit, but you know she'll make a move before I'm ready to defend myself. And unless you've got some magical mace in your pocket, this all feels pretty, well, too little too late. But, I—I don't want to let her steal my gifts. They're mine," I say, feeling a bit defeated.

"I know, Ember. Believe me when I say I questioned myself daily about keeping you innocent in this situation. Still, it was the only way I could keep you safe. I know it feels overwhelming now. I feel it, too! But to start is all we can do."

"That's not going to happen! That woman is at least partially responsible for my mother's death. She will not rob me of everyone I've ever cared about. I will not let her harm either of you as well."

While Kenyon's anger startles me, I can't help swooning at his pronouncement. He cares about me! Though the circumstances aren't ideal, my heart swells just a little.

"I just don't think anything we do will stop her," I reply, hoping I won't make them mad. But really, it's my life in danger, so I shouldn't be so worried about their feelings as much as my life.

"We'll see about that," Kenyon says, grinding his teeth with resolve. "But for now, there's this." He pulls a small metallic object from his pocket, presenting a heart-shaped locket. It's not just a lame gold heart, though. It's enameled red and has golden frames crowning the heart. It's so much like the painting on my boots! Opening it, he reveals an internal space filled with mechanics. As he draws a rune above the tiny gears, they whir to life, one gear spinning another, causing small chips of quartz crystal to shimmer momentarily. Closing the locket, he turns me by the shoulders, facing away from him. Then he lays it on my chest and fastens the clasp.

"I made this while you were with the Sister learning to spin. This will let us track you if she does manage to get her hands on you." He steps back, examining his creation. Before I can even thank him, he turns to Whit. "Do you have any thoughts about how to stop her?"

Before Whit can answer, I interject, "Umm, thank you. This is a beautiful locket, and I really appreciate you making such an amazing thing for me. But—I do not appreciate being spoken about like I'm not even here."

Then Whit replies to his question as though I haven't even spoken. "Unfortunately, I do not, and I believe we will see some attempt sooner than later."

In exasperation, I turn and walk away from them. Apparently, I don't even need to be there, so why should I bother? Maybe I'll just walk myself back to the Temple and confront Phaedra, get it over with. When they finally notice I'm halfway down the street, they run to catch up.

"What in the Nine Worlds are you thinking walking off alone like that, Ember?" Whit demands.

"I'm not going to stand by as you two talk about, around, and over me! I'm right here! And, this is all about me, after all, and while I know I can't protect myself, I at least get a say in this." Reining in my anger, I try again. "I appreciate your efforts to keep me safe. But we need to figure out something I can do to defend myself when it happens. And I can feel it. It's going to happen." I know this contradicts my previous statement, but it's this, or I might as well give up and seek Phaedra out and hand over my abilities. I'm not calling them gifts anymore because they don't feel like gifts. Plus, they're mine, and I won't go down without a fight!

"How do you know, Ember?" Whit looks worried.

"I can't exactly explain it. It's like I feel a pull. It's like we're connected by a cord or something. She's tugging at it every now and again, like she's testing it."

"Interesting," Whit replies. "I think the only thing we can do is to continue your training. These things have a way of working themselves out in unexpected ways. After all this time, I refuse to believe it's your destiny to succumb to Phaedra's machination."

"For now, let's go home and renew our lessons in Runic magic," Whit continues. "Perhaps we can jog your memory enough to rekindle the knowledge you learned as a child."

Great, that'll save me: rudimentary runic magic. I don't say it aloud.

Walking back to the car and settling into the back seat, I feel antsy, like I want to crawl out of my skin. Waiting is always the worst part. Weirdly, it reminds me of when I lived with the Osborne family, when I waited for Whit to pick me up and deliver me to another family. The remembered feelings of rejection and fear of what was to come flood my chest with heat even now, twisting my stomach just as it had while I sat in the foyer of the Osborne house. My fingers naturally gravitate to my cuticles, and I begin picking at them. Mrs. O.'s face is vivid in my memory, sitting next to me on the floral jacquard bench, my soon-to-be-former foster sister Rhonda playing piano in the music room. The notes came haltingly, accompanied by the voice of Rhonda's tutor chastising mistakes. Pachabel's Canon in D will forever be the soundtrack of rejection.

The unusually cool autumn brought sunset earlier and earlier. I looked at my lap, fidgeting with the mittens I'd just finished knitting when the headlights of Whit's car illuminated the driveway.

"You know this is not about you, right, Ember? Rhonda is just in a place where she needs all my attention, and we'd be doing you a disservice by depriving you of a family that can be there for you..."

Ugh, enough of that! The words fade away as I forcibly pull myself from the memory and back to what's happening now.

"You look so lost," Kenyon says as he slides into the seat next to me, grabbing my hand. "I'm sorry you felt ignored out there. I'm just worried."

"I know. I'm worried, too."

"We're going to do everything possible to keep you away from Phaedra."

"I know, but it's going to happen anyway. I have to face her no matter what. So in some ways, sooner is better than later. I just hate all this waiting," I confess.

Before Kenyon can say anything, both Whit and Zandi open their doors and climb in, interrupting us,

"Please take us home, Zandi," Kenyon says, and the vintage Jaguar pulls away from the curb in silence. The quiet nature of the cars in Elysia surprises me again. "Man, it's crazy how quiet this car is. It's going to take me some time to get used to how different everything is here—"

———

My thoughts are stolen from me as my entire body is suddenly stiff, wracked with tension. My jaw feels locked in place.

My vision goes white, and I'm not even all that surprised, though this feels different, more forceful. I expect to see some ancestors materialize. But no ghostly figures swirl into view today because it's Phaedra. Of course it is.

We're standing face to face, neither of us saying a word, until finally I break the silence.

"What do you want from me?"

"Everything. But for now, I'd settle for you minding your business."

"You've got to be kidding me! After all this, you want me to mind my business. How 'bout you leave me alone, and I'll never bother you again!"

"Insolent! Is this how Addi raised you?"

"Your outrage is wasted on me. I know everything. I saw your fight with Kenyon's mother. I saw how you left her to die."

I know I should be scared. I mean, she's pulled me into Onirique in the middle of the day. But I'm too angry to care right now.

"She was destined to die. That should be painfully obvious to even you."

"Why did you pull me into Onirique? And how, for that matter?"

"Because I can—" she replies, smug satisfaction coloring her words. Before I can say or do anything, the spell is broken.

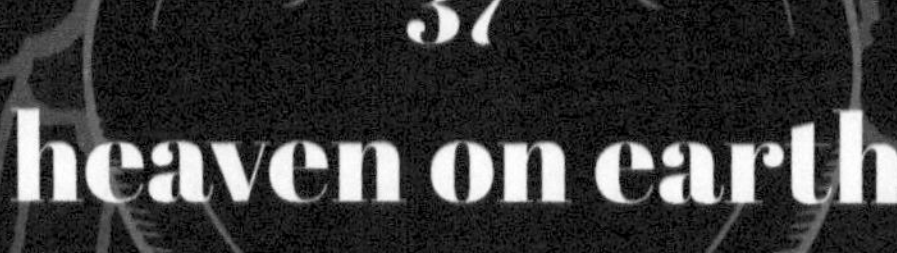

37

heaven on earth

Ember

"Ember! Ember! Are you all right?" The panicked voices of Whit and Kenyon filter their way through the receding mist, clearing my senses.

"It was Phaedra. She pulled me into Onirique. It's a threat to show me she can do whatever she wants to me, whenever." My head feels foggy, like my brain is shrouded in some remaining mist from Onirique.

Let's get you home. I intend to cast new protective spells and wards," Kenyon says.

"I'll help!" Whit chimes in.

Once we get home, I realize I won't do anything but get in their way. I'm super tired so I decide to nap. I'm not into napping normally, but it's been a day full of extra.

The chanting fades quickly, but I try to hold onto the sounds, listening for specific words, anything I can take away from this, but it's all too elusive. The words and accompanying haze of white fade, taking with it all memory of Onirique. It's replaced by a hand at my waist, gently shaking me awake.

"Ember, wake up. You fell asleep while Whit and I were weaving wards and protection spells on the house and grounds."

I arch my back and rub my eyes. "What time is it? How long have I been sleeping?" I feel disoriented. I'm not a good napper. I never feel quite right after I wake up.

"It's been a couple of hours; it's about 4:00." He leans over, his lips brushing mine, teasing out the moment until I wrap my arms around him, deepening into a full kiss. I breathe in his scent, taking in as much of him as possible. Pulling him in closer, a low sigh escapes as I bite his lip.

His arms wrap tighter around my waist, pulling me toward him into a sitting position. "As I was about to say, all the wards and protections are in place. There are not many who could break them."

"I really appreciate all that you have done to protect me. But, she'll find a way," I reply, not really wanting to talk about wards or charms or Phaedra, for that matter. My eyes linger on his mouth, craving another kiss.

Instead, I ask, "So, what's the plan for tonight?"

"Well, Zandi reminded me I accepted an invitation to a friend's art exhibition this evening. But in light of everything, I think I should stay with you here, where I know you're safe."

He says it all like it's no big deal, but there's hesitation in how he says it. So, I push him, trying to wrangle a bit more information out of him.

"I don't want you to give up your plans and be stuck here, protecting me, giving up your social life. What I wouldn't give to have one! You should go. Whit will stay with me. I'm sure he has some magical chops left."

"I have no intention of leaving you anywhere."

"Maybe I could go with you instead of hanging out here. I mean, do you really think she's going to show up at some art show and nab me in front of a bunch of people? We'll probably be safer around a bunch of people."

"It is an important opening, but I don't know. Seems risky." He's torn, weighing the pros and cons, so I push on.

"It would be a great opportunity for me to meet some of your friends and artists, and I'm sure there'll be some bougie scene-makers as well. Plus, I'm desperate to do something normal in this place."

"How do you know there'll be bougie scene makers there?"

"Aren't there always bougie scene makers at art galleries?"

Kenyon thinks for a moment, then his face changes, a smile flickering across his eyes. "You're not wrong. A lot of my friends will be there, too. And I did promise I'd attend. So, you'd better figure out what you want to wear."

"Really?!" You're sure you want me to meet all your friends, considering—"

"Ember, don't get weird about it. It's no big deal, and I don't care about any of that stuff. I especially don't care what anybody thinks of you or me, for that matter. I've lived under the shadow of my bereft father for as long as I can remember. I've learned how to steel myself against gossip."

"Then I'd love to go!"

"Perfect."

"Where is Whit anyway?"

"He went to speak with his brother, saying he needs to get his affairs in order and something about doing more to protect you."

My stomach drops and my breath quickens as I realize this is our first time alone. Originally I'd gone to Kenyon's room to curl up in his bed, wanting to be nearer to him. It felt safer somehow than my own room. It's a lovely room, but it feels like all the rooms in all my foster homes: nice but generic, a guest room lacking true personality. Laying in his bed, I can almost feel him, surrounded by the heady scent of the warm, musky amber he wears. Plus, he's like the only person here who hasn't lied to me, so I guess that makes me trust him even more.

His arms still wrapped around my waist, he pulls me closer, lifting one hand to my face, cradling my cheek. The warmth I see in his eyes nearly takes my breath away.

He lightly runs the tips of his fingers down my cheek to my lips. His rough, calloused thumb glides along my bottom lip. There is something so intimate about the way he's touching now. My desire to be closer to him is overwhelming. I want him to kiss me. The anticipation of what's to come is both sweet and tortuous.

"You're so beautiful," he says. But he makes no move to kiss me, instead caressing my lip with his thumb. I do the only thing I can, switching our positions, rolling gently on top of him. I kiss him. Putting my hand on his chest, a shiver runs the length of my body as his arms wrap around my waist again. His warm hands find the hem of my shirt and slip underneath to stroke the small of my back. I shudder, pleasure mingling with the tickling sensation of his fingertips, goosebumps springing to life. I let my legs slide down onto either side of his body. I deepen our kiss, needing more of him. I can't get enough of his touch, his sighs, his smell, the feeling of safety I have when I'm with him.

Finally breaking the kiss, needing more from him, I sit up, cross my hands around my sides, and grab the hem of my shirt, pulling it over my head. My hair lifts with my top and falls again around my face. Shaking my head, I push my hair out of the way. I don't care if he sees my spots. His magical tattoos pulse a little brighter and my spots pulse in time.

I throw my shirt onto the gigantic bed and unbutton his, revealing his bare chest. Sitting halfway up, he pulls the collar at the back of his neck. It slips off over his head, and he wraps his arms around me again, pulling me into a passionate kiss. Before I realize it, I'm on my back. He whispers, "Are you sure you want to do this?" His voice is thick and hesitant.

"I am. I want to be with you. I will not face the possibility of losing everything to Phaedra without knowing what everything is." Looking deeply into his eyes, I try to convey the conviction of my decision. At this, he stands up, pulling me with him. My stomach flips at the sound of his breath catching. Our lips meet again, but this time it's sweet and slow.

His fingers work at his belt, then the button of his pants, and then mine. I flinch slightly as his pants hit the thick wool rug under our feet with a dull thud from his belt.

I had been brave about pulling my top off, but it's an entirely different matter stepping out of my pants. And while I know this is what I want, I'm still self-conscious standing here with him, undressed. I've never been fully exposed with another person. As his hands run the length of my body, my skin tingles with every curve he touches. Every nerve in my body feels more alive than ever before, and my nervousness ebbs away.

He pulls away. "Open your eyes, Ember." He's so self-assured and calm in this. He's not rushed or impatient with me but kind and thoughtful. I look over his perfect body. His tattoos coalesce into a solid shape, traveling from the tops of his hands, up his forearms, and onto his biceps, their ordinarily dim light reflecting brighter. Do they respond to his emotional state as well as work with magic? I could spend hours studying them. They no longer make me uncomfortable. I'm not sure when I stopped caring about my magical marks, but these make me see beauty and possibility instead of shame or embarrassment. As though thinking about the magical markings calls his attention to mine, he looks at my bare chest. The starburst pattern leftover from my initiation in the ancestor's cave pulses under his gaze. "When did you get this? I assume it didn't happen when your forehead markings did."

"It appeared after my Vision in the Temple when I passed out. It has to do with the experience in the Vision. But let's talk about it later. Thinking about all that is kind of a mood killer."

"Of course. It's beautiful. I've never seen this happen from an experience in Onirique." He bends his head and kisses the new marking. It sends my heart soaring, beating faster in response to his intimate contact.

"Well, you know me, keepin' it unique..." Self-depreciation is my only tool to distract from the weirdness I feel about having this marking. I wonder if it's permanent or will return to normal. I'm not sure which I would prefer.

He strokes his hand down my cheek again. "Hey, you ok?"

"Yeah, I'm ok," I answer, looking deeply into his eyes. He's opened himself completely. I can see into him. Or, it's more accurate to say, I can feel into his thoughts and feelings. It feels like that mind-meldy thing, Erindring, but we're not sharing consciousness. We're sharing feelings and sensations. I feel his unspoken feelings for me, as well as my nervousness, but that's not what I want to feel, so I push it aside. Focusing on him, I sense a hollow place where the memories of his mother live, and the sadness surrounding his father. His secrets are bare for me as he stands unguarded and unflinching.

I wrap my arms around his neck and his arms encircle my waist, lifting me off the floor and onto his bed. He's my first. Not knowing what to expect, overheard words of the girls at school echo in my ears about how it hurt and was over quickly. Their words cause me to tense up, my body stiff against his. He feels my hesitation, and stopping, he asks, "What's wrong? Have you changed your mind? It's ok if you have."

"No, I'm just nervous. I've—never done this," I answer, trying to open myself up to him the way he has. Maybe if he can feel my feelings, it'll be easier. I wonder if he can feel the flutter in my stomach or my awkwardness at admitting my inexperience, though I'm sure he was already aware of that. Before I lose my nerve, I push on, saying, "We need protection. I mean, I'm—I'm not on the pill or anything." I stammer, "I—I wasn't really expecting to be in this position anytime soon. I'm not exactly popular at my school..."

"Hey, it's ok, I've got that covered," he says as he reaches into a drawer beside his bed and pulls out a foil packet. "I'm always careful." However, this admission doesn't make me feel better. It makes me wonder about the length and breadth of what always careful means. But I push that away too. It's obvious he's experienced, and I'm glad for that. No awkward fumbling or race to the finish line for us.

He pulls away from me, looking deeply into my eyes for a long moment. Putting his hand on my face to cradle my cheek, his sweet gesture endears him to me further.

"You may not be popular at school, but they don't see you properly. You don't belong to their world. You belong here with me, and now that you're home, everything will change. Welcome home, my love."

Every sense, every cell, every neuron, every impulse flares to life. I feel seen for the very first time, without all of the preconceived assumptions other people put on me. It's everything.

He kisses me again, and my whole body responds. Nothing exists outside of us. Lengthening my neck, my head angles back as his kisses migrate. Honestly, I hadn't expected it to feel so good. My heart feels too big for my chest. My breath comes faster, erratic as he lays kisses over my body. Every touch from him brings a greater response than the previous one. Everything about this feels right. But before I can dwell on those sentiments too long, my mind is lost to thought. My body and breath and him are the only things that exist.

Opening my eyes, my breath catches at the intensity on his face as his mouth moves to mine again. Every inch of our bodies and our magic is drawn together in unison. We move as one until there is only light and heat and us, our spirits bonded to one another.

38
tower of strength

Kenyon

I lean against the wall waiting for her. She takes my breath away. Her hair shines as the light hits her bangs; her red lips stand out in the sun streaming through the window. I hear the rustling of an underskirt that I assume creates the bubble shape of her dress. I assume some kind of magic is at work, making a wide collar stand up above her shoulders with sleeves that end on her forearm. I love this outfit! And I make a mental note to thank Zandi for arranging a perfect wardrobe for my girl. Looking her up and down, I'm delighted to see her wearing her painted boots and long knitted scarf, both of which I'm pretty sure she made. I don't want her to change for this world. It doesn't really deserve her.

I guess I've been staring for too long in silence because she asks, "Is this ok for the thing tonight? Is it too much? I could go change..."

"No! You look amazing. So amazing, in fact, that you left me speechless."

"Oh, in that case, you look amazing, too," she says, a hint of a blush creeping up her neck to her cheeks. "Your suit looks custom-made—oh, duh, of course it is. Feelin' like I'm the smartest over here."

I look down at my long black wool and leather jacket with no collar and fitted pants with a hint of tone-on-tone tartan. A black tee and boots finish it off. Between the two of us, I want Ember to be the main attraction tonight. I'm hoping that if enough people notice her, it'll be harder for Phaedra to make a move against her. So I dressed accordingly—nice enough to be her date but subdued enough to let her shine. Which she would've done anyway.

As we walk through the door, the sight of my black 1956 Alfa Romeo Giulietta Spider convertible waiting for us makes Ember's eyes widen, and I can't help but smirk.

"Wow! This kinda looks like the sports car version of the other car you own. Wait, how many cars do you own, anyway?"

"Just a few. As you know, that old Jaguar belonged to my father, so I don't have the heart to part with it. Plus, it comes in handy for more than two people. I also have an old Mini Cooper I picked up a few years ago and a '56 Ford Thunderbird. Safe to say I like two-seaters, I guess. But this? This car is my baby. I've made a lot of modifications to her." I walk her to the car's passenger side and open the door.

Ember turns and kisses me. "Thank you for tonight. I'm glad it was you, here and now. And I'm super excited to do something normal for a change that doesn't involve *her* or the worry of what she'll do next. In fact, I refuse to think about her anymore this evening." She sits in the car. "So, you have a Mini Cooper? That is *so* rad! What color is it? Will you take me for a drive sometime?"

"It's British Racing Green. And, anything you want, babe, let me know when you want to go." And I mean it. She could have the thing if she asked me for it. All I want to do is make her happy.

Ember hasn't paid much attention to scenery during other car trips we've taken so far, as there is always something to divert her attentions. As we round the corner into the bright lights of the city proper, her breath catches. "This is amazing! All this, the city, the lights, the fact that the stars are somehow still visible." She turns her face from the sky toward me, and the wind whips her hair into her face. Pushing it back, she just stares at me.

"What is it?" I ask.

"You. You're amazing." Before she can say anything more, I turn into the driveway and park the car.

As we walk toward the building, a peal of shrill laughter sets my hackles on edge, and I know that laugh. I hoped to introduce Ember to some of my friends, but apparently, that will have to wait. Her eyes dart over the structure, taking in the flat roof. "Glass Houses..." But it's mumbled under her breath.

"What did you say?" I ask.

"Oh, sorry, it's a saying one of my foster parents, Mrs. Gates, used to say. You know, 'Those who live in glass houses shouldn't throw stones.' Ironically, it's the name of an album that Mr. Gates was super into. They were both pretty hypocritical, though. She was super suspicious that he was cheating on her, but *she* was actually having an affair. It broke up their marriage and sent me to a different foster family. It was actually the second time it happened. Anyway, this building, it's like a glass house. Whatever, It was like eight years ago. And I never liked the album anyway."

She's rambling nervously, babbling, so I try asking her something in hopes of distraction, "How many foster families did you live with?"

She hesitates, "I don't know—a lot. Why? Does it matter?"

Well, that was the wrong thing to say. Sensing her unease, I turn to face her and halt our progress toward the show. Dipping my chin, trying to make eye contact with her as she stares resolutely ahead, I say, "Of course it doesn't. Where you come from and how you got here is no concern to me. The only thing that matters is that you are here now. So please, just be here with me." I'm almost pleading.

"I'm here; what are you talking about?" She asks.

"You're here physically, but something is pulling you away from me. Please do not let your past come between us. For that matter, don't let my past come between us, either. You have me, every part of me. You've conquered me, and I'll be yours as long as you'll have me." And the suspicious look that crosses her face concerns me, but I can do nothing to prevent what I know is coming.

"B—But, there's so much you don't know about—" I cut her off with a kiss, and it's demanding and fierce, like I'm trying to impart everything I can't say to her right now. I know this kiss needs to be brief. We have an audience already.

Reaching for me, she slides her arms in mine, and my stomach jumps. I know it's just nerves, but she's quickly becoming my everything. Bracing myself as I hear the laughter again, I head toward the building with a sense of foreboding I can't shake. We reach the wide poured concrete steps surrounded by meticulous landscaping and tiny, exotic-looking miniature trees. The door opens, and a well-dressed older woman emerges and spots us. Before she can speak to us, though, my ex-girlfriend appears from behind someone she'd been talking to, saying, "Kenyon! I was beginning to think you wouldn't make it to your best friend's event! Everyone will be so happy to see you. And who is your friend?"

"Charlotte St.James, Romulus Amato, this is Ember Wright. She has recently joined us here in Elysia." But before I can tell Ember who Charlotte and Romulus are to me, Lottie cuts me off. "Oh, the new girl the entire city seems to be buzzing about." Spite colors her words. "I was just speaking with Zöe, and she was telling me that—" She pauses, looks at Ember, and says, "What's your name again?"

"It's Ember," She replies curtly.

"Yes, the Ember that was raised by the Ordinaries. How unusual. This must be so overwhelming for you! I'm sure that Kenyon is doing all he can to show you our fair city and a good time," Lottie says, her voice dripping with saccharin. Ember's face flushes crimson at the insinuation.

"That's enough, Lottie!" My reprimand is terse as I tug on Ember's arm and step forward. "Bitterness never suited you," I say over my shoulder, walking away. "Rom, we'll catch up with you later."

"Don't worry, Ember, not everyone here will be awful. Obviously, Lottie and I have a history. She wanted it to last, but we weren't suited or destined. But don't worry, this party will not be littered with all my exes....hopefully." I laugh nervously.

"What was that?" She asks.

"Oh, nothing. But I'm beginning to wonder if this was a mistake," I say, noticing the distressed look on Ember's face.

"No, I'm sure it will be fine. I mean, how many ex-girlfriends can we run into at one time?" She jokes in a manner that I'm sure will provoke fate.

"No, I'm sure it'll be ok," I say, trying to reassure myself as much as her.

Poured concrete walls host the massive mounted canvas art panels greeting us as we enter the building. The canvases are ablaze, featuring violent streaks of paint imbued with magic.

"Kenyon, what is this show about? And who are the artists show-ing?" Ember asks.

I tried to minimize the details of this evening's event at first. I didn't want her to realize what a momentous event this is for my friend. But Lottie let that secret out, and what Romeo has accomplished is worth celebrating. And I'd be a poor excuse of a best friend to miss this show, so I was relieved when Ember fought me on staying home. Now I'm reconsidering the wisdom of introducing Ember to my entire friend and peer group all at once. There is no escaping it now.

"This is my best friend Romulus's disquisition and exhibition for completion of apprenticeship into the Honourable Guild of Arts," I answer.

Awareness lights her face. "Why did you play this off as just some art show when you told me about it earlier? This show seems like a big deal."

"I didn't want to make a big deal about it. Your safety is more important than the opening reception. Romeo is my best friend and would understand my absence," I reply. But this show is a big deal. His art is the most innovative example in the re-emergence of Artomancy. But as she intuitively understands the importance of this showing, I decide to share the details with her.

"Wait—what? Like legit, you call him Romeo? For real?" She asks, stifling a giggle.

"Well, technically, his name is Romulus, but we've all called him Ro, or Rom, or Romeo for years. Sorry, I guess I introduced him by his proper first name earlier." I look at her quizzically, wondering why the use of his nickname strikes her as humorous.

"O Romeo, Romeo, wherefore art thou Romeo?"

Suddenly, I understand that she's quoting literature by the Ordinar-ies. "Well, I guess it's inevitable that the worlds of the Ordinaries and la Magie will sometimes reference one another. But Romeo is a good friend, so please don't laugh at his name." I regret my words almost instantly as I see her face fall with my reprimand. But I soldier on, saying, "The practice of Artomancy had long been forsaken in favor of the more straightforward divinatory arts practiced by those of the Guild of Liminal Space. But Romeo has nearly single-handedly reignited the public's interest in the subject. He's worked for years, and most of his prophecy paintings have manifested into reality in one way or another. You might find a conversation with him quite fascinating at some point.”

“Wow! That’s pretty impressive for someone so young. Being responsible for basically bringing that back from the dead must be a lot to carry.” She pauses, and I wonder if she’s feeling a similar weight at being a dually gifted oracle. It’s rare to inherit more than one of the foresight gifts.

She stands to the side of a painting, noticing the light-imbued aura of color emanating from the canvas for several inches. “This is an incredible technique!” She whispers excitedly to me. “It would never occur to me that magic could be embedded into the paint! I totally want to try it.”

“One more thing I look forward to seeing as you grow into your magic,” I tell her, wrapping her in my arms and kissing her temple. I close my eyes and imagine her potential as she discovers every aspect of her abilities.

“Well, look-a-lookie here,” comes an intruder’s voice from behind. Turning, I’m disheartened to see the biggest busybody I know.

“Ah, Mrs. Cromwell, it’s lovely to see you. Let me introduce you to my girlfriend. This is Ember.” Even as I say the word girlfriend, there’s a fluttering in my chest.

“Oh, dear boy, I’ll admit I’ve had a bit of tête-à-tête about this young woman. She’s become quite the topic of conversation, if I’m honest. So, it’s a pleasure to meet you, Ember. That’s quite an unusual name.”

“It’s actually short for December.”

“I see! That’s so unexpected. I’ve never met anyone with that name.”

“Oh, you know, it’s because of my cold, cold heart.”

A bark of laughter escapes Mrs. Cromwell. “Clever girl.”

“Well, I don’t wish to be rude, but we have a lot of art to view. It was nice to see you, Mrs. Cromwell,” I say, pulling on Ember’s arm. “Ugh, that woman is so dreadful. I hope this isn’t a portent of what the evening will be like,” I say once Ember and I can navigate away.

“Uh, yeah, lemme just track down some scandal-water, so I can enjoy all the gossip going on about me.”

And all I have to do is look questioningly at her, and she explains. "Oh, scandal-water is a euphemism for the tea served at tea parties held for gossiping."

"I see," I reply. "That sounds about right."

"Whew, I thought you might be mad at me for being rude to her," she says, returning to the previous topic, "I'm so used to people bustin' on me for one thing or another that I guess I got defensive."

"No, I have a sinking feeling that you- and now, we-have been a topic of many conversations over the last few days. It's my least favorite thing about my position and family lineage. News travels quickly, and there seems to be no escaping it." I pause. "You know what? Let's just get outta here. I don't want to subject you to any more of this."

"No, I don't want to let these people think they've intimidated me into running away. They haven't got anything new to show me. This is an old hat for me, just like a day at school with bullies, only they have better clothes and magic." She shrugs her shoulders, giving me a lopsided grin.

"It seems like a lot, Ember."

"Trust me, I got this. It's a storm in a teacup, and I know how to snark back if I need to, but I'll try to keep it polite. I just don't want to embarrass you. How would it look if your first outing with your new girlfriend ended so quickly or humiliatingly?"

"Ok, but let me know when you've had enough," I reply, resigning myself to a very long evening ahead of us, knowing that was my last shot at convincing her to leave. Any more attempts, and she'll question why I want to go so bad.

"Can we look at more of the art? I thought it was really cool. The best part of all this, actually. I mean, other than being here with you."

At her sweet words, I wrap my arm around Ember and kiss her temple as we walk toward another section of canvases. "These are more minor works by Romeo. Though ironically, they point to more cataclysmic changes within la Magie. Big things, small packages, I guess."

As we stand taking the art in, Ember inches closer to one piece. It foretells the impending danger of over harvesting the crystals from the cave structures. Damaged and decaying crystals are depicted as fractals, painted at incongruous angles that warn of instability in their matrix. That's the gist of what the placard next to the art says, anyway. Moving closer to read it with her, I fail to notice someone I'd rather avoid, standing behind us.

A delicate voice speaks my name, and I turn to see Emiko Mori. This isn't going to be good. She's no longer dressing in the traditional Shinto garb. Instead, she wears an outfit in the theatrical style of the Harajuku region. Her hair is now white, gathered into messy buns atop either side of her head, with heavy bangs along her forehead. A dress made of layer after layer of white lace paired with her painted white skin gives her a ghostly appearance. And I know Ember is going to love it.

As predicted, when she turns and looks at Emiko, her eyes widen, and I can practically see cartoon hearts in them. So, I do the only thing I can, I introduce them, hoping Emiko isn't holding a grudge.

"Ember Wright, this is Emiko Mori." And I turn to address Emiko, saying, "Hello, Emiko. You look well." It's stilted and awkward, but unfortunately, it's the best I can do here.

"Thank you," she replies stiffly, extending her hand toward Ember, who shakes it, saying, "It's nice to meet you."

"How goes the revolution?" I ask before they can start any kind of conversation.

She gives me a warning look and says, "Our movement toward the more powerful traditional Miko roles progresses well. I'm no longer at the Temple, and we are gaining in numbers. Thank you for asking."

"Glad to hear it." I'm still fumbling, our awkward but amicable breakup standing between us like another person. I'm grateful when Ember interjects, "I could not be more into your outfit! You look awesome."

"Thank you," Emiko replies starkly.

"I wasn't aware that you and Romeo remained in contact after—" I don't finish that sentence, though. Where I leave off, hoping to avoid the subject I accidentally broached, she doesn't hesitate.

"After you and I broke up? Yes, occasionally we did. Our practice of metempirical trances is not dissimilar to Romeo's Artomancy practice. I'm intrigued to see the outcome of his years of work." She looks around. "Well, I'm off to find Romeo and speak with him. Sayōnara."

Before she's even said Sayōnara, I feel Ember's eyes on me, appraising and doubtful.

"It seems like you're having kind of a rough night. I know I wouldn't want to run into a bunch of ex-girlfriends when I'm out with my new girlfriend who doesn't know I've dated a ton of girls before her." She says it all in that single-sentence way that tells me she's half-joking and half reprimanding me. And to be fair, I suppose I deserve it.

I cannot hide the sheepish look on my face. Thankfully, she resumes our previous conversation. "Let's move on to a new section. Romeo is quite talented. Even beyond the Artomancy business."

As we round the corner into a sculpture gallery, I see the one person I was really hoping to avoid. She walks right into us.

"Oh, for the love of the Nine Worlds!" I quietly curse under my breath, but I attract Ember's attention, so she's blindsided as Miranda says, "Well, well, well! If it isn't my no-show date and the girl he stood me up for!" Spite turns her delicate features hard. She looks between us, her vibrant orange curls a ring of flames around her face.

"I'd watch out for this one, sweetheart. He has the attention span of a gnat."

"Enough, Miranda! I didn't purposely miss our date; there was a life-and-death emergency with an old family friend."

"Oh, I know all about the 'emergency,' but tell me, Kenyon, did your 'emergency' take you three days to sort out?" She makes air quotes every time she says the word, and it almost makes me glad that I missed our date.

"Or perhaps you lost your Oculus device and couldn't contact me in all the 'emergency-ness?'" She rolls her eyes. I open my mouth to respond. "You know what? Never mind. I don't even care enough to listen to your excuses. I was only ever looking for a good time, anyway. And the entire city knows you're just the man for the job..." She turns on her heels after dropping her emotional napalm bomb. I know the words hit their target as I look at Ember and see a litany of shock, disgust, and irritation cross her face.

<h1 style="text-align:center">39
atmosphere</h1>

Ember

Moving in slow motion to face him, I want to demand answers. He literally said this wouldn't be a party full of his ex-girlfriends, but that seems to be exactly the case. He looks like he's bracing himself for what's to come. But, as I stand here, trying to think of what to say, a hypnotic voice calls me, beckoning me to go to the next room. Looking back at him, I just shake my head and walk away. Honestly, it's the only thing I can do at the moment.

Entering the side room, I'm grateful the lights are dim. I hear a band playing but can't see them through the people standing and swaying or dancing. I need to get lost in the crowd for a while, maybe even dance, too. I move toward a far corner of the room and sit on a slatted wood bench. The music is a litany of new wave songs from the early '80s. Staring at my cuticles as I mercilessly tear them, I realize it's ridiculous that I'm upset with him, and I'm taking it out on my own fingers. I should really wear gloves or something. Before I can stop myself, I feel a sharp pain in my finger. "Ouch! Oh great." There's a drop of blood standing at the edge of my cuticle. Maybe my ancestors can pull me into Onirique again. "That would make tonight complete..." But this time, I wipe my finger on my leg, pushing it into the spot hard to prevent any more bleeding. No way am I letting my blood out of my sight.

Before I realize what's happening, Kenyon sits down next to me. "I'm so sorry, my Luv!"

"Don't call me that," I retort. "How many of your other girlfriends do you also call Luv?"

"None, because none of them are or have ever been my girlfriends," he says with complete sincerity. "Perhaps I should've told you about my history before—before we were together, but it changes nothing. At least not for me."

"Perhaps? Perhaps?! Yes, perhaps you should have. I mean, you literally stood up another girl on the day you gave me the watch. I mean, obviously, I'm glad you did because otherwise, Whit would be dead. But still, this feels like a lie of omission."

"And when should I have told you, Ember? When we got to the Temple, or maybe when we were about to bear witness before the Convocation of Esteemed Elders? We haven't had much free time, have we?" He's gotten defensive. Not only is this the wrong time and place for an argument, but I'm also not in a position to judge him, what with my evil incarnate mother trying to get me and my lying liar father.

My shortcomings don't excuse his, so I forge onward rather than let any of those facts stop me. "Oh, I dunno, perhaps before you slept with me?"

"Were you under the impression I was inexperienced?" A sarcastic undertone colors his words. "Either we can accept and love one another, flaws and all. Or I feel like we need to give each other detailed accounts of every conceivable upsetting thing we'd done. I know which I'd rather do, but the choice is yours." His voice has softened, and the hard glint in his eyes only moments ago is gone.

His use of the word love surprises me. I mean, I know I'm crazy about him, and I felt the depth of his emotions while we were together. I guess I just don't trust that his feelings can endure. It's all too fast, too soon, even though I want them to be true. But I let it go, knowing this conversation is not finished.

When Kenyon wraps a tentative arm around my shoulder and guides me to stand, he hugs me. Even though I haven't really responded to the ridiculous all-or-nothing scenario he suggested, he doesn't seem ready to push me. I'm still out of sorts with all of tonight's revelations, but in reality, his offenses are minor compared to all the other betrayers in my life. I'll let it slide for now.

Kenyon steers me deeper into the open expanse of the room. A near-perfect rendition of "Time (A Clock of the Heart)" by Culture Club is sung by the most mesmerizing contralto voice I've ever heard, matched only by the singer's seductive movements. Golden brown arms move through the air in patterns while their hands glide and turn, twisting an invisible ribbon. Long narrow dreadlocks sway in time with the movements of their hips while their face remains skyward. Honestly, I cannot discern if it's a man or woman singing–until, that is, my eyes lock onto a very familiar pair of knee-high Doc Martens. Masculine plaid pants hang low on her hips, rolled at the calf, revealing the silhouette image of the Three of Swords I painted on the back. She turns with fluid grace, revealing a button-down shirt, a waist-hugging vest and necktie that complete her getup. My best friend Nico is singing with this band. I knew she could sing but didn't know she was a total badass about it.

She doesn't see me. Her attention seems focused on Romeo, whose rapt attention she also commands. His kohl-rimmed dark eyes are locked with hers as he brushes near-black hair from his face. His olive skin is warm against his gray shirt. But that's when I finally notice he's wearing some kind of skirt and pant combo unlike anything I've ever seen. And in the dim light, I spy glints of light reflected in the glittering gold nail polish he's wearing. I wonder if he's imbued it with magic, like his paintings.

Finally, when Nico looks away from Romeo, our eyes connect, and her eyes widen in surprise. As the song they're playing ends, they launch into "Promises Promises" by Naked Eyes.

"Geez, I know Romeo loves New Wave music, but did he tell her that's all she's allowed to sing this evening?" Kenyon quips, startling me out of my surprise at seeing her. Now I understand. They know one another, and well.

"I know. I was kinda wondering about that. I didn't think she was that into it. Whenever we hang out, she's usually listening to old Blues records," I reply, trying to play it cool til I can figure out their relationship. It would crush me to find out they, too, had once been a thing.

"Oh no, it's Romeo, it's his party, so they're playing what he wants.

But, it seems like she's really tryin' work something out up there, though." I see him scanning the crowd until his eyes land on Romeo.

"Wait—what?" I ask. "What's going on with her, and how do you know?" I ask, blowing my momentary cool.

"Nico is a Novitiate in the Vala, but she's only doing it to satisfy her parents. They were friends with my parents before my mother died, and we grew up together. She's never been that committed to her gift and add to that, she and Romeo have been in the Worst-Kept-Secret relationship for years. Apparently, they're going through something, though."

"Again, wait—what? How well do you know Nico?" I ask more pointedly, looking between the two of them.

"As I mentioned, our families know one another. She's like a sister to me."

"So why didn't Whit recognize Nico? I mean, she's been my best friend for a few years. And while he did say there was something familiar, he never seemed to figure it out."

"Well, as far as I know or have deduced, my father and I are the only people he really kept ties with. Plus, Nico is a year or two younger than me. My mother was gone before she was born. But her parents remained friends with my father. They often included us in family gatherings and holidays since it was just my dad and me. It was really my only glimpse of what a normal family must be like."

"Well, there's something we have in common," I mumble under my breath as I look between Nico and Romeo. Everything from the expressions on their faces to their tight body language expresses their turmoil.

When the song ends, Nico says, "Thank you, we'll return after a short break." And she walks away. I have the urge to follow her and confront her. While privacy might be hard to find in the middle of a party, it's better than at the Temple. I excuse myself to pursue her, but as I see her, I notice she's already engaged in a heated discussion with a woman that looks just like her. Obviously, they're sisters. A small gasp escapes my lips. "Twins?"

The realization that I know next to nothing about this person who's been my best friend for years feels like the perfect addition of suck to this sucky night. Has she told me anything that is actually true?

Before I can decide my next move, she turns abruptly from the girl, her head downcast, and walks right into me. Looking up, she blinks her surprise. "Look, I know you've got a right to have beef with me too, but I can't take another person telling me how I've failed them right now. Can you just be my friend for a minute before you yell at me? I've got the morbs." Her voice sounds small and quiet, and the unshed tears in her eyes remind me that she's always been there for me. Plus, using our Victorian slang, "Got the Morbs," is like a direct line into my heart. My grievances can wait.

Wrapping my arm through hers, I walk us toward an empty corner of the room. "Why so glum, chum?"

"It's too complicated to get into at the moment with all the ins and outs and politics of this world, but no matter what I do, I'm going to disappoint or anger someone I love. My mom's ready to throw down 'cuz I'm not joining the Vala. My sister's gonna slay me over her latest complaint. And I feel completely lost. I mean, I have been living a double life, or maybe a triple life..."

"Wow, that's a sucky place to be," I respond, trying not to invest too much into things I don't know anything about and can't fix.

"You got that right." She says as she wraps her arms around me in a hug. I hadn't been expecting it, and it takes me a second to respond in kind, but I do.

"Thank you for just being my friend. I know I don't deserve your compassion or understanding, but I appreciate it." She steps back.

"Is this about Romeo?" I ask. I work to stifle my giggle at the name.

"I know, I know," she says. "People in this world either aren't very aware of the literature of the Ordinaries or don't care. But beyond that, what do you know about him?" she eyes me suspiciously.

"Oh, Kenyon introduced me to him when we first got here. I know he's Kenyon's BFF and about the whole artomancy thing. But that's about it. I also got to meet Lottie as well." The corners of her mouth turn down at my mention of Kenyon. "What, what is it?"

"I feel like I'm in enough hot water with you, so dissin' Kenyon is not on my to-do list. But—how many of the girls here tonight have you met?"

"Enough to know that Kenyon has a lot of exes."

"Exactly. It worries me that he's latched on to you."

"What do you mean?" I know it's wrong to play stupid, but anything she can tell me might help me figure out what to do.

"Well, he was with you at the Temple, and word 'round the campfire is that you and Whit are staying with him. And it's just—he is definitely charming and dates a lot. I don't want to see you get hurt."

"You mean any more hurt than I've already been?" I retort. "Sorry. I didn't mean for that to be such an accusation. But now that we've come to it, what the what, Nico? You've known this entire time about everything, and you've let me flounder around when you could've let me in on the secret. I mean, is anything you've ever said true? Do you even like me? Or was I just an assignment? A mission?" I can't keep the hurt from creeping into my voice.

"I'm in my last year as a Novitiate with the Priory, and Sister Lisoń sent me to keep watch over you. So in the beginning, yes, it was an assignment. But you are my best friend, and it has been killing me to lie to you all this time. I love you, Ember. Please forgive me," she says with complete sincerity. I can't help but feel for her. Everybody else who has deceived me did so by choice. She didn't.

"I forgive you," I say. Her face reacts in surprise at my declaration. "I'm kinda surprised myself, but I need a friend here, and you've been my best friend for too long to give that up."

"So what are you going to do now that you're here?" she asks.

"Well, that's the million-dollar question, isn't it?" I answer her question with my own. "I mean, apparently my long-lost, not-so-dead mother is out to get me, and Whit is now Addi and oh, in love with one of the Draíodóir. I don't know what Whit's, I mean Addi's, plans are, and honestly, I don't think I'd be comfortable with him now anyway. Obviously, I can't stay at Kenyon's hous—"

"Ember, my plans haven't changed. I'm getting an apartment and still want you to be my roommate."

"What—really?"

"I mean, the apartment will be here in Elysia, not in les Dormeur. Everything else is pretty much the same as before. You're my best friend, and I need you in my life. There's a lot I have to tell you."

"Um, there's a lot I have to tell you, too. Particularly about Kenyon," I reply.

Before I can get into it, Kenyon decides it's time to join us. The hand he puts at the small of my back feels possessive. As much as I like being touched by him, it makes me bristle. It's a bit too possessive and Alpha-Male for me, especially for someone with such a long dating history. Maybe it wouldn't feel so questionable if I weren't so keenly aware of all his former flames and flings. So I take a small step forward, because no matter how strong the connection I feel, there's no guarantee that it isn't fleeting for him. I've had too many rugs pulled out from under me already.

"Listen, I've been thinking about taking a trip down to Acadia and New Orleans that my Gradmère is encouraging me to take for—reasons. Would you consider coming with me? It would be a chance to get to know each for real…"

"Really?" I ask, unable to hide my excitement about this idea.

"Of course!"

"Then yes!"

"Alright, talk later. I've gotta get back for the rest of our set. More bitter love songs to sing." The laugh she lets out and her melancholy look hint at the hurt she's trying to mask as self-deprecation.

As soon as she returns to the stage, the mood changes as the band launches into a rousing version of "Change of Heart" by Cyndi Lauper. I'm amazed as I watch her belting out lyrics, and she's feeling every bit of them.

Kenyon's breath tickles my ears as he leans in. To my great surprise, he's quietly singing along with the chorus. Returning my attention to Kenyon, I step away and face him. "Remember when you said this wasn't going to be a party of ex-girlfriends?" I can't hide the edge in my sarcastic tone.

A mix of emotions crosses Kenyon's face: hurt, embarrassment, and maybe even shame. "About that—" But he's cut off as slender fingers with perfectly manicured long fingernails curve over the edge of his shoulder. Kenyon turns abruptly to face Lottie. Because of course it's her. Raven hair hangs heavily down her back. Icy blue eyes focus solely on Kenyon, her tall willowy frame complimenting Kenyon's lean muscular body, making me feel too short and too curvy. My short fingernails, chipped nail polish and bleeding cuticles starkly contrast hers, an annoying metaphor for all our differences.

The music changes again, eerie and alien tones of a Moog keyboard breaking the momentary silence. Nico sings Tubeway Army's "Me, I Disconnect from You." The shift in energy in the room sets my nerves on edge, the atmosphere is suddenly charged, and I decide it might be time to go. But the knockout babe, Lottie St. James, seems to think otherwise.

"I'm going to use the ladies and give you some space to get this handled. If that's what you want." I point between the two of them before walking away.

I hear Lottie say to Kenyon, "Come with me for a minute, Kenyon. I'd like to speak to you about something privately." She tugs his arm, pulling him to a vacant corner.

"I can't imagine what you need to talk to me about." His voice is hard and dismissive. "I think our ending—" But that's the extent of what I hear as I walk away. And I'm more confused than ever. Her resurgence into my night brings all my hurt feelings and questions screaming back to life. He seemed so into me, not Lord Casanova McQuiston of the Court of Libertines and Heartbreakers with a little black book that rivals the regular phone book. Not sure I'd have been so anxious to get horizontal with him if I'd known.

"Whatever!" The word comes out as I shake my head at my ridiculousness and decide to go ahead and get over it. Nothing I can do about it now; besides, this may not be as bad as it seems.

Walking out of the bathroom, I can't find Kenyon until I do, across the room, sequestered away with Lottie, her hand lightly placed on his forearm. My jaw is rigid, teeth grinding, lips pressed in a hard line. Lottie leans in and presses her lips against Kenyon's.

"So much for declarations of devotion!" I mutter under my breath, turning away. "I can't even deal with this right now! I'm sure it's all her; she's obviously still into him. But, I just can't deal with her again..." I mean, I do want to run and punch Lottie in her too-pretty face. Instead, I walk to an open door I spied at the side of the building, deciding I could use a moment alone to cool off, my anger at Lottie roiling.

Stepping outside, the cool late May air surrounds me, causing little goosebumps on my forearms. My eyes wander up to the sky, and my breath catches in my chest. The stars blaze above me. Never have I seen them shine so brightly. Though there is no visible moon, I can't stand the dark moon phase. The sky feels so lonely.

Without warning, the hair on the back of my neck stands up. My skin tingles in apprehension. Squinting my eyes and looking into the area in front of me, a motion at the edge of my vision catches my attention. My head turns in that direction. Another movement in the opposite direction, and my head whips around again. It feels like all the blood in my head is ebbing away. My mouth is dry.

"Well, this is dumb; just go inside and find Kenyon. Staying out here alone is like hanging a neon sign over my head, asking to be a victim. Don't be the dumb girl in the horror movie who stays to investigate the danger," I reprimand myself.

Turning on my heel to go back inside, my breath catches in my throat. Suddenly, my lungs feel like they're shutting down. My hands fly to my throat, and my mouth opens and closes, trying to scream or even breathe, but nothing happens. I try to take another step forward to knock on the door, or to do anything. But the hands gripping my neck from behind won't allow me to move. I try throwing my legs at the slider, but my body is yanked backward instead. A hand snakes around my face, and I smell something sweet. I struggle harder to escape, but it's no good; dark spots speckle my receding vision, narrowing to a small tunnel until everything is black.

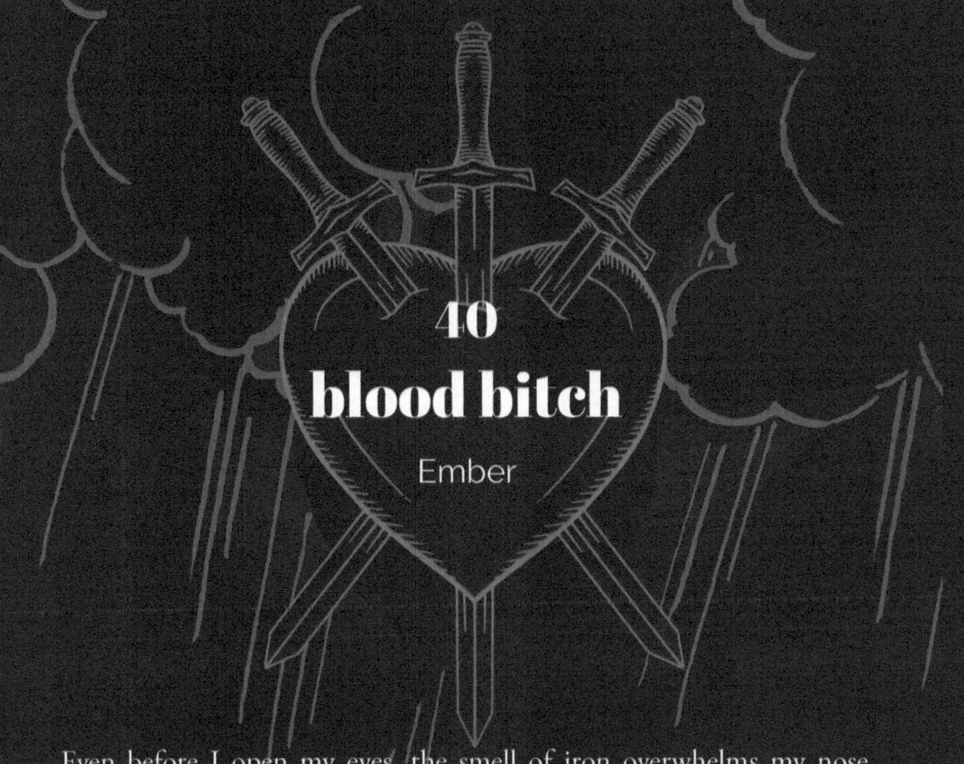

40
blood bitch

Ember

Even before I open my eyes, the smell of iron overwhelms my nose, accompanied by a beautiful soprano voice that cuts through my brain fog. The melody is melancholy and forlorn, resonating and reverberating, telling me that I'm not where I'm supposed to be. I shift my hands at the pinching pain at my wrists and ankles. I'm rewarded with the sting of scratchy rope fibers burrowing into my skin. I breathe deeply, my stomach twisting painfully with a wave of nausea. Everything feels so wrong. Slowly, I open my eyes to eerie darkness. As my blurred vision clears, I focus on small areas illuminated by lanterns or torches. They cause the dim light to refract as far as I can see. And finally, I see it, the wrongness. I recoil, repulsed by the gelatinous blood encircling the space to create a summoning circle around me and Phaedra. There's not a single doubt that it's her blood. Am I lying on a bed of nails? A thousand points of sharp stab my entire back. Her voice swells and washes over me. It really is beautiful, even with its edge of menace.

The cadence of the melody changes, somehow demanding more, carrying and filling the space, reverberating in supernatural ways. The voice singing the melody is familiar, like something I've heard in my dreams or a ghost from another life.

Narrowing my eyes, I try to make out what the sharp lines belong to, but my vision is still too blurry, the low light yielding only shapes. Looking down, I notice that I'm lying on what must be hundreds of tiny pointy crystals. Ah, I guess that means we're in the Crystal Cave Whit told me about. I try again to wiggle my hands, hoping to gain enough leverage to free one, but it's no use. The rough rope rips into my skin again, and I wonder bleakly how long before I bleed. My heart races as my breath becomes ragged, a thin sheen of sweat on my face.

I shiver as the song stretches into a higher range, no longer soprano, more like a whistle. As the sound escalates, I cannot take it anymore. I want to cover my ears, to escape the sound and give my senses a break, but I can't move. This whole wrist-tied-up thing is getting pretty old.

Finally, the voice stops, and Phaedra, nearly glowing in the dark, turns to face me. Within seconds her breath is on my face, hot and foul-smelling. I recoil, but undeterred, Phaedra moves closer. "Good, I'm glad you're awake. I want to give you one last chance to join me. We could have everything. There is so much I can teach you. Don't be stupid." Bits of spittle punctuate her words, landing on my cheeks.

"Of course it's you. It's always you. It was stupid to think I could just have a nice time with my boyfriend without you fuc—"

"How dare you speak to me like that!"

"Why is everyone always so damn worried about my language? Never mind that we're surrounded by your blood and you're going to try to steal my powers again. We should definitely worry about the swearing!"

"Well, you could at least try to be respectful in the presence of your mother! Please consider the wisdom of joining me. Give me access to your gifts, and I promise it will be painless. All you have to do is open your mind and let my consciousness merge with yours. I'll hear the echo of your True Name, and then I'll take just a small portion of your gifts. You won't even know they're gone. After all, you've never really had access to them anyway. We could be a team. I love you and don't want to do this, but you are forcing me to take what I need." Her tone is plead-ing, her words rushing with her request.

I scoff at her declaration of love. "Why is it so important that you have my gifts, anyway? You seem powerful enough to do anything you want. Why does this one thing matter so much to you?" My heart pounds in my ears.

The anger I see in her eyes builds as she swiftly raises her hand and slaps me across the face.

"I don't need to explain myself to you! I'm your mother. You should be willing to share your gifts with me. After all, I gave them to you, and I can take them back."

I lay still, stunned by the sting on my cheek, yet compelled to respond. "You are not my mother! You have no right to discipline me or even touch me! You may have given birth to me, but you're no mother."

Ignoring my retort, Phaedra continues as though nothing happened, standing tall. "I am powerful, but the gift, the Völuspa, has eluded me. In any real and substantive way, that is. The Fates played a cruel joke. My real mother was a gifted seeress, and I've created daughters with powerful gifts as well. Clearly, the Fates passed my power to you and that ungrateful excuse of a daughter I gave life before you! So, let me be clear. I. Will. Have. My. Gift. Back!"

"Wait! What?! I have a sister?" I gasp, interrupting her.

Again, she ignores me. "I've been forced to rely upon the draíochta of my underlings to continue at the level I need as Prioress. I must have that power back again! I cannot go on, borrowing the Sight like a beggar. And I refuse to use Amplicon anymore, harvested or synthetic. I need my draíochta intact." Her words are urgent, her voice determined.

"Yeah, Whit–I mean Addi–told me all about Amplicon, said it burns away the mitochondrial DNA's ability to manifest magic. Tell me, Phaedra, how much of your magic have you sacrificed to get you where you are? Was it worth it?" In my anger, I can't stop myself from taunting her. "You know, after our meeting, I found the room where you tried to steal my magic. It made me puke."

"What a vulgar child you are. If you join me, that will need to change." Her words are so calm, so matter of fact, like my life isn't hanging in the balance.

"It made me so sick that I ran and ended up on the docks, where some Ratbag tried to overpower me to do that little magic trick where you steal the powers of another. And you know what? You are no different than that Todger. No better than a thief."

"Again, I tell you, if you willingly share your gifts, I'll leave you enough, but if you force me to take them, I will have all of them. But I will have them, one way or another. The choice is yours. What you lose in draíochta, you will more than gain with what I can teach you. You have no idea how powerful I am in this community."

"Wow, it's like I'm not even speaking. I mean, can you even hear me? While I might not lose too much of my magic, I would lose one hundred percent of my soul. The price is too high."

I'm so dizzy. If I weren't lying down, I would fall down. "And as far as your powerful connections go, I know you mean Rémy? I'm aware of your connections."

The idea of sharing my consciousness with Phaedra, letting her into my mind, sharing myself, my memories, or the initiation in the ancestral cave, makes my stomach roil. Plus, the bond I share with Kenyon and the sweetness growing between us is definitely not something she needs to know about. "I will never give you any part of me or my magic!"

"So be it!" she retorts angrily, grabbing my wrist and pulling a ceremonial-looking dagger from a thigh holster. A sharp pain lances through my thumb as she cuts me. She squeezes the cut and blood trickles over my fingers and onto the floor. I roll over and see it travel the short distance to join her blood in the summoning circle. When my blood reaches hers, a luminescent pulse shoots through in a glittering show of magical energy. I'm connected to her circle.

"Why did you do that?" I demand.

"The merging of our blood will facilitate the merging of our draíochta that is to come."

"So, that's it? You're just gonna steal my gifts?"

"I gave you the chance, but you refused. Choices have consequences, sweetheart. You're about to get yours."

Without another word or second thought, she moves away from me and circles the room again. Her voice fills the space, echoing as it reverberates off the thousands of crystals in the cave. She raises her hands. The crystals begin to glow as she sings to them, her light and magic merging together.

A low hum comes from the crystals, ambient noise growing. Everywhere I look, crystals of every shape and size emerge from the floor, the walls, the ceiling. The pain in my back throbs with their movement. Not all crystals vibrate, though. I know they are not on her side yet.

With the smaller ones visibly vibrating, their neighbors begin to vibrate in sympathetic resonance. Singing louder with every step, Phaedra paces the cave, finally sparking the larger Lemurian Seed crystals to life, activating them to a higher level of attention. My memory plays a sound bite of Whit telling me they are the Keepers of Memory. They contain magical knowledge, imbued with the awareness of generations, creating an ambient intelligence. I feel their intelligence awakening. I just hope they know the difference between right and wrong, or at the very least that they won't succumb to Phaedra's entrainment.

Their energy thrums in my body like a second pulse of blood rushing through my heart.

Thump-thump, thump-thump. Thump-thump, thump-thump.

Each Lemurian Seed crystal now vibrates and sings with Phaedra. Tiny sparks of electricity dance at the tops of the larger crystals. Power surging, they amplify energy as they make it. Sparks spread like lightning strikes from one crystal to another. But it seems like the energy isn't stable as it surges and contracts beyond her control. As their powers multiply, they awaken my own. My untapped magic courses through my nerves and veins, pulling in time with my blood. A sunburst of light blazes to life on my chest.

Phaedra turns suddenly to face me. "Good, I feel your magic awakening." Then her eyes travel to my chest. "Ohh, what's this? How did you come to have a magical mark over your heart? What an intriguing development. Alas, I'll have to live with the disappointment of not knowing how you got that, because it's almost time. If you open yourself to me, it will hurt less."

Phaedra resumes her song and her voice changes. All sweetness in her melody disappears as it turns into something else, creating chaos within the vibrations. The crystals' tone and pitch lose their coherence. They sound in notes that disagree so completely that it sets my teeth on edge. They clang louder and louder, filling the echoing space and projecting dissonance at me. The jarring sounds make my muscles twitch. I can't tune them out.

She pulls something from an unseen pocket and blows on her palm. Then I see it: she's got a bobleverden encasing her. I can't hear her anymore, but the crystals continue to sing on their own.

Some of the tones drop off and I begin to ache. I don't know if it's tone or frequency or pitch, but whatever it is, I can't hear it anymore.

More sounds deepen. Finally, they disappear too. Eardrums throbbing, skin prickling, my senses are alight with the sensation. Tightness constricts my brain, aching as my body curls into a ball, trying to protect itself. I taste bile. My vision blurs and I feel dizzy all over again. Beads of sweat pop up on my forehead and trickle down my temples. And it's only been a few seconds.

I try to figure out how to save myself, but my brain can't function. It's like walking through water, thick and distorted. It feels like I'm being ripped apart as the prickling sensation deepens, energy seeping in and attacking me. But energy surges through my chest. My energy. I look down to see tiny fissures of light, like cracks in a sun-baked desert, illuminating my sweaty skin. It's my magic, my draíochta shining from within.

My magic, now fully awakened, rises to meet the energy and vibrations of the crystals. I look over at Phaedra. How can she be perfectly fine watching as my body is literally coming apart?

As the light escaping my body brightens, tiny fissures widen into larger cracks, pain rising, noise rising, light rising.

Suddenly, it's gone. I might be dead, but I can't be sure.

———

This place is unnervingly familiar. I mean, I've been here several times in the last few days. But this time, I'm also acutely aware of still being in my body as well as Onirique. I feel the pain as an echo, yet watch it with the eyes of an observer, seeing the scene through both my own eyes and from above my body. Turning my head left, then right, nobody's here with me, but echoed words from a previous meeting ring in my ears.

Just as before, voices reverberate, questions and answers at once. But I can tell it's not the Grandmothers this time. As I look into the whiteness, a shape takes form, and I stand before a lone woman. She stands with enormous wings spread. She is no angel, and not Grandmothers, Ancestors, or Disir. This woman is a warrior, toned and muscled, wearing a golden chest plate. Her armor gleams dully, and everything else she wears looks like scraps of leather sewn together into makeshift clothes. A thick braid of white blonde hair cascades over her shoulder, intertwined with bits of bone and sharp quills. Painted black runes cover her brow bone, artful and fierce, transitioning into a thick band of black that engulfs her eyes and upper cheekbones. Brutal and beautiful, I'm pretty sure she's a Valkyrie.

She silently takes me in, and I think she's examining my soul. I feel when she's made her decision because her attention is drawn to the ghost-like figures slowly taking form.

Disembodied voices speak to one another, one question replaced by another.

"Will she fight for what's hers?" One voice asks

"Is she strong enough?" Another asks in return.

"Can she see her light?" A voice demands, only to be answered with another question.

"Or does she only see the cracks?"

"Is her heart that of a warrior?"

Then, in one voice: "What is your choice?"

"Do I have one?" I whisper.

"Relent and relinquish your gifts; we will take you away. You will feel no pain." The words echo, hanging in the empty space.

"Or fight."

"How would I even begin to fight? I don't know how to use my magic!"

"To understand this moment without the trappings of future or past is powerful. Within the span of a breath, you may harness the ability to change your fate..." Verdandi's words echo back to me. I'm unsure if it's from my memory or the Valkyries are speaking to me, but it doesn't matter.

"The choice is yours. Come with us or claim your gifts with everything you are, every part of you. Your skill, your heart, your fight!" The Valkyrie says after Verdandi's words fade away.

"Like it's that easy. You know, live in the moment, don't be afraid and claim my gifts, and fight. What could be simpler?"

"It will not be easy." Her tone is harsh as she looks into my soul, evaluating me.

For the briefest moment, I think about how easy it would be to stay here to let the Valkyries take me away, to avoid the pain invading my body. But fast on the heels of that Sight come images of Kenyon and Whit and everybody else for that matter, who might suffer at the hands of Phaedra with heightened powers. My choice is clear. I might die trying, but if I stay here, I'll definitely die, and I'm not ready to give up.

"I'll fight for wh—..." But before I can even finish my sentence, Onirique is gone.

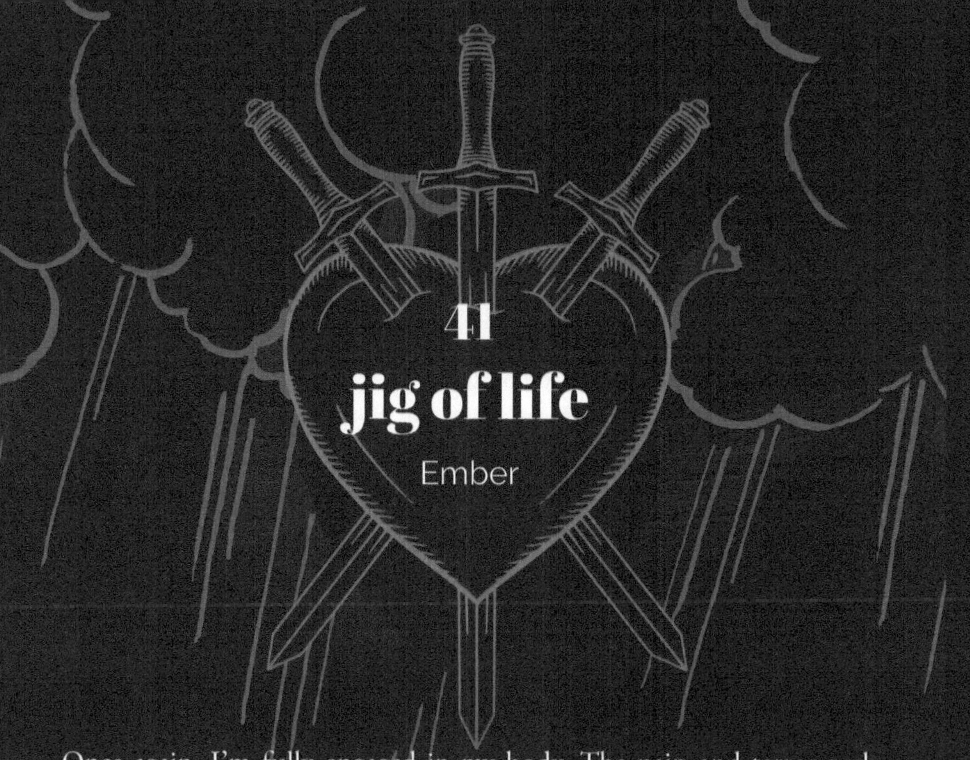

Once again, I'm fully engaged in my body. The pain and terror rush back now that Onirique has disappeared, and my senses are overcome.

But this time I know what I'm getting into. The words of Verdandi play in my mind again as they had in Onirique moments ago: "To understand this moment without the trappings of future or past is powerful. Within the span of a breath, we may harness the ability to create our own fate..."

Then the Valkyrie echoes in my mind: "Claim your gifts with everything you are." Defiance swells within me, overtaking the external sensations as the light blazes through my hot skin. Taking a breath so deep that it fills my diaphragm completely, I seek to use my True Voice to declare my powers for me alone, but my breath falters at my throat. How do I claim something I don't even understand? Before I allow panic to take hold, I replay the words of Verdandi again. I visualize a single moment stretched out into infinity, lights sparking around me. I focus on my throat, on the vibrations, the words that should have emanated from my vocal cords. Still nothing. Panic hovers at the edge of my consciousness. Moments ago, I was ready to wrap this thing up and go home. What went wrong?

Suddenly, pain flares in my heart, becoming the only thing I can feel. I'm struck by an image of myself, seeing the heart that burned my old self away in the ancestral cave: the moment my new heart took hold of my body and mind, the flames blazing from the top but never burning the heart itself.

That! That is my true power, my essence, my True Voice, which doesn't start in my throat.

There is only this moment.

I push all my pain, my memories, my regrets, my nightmares, my fear of Phaedra, and finally my hope for my own future into a single point of focus. My body is the magic. The pain in my chest transforms, the white lines etched into my chest cracking open as fire and light shoot out of my chest, an explosion of heat and magic and prayer, blinding shards bursting through my chest like rays of the sun. The light meets the blood of the summoning circle.

It's her blood mixed with mine, the blood that gave me life beating through my heart. But it's not hers anymore.

The fire traveling with the light catalyzes my blood in that circle, shifting the power from Phaedra to me. It's my energy and magic that occupy it now. The crystals are now mine to command, too. The fire blazes and flares illuminate my vision. As I look at the crystals, the light of my fire dances in them. I look down at my chest, my fiery heart from the cave blazing fully. I feel its flame in every part of my body, consuming all my doubt and fear. This is it. This is my truth. I open my mouth and the fire travels up my throat, pushing the words forward.

"I belong to me!" I reflexively hit my chest with my hand and the light from my fire grows brighter. "My body!." Another smack of my hand to my chest. "My mind!" Smack. "My power!" Smack. "My heart!" Smack. "My heart beats fiercely and burns brightly. It belongs to me!" As I speak my truth, I project my will, shifting the dissonance to harmony and breathing a sigh of relief as the ringing in my ears lessens. Phaedra looks at me in silent bewilderment as my light meets the crystals. Fissures of light that once traveled along my skin knit back together.

Light ricochets and travels to another crystal across the cave, reflecting to another crystal and again to another, over and over, until the room is a labyrinth of golden light rays. I feel them all, each drawing from my heart fire.

As the light multiplies around the room, I gaze into a large crystal, seeing the young Embers I saw in the cave. I turn my head and in another crystal, I see older versions of myself. At the crossroads of this moment, these crystals are conduits to all versions of myself, whispering secrets and undiscovered truths. They beckon: "Claim what belongs to us, that we may live." We stare at each other, and again, as in the ancestral cave, we speak in unison.

"I belong to me! My body. My mind. My power. My heart. My heart beats fiercely and burns brightly. It belongs to me!"

The words are simple, but the truth of them spoken by every incarnation of me, together, carries the strength of my will. Finally, I feel compelled to say the words once more.

"I belong to me! My body. My mind. My power. My heart. My heart beats fiercely and burns brightly. It belongs to me!"

I close my eyes, feeling the words deeply, as something inside me locks into place, intensifying the heart fire. I open my eyes, only to see Phaedra shield hers as the light grows too bright for her. As illumination bounces from one surface to the next, my power continues to grow. In a final surge from my rapidly beating heart, one last blast of light travels around the maze, picking up speed. My magic travels along with the light; my magic is the light. When it reaches the largest crystal in the cave, it doesn't reflect to another surface. Instead, the light and magic enter, energy bouncing around the interior surfaces, getting brighter with every impact.

As the fire finally dissipates from my chest, I gather all my will and conviction, willing the ropes on my wrists to unravel. Instinctively, my hands push a ball of energy at the crystal. The shock of its force is absorbed as rays of rainbow light shoot out at Phaedra, bursting her Bubblevarden, circling her faster and faster until the light turns white again, spinning around her like a tornado. The vortex pulls iron from the blood on the ground. The liquid parts fall away, turning the light a sickly gray color. It rotates so quickly I can barely see her anymore, only catching glimpses of her face, contorted in agony, her body writhing. As the cloud tightens around her, the iron, now sharp shards of metal, cuts her face, then hands, then body, the darkening gore staining her woolen gown.

Without thinking, I reach for the iron shards. I feel their acquiescence as I make a fist, thrust it forward in the air, and envision the tiny missiles doing the same. They mirror my action, landing a throat punch at Phaedra. It's not enough to kill her, just knock the wind out of her.

Phaedra opens her mouth to scream, but no sound escapes. She tries again in vain. Raising her hand and tracing a rune in the air, she tries one last time to dissipate the vortex. Before she can finish, though, it lifts her off the ground, her feet hanging limp and useless. The last of her blood is pulled into the whirlwind and hits her all at once, striking like a bolt of lightning.

Phaedra falls to the ground.

So do I.

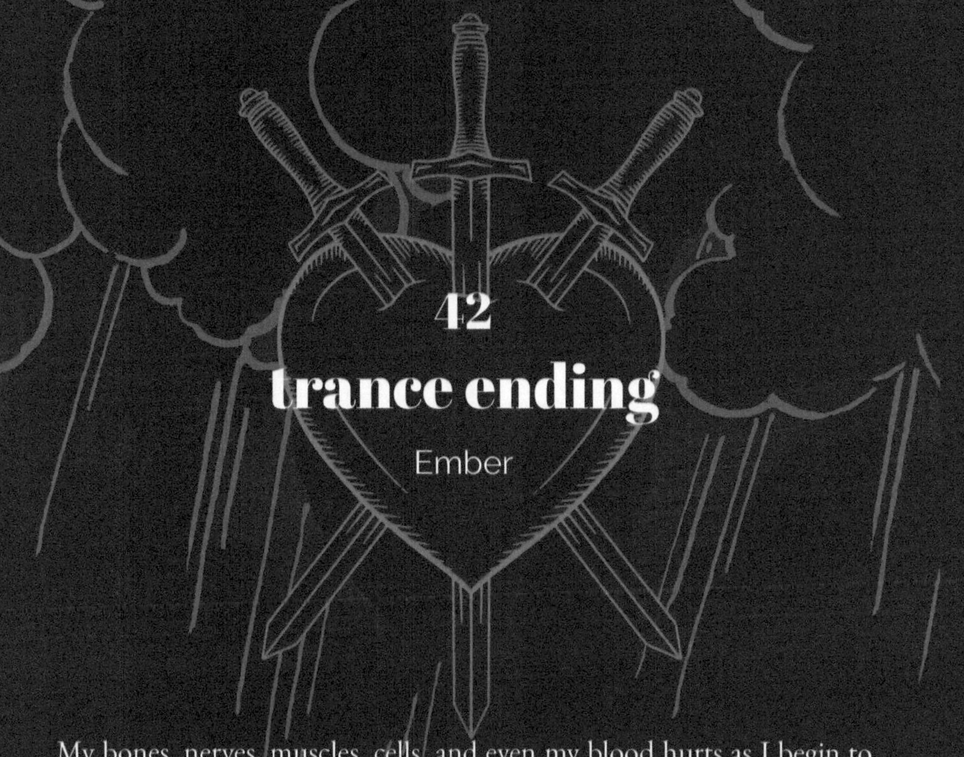

42

trance ending

Ember

My bones, nerves, muscles, cells, and even my blood hurts as I begin to stir. A moan escapes my lips, and there's a cool hand touching my face, rubbing my cheek. "Ember, can you hear me? Ember? Ember?" The sound is muffled, though. The insistent voice will not stop calling my name. "Ember, wake up, please." This time it's pleading. Why is the voice so far away?

I slowly open my eyes. Spots, like the after-effect of a camera flash, darken my vision. Kenyon and Whit's faces hover above me. A protest escapes my lips as Kenyon shifts my body to a semi-seated position, leaning into his.

Whit still sounds distant as he asks, "Are you alright? Can you speak?"

"Ouch! My everything hurts. So batty-fang!"

Whit laughs, looking at Kenyon, explaining, "It means 'damaged to an unusable state.'" He chuckles as he shakes his head. "I swear, Little Rose, the people around you need a Universal Translator to understand you sometimes." In a move so uncharacteristic of him, he grabs my hand and kisses my palm. "Thank the Nine Worlds, you are ok!"

"Yeah, she said that one other time, but thanks," Kenyon answers. But his demeanor is not as relaxed or happy as Whit's. Then it occurs to me that I was abducted at a pretty tense moment between us.

But I can't deal with that now, as panic replaces everything. "Where's Phaedra?"

"We don't know where they've taken her. They saw us as we approached; several of the Sisters were carrying her away," Whit answers. "Though we did not pursue them for want of finding you. I suspect they might've taken you as well, if they'd had the time."

"All this can wait. She needs healing right now," Kenyon says.

"We should bring her to the Draíodóir. They are the best healers in Elysia," Whit says.

I violently shake my head. "No! No Temple."

"Right—I'll call Aaric and see if some of the Brothers will make a house call." Whit's voice is the last thing I hear as I lose consciousness.

When I open my eyes again, I'm lying on the bed in my room at Kenyon's house. The soft bedding feels cozy and I'm reluctant to move, but I'm not alone. A small group of Draíodóir is also in the room, their hands pressed together, laying lightly on my extremities, faintly glowing. Glittering light sparks as they occasionally draw runes above me. My vision clears and the once opaque black spots are now a transparent grayish color. Though it's better, there's still an uncomfortable ringing in my ears, but I can hear at full volume now.

Gingerly, I test my arms and legs to see how much pain moving will cause. With great relief, I discover the pain isn't nearly what I feared. At my movement, the Brothers back away, and the Prior helps me to a sitting position.

Before I can even ask the question, Whit begins giving me a rundown. "It's Sunday morning, Ember. The Brothers have been here most of the night healing you. Sister Vadoma buzzed on the Oculus to let us know she's in charge of the daily duties of the Vala for the indefinite future. Phaedra's most trusted acolytes stand vigil, guarding her door, allowing only select Sisters to see her, saying that she is in isolation preparing for the ceremonial Investiture of the Sacred Spindle. While it's common for a head of an Oracle Society to go into solitary contemplation to reflect upon the Order's future, these retreats are normally planned ahead of time."

"Of course she is..." Kenyon says, with absolutely no sarcasm.

"The Sister also asked me to relay a message. She would appreciate knowing the details of your encounter," Aaric adds.

"Wait, how did you know where to find me last night?" I ask, still trying to sort everything out, "I'm not wearing that necklace you gave me."

"After a short time, I realized you should've rejoined me. I'm so sorry that I got caught up in the intrigues of others when I should've been more attentive to you. If Phaedra had—I can't even say the words. I don't think I could've lived with myself."

"It's ok. Like I said before, this was kinda inevitable."

"So I got ahold of Whit. A short time later, power fluctuations began all over the city." Kenyon hesitates at his next words. "And because of our spirit interaction as children and our recent connection, there is a part of you in me and vice versa. I felt that you were in danger. I put these two facts together and took a leap of faith. I also assumed that Phaedra would need to draw in more power than she could access on her own."

My eyes widen with surprise as he references our connection in front of Whit and the Brothers. The heat of a blush creeps up my chest to my cheeks. Reflexively I shoot a look toward Whit to gauge his reaction.

He throws his hands up in a "hands-off" kind of gesture. "You're nearly an adult. Your choices are your own."

Kenyon awkwardly clears his throat and continues. "Anyway, we headed to the Crystal Cave and as we neared the entrance, we saw some of Phaedra's underlings carrying her away. I don't think she was conscious or doing all that well, to be honest. Whatever you did, it seems to have cleaned her clock...at least for now."

"What did you do?" Whit asks.

"It's kinda weird and hard to explain. But Phaedra was going on and on about how I should change my mind and join her. If I opened myself up to her willingly, it wouldn't even hurt when she stole my gifts. She kept trying to get me to agree, and I keyed into the fact that there's a lot of power in my willingness to relent. So I told her I'd take a hard pass on joining her. And this is where it gets weird and all magic-y..."

I tell them most of what I remember. I mean, I don't go into all the details. Sharing the encounters with the Valkyries and the wee little Embers to the elderly versions of me feels too personal. I already feel exposed.

Both Whit and Kenyon are surprised at how it all went down. Looking between the two of them, I say, "I know! It was crazy."

"Indeed," Whit agrees. "But, I don't believe we've seen the last of Phaedra. She's in seclusion, nursing her wounds. When she recovers enough power, she'll be back.

"I'll be back!" I say, in the worst impression of Arnold Schwarzenegger ever. But, dang, the mood in here needs to lighten up. I mean, I won! I did it, I beat her, and I don't even know how to use magic.

Giving me a look, Whit continues, "I imagine she'll siphon power away from her underlings to accelerate her healing."

"Well, I'm assuming it's not going to be today, and I really need to get some more sleep. I mean, I was almost grinning at the daisy roots."

"Very well, get some rest." Whit says as he turns his attention to Kenyon, saying, "It means dead. Grinning up at the daisy roots means dead." He then turns to Brother Aaric, saying, "Aaric, a word in private, if you have a moment." And because I'm already in my room, I lay down, burrowing deeper into the bed. Kenyon sits down next to me as Whit and the Draíodóir leave.

Before Kenyon has the chance to say anything, I look at him, saying, "Listen, I'm not mad at you about last night. I'm not exactly ok, either, but I'm not mad. I just—have a lot of thinking to do. I'm not sure where we go from here. But now is not the time. I seriously do need to sleep, but I don't want to sleep alone. Can you just lay here behind me and cuddle into me?"

"Anything you want, Ember." He says as he curls up behind me. We lay there in silence, our breathing is deep and rhythmic, and I think he's asleep. Until he breaks the silence, in the faintest of whispers, he says, "I love you."

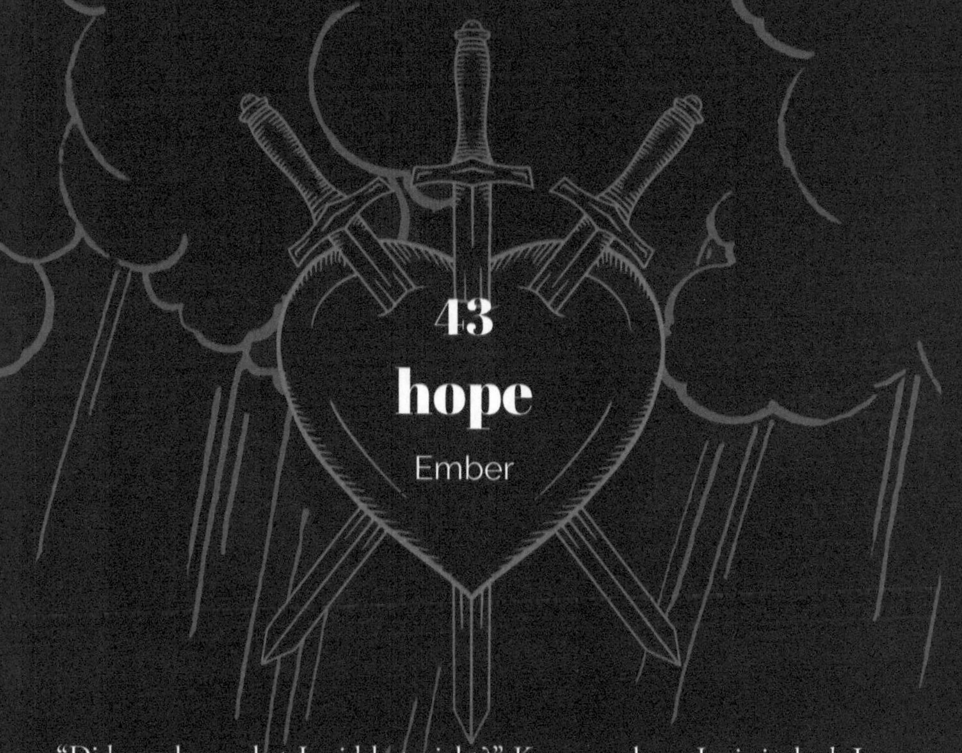

43
hope

Ember

"Did you hear what I said last night?" Kenyon asks as I stir in bed. It doesn't seem fair to hit me with heavy questions before coffee. Still, I won't leave him hanging.

I roll over onto my back and sit up in a crossed-leg position facing him. "I heard you. But, I'm not sure that love is enough."

"I'm sorry that I didn't mention my somewhat notorious dating history, and I'm sorry that it complicated the situation, allowing them time to abduct you. But I want this to work with you! I feel things I never believed I could feel for another person—-for you. I don't want to lose this, so what can I do?"

"Don't you get it, Kenyon? I've spent my whole life desperate to be loved, only to be spurned or turned away, while you—-"

"But that's exactly what I'm offering you!" He interrupts, his voice tinged with exasperation.

"Please, don't interrupt me. This isn't easy for me to say."

Kenyon puts his hand on my cheek. "Sorry."

I put my hands over my face taking a second before I speak. He just doesn't get it. I've spent a lonely life yearning for nothing more than love and acceptance, only to be rejected over and over again. He's spent his life running from those things while having every opportunity to accept love. And that scares me.

"This sounds so lame—But I've always been conflicted. Both seeking love and being terrified by it, I watched my father become a shell of a man after my mother died; his love for her gutted him in the end. Growing up that way, with a father only going through the motions out of obligation, made me like a Hungry Ghost, driven by intense emotional needs but seeking to fulfill them in an animalistic way. I wanted to be self-sufficient but needed what scared me the most.

"I've never found the right person or relationship to fill the void left by the absence of family. So, I dated around—-a lot, trying and failing to find what was missing. I realize now that I can't expect someone else to make me whole, but I'm asking you to help me find the missing pieces and learn to be a better man."

He falters just a bit, but continues. "So, I hope you can forgive me, and we can move forward. There is nobody like you, and I only want you!" Before he can continue, I put my hand up to stop him.

"I believe you, Kenyon." And the sigh that escapes his lips only makes this harder. "I believe that you mean every word you say, but for how long? I don't wanna be hurt—"

"But I'm not going to hurt you! All I want to do is love you."

Rather than reprimanding him for interrupting me again, I let my frustration take the wheel. "Urrgh! Don't you get it? I don't know if I can handle being your first real relationship." And even as soon as the words leave my mouth, he flinches away and I'm sorry I said them so bluntly. I gasp, rushing to say, "Oh geez! I'm so sorry, that was mean." The look on his face tells me it was a direct hit in the soft places he hides away.

"I didn't mean for that to sound so cold. I'm just scared and I don't think I could handle another heartbreak right now." A mix of desperation and hope in his eye, he slides this hand down my arm to rest his hand on mine, intertwining our fingers.

"I know I have a lot to learn about being a good boyfriend and how to have a relationship, but I'm ready for this. Please trust me!" He replies. "You own my heart."

"Well, that's hard to argue with, so dating it is. But, I want to slow things down, get to know each other, have more fun, be less serious—"

"So what does that mean? Are you planning to date other people while we're having our not-too-serious relationship? I want to share everything I feel for you, with you. I just told you that you own my heart. I'm committed to seeing this through, but I can't do it alone."

"You're putting a lot of pressure on me, given that I just had my entire world flipped upside down and my mother tried to kill me. Again."

"I get it, but—"

I raise my voice to stop him. "No! It's not your turn. I wasn't finished!"

He puts his hands up, offering his surrender.

"Plus, I think you misunderstood me. I'm not talking about dating other people. I just want to get to know you without all this pressure. My life has never been stable or in my power to control. I need to be the one behind the wheel for once. So, I'll date only you, but we're taking it slowly."

"I guess if that's what you're offering, I'll take it, but I'm going to do everything in my power to prove myself and win you over completely."

Before I can reply, there's a knock. I hear Whit behind the door. "Ember? Wakey wakey, we've got some decisions to make, sleepyhead."

"Ok, gimme a minute."

"See you downstairs and bring Kenyon with you."

After a quick trip to the bathroom to become human again, I walk toward the door. Knitting needles sit on the chair, beckoning me to pick them up. I impulsively grab them, along with the 'Vision Yarn.' I don't know where the needles came from, but I'm due for a day off and the yarn is mine now.

When I asked Sister Vadoma about their shawls, she told me they're made of yarn that they spun as novitiates, plus yarn their mentors have given them, joining the past and present of the lineage together. I don't know how to weave and I'm not super interested in joining the Vala, but I should start knitting something. In a way, it's super creepy. It's connected to Lena's death, but it's also part of my journey now. There is no amount of wishing that away. After last night and my near death, I need to process all that mess and figure out my next steps. Knitting always helps me to feel better and get things figured out.

I find Kenyon and Whit sitting at the table with a huge breakfast spread waiting for me.

"Alright, Pops, lay it on me," I say as I sit down and look at Whit, trying on a casual expression of our new relationship, wanting to see how it fits. It doesn't.

Whit replies, unimpressed. "Ember, we must take the events of last night to the Convocation of Esteemed Equals."

"You can do whatever you want. I'm not going! You know how that's going to be, sitting there through all their formal proceedings, lots of titles to be acknowledged, announcing and preening, and it's going to be all cumberworld: sitting there taking up space and being useless. Then Rémy will declare what we're saying is 'Preposterous!' Then he'll ask what proof we have of what happened, which we don't have. And then we'll be dismissed and probably chastised for wasting the Convocation's time."

"You're right, but I'm just incensed at the idea of her getting away with what she did!" Kenyon interjects.

"Well, it's not exactly like she got away with anything, did she? I mean, I kinda accidentally kicked her ass! You guys said that her minions had to drag her out of the Crystal Cave, and now she's in 'seclusion' or whatever. My guess is that our kerfuffle took it outta her. But I do understand what you mean. And I feel like this is not the last time I'll have to put the smackdown on her."

"We'll let this lie for now," Whit says. "But in the meantime, some decisions must be made about all our futures. Now that the immediate crisis is over, it's time to begin your magical education. Perhaps tutoring?"

"I guess there's a lot I need to catch up on before I can apprentice into one of the Guilds and start my life here in Elysia."

"I know some very qualified teachers who could be persuaded to adapt their curriculum to meet Ember's needs," Kenyon says. I'm overwhelmed with relief—a plan is at hand.

Changing the subject, I ask, "What are you going to do now, Whit, without the shop?"

"I haven't decided. Perhaps I'll open up a version of Mr. Whitley's Emporium of Curiosities and Oddities here in Elysia. There always seems to be a need for trinkets from the ordinary world here."

"Um, can I work there, too?"

"Of course you can. It wouldn't feel right with anyone else at the front desk, dressing mannequins or torturing me with their musical selections."

"Perhaps I can intern in a guild dedicated to fashion, you know, for the remaking of clothes and knitted items. I think this place could use a bit more sass if all the Gnashgabs and Gobermouchs at that Art reception are any indication of what this town is like. It's all so normal and conforming in its way."

Whit looks to Kenyon without missing a beat. "Constant complainers and nosy, meddling people, respectively."

I continue my previous thoughts. "Yes, I think Elysia is a perfect place for me to launch my career as a clothier or a sartorialist. I mean, we can have the same deal as before, right?"

"Of course we can, Ember. I'm pretty sure they're not going to know what hit them."

As Whit dreams of his future shop, I begin to cast on stitches. Looking up from the yarn, I see Kenyon's eyes locked on me, but I look away before it becomes too intense. I can't even deal with Kenyon's declarations right now.

As I escape thoughts of Kenyon, they return to Phaedra. I know she'll be back and I haven't forgotten about the half-sister situation she mentioned last night, either. But I'm positive that it will unfold without any help from me. Maybe it's time for me to dream about my future, too.

I don't get very far before the doorbell rings. Without thinking, I look back at Kenyon, my unasked question of who could be here mirrored on his face as he excuses himself to answer the door.

As a minute ticks by, I can barely contain my curiosity. I mean, there's no way it's Phaedra, so how bad could it be?

Kenyon returns with Nico, who always looks amazing. She's wearing a sleeveless white knit top she made during our many 'knit nites' with bright blue banded arm holes. An orange knitted piece encircling her neck peeks through a cutout just above her chest, hanging to her mid-thigh. Only Nico could make White harem pants and orange platform shoes look that right. Baby blue panda ear buns perch high on her head, her oval sunglasses propped at a careless yet somehow perfect angle. I need to take lessons on how to be cool from her.

"Hey, Em. You're lookin' a bit rough this morning. But the entire

Priory of the Vala is alight with gossip about last night. And, from what I hear, Phaedra is a whole lot worse than you, Chuckaboo."

"Chuckaboooo!" I exclaim in return.

Whit quickly offers, "It's a close friend," which of course Nico already knows.

"Nicoletta, my favorite maven of ostentatious fashion choices, what brings you here to brighten our doorstep?" Whit asks before I can do the same.

"Hey, Mr. Whit... should I still call you that?"

"Yes, it's just fine."

"I've come to take our girl on an adventure today. I think she could use a break."

Nico looks at me hopefully, and I can't help but smile back as a gigglemug takes over her face. "Oh yeah?" I ask.

"Totally!"

I look at Whit out of habit, like I need permission from the adult in the room. I realize that I'm an adult in Elysia and don't need anybody's permission. A look of apprehension, quickly replaced by a neutral expression on Kenyon's face, tells me he's worried about what we'll get up to today. But honestly, that's his problem. An adventure is exactly what I need.

"Whatcha got in mind?" I ask as I move my eyes away from Kenyon to hers.

"It's a surprise! Grab your bag and let's get outta here!"

My bag sits by the door, waiting for my next decision. I guess Kenyon or Whit grabbed it from the cave as they carried me out.

I look at Nico, who's already opened the door, my bag dangling off her fingertips, mischief in her two-toned eyes. The leaves of a maple tree frame her outline as the sunshine streams in the door around her. They sway in the breeze, inviting me outside.

"Will it be fun?" I ask.

"Duh. Of course it'll be fun! You're with me."

Having some fun seems like the perfect thing to do today. I can contemplate my future tomorrow or another day. I look to Kenyon, resignation easy to spot in his blue eyes, as he says, "Better shake your tail feathers! Nico is an unstoppable force of nature." He waves his hand once to say goodbye.

I look back to Nico.

I take a step toward the door. "Weeell, I had planned on sitting and knitting, and ya know, contemplating my future and all that, but this sounds like more fun. After all, life is for the living, and I had to Shake a flannin last night to survive a lot of skulduggery to be counted amongst the living."

"It means 'fight to avoid underhanded trickery,'" Whit chimes in on cue.

"Yeah, that's what I said. I kicked ass!"

ember's lexicon of victorian insults and curses

Addle Pate-An inconsiderate and foolish fellow.

Batty-fang-To damage something to an unusable state. Well thrashed and unusable.

Blowsbella-Old English insult for an unkempt woman.

Blunderbuss-Stupid blundering fellow. A short gun with a wide bore.

Chuckaboo-A nickname for a close friend.

Cumberworld-Someone who's so useless they just serve to take up space.

Death's head upon a mop stick-An emaciated person, miserable and unwell.

Eyes on stalks-When your eyes are wide open with surprise or amazement.

Fizzing-First-rate, very good, or excellent.

Fopdoodle-Stupid person.

Fustilarian - Someone who stubbornly wastes time on worthless things.

Gigglemug-A person who is always smiling.

Gnashgab-Constant complainer.

Gobermouch-An old Irish word for a nosy, meddling people.

Got the Morbs-Temporary state of melancholy.

Grinning at the Daisy Roots-Dead, literally grinning up at the flower roots covering the coffin.

Jackanapes-Pert ugly little fellow, an ape.

Kerfuffle-A fuss or commotion caused by conflicting points of view.

Ninnyhammer-A fool or simpleton, aka a ninny.

Ratbag-Generic term of abuse, a rogue.

Scandal-water-Tea served at tea parties that focus on gossip and scandal.

Shabbaroon-A shabby ill-dressed fellow, or a mean-spirited person.

Shake a flannin-Fight

Skilamalink-Secret, shady, doubtful.

Skullduggery-Underhanded or unscrupulous behavior; trickery.

Storm in a teacup-An overreaction to an unimportant incident.

Suggestionize-A legal term from 1889, "to prompt."

Throttlebottom-Futile and inept person in public office.

Thunderation!-Variant of damnation.

Todger-Euphemism for male genitalia.

Umble-Cum-Stumble-Low-class phrase means "thoroughly understood."

Zounderkite- total idiot who makes awkward and clumsy mistakes.

characters and the world

December (Ember) Wright
Nico (Nicoletta) Jones, Novitiate, Priory of the Vala .
Honourable Guild of Liminal Space.

Mr. Whitley (Adair Whitley Wright)
Aka Whit or Addi

Kenyon McQuiston, Honourable Guild of Innovation.

Prior Aaric Aumont, Priory of the Draíodóir
Honourable Guild of Liminal Space.

Brother Imanu, First Steward, Priory of the Draíodóir
Honourable Guild of Liminal Space.

Prioress Phaedra Rule, Priory of the Vala
Honourable Guild of Liminal Space.

Sister Vadoma Palgrave, First Cleric, Priory of the Vala
Honourable Guild of Liminal Space.

Magðalena (Lena) McQuiston, née Lalonde.
Kenyon's mother

Merrick (Merry)McQuiston,
Kenyon's father

Sister Zola Ragana, Priory of the Vala.
Honourable Guild of Liminal Space.
Ember's Art teacher

Théo Wright, Honourable Guild of Tektōns

Whit's brother

Samara (Zandi) Zandi, Honourable Guild of Civil Service,
Kenyons assistant

Sister Ordonna, Priory of the Vala
Honourable Guild of Liminal Space.
the Prioress' most trusted Devotee Laureate

Romeo (Romulus) Amato, Honourable Guild of the Arts
Nico's secret (not so secret) boyfriend

-Convocation of Esteemed Equals-

Each of the thirteen guilds of every magical city appoints a leader who is among the most influential of their respective guild. That leader has a seat on the Convocation, which is responsible for the city's governance. The Leader or Primus Inter Pares also serves on an additional Convocation composed of their equals and led by the Chancellor of the Commonwealth of Atlaria. In addition to each guild's participation in the Convocation, they serve as the regulatory body for the industries and occupations they oversee and education through internship programs.

-Aadya Varma - Chancellor of Commonwealth of Atlaria

-Convocation of Esteemed Equals for Elysia-

-Remigius(Rémy) Châstellain,
Starosta of the Vede Mecum of Allthings,
Headman, Honourable Guild of the Arcane.
Justiciar, Primus Inter Pares, (First Among Equals) Convocation of
Esteemed Equals

-Venerable Magister Idris Pritchett, Luminary Innovator,
Headman, Honourable Guild of Innovation.

-Venerable Magister Pan Ling OuYang 巫,
Wěiyuán Zhǎng of the Wu Oneiromancers,
Readers of Dreams and Walkers in the Dreamland
Headmistress, Honourable Guild of Liminal Space.

-Venerable Magister Majordomo Denma Beridze, Tempestarii and
Master of the Storm Callers, Headmistress, Honourable Guild of
Stewards

-Venerable Magister Alexander deVilbiss,
Master Expressionist and Fine Artist
Headman, Honourable Guild of the Arts

-Venerable Magister Legate Erastus Manning
Civil Defense Ministry
Headman, Honourable Guild of Civil Service

-Venerable Magister Cornelia de Lange,
Master Alchemist
Headmistress, Honourable Guild of Healers and Alchemists

-Venerable Magister Vesta Parker,
Votary of the Alliance of Pragmatists, Quidnuncs, and Morality
Guardians
Headmistress, Honourable Guild of Future Destiny

-Venerable Magister Hakeem Bayon,
Labor Council Director
Headmaster, Honourable Guild of Laborers

-Venerable Magister Eila Egan,
Conditor Scholar and Head Arkhitéktōn of the Masterful Union of
Arkhitéktōns
Headmistress, Honourable Guild of Tektōns

-Venerable Magister, Vedovus Claeg,
Sophist Laureate, Order of Pythagoras,

Headman of the Honourable Guild of Wisdom and Academe

-Venerable Magister, Diana Tierney, Barrister Advocate
Headmistress, Honourable Guild Advocates, and Protectors

- Venerable Magister, His Beatitude, Prèt Luis Reyes,
Catholicos, Sacrament of the Sacred Heart
Headmaster, Honourable Guild of Diversified Holy Houses

-Commonwealth of Atlaria-
-Capital Cities-

Elysia (America)
Zealandia (New Zealand)
Akrotiri(Greece)
The Hanging Gardens of Babylon (Iraq)
Shangri-La (Kunlun Mountain, China)
El Dorado (South America)
Tuatha Dé Danann (Ireland)
Zerzura (Saharan city)
Kitezh (Russia)
Kalahari (South Africa)
Thinis (Africa - ancient Egyptian city Abydos)
Tenochtitlan (Mexico)

terminology, pronunciation, and concepts

-Amplicon - A drug that, when taken, can temporarily amply the user's ability to wield magical energy through impermanent enlargement of mitochondria within the user. There are two ways of producing the drug. It can be harvested from quartz crystals or by voluntary or forceful human extraction. The quartz-derived variation is more powerful but burns out the user's ability to wield magic over time. The stolen variety poses no threat to the user, but its effects are not as great.

The science behind the concept: In molecular biology, an amplicon is a piece of DNA or RNA that is the source and/or product of amplicon or replication events. This plays a vital role in the evolution of genes.

-Artomancy - This practice attempts to connect this world to the realm of the unknown. Magical figures, shamans, prophets, or artists created figurines, masks, and paintings to bring dialogue between themselves and spiritual forces. These pieces illustrate their beliefs, which include ritualistic spells to foretell the future, increase crops, or influence fate.

-Bobleverden - Norwegian word meaning "Bubble World." In this context, the bubble world traps sound within the sphere to create privacy.

-Confractio Anima - Latin words meaning wrenching soul. This is the basis for a spirit-shattering spell that allows for magical thievery in the magical world.

-Currency - In the magical world, money can be coinage:

-Aeris - Latin, copper.

-Argenti - Latin, silver.

-Aurum - Latin, gold.

It can also be energy collected from crystals compressed by a piezo-electrometer. Measured in Joules, the energy is stored under pressure in a vanadium battery, usually called a Vanadium for short. Therefore, this currency represents a decentralized banking system and is untraceable and nontaxable.

-Disir- pronounced "DEE-sir," are female spirits often portrayed as female ancestors who protect a particular person, group, or location.

-Draíochta - (dre-oct-ta) plural Gaelic word magical powers.

-Furta Spiritus - Latin words meaning theft of the spirit, the second part of the magical theft spell.

-Geasa droma draíochta - Binding spell.

-Lemuria- Lemuria, known as Mu or Lemuria, was a peaceful highly-developed spiritual civilization according to the legend. Existing many millennia ago in the area of the South Pacific, now buried deep beneath the sea.

-Lemurian Seed Crystals - The Lemurian were believed to have foreseen a cataclysmic event. They prepared the Lemurian Seed Crystals to preserve their knowledge and traditions.

-le Labyrinthe de Magie - Street fair located in the central district of the cities of Atlaria.

-Ley Lines - Invisible but deeply powerful lines imbued with electromagnetic energy that encircle the Earth. They connect important and sacred sites worldwide.

-Maleficium - to harm with witchcraft.

-Mitochondrial DNA - DNA that metabolizes food into energy but also converts the magical energy given off by the Ley Lines surrounding the Earth and amplified by the Crystal caves. This creates an ability for the person to wield magic.

The science behind the concept: Mitochondrial DNA are structures within cells that convert energy from food into a form that cells can use. Each cell contains hundreds to thousands of mitochondria which have a small amount of their own DNA. This DNA is passed on only through maternal lines.

-Norn - The Norse goddesses of Fate live under the world tree Yggdrasil where they weave the destiny of humans. The three were named Urd, Verdandi, and Skuld, representing the past, present, and future. They are the ultimate prototype for the Norse witches, the Völva/Vǫlva (the predecessors of the Vala in this book), as they spin and weave. They are the strongest among the supernatural beings in the Norse pantheon of Gods and spirits.

-Oneiromancy- The interpretation of dreams to foretell the future.

-Onirique - Mystical realms where Ancestors and other Spirit beings dwell, as well as a plane of existence visited in the dreamtime where adept magic practitioners can spell cast.

-Piezoelectricity - The electricity that results from external mechanical pressure is applied to crystals, certain ceramics, and biological matter like bone or DNA.

-Piezoelectrometer - A device that applies pressure to crystals to create piezoelectricity. The device also acts as a conduit, transferring the acclimated energy to a storage device.

-Pledge vows of Convenance - Get married.

-Seiðr - The pronunciation of Seiðr varies from country to country but is commonly pronounced as SAY-dr in English. Was a Norse magical practice in the late Iron Age. It involved the telling and shaping of the future utilizing a wand or distaff and song to enable Shamanic Visions. Part of this ritual involved contact with the Norse Fates or Norn. The specifics of the practices are debated, as with many things from Norse mythology, conflicting facts have been presented as evidence. It's speculated that the distaff was used for spinning yarn in addition to the weaving they performed. A practice also associated with the Norn, who spun and wove fate.

-Sgian dubh - (skee-an doo) is a small, single-edged knife from Scotland. This all-purpose knife was used for eating and preparing food and for other day-to-day uses and is now worn as a part of traditional Scottish dress. It is usually worn on the side of the dominant hand, tucked into the top of the kilt hose with the upper portion of the hilt visible.

-Vanadium devices - Batteries that can store large amounts of energy almost indefinitely without deterioration

-Vegvísir - (Vegg-vee-seer) means "that which shows the way" in the Icelandic language.

- VoceInvocare - The Truthsayer's ability to infuse their voice with the true conviction of truth.

a note from the author

When I began working on this book, I used folkloric magical traditions from European history because that's where my ancestors came from. Specifically, I chose Celtic and Norse mythologies; I loved the connection of fiber craft to the Norse witches, who were practitioners of Seiðr. It blended my love of knitting with their ancient shamanic traditions. As an American, I wanted to explore that ancestral connection.

However, in the years since I began this book, it has become clear to me that racists hide white supremacist beliefs in their version of Norse Pagan Revivalist traditions. Because of this, I want to take this opportunity to denounce racism and white supremacy. I do not, nor does this book, support hatred.

America has a long history of oppressing people of color and a complicated, revisionist relationship with that history. There is a temptation for some to believe that because they do not behave in outwardly racist ways, the burden of white privilege should not rest on their shoulders. But we have an opportunity to change our mindset and understand that we can begin dismantling systemic racism. We have an opportunity and an obligation to change.

As Americans, most of us are descendants of ancestors from at least two different countries. We live in a cultural liminal space, and the search for identity in America is profound. I wrote a uniquely American story recognizing that people who immigrated here brought their beliefs, traditions, and god/s. But those things evolved with time. The denizens of my world are also of mixed race and heritage and their culture, rituals, and traditions have evolved.

In the Commonwealth of Atlaria, magic is a constant, and a person's method to catalyze it is unique to their secular or spiritual traditions or beliefs. The Priory of the Draíodóir and the Vala are open to anyone. If someone has the gift, they are welcome. And you, too, are welcome in my world.

about the author

Bethany Grenier
Artist · Author · Hairstylist · Knitter

heartofember.com
bethanygrenier.com

———

If you liked this book, please consider reviewing it
on your favorite book platform or sharing it on social media.

———

Each chapter name is also a song title that predicts some aspect of the
chapter. If you'd like to listen to the songs, check out the
Heart of Ember playlist on Spotify.

knitting pattern for ember's scarf

Photo by Anisa Williams

This scarf is a variation of a striped scarf. Rather than a contrasting color, this uses a row of yarn overs to separate garter rows of equal size to create stripes. A picot cast on and cast off replaces traditional fringe. Though you could replace the picots with fringe. The extreme length of this scarf, 10 feet, is a nod to the Fourth Doctor in the Doctor Who lineage, a favorite of the character (and the designer). You may knit it to any length you like.

Difficulty Level
Advanced Beginner

Skills Required/Techniques Used

- Knit & purl
- Picot CO & BO
- Yarn overs

Materials

Plucky Knitter Primo Finger, 385 yards 75% Superwash Merino, 20% Cashmere & 5% Nylon Colorway, Morticia.
or
Plucky Knitter Feet Fingering, 425 yards, 90% Superwash Merino, 10% Recycled Nylon Colorway, Morticia

This pattern has a lot of texture and is best suited to solid or tonal colors. Variegated yarns can overpower the pattern.

Notions

• 3.75mm/US 5 or 6, Smaller needle gives a more compact and smaller scarf. Larger needles will create a looser fabric.

• Needles-straight or short circular as you prefer

• Yarn needle

Gauge

Gauge is not as important as consistent tension, to create a uniform fabric with consistent straight edges.

Finished measurements

Dimensions: 10'x 4" or so that it wraps around the neck and reaches mid calf in front and back. Though the measurements will vary depending upon which blocking method you choose. If you desire a wider version, follow the pattern basic, just cast on more stitches. Just be sure to CC on one final stitch, so there are an odd number of stitches in the stitch count.

• Before you begin...

Please read pattern before you start. Once all stitches are cast on, a pattern quickly establishes itself as a 6 row repeat. However, it is important to note that the pattern alternates every 6th row. So it's 5 rows of garter stitch, slipping the first stitch of every garter row, then, alternating rows on 6, 12, 18, 24, etc...

Picot Cast On

• Make a slip knot and place St. onto needles.

• CCO 3 Sts. Bind off 2 Sts. Place remaining stitch back onto left needle, 2 Sts remain.

• CCO 4 Sts, bind off 2. Return remaining St. to left needle, 4 Sts.

• Continue this process until you have 22 Sts.

• CCO 1 Final St.total 23 Sts. And 11 Picots. This   Picot cast on differs from others, there will be one St. Between all picots.

• Work Row 1. (For this first row only, knit all stitches, once completed turn to knit Row 2 as written. All subsequent rows are worked as written.

Repeat rows 1-12 until scarf reaches 10ft.or desired length.I found it helpful to place a locking stitch marker to demarcate Row 6 on the WS of fabric. Move St. marker every other 6th row to track if you are working Row 6 or 12.

Finishing

• Repeat rows 1-4
• WS-CC 2sts, BO 4.
• Move St. back to left needle.
• Repeat until 2 st. remains. Bind off last stitch in pattern. So, for the last picot, you will bind off 5 Sts. 11 total Picots.
• Break yarn and pull through remaining live St.
• Weave in tails.

Blocking

There are two ways to block this pattern, depending upon the desired outcome and the yarn used. I made two samples and blocked them differently, achieving two types of fabrics. The first sample was done with Plucky Knitter Primo Fingering. This one, I wet blocked so the picot cast on could be straightened and lengthened and the yarn could bloom and set into its knitted pattern.

The second sample I knitted on Plucky Knitter Feet. This yarn doesn't have cashmere in the blend; consequently, there isn't as much loft.

I steam blocked this version. With my iron on the silk setting and the steam set to full, I pulled the finished fabric as I steamed it. It was kind of an experiment, and I love the final result. The stretching and steaming narrows the fabric in both length and density. This makes for a much lighter weight scarf while making the edges more uniform. Nice for warmer weather. If you choose to steam block, I recommend pinning the picots in place and then steaming, to avoid any steam or contact burns.

This pattern is also available as a free download on Ravelry.

https://www.ravelry.com/patterns/library/heart-of-ember-embers-scarf